time

a novel

Janessa Burt

TIME
Mirror: Book Two
Copyright © 2015 by Janessa Burt
All rights reserved.

This is a work of fiction. Names, characters, businesses, places, events,
and incidents are either the products of the author's imagination
or used in a fictitious manner.
Any resemblance to actual persons, living or dead,
or actual events is purely coincidental.

Published by Janessa Burt

Cover illustration © Richard Larsen

Cover design © Sarah Hansen, Okay Creations

To
Brittany, Katie, and Sophie
None of these books would exist without you three.
I owe you more than you know.
I love you girls.

chapter one

Going through the mirror feels the same as before—cold and dizzying.

I feel myself hit the ground. This time I land on my feet, but just like before, I can't hold my balance and fall on my back. I can't be too upset, though. At least I landed on my feet at some point.

I see Shane first. Through the dimming light of the setting sun, I see his finger up to his mouth gesturing for me to stay quiet. I watch his eyes cautiously scan our surroundings. My breath quickens as I look over my shoulder, terrified I'll see someone who shouldn't be here. But then I hear Shane exhale a relieved breath, then his low chuckle.

"Grace, are you okay? That was some landing," Shane laughs as he helps me sit up.

As I sit up, I know, just by the feeling, that I'm home. Pine trees of my childhood surround us, though there's no snow on them. The tree house Dad and I built when I was eight is still here, slightly decaying from no use.

Mom pops her head in my line of sight, worry painted all over her face. "We were so worried about you. We've been waiting for a few hours. I was about to go back for you, but thought you needed some time to say goodbye to people . . . to Miles."

At the sound of his name, my stomach lurches into my throat. "Miles. Where's Miles? Did he make it here?"

"I am here," Miles says as he moves from behind Shane. His face has absolutely no color, his hands are visibly shaking, and his eyes are incredibly wide.

"Are you okay?" I ask, reaching out and taking his hand.

"Um . . . well . . . I followed you through a mirror," he rambles, his eyes getting bigger. "I followed you through a mirror," he repeats in a whisper. He rubs his neck, his face looking like he's seen some gruesome crime.

I smile at him, wondering if this is what I looked like the first time I went through. Then a thought comes to mind, and I instantly scowl at him. "Did you land on your feet?"

There's still no color in his cheeks, but his eyes slide over to me, and his grin is slow and arrogant. "How else would I land?"

I glower at him in jealousy. That was my fourth time going through and I still landed on my back. That big smile spreads across his face, and his eyes tell me that he's on the verge of laughter. Raising his hand to my hair, I feel a small tug, and then I see him roll a twig between his fingers. If I wasn't so happy to have him here, I'd be embarrassed.

"Grace, we can talk about your clumsy entrance later. We have more important matters to discuss." Shane laughs while ignoring the annoyed stare I'm giving him. "No one jumped, but I need to check out the house before you three follow."

"I'll come with you," Mom says to Shane, which instantly puts his back up.

"No. You stay with Grace. Let me make sure it's safe."

Mom cocks an eyebrow and slowly folds her arms across her chest. I know that maneuver. She can somehow change your mind without saying a single word. Shane and Mom become locked in an intense stare down, and I fight a smile when Shane sighs, giving up.

"Grace stays," Shane orders, pointing a glare at me that tells me not to argue. "Give us a five minute head start, then come up. I'll watch for you."

Mom smiles smugly, hugs me, and then she and Shane follow the path that leads to our house. After they disappear through the trees, I turn back to Miles. Impossibly, I think he's lost more color.

"Grace, where are we?" he asks, his eyes bouncing from one thing to another.

"We're in Oregon," I tell him. When his eyes only get more confused, I explain further. "It became a state in . . ." oh shoot, ". . . uh . . . the 1850s."

Hopefully. I watch him try to take in everything, and when I see his growing panic, I smile.

"I am happy you are finding humor in this," he says dryly. "But may I remind you of how you looked when I first saw you?" He smiles when my mouth turns down. "Your eyes were wild with fear, you had twigs in your hair, mud dotting your dress, and a permanent scowl on your face, not unlike the one you have now." He catches my hand before I walk past him. "And as you can clearly see, my hair is twig free, I am not coated in mud, and I could never scowl at you while you are doing it so well for the both of us."

"It's not a contest."

"Only because you would be losing."

I try to glare, but his smile is too contagious. "Come on." I wrap my hand tighter in his and begin leading him up the hill.

Were the hills always this steep? My lungs are burning as we make our way up the switchbacks to the house. In all my memories of going down to the tree house with Dad, I never remember it being this hard. Granted, I'm bigger now and, regretfully, not as active. But heavens, I'm pretty sure I'm going to end up with my face in the dirt when I collapse to the ground.

"I can't breathe," I sputter through horrible sounding breaths. Why can't I remember this hill?

"I can hear you breathing. Rather loudly," he adds. I look over just in time to see his eyebrow arch and his grin. "Would you like me to carry you?"

"No, I wouldn't," I mutter under my breath. I don't need his help. I just need the hill to be smaller. Tripping over my dress isn't making anything easier. And I can barely see now that the sun has set.

Because I've felt it before, I immediately freeze when chills run along my skin. This isn't the breath-on-my-neck feeling. This is the nails-scraping-across-my-nerves feeling that tells me Miles and I aren't alone.

"What is it?" Miles whispers.

I hold my finger up to my mouth and slowly look over my shoulder. It's too dark to see more than a few yards behind us, but the dark holds secrets—secrets I don't want to find out.

3

"Grace, what—" Miles' head whips to the right at the sound of a twig snapping. We both turn to the trees behind us and hear slow, heavy footsteps crunch along the frosted leaves, getting closer, louder. Sweat forms between my hand and Miles' as we both take quiet steps backward.

The footsteps stop, only for a moment, and then begin to race. Right for us.

"Run," Miles whispers, letting go of my hand and pushing my back. "Go!"

We both take off in a sprint, but the footsteps behind us are faster than ours. They're weaving in and out of the trees. I hear them to my right, and then behind us, and then to my left.

And as I run, my thoughts begin piling on top of one another.

Someone jumped.

Someone jumped, and they're here.

And then another thought comes, twisting my already knotted stomach. If someone followed us, there might have been someone already here waiting.

"Mom!" I scream, pushing harder up the hill. "Shane!" I can't lose them again. I won't. Tears cause my vision to blur as I race toward home.

"Grace, keep running. I'll—" He stops talking the same time the sound of his footsteps disappear from behind me, and then I hear his low laugh. I turn around, wondering what could possibly be funny in this situation. Miles is a few yards down the hill from me, bent over, grasping his knees while he catches his breath between laughs.

"Why are you laughing?"

"Gracie, I fear we are both overly suspicious." He straightens and smiles at me in a way that makes the fear slowly begin dissolving. Then he turns and points down the path a ways, and I see a small herd of deer leisurely strolling through the trees.

That's all that was? I feel stupid for overreacting, but a laugh bubbles up in my throat. Soon Miles and I are both bent over laughing.

He throws his arm around my shoulder and guides me up the hill. "Perhaps we should agree to never speak of this to anyone."

"Agreed." I lean into him more and attempt to push away the paranoia of someone watching me, and I refuse to itch my neck when that cool breath runs down my spine.

"Grace!" Shane yells. His footsteps fly down the path, and I see him barrel around the bend in a panic. He crashes into me, gripping the back of my dress as if he'll keep me safe the tighter he holds. I gently pat his back and then close my eyes and let myself love this moment. "Are you okay? What happened? I heard you scream and came as fast as I could."

I push back so he can see my smile, hoping it will erase his fear. "We heard footsteps. We thought they were chasing us, but it was just a herd of deer."

I look away from Shane's annoyed stare. Miles clears his throat and avoids eye contact with him too.

Shane blows out a breath and slaps his hand against his chest. "You took ten years off my life."

"Sorry. I screamed for you because I thought someone was here, and maybe someone was at the house waiting." Shane's eyes meet mine, and there's an understanding in them that instantly calms my beating heart. He knows what it feels like to be scared for family—to live in fear that at any moment, everything can change.

"We were just to the house when we heard you—"

"Grace!"

Shane rolls his eyes and sighs. "Women," he grumbles under his breath, then steps aside so Mom can crash into me. "I told you to stay up there," he scolds Mom.

"I'm surprised you thought I'd listen." Mom takes my face in her hands and examines me. "You're alright?"

"I'm fine."

She pulls me back into a hug. "What happened?"

So I have to tell another person that I freaked out, because a harmless herd of deer decided to take a stroll through the woods. Once that embarrassing story garners enough laughs from Mom and Shane, the four of us head up the rest of the hill.

My nerves tingle at the thought of going home. When I left before the Rockwell ball, I had no parents and an uncle who acted indifferent. Now

I'm going home with Mom, Shane, and Miles. As excited as I am to be back, I'm thrilled for Mom. Her and Dad built this house. They actually patterned it after Rockwell, though it's not even close to the same size. It's going to be interesting to see the house now that I spent time living in the real Rockwell.

But more than anything else my excitement is for Miles. When I went back to Rockwell, I knew a little about what to do. Luckily I had read and seen movies based on that time period, so I had a small clue of how to act. But Miles came here with me not knowing a single thing about it. My thoughts shift from one invention to another that will be new to him.

The trees begin thinning as the ground levels. Mom smiles as we step out of the trees, she takes my hand and says, "It's so silly, but I forgot how beautiful it is."

It really is a beautiful house. It rests on a knoll that overlooks the city. If it isn't rainy and cloudy, which is rare, you get a great view of Mt. Hood.

The cobblestone drive wraps through the trees and circles a small fountain in front. My parents liked the privacy of the large pine trees that shelter the house, so after a few years, they planted a lot more. Everywhere you look there are pines. In the back of the house is a large gully, so we really don't have any neighbors, at least not within close proximity.

"Let's find something to eat," Mom says, which gets an automatic smile from Shane and me. I let them get a ways ahead before I take Miles' hand and lead him up the driveway.

"Miles, before we go in, you need to know there are a lot of things here that you've never seen, a lot that have only been invented in my lifetime. If you have any questions, or are feeling overwhelmed, you need to come talk to me. I don't want you to feel uncomfortable here." He took a big leap of faith walking through that mirror with me. I'd hate it if he regretted that decision.

"After going through that mirror, I am sure there is not much that can surprise me," he says confidently.

I only laugh. He's in for so many surprises. We step inside the house, and I instantly smile at the feeling only home can bring. It's better now that Mom's back. This house is all I've ever known. Mom and Dad moved in the fall before I was born, so this is it for me. It was hard to live here after Mom "died," but just knowing she's back makes the house warm again.

Through the entry way is the living room, and the entire back wall is windows. Dad loved to see the trees change with the seasons, and Mom loved looking over the valley and watching the sunsets. Through the windows, I see the last bit of light coloring the mountains slowly fading.

Walking further into the house, I flip on more lights so Miles can see everything better.

"Incredible," he whispers as he walks over to the light switch. Slowly, he flips the switch off, then back on, and then back off. I was so excited to show him things like cars, phones, and airplanes that I forgot about the everyday things I take for granted. He's never seen electricity before. After a few more minutes of switching the lights on and off, he turns to me with excitement. "Does it stay on all the time? Does it run out?" He flips it off and on again, and the flashes are beginning to hurt my eyes.

"The light bulb that holds the light will eventually run out. You replace them and it's as good as new. As long as the switch is up, the light will stay on." I pull him away from the light switch to spare my eyes. We go through the living room, and I watch Miles as he studies everything. Some things aren't new to him, but the style is so different it all enthralls him. He walks to the window and looks around the back of the house, his brows furrowing further.

I fold my arms and lean against the wall growing increasingly curious. "What are you thinking?"

"I am thinking that either I have gone completely mad, or this is indeed real. I am not sure which conclusion I have come to." Glancing over his shoulder, he sheepishly smiles at me.

"Hopefully this is all real, or I'm just as insane as you." Didn't I think that I was going crazy when I landed in Rockwell? His feelings are something I can empathize with. I offer him my hand and lead him to the kitchen. Shane and I left weeks ago for England, so I'm not sure what the food situation is, which is too bad considering I haven't had a decent meal in too long. Yes, the food at Rockwell was good, but there was always so little of it I felt I needed two servings of everything just to be remotely full.

Mom has the same idea as me. She's rummaging through cupboards when we come in. "What did you guys eat? There's nothing in these cupboards, and don't even get me started on the contents of the refrigerator." She shudders as she returns to her search for something to eat.

When I open the fridge I can only laugh. Most of the items are expired, and the ones that aren't probably don't even have an expiration date. The fridge consists of already made dinners, cheese, milk, eggs, and deli meat. I poke my head around the fridge to see if anything is edible when I feel Miles behind me. Trying to be inconspicuous, I move to the side a bit so he can see inside. He raises his hand and holds it up so he can feel the cold temperature. I pretend not to see him but can't hide my smile.

"That's it. I'm ordering delivery." Mom turns the computer on, strumming her nails against the counter as it boots up. When it flickers on, I see the screensaver hasn't changed. It's a picture of my parents and me standing in front of Rockwell. I was fourteen and it was the last time we went with Dad. That year I complained the entire trip of being bored, how rude my parents were for taking me away from my friends over New Year's Eve. Had I known that was the last vacation with Dad, I would've never left his side.

"What happened to Rockwell?" Miles asks, looking at the picture that shows the Rockwell I know—only half of it.

"There was a fire that took the wing of the house," Mom explains. "I've never dived into the history of the fire before. Most documents don't have any clues into what happened. I don't even know the year."

He's so stunned by the picture, he stares and then reaches for it, but pulls his hand away as the computer tips back when his fingers knock against the screen.

"Miles, do you remember when Shane spoke of a computer that he needed to get into?" I ask. He nods, and I try my best to describe what I really know nothing about. "That's what this is. A computer. It holds information and can help you find things you're looking for. Like, at the moment, we're looking for a pizza place that delivers."

"Chinese," Mom corrects me as she pulls up a list of restaurants close by.

8

"How do you get inside?" Miles studies the computer. He wraps his body around the desk so he can see the back of the computer, and he begins curiously pulling at cords.

"You don't physically get inside. It stores things, um, just like our brain. We don't have to physically go inside our heads to recover memories or information, right? It's the same here, it holds memories or information and with a little navigation you can have that information on the screen here." I point to the screen feeling really inept at explaining the workings of a computer. I know how to point and click, but ask me how it actually works and I'll only laugh at you. He continues to watch the screen as Mom orders our dinner over the phone.

"Mom?" I ask when she hangs up the phone.

"Yes?"

"Will you please help me get out of this dress?"

She turns to me, surprised, and then laughs. "I have been wearing one for so long I forgot I was even wearing it. How exciting to be rid of it. Lets go."

I turn to Miles before following Mom, but he waves me off. "I will be fine, Gracie," he answers before I can ask.

"You can sit on the couch if you want. I won't be long."

He rolls his eyes letting me know I'm being overprotective and sits down on the couch. Our family room and Miles don't match. Although our house isn't way modern, it's definitely ahead of Miles. His waistcoat, cravat, and tall boots don't blend in with the style. If it's possible, his olden-day clothes actually make the room look fancy. I shake my head and laugh and then follow Mom upstairs to my room.

"I'll bring some gauze up for your stomach," Mom says as she unlaces the back of my dress. "After you shower, we'll get it bandaged up again."

When she leaves, I unwrap the layers of old gauze around my stomach and cringe when I see the wound. It's not infected, but it looks disgusting. Stepping under the steaming stream of water, my muscles loosen and the joy of being back increases. The smell of my coconut shampoo is relaxing, and I apply the conditioner twice so I can give my poor scalp a break from the constant pulling it received. When the water loses its warmth, I know I've been in long enough.

Wrapping a towel around me, I step out of the shower and instantly glue myself to the ground. My first thought is to jump back into the shower, but I don't get a chance. Miles turns in my direction just as I tell myself to move. Once he sees me, his eyes widened in a horrified panic, and he quickly turns around.

"I am sorry, Gracie. I . . ." His voice trails off when he looks up and sees me through the mirror. Oh, I feel bad for him. His eyes hold pure terror as he bolts from the bathroom. Laughing a little, I decide to get dressed before doing my hair.

I walk to my closet and scan my clothing for too long. Looking at all of my clothes has me self-conscious. Miles is used to seeing women in dresses only, and on top of that, he never even saw women's ankles. Now he's going to see me in pants and a t-shirt.

After too much fussing, I decide on black yoga pants and a cream, long sleeve sweater. When my hair is brushed through, I, again, get self-conscious. Women don't wear their hair down where he's from. I contemplate putting it up, but think better of it. If he's going to be here, he needs to get used to the differences.

Taking a big breath, I step into the kitchen. Miles is sitting across from Mom, watching her unload takeout boxes from the brown bag. He catches sight of me out of the corner of his eye and quickly stands, but he's too shaky, and he stands too fast. The chair crashes to the ground behind him.

"I . . . um . . ." He turns and picks up the chair while Mom gives me a sympathetic look. He looks at me, his eyes roaming down my body and then back to my eyes. Not in a creepy way. It's out of genuine interest. A faint blush creeps along his cheeks as he quickly looks away. I sit and pull him down into the chair next to mine. His hands rub up and down his thighs as he looks at just about everything but me.

Taking his hand in mine I smile at him. "Are you alright?" I have a feeling I'm going to be asking him this question a lot.

"Yes. I am sorry about that. Upstairs. Madam Clary told—"

"Miles, please call me Carolyn," Mom says.

He swallows hard, forcing her name to come out. "C-Carolyn showed me which room was to be mine. I was curious and began looking around. I did not know you were in there before I came in. I assure you I did not."

"I believe you and wish you wouldn't worry about it. No harm done." I overcompensate on the smiling so he knows it's okay.

"It was my fault really," Mom says. "I put him in the room next to yours with the Jack and Jill bathroom. I didn't think about you two sharing a bathroom." Mom's brow furrows as she thinks about it more, then continues separating the last few containers. "I'll go get Shane. After we eat, we should all go to sleep. It's been a long day, and I'm sure our days ahead will be just as . . . entertaining." She sneaks a glance at Miles, which he doesn't miss. Laughing, she strolls out to find Shane.

Being back home has unfortunately brought back my manners, or lack of. When I see Miles looking at me, I cringe at what he must be seeing. My legs are pulled up to my chest as I lounge in the large chair. Eating straight from the box, I didn't even offer him some. I'm sure I look like a barbarian.

"I'm sorry. I'm being rude." I set the container down and go get plates and silverware. Putting a plate in front of him and myself I sit back down. "What would you like?" Grabbing the containers, I open them, showing and explaining to him the contents of each.

"I will have what you have," he says.

I hesitate for a moment, then sigh and start loading his plate. I'm having a lot of everything, and if Miles is going to stay here with me, he's going to have to get used to my eating habits.

As I'm piling food on his plate, he stops me. "Do you normally eat off plates?" he asks.

I wince at his perception of me. "Yes, we always eat off plates, with silverware. I was just being impolite."

"Gracie?" He stops my hands from fumbling with the cartons, and pulls them down into his lap. "I do not want you to change because I am here. If you eat from the boxes, I want you to. I will even join. And if you usually wear your hair down," he strokes my hair, then puts it behind my ear, "then please wear it down. It is lovely, and you have been tugging on it since you came in."

My shoulders sag as I blow out a big breath. "I'm sorry. I'm trying to make you comfortable. Things are so different here."

11

"I can see the difference, but I will never be comfortable here if you are not. You need to be Gracie, and I will learn from you. Now, which is your favorite? I will start with that."

I hand him the box of Kung Pao and relax as we pass each other different containers to try.

Mom and Shane come down to eat with us, and gratefully, Shane's manners make me look elegant. He scarfs his food in what seems like seconds. Miles watches him with wide, curious eyes.

When dinner ends, I help throw away the boxes because, of course, the food is gone, which is why my stomach hurts beyond what I thought capable. I'm not sure if it's because my stomach has shrunk from being at Rockwell or because I ate way too much Chinese.

After the kitchen is clean, Mom hands me a pile of clothes. "These are some of your father's old clothes. Miles is quite a bit bigger than he was, so I tried getting clothes that could fit different sizes. There are mostly basketball shorts, pajama pants, and t-shirts in here. They will have to do until I can go shopping tomorrow."

It feels weird to hold Dad's clothes, so I tuck them under my arm. "You're going shopping? Isn't that going to be hard when no one is supposed to know you're alive?"

"I'll disguise myself." She waves me off as she wipes down the table.

"And how are you going to pay for the clothes? I'm pretty sure your credit cards are expired. And how will you shop for Miles without him being there?"

"Don't lecture me, Grace." The teasing she aimed for is overshadowed by annoyance. "I already asked Shane if we could go. He'll come with me and I can use his cards, fully intending to pay him back once I come back from the dead." We laugh as she pushes me from the kitchen. "And I've been making Miles' clothes for a year. I'm pretty sure I know his measurements by now. And I'm also sure I can pick out clothes better than him. Give those to Miles. There's also a toothbrush in the bathroom for him. You'll need to show him the toothpaste, but he knows how to brush."

"I hope everyone knows how to brush," Shane says as he walks into the kitchen.

My face burns as I pull at my hands and ask what I've been putting off asking. "Shane, while you're here, I was hoping you could do me a favor." I talk so quietly he has to walk closer to me to hear. "Um . . . well . . . I was wondering if you would take a minute with Miles and teach him some things." He doesn't understand right away, so I look at my feet and awkwardly keep talking. "Like how to use the shower, and um . . . the bathroom?" Visions of that demoralizing chamber pot flash through my mind. I'm comfortable enough with Miles to teach him a lot of things, but anything that has to be taken care of in private is off limits.

I jump at Shane's loud laugh. He slaps my back and through chuckles, says, "I think that's only fair. I'll take him upstairs now." I smile at him, then watch Shane leave, laughing. "Miles, come with me upstairs. I need to show you a few things," he says from the other room.

"I didn't think about those situations when I asked him to come."

"It's a good thing we have Shane." When Mom says it, I know she means it. We'd all be lost without him.

My shoulders sag in relief when Shane comes back and gives me a nod that *that* situation is taken care of. "I just gave Miles the same rules I'm giving you," he says, standing in front of me so I can't look anywhere but him. "If you leave the house, I need to know where you're going. Be careful where you take Miles, and be aware of the consequences your actives may have. A hospital visit for him would lead to questions we don't have answers to." I nod, gulping down the sudden lump of reality in my throat. "No one can use the mirror . . . wait." He holds up his hand when I open my mouth to protest. "No one can use the mirror until I can get it fixed. I just discussed it with Miles, and he's fine with it."

Shane releases a breath and loses his scary protective uncle face when he smiles. He lays his hand on my shoulder, giving it a gentle squeeze. "I promised I'd keep you and your mom safe, but you two need to do your part so I can keep that promise. Okay?"

I nod and manage an, "Okay."

Miles is sitting on the couch when I go into the family room, so I drop the pile of clothes next to him.

"These will have to do until my mom gets you some new clothes."

13

"What is wrong with the ones I have on?" He looks down, confused.

"Nothing, but I'm pretty sure no one has cravats anymore. And as much as I love your waistcoat and boots, I'm afraid they've gone out of style as well."

"I am trading my trousers and cravat for these?" He holds up the basketball shorts, twisting them around in his hands.

I laugh and pull them down. "These are only pajamas. Clothes you wear to bed. My mom is shopping tomorrow. You'll have your trousers back, but they'll be different."

He nods as he looks through the pile of clothes. A lot of the t-shirts have graphics on them I have to explain. I tell him about the current styles of clothing more as we walk upstairs and into the bathroom. I pick up my toothbrush and dramatically put on my toothpaste, so he can see how to do it.

"Give me some credit, Grace." He chuckles as he snatches the tube from my hands.

The tension in his body is clearly visible when I walk into his room with him, so I'm quick. "If you get too cold there's another blanket in the closet. I'll keep the bathroom doors cracked in case you need something. Also, if you—"

He bends down fast, picking me up around the waist and hugs me. "Will you please stop fussing over me? If you have not noticed, I managed to dress myself this morning, although not according to the latest fashion trends, or so I am told. If I need help, I promise I will ask you, but please stop worrying about me."

I pull away so I can see his face just in case he's trying to sneak something by me. "Okay." I kiss his cheek quickly then walk away. "Good night, Miles."

"Good night, Grace."

I leave the door open a bit so I can hear if he needs anything. Exhausted, I fall on my bed and smile at the familiar smell of my laundry detergent. How funny that I'd miss something so small. My heavy eyelids fall shut, and I listen to the house begin to settle for the night.

14

My eyes snap open when I hear the short beep of the house alarm, indicating an opened door. Peering at my nightstand, I see it's almost midnight. It's probably Shane making sure everything's locked up for the night. But the nerves in my stomach won't settle, so I push off the blankets to go check.

I slip out of bed, quietly open my door, and have to bite my tongue when I see Shane soundlessly maneuver down the stairs with a gun in his hand. Instinctively I follow, fear for myself taking a backseat to fear for Shane. Every creak of the stairs or groan of the house has my breathing coming in quick, shaky spurts. My heart is pounding so loudly I'm worried someone will hear me before I hear them.

I jump when a woman's scream comes from the kitchen.

Mom.

I run down the hall and carelessly barge into the kitchen and immediately stop when I'm staring at the barrel of a gun.

"Grace!" Shane growls, slapping his gun onto the counter. He rubs his hands aggressively over his face while he continues to glare at me. "What are you doing down here?"

"I heard the alarm and followed you downstairs." And by the look on his face that wasn't what he wanted to hear. "Who screamed? I thought it was Mom."

Shane sighs and steps to the side so he's no longer blocking my view. Beth is pressed against the fridge with her hand over her heart, not an ounce of color in her cheeks.

"Beth." Pushing Shane aside, I run to her.

She meets me halfway and catches my face in her hands. "Are you alright?" she asks between sobs, moving my face around to look at every inch of me. "I've been so worried about you." She pulls me tightly against her and continues to cry into my shoulder.

"What's happened? I heard screaming and . . ."

As soon as I hear Mom's voice, I feel Beth's breathing stop, her skin go cold. I pull away to see her face, but she isn't looking at me. Her eyes are

15

wide in disbelief as they fix on something behind me.

"Carolyn?" Beth chokes.

Mom steps into the light of the kitchen, and smiles. "Hello, Beth."

Beth's face goes slack, and the red that came to her cheeks when she saw me is now gone. She opens her mouth, but then shuts it. Her legs are shaking, so I wrap my arm around her waist and lead her to the couch. Her eyes stay on Mom, locked on a ghost. I can empathize with Beth; I felt the same when I saw Mom walk from the back of her shop.

"Are you alright, Beth?" Mom slowly walks to her with her hands raised so she won't scare Beth more.

"How did you . . . where have you . . . are you real?" Beth's body is still, but when Mom sits beside her, Beth flinches away. Beth looks over at me with the same wide eyes. "How did you get back? I'm so sorry I sent you. It was the only thing I could think of at the moment." With shaky hands, she pinches the bridge of her nose like she's trying to concentrate. After a moment, she looks up, and her eyes narrow at Shane. "I thought you killed Carolyn."

Shane sinks into a chair across from us, his face somber. "I know."

"Why didn't you say anything?" Beth yells, wrapping her arms around herself. "For over a year, I've been living in fear that you'd go after Grace next. Do you know what it felt like? Leaving this house knowing she'd be alone with you? I was terrified that when I came back, you'd come up with some excuse for Grace's disappearance." She closes her eyes and tries to control her breathing. She glances back at Mom, her eyes filling with more tears. "Dan told me, right before he died. He told me if I ever thought you or Grace needed protection that there was a way to keep you safe." Beth hesitantly lays her hand over Mom's. "I thought he was crazy, but he showed me once. He told me not to tell you because you'd be angry with him for trying to control situations he has no business controlling."

Mom laughs, sandwiching Beth's hand between hers. "That sounds like Daniel."

"Although the situation was never so desperate, I appreciate you helping Grace that night." Shane's mouth turns up at the side into a small, albeit forced, smile.

16

"I'm sorry. She was so scared, and the only thing I could think of was taking her up to the attic. If I had known . . . "

"Beth, we aren't accusing you. I'm trying to thank you." Shane relaxes and sits back, and instantly the room is more pleasant.

Beth lays a hand over her heart, still gripping Mom's hand. "I came over, because I was alerted that the alarm was triggered. I didn't expect you two home for another few days." She lets out a shaky breath. "I didn't expect to turn the corner and be met with a gun." She laughs a little, then her brows scrunch together in confusion. "Who are you?"

I follow Beth's gaze and see Miles standing in the doorway of the room, unsure if he's supposed to come in or not. I wave him in, and he goes to Beth first.

He stands in front of her and bows. "It is a pleasure to meet you, Beth."

Beth watches him bow, and hesitantly smiles. "You too?"

Miles sits down next to me, and I turn to Beth to explain everything that happened at Rockwell, from Annie and Miles to Harry and Hannah.

chapter two

If I didn't love him so much, I'd be jealous at how well Miles adapts to situations. Either he's great at hiding his fear, or he's able to take in change and surprises with an annoying amount of skill. Whenever he learns something new, I can see in his eyes how he studies it and files it to memory.

"I do love your hair this way." Miles rubs his hand over my hair, tugging on the end with a smile. "Although the contraption you use to get it this straight terrifies me." He looks down at his bandaged fingers—the ones he used this morning to pick up my straightener. While I was using it.

I laugh and grab his hand, leading him downstairs for dinner. For going through the mirror just yesterday, he's sliding into the groove of things really well. He's learning that you don't wake me up before the sun is up, it's not common practice to stand every time a woman comes to or leaves the table, people don't bow anymore, and women can dress as they please, although I'm sticking to pants and long-sleeve shirts for awhile.

"How are you holding up, my boy?" Shane asks Miles as we sit down for dinner. I laugh and internally cringe at the scene we're creating for Miles. His dinners were brought to him ready to eat. I'm sure people didn't talk with food-filled mouths or eat with their legs pulled up to their chest, like I am now.

"I am doing fine, thank you. My father warned me things would be different."

"He did? When?" I make sure to swallow my food before asking.

"Right before we came here, when you asked me to speak with him about Thomas. He gave me some advice about traveling here with you. I was arrogant to think I had already seen it all after watching you walk through the mirror. I can see now I was mistaken." Miles takes a small bite of food.

"What about Thomas?" Shane puts his fork down. His elbows rest on the table as he presses his fingertips together. Though his voice stays calm, his face is brimming with disgust.

"After you and Mom went through the mirror, I followed, but it took me six years ahead of the time I'd spent at Rockwell. I found Miles and had a misunderstanding." I glare as my eyes slide over to Miles. I'm still not over him leading me on about being married. He only laughs. "I found out that Thomas had stayed around and . . ." We changed the future by changing the present. I know Annie is alright and will hopefully stay that way, but saying it out loud makes it too real.

Miles explains the situation for me. "Grace learned that Annie and Mr. Wilson were killed by Thomas."

Mom gasps and Shane's face stains darker until it goes red.

"Miles told me he had searched for Thomas but couldn't find him. When I got back, I asked Miles to talk with his dad and Matthew to make sure the family stays safe." I hope that it is enough to keep them protected.

We eat in silence for a bit while Shane mutters under his breath. Some words I catch, but by the look on Mom's face, he probably shouldn't be saying them. Others are of regret and blame.

"What is that noise?" Miles asks, twisting in his seat to find what's beeping.

"Grace's cell," Shane mumbles, stabbing at his food. "I shipped all your things from England before I went back through the mirror to Rockwell. Package came just before dinner. Your cell was dead, so I plugged it in."

"We got Miles a cell today." Mom talks quietly, probably to apologize for the way Shane and I eat. "And some clothes."

"Some clothes," Shane repeats, laughing. "More like an entire department store."

Mom lifts her chin in the air. "He can't keep wearing his cravat and boots, now can he?"

Miles awkwardly straightens his cravat. "Thank you." Then he leans over and whispers, "What is a cell?"

I hop up and grab my phone, flipping through the texts, erasing the *Merry Christmas* and *Happy New Year!!* texts I received from people, many of which I haven't spoken to in years. One text catches my eye though:

Grace, if you don't answer my texts I swear I'm getting on a plane and coming to England. Shane told me (after an embarrassing number of times calling *his* cell phone) that he'd have you call me when you got back. If you come home and don't call me, I'll show up causing a scene. I'll bring Stella and Kallie with me as reinforcements.

The next text says:

And you better have brought me chocolate from England.

Bridgette.

It's so good to hear from her. She has a way of turning any mood into a happy one. We were best friends since before I can remember. In elementary school we met Stella and Kallie, and the four of us stuck together. After Mom died, or when I thought she died, those three were there for me. I'm surprised they still want to talk to me after the way I treated them. Avoiding them was a lot easier than facing their sympathy. I knew that if I let them come around, they'd force me to talk about it, and I would cry, and that was after I had promised myself I wouldn't cry anymore.

I haven't talked to them in over six months. It shouldn't surprise me that they still care about me.

I smile and hit reply.

Me: Bri, I just got home yesterday. My phone has been off for the holidays. How are you?

"Who is Bri?" Miles asks. "And what is that you have in your hand?" He pokes at my phone, his hand flinching back when it beeps at him.

"This is a cell phone, and Bri was my best friend growing up." My phone vibrates, and before I can read it, two others come in.

Bri: How I am is not important. What is important is if you brought me chocolate.

Stella: You're home? When are we getting together?

Kallie: I'm so glad you're back. How was England? Did you meet a cute British guy?

Geez, I've missed these girls. I reply back that I didn't bring any chocolate, I'm free tomorrow, and yes, I did meet a cute British guy. I put my phone aside knowing that piece of information will spread like wildfire. I'm not disappointed. My phone begins beeping incessantly.

"Is that Bridgette?" Shane asks.

"Yeah."

"Hold on a second." He leaves the table, and I glance at Mom, but she shrugs her shoulders not knowing anything. When Shane comes back, he hands me an envelope. It's addressed to the Gentry family. I open it and gape at the invitation in my hands.

"Bri is getting married." The words sound strange coming out of my mouth. I knew she was. I saw the invitation she posted on Facebook before I went to Rockwell but seeing the invitation in my hand is different. She's marrying Peter, her boyfriend since the eighth grade. Those two have been dating for so long they became grouped together as one person. I quickly pull out my phone to text Bri.

Me: You have a lot of wedding explaining to do. Breakfast tomorrow? Ask Kall and Stella.

Bri: I will annoy you with wedding details, but only if you give details on the souvenir you brought home.

Me: Deal

We finalize our plans to meet in the morning as I continue to eat.

"They sent a save-the-date about a month ago," Shane says. "Since they're getting married up at the lodge and having celebrations before the wedding, they mentioned there were rooms available for wedding guests. I reserved one for a few nights in case you'd like to go, Grace. I think the wedding is the end of January."

"Thanks, Shane. That was really thoughtful." I put the invitation beside my plate but keep staring at it.

"I should tell you the reason behind it was purely selfish. Originally, I booked the room for you and Landon to stay at in case you accepted his offer and he followed you here," Shane confesses.

"You booked a hotel room for Grace and Landon to stay in? Alone? Shane!" Mom is shaking her head as she stabs at the food on her plate. This situation is getting extremely uncomfortable considering Miles is sitting next to me.

Shane laughs. "Dan would have come from the grave and killed me himself if I'd done that. The hotel room is a suite, which has four separate bedrooms and a common area. I booked the suite so I could be chaperone. Although going to weddings is like having teeth pulled." Shane shifts into his grumpy mood and grumbles under his breath.

Dinner ends and it takes awhile for me to feel comfortable moving. I forgot what it's like when Mom cooks. I always eat too much.

"Get Miles' phone set up so you both have one in case something happens." Mom pushes us out of the kitchen, and I just laugh when we walk into the family room and see the mountain of purchases. There has to be a bag from every possible store. I rummage through them and quickly realize they aren't for me.

"I think we have your new wardrobe, Miles."

"I couldn't help myself." Mom walks in to defend herself. "Everything I saw I thought would look good. Of course I favored blue to match his eyes, but I couldn't pass anything black. Then there were these aisles of reds, and I just lost control. We don't have to keep it all, but at least now he has options. Lots of options." She sheepishly grins. She pokes her head around

22

the bags until she finds the one she wants. "I thought of getting him the most basic, but it might be better if he matched yours. And if they make these smart phones easy enough for me to use, anyone can use them."

I catch the bag she tosses to me and pour the contents on the couch. Phones are one of the things I'm most excited to show Miles. My impatience is apparent as I mutilate the box to get the phone out.

Miles sits down beside me as I turn it on and start programming numbers in it. As I set up his phone, I try explaining what it is and how to use it. Throughout my description of the phone, I'm reminded that I should've listened more intently in history or science. My commentary of the phone's inner workings consists of basic intelligence. After successfully failing at explaining what it is, I give up and just show him how to use it. He sits quietly beside me, analyzing every word and action.

"Texting is just like writing a letter. You have all the letters on the phone here, and you hit one just as you would write it." I show him how to write Miles and Grace in the text box and then how to send it. When my phone beeps his eyes intensify with curiosity. Showing him my phone, he reads the words I wrote in his phone. The more I explain how it works the more incredible it becomes to *me*.

"May I try?" He holds his hand out for the phone, and when I hand it to him, he stares at it for a moment before trying to write. The phone looks so small in his hands, which makes it hard for me to see what he's writing. After some time passes, I worry that he isn't entirely sure of what to do but is too embarrassed to admit it. My phone beeps just as I'm about to ask if he needs help.

The word *hello* appears on my phone, making me laugh. It took him a solid minute to write that one word, but he's trying. I write back and watch his face change with the amazement of what he's doing.

"This is astonishing. Can I write anything to you anywhere? What if you were out of the house?" he asks.

"If you were here and I were in a different country, I would still get it." Okay, I'm showing off a little bit, but I can't help it when I see how excited he's getting over something I've used everyday but never thought twice about.

We continue the phone lessons until I see his blinking begin to slow and his yawns getting longer.

I get to my feet and hold a hand out for him. "Let's finish this tomorrow."

After saying good night to Miles, I crawl into bed. My phone beeps before I drift too far.

Miles: Good night

I smile and tell him good night. Rolling over, I pull the down comforter up to my chin, forming into a ball. My phone beeps again. I'm going to have to explain texting etiquette to Miles.

Miles: I love you.

I thought I was passed the point of Miles causing butterflies, but three simple words have my stomach fluttering.

Me: Love you, too.

chapter three

There have only been a handful of times in my life when I've known I was dreaming. The last time was at Rockwell, and it affected me in such a way that I'll never brush off a dream again. Whether it's the familiarity of the dream that catches my attention or the feel of it, this dream won't soon be forgotten.

I remind myself that I'm in a dream as I stare at my reflection in the mirror. The mirror used to scare me, and I guess it still does, but it isn't the same fear as before. It holds an uncertainty and a mystery that's begging to be solved. Inching closer to the liquid glass, I can hear my heart pounding in my ears, trying to drown out the pleading in my brain telling me to stop. The cold hits me when I step through but only briefly. I'm warm again by the time I open my eyes. As soon as I look around, I'm more confused than ever. I stepped through the mirror only to end up right back in my bedroom. It's dark, but my room is unmistakable.

I turn back to the mirror, and I look just as I did a moment ago—no time has passed. Guessing I went through wrong, I step through again and subsequently land back in the same spot. My irritation for the situation is climbing, and I impatiently throw myself through the mirror. Every time I end back in my room, and every time makes me angrier than before. As a result, I throw myself harder through the glass.

My knees hurt when I land on the ground after my last jump. The green shaggy rug underneath me tells me I'm again in my bedroom. Pushing off my knees, I turn and stare at the mirror. I watch as I try to catch my breath and wonder what it is about the mirror that makes me feel so rattled. It silently begs me to enter. I can feel its pull. But my impatience for literally running around in circles is much stronger than the mirror's allure. Folding my arms, I sit down and rest my back against the foot of my bed to wait until I wake up and can finally be done with this dream.

But my reflection doesn't sit down. It stands, staring down at me, tilting its head as if she—me—is studying me.

Then, so quietly, she whispers, "They're coming."

And then I watch, unmoving, as my reflection turns and vanishes into the darkness of the mirror.

My eyes fly open, and I immediately sit up and drag in sharp, painful breaths, shaking my head to wake myself up further. My heart rams against my ribcage, acting like it's going to beat its way out of my chest.

"Just a dream," I say to myself, but I cautiously watch the mirror for awhile to be sure. "Just a dream," I whisper again, lying down and turning my back to the mirror.

I squeeze my eyes tighter when I feel that chilly breath crawl across the back of my neck. Trying to ignore it, I pull my blankets up over my head and begin counting, each number I say coming out shakier than the last.

I fall asleep with red scratches across my neck from trying to get rid of that horribly familiar sensation that I'm not alone.

* * *

"Grace?"

With effort, I pry my eyes open at the sound of my name. Miles is sitting on the side of my bed with my phone in his hands, frantically trying to turn off the alarm. With even more effort, I sit up and take the phone from him.

"I am sorry. I heard the noise and followed it in here. But I could not make it stop." He runs his hand through his hair trying to wake himself up. Once I'm fully awake, I notice what he's wearing, and it isn't his usual clothes. He's wearing red and black plaid pajama pants with a short-sleeve black T-shirt. If my mouth isn't hanging wide open, I'm amazing, because that's what I feel like doing. He looks so different in normal clothes. Bigger, somehow, but still just as handsome. As a result, I can't form complete sentences.

"Um . . . thanks." Clearing my throat, I slide out of bed. "I set my alarm last night, so I'd be on time for breakfast. Whoever thought eight o'clock was a good time to meet was severely mistaken." I didn't go to bed too late the night before, so I shouldn't be this tired, but I'm skeptically eyeing the clock on my nightstand in case the time was changed. I pass the mirror quickly, not wanting to see my reflection in the glass this morning for two reasons. First, I'm sure I look terrific after a night of no sleep, and second, I'm not one hundred percent sure my reflection won't walk away from me. I shudder at the memory of my dream, so I hurry to my closet to pick out an outfit.

"Do you want to come to breakfast with me?" I ask Miles.

"No, thank you. I believe you need this time with your friends, and Shane offered to give some explanation on the mirror. I am interested in the time your father spent at Rockwell."

"Okay." I only just thought to invite him, but now that I know we're going to be away from each other for the next few hours, I feel surprisingly sad.

Miles leaves to let me get dressed, and I'm sure he could have dressed himself three times in the amount of time it takes me. The dream flickers through my mind like photographs in a slide show, and I feel just as unsteady now as I did in my dream.

Mom is stirring something delicious when I come into the kitchen. When Miles enters from the opposite side, I quickly turn to Mom for help. Remembering how embarrassed I felt when I did something out of place at Rockwell makes me empathize with Miles now. He comes in wearing a different pair of pajama pants—navy and black checkers—with a button-down, blue, pin-stripe shirt. If his outfit wasn't bad enough, he added black dress shoes to complete the ensemble. Didn't anyone tell him what pants are for what? That was probably my job, and by the look of him, he has no idea.

He notices my look to Mom and her struggling to keep a straight face.

27

"What have I don't wrong?"

"Grace, you're going to be late for breakfast, and it seems you have enough to apologize for with those girls. I'll help Miles. Go." Mom knows by the look I give her that she's appreciated. I kiss Miles' cheek and slip outside just in time to explode with laughter. The image of him walking into the kitchen with his commanding presence in pajama pants and a dress shirt will always be a source of entertainment for me.

I hop into my car, laughing all the way to breakfast.

Walking into the bagel shop is nothing new to me. I worked here for a summer when I was sixteen. The girls would come in every week and tempt me into giving them free donuts and bagels, and I caved every time. This time walking through the doors is rejuvenating. I'm a different person than all those years ago.

I see them in the corner, heads together, whispering about something. Just seeing them makes me feel sixteen all over again.

Bridgette and I have been friends forever. She's the kind of person that when you're around her, you can't help but be happy. Stella and Kallie came in later, and the four of us just stuck together. Stella is one I go to when I need help with anything. Whether that was homework or a personal problem—her advice was priceless and always needed. Kall is a ball of fun energy. She can make anyone laugh, and you always seem to be carefree when around her. After Dad died, our friendship only solidified. They showed up when I didn't want to see anyone, but they knew I needed them. After Mom was gone, I cut them out of my life. Looking back, I think they only reminded me of a Grace that once was, and after my parents were gone, that Grace was gone.

None of us look anything alike. Kall has fire red hair that only adds to her dynamic personality. Stella has straight black hair that always looks professionally done, even if she claims she just crawled out of bed. Bri is blonde and keeps it short but somehow even short it looks elegant. Then there's my brown hair that's usually out of control, because I still can't figure out how to work with my mane.

I snap out of my thoughts when I hear my name and then have only a second to brace myself before I'm bombarded by them. If I were watching

28

this greeting from the outside, I would think we're crazy—a bunch of girls sobbing at the sight of each other. But I only grab at them tighter when I let myself feel how extremely happy I am to see them.

"Grace, I'm so happy to see you," Bri says, hugging me.

Then Stella hugs me. "I can't believe you're here. How are you?"

Kall pokes my arm. "Girl, lets get you a donut. You're rail thin."

I laugh as they, as a group, take me by the hand and lead me to the corner table.

Wiping the tears from my eyes I smile at them. "It's so good to see you guys." I watch as the smiles on their faces grow, and the acceptance I feel from them has me smiling bigger.

"How are you?" Bri asks.

It's nice that, for once, I don't have to lie. "I'm good. I really am."

"This has nothing to do with your British souvenir, would it?" Kallie flashes her too-perfect smile at me.

"Kall, we agreed we would make sure she was fine before interrogating her." Bri defends me against the onslaught of questions I'm sure is coming.

"I did wait. She just said she was good; therefore, the interrogation has begun," Kall answers like it should've been obvious.

"I'll answer any question you have after I get some food and Bri tells me every detail about the wedding," I say.

"I'll bore you, and these two have heard everything already."

"No one gets bored hearing about their best friend's wedding." Stella nudges Bri's arm.

I order enough breakfast to feed two and listen intently to every detail of the wedding. It sounds magical, a wedding in the mountains. Snow just fell last weekend at the resort, which means the scenery for a wedding will be picturesque. I wasn't lying when I said I wanted every detail. I quiz her on her dress, flowers, food, dancing, and her cake. After hearing her describe her three-tiered, chocolate buttercream cake, I decide I do need that donut.

"Okay, enough about the wedding. You'll see it all in just three weeks. Oh, is it really three weeks away?" Fanning her face, Bri begins breathing irregularly. Stella pushes a glass of ice water over to her, and Kallie pats her back. I'm guessing this reaction is normal.

29

"Enough about me." Bri sits back and waves a hand in the air. "After this month you will all be sick of me. We want to hear about you, Grace."

"What she means is we want to hear about this new man." Stella laughs as she motions to the waiter to put the donut in front of me. Uncharacteristically, I become shy in front of them. What do I tell them about Miles?

"You're blushing! You're killing me, Grace. Spill it!" Kallie demands to the amusement of the others.

"What do you want to know?" I ask.

"Oh, I don't know. Where did you meet him? What does he look like? How did you meet him? Why is he here? Do you two have plans for the future? When can we meet him? Is he coming to the wedding? Why have you not—"

"Kall, let her breathe." Bri punches her in the arm.

I laugh and try to answer the questions as honestly as I can. "I met him at Rockwell. When I came home, I asked him to come with me, and he did. I don't know about a future with him. All I know is the way I feel about him would make any future without him quite depressing. You can meet him anytime, because I've already warned him about you three. I'm not sure if he's coming to the wedding, since I just found out about it yesterday." Satisfied with my answer, I sit back and dive into my donut.

"Give me a break, Grace. I've never known you to blush and just the mention of his name has you going rosy. Give up the goods." It's Stella this time calling me out.

"I don't know what you want me to say."

"How do you feel about him?" Bri is kinder than the others when she asks.

"How do I answer that? At first, he bugged me. He teased me, and because of the situation I was in, I had to deal with it. But after awhile I saw that teasing me was his form of flirting, you could say. We got in a carriage, I mean, car accident, and after that I found that I cared about him much more than I should. Then, there was the Rockwell Ball where we danced, and I fell for him without even knowing it. I tried leaving, going home without him, but I wondered what my future would hold without him, so I

30

went back and asked him to come with me. And he came. I'm still asking myself why he came."

"Did you waltz with him?" How is it possible for all three to ask the same question at the same time?

"Yes, I did." The squeals erupt again, and I feel myself ease into the moment.

"Please tell me you're bringing him to the wedding. Your uncle booked a place up there for you and RSVP'd yes for three. So, you're locked in. What am I going to do with three extra plates of lemon butter chicken with vegetables?" Bri sighs like two extra plates going to waste is criminal.

"I wouldn't miss it."

Breakfast passes without a care as they catch me up on what everyone is doing. I'm happy to hear they're all happy with where their life is. All three are in school, working, and because of who they are, their social lives are demanding. It's only when I glance at my phone after it beeps that I realize the time.

Miles: I am sorry to interrupt your breakfast. This phone will not stop making noises and the more I try to quiet it the more it defies me.

I've spent two hours with my girlfriends, and as much as I like being with them, I'm ready to go home.

Miles: Alright I confess. While the phone is in fact beeping it was just a ploy to send you a letter through the phone. I miss you.

I look up from my phone and see them beaming at me.

"You need to go, don't you?" Stella smiles at the other two.

"Um, yeah. He's new here, so he doesn't know his way around yet." That definitely is not a lie.

We hug each other again and irrationally cry.

"I'm so happy you're home. You look happy," Bri whispers as she hugs me.

"It's good to be home, and I really am happy."

The three of them watch me

leave with arms linked. I turn back before I shut the door behind me and grin, knowing those girls will be by my side forever.

* * *

My car flies up the driveway, and as I take the corner toward the garage, I have to hit the brakes before running Miles over. He's unfazed by his almost-demise as he looks over my car.

I lean across the car and open the door for him. "Get in."

Cautiously, he crouches down into the passenger seat. His legs barely fit; they're scrunched between the seat and the dashboard. He's wearing dark blue jeans, the same blue button up shirt and black shoes. His hair is swept back off his face, but some strands are trying to rebel and fall across his forehead. I know I'll never get used to seeing Miles in jeans—not that it's a bad problem to have. Without his coat and cravat, I can see how strong he is. Maybe Mom didn't get the right size, because his shirt is a tad tight around his arms, or maybe that's the purpose of the shirt.

Miles' eyes are laughing as he watches me look him over. "Have I gotten it wrong again? Your mother helped me." Becoming uncomfortable, he tugs on his sleeves and straightens his collar. My fingers wrap around his chin as I turn his face to me.

When he looks at me, I see the uncertainty he feels, and I want to make it go away.

"You are doing incredible here, Miles. The reason I looked at you that way was not because you did something wrong. I was only surprised when I saw you in these clothes. It makes it feel more real that you're here with me. As embarrassing as it is, I think I was gaping at you."

The corner of his mouth twitches. "Gaping? If you are not careful, Gracie, I may start feeling like an object around you."

I tap his nose and laugh. "Only if you stay so pretty." Reaching across him, I take the seatbelt and bring it across his chest, but he catches my hand. Looking up, I see the uncertainty from before is gone.

"You look happy." He brushes the hair from my face.

"I am happy."

32

There's warmth in his eyes as he leans forward and kisses me. It isn't a long kiss, or deep, but it's powerful. It's just long enough to send my thoughts swirling, and my plans for the rest of the day become only a memory. He sits back in his chair and watches me as I try to buckle his seat belt. After the third time missing the slot, I calm down enough to concentrate. How hard is it to buckle a stupid seat belt? When I hear the click, I sit back and sigh.

"Why are you still so nervous around me?" he asks, finding the humor in it.

"I'm not nervous." Shifting the car in reverse, I turn my head and back down the drive.

"That may have worked on me when we first met, but I know you now. The changes in your face are what give you away. You do not look at me, but I know you want to. You fiddle with your fingers when you cannot find the right words to say. Sometimes, if your nerves get really bad, your hands tremble." He reaches over and takes my hand from my lap, and even with my arm flexed, I can't stop it from shaking.

"Why is that? Why are you nervous?" As if my thoughts weren't already jumbled, he raises my hand to his mouth and kisses my palm.

"It's not you that makes me nervous. It's the way you make me feel that has me nervous." Taking my hand back, I grip the steering wheel tightly. It's hard to concentrate on the road when I know he's looking at me. We need to change the subject and come back to it at another time, hopefully when I'm not driving.

"If you don't mind, I'd like to take you somewhere," I say.

"I do not mind. But if you would please tell me, what are we traveling in?" His gaze moves around the car, and he presses buttons on the console like a small child.

"This is a car, our version of a carriage."

"You do not need horses to pull it?" Watching the other cars pass us, he gets more confused.

"The horses are under the hood." Laughing at my incredibly lame joke, I push the gas a little harder.

It's a nice drive. There are moments we talk, and others that we're

33

content just being with each other.

"Have you ever seen the ocean?" I ask.

"No. We did not travel much because my mother loved being home. When it came time for me to take my tour, my father had been absent for a few years, so I could not leave Annie. She made me promise I would take one this coming spring. But then you came. It seems I am able to take my tour after all, just to different places."

After an hour, I flip on the radio and find a station that has classical music. No need scaring him with some of the music of today. He only smiles when he hears the music, sits back in his chair, and watches the land fly by.

When we arrive, I pull into the small parking lot and discreetly watch Miles get out of his seat belt. Secretly, I'm hoping he'll get stuck, but he pushes the button and is soon free. Once outside, I take his hand, and we head to the lighthouse. The smell of salt and fresh air blows around us as we make our way to the look out. You can hear the ocean, but once you see it, the noise goes up an octave. Watching the violent waves crash into the cliffs is calming to me. Taking a deep breath, my body relaxes as I think of all the afternoons I spent here with Dad.

"My dad used to bring me here when I was younger. There were so many things he loved about this place." Looking out at what seems like never-ending ocean, I feel like Dad is here.

"What were they?"

"Come on, I'll show you."

I lead him around the tourists taking pictures and sit down on a bench nudged up against the railing. Motioning for Miles to sit next to me, I turn to the horizon and smile. Just below us is the reason Dad brought me here and what I was hoping to show Miles.

"Miles, look over there. Do you see those birds?" I point out just below where we're sitting to two bald eagles flying circles around each other. He nods and watches as they swoop around one another, and then with a force that looks too great for their small frame, they fly higher. "Watch them."

I've seen this done so many times, but it never gets old. The eagles are climbing to the clouds, weaving in each other's paths to stay connected. At

34

the height they think is adequate, they stop flying up and begin circling each other. Smiling in anticipation, I turn to Miles to watch his reaction. When his eyes get wider I know he sees it. Looking back, I see the two birds diving toward the earth with no hint of stopping. They hurtle toward the ground at an alarming speed, but it's not this that's so beautiful. If you look closely, or have seen it enough times, you can see them holding on to one another. Their talons clasp tightly as they spin toward the ground. Miles stands up so he won't lose sight of them when they drop below the cliff's edge. I see the worry in his eyes as the eagles soar toward the water, and then see the relief when they break apart at the very last second. Their wings catch the wind, and then they find each other again to fly off.

"My dad used to bring me here to watch the eagles when they would court. He told me they do things to impress each other. Sing songs, fend off other eagles, or do acrobatics in the air. Once there is a connection in place, they fly together. One never leads the other, they fly as a pair, usually flying around one another. They then fly really high and hold onto each other as they plummet to the ground. I'm not sure why they do this, but my dad said it was a sign of trust. They could fall together. They trusted the other to let go when the time was right to save them both. After the fall, they find each other again and fly off. Some pairs do this continuously through the courting period, others only have to do it once.

"Bald eagles choose a partner, and they're theirs for life. They take their partner home to where they were born and start a home there. But they both came from different homes, so one has to make a compromise and live with the other, away from their home."

I didn't realize when I began, but I could be explaining Miles and me at the moment.

"My dad loved these birds because they were one of few animals who stay with one partner throughout their life. He loved watching them show off and eventually fall for each other. He said it reminded him of trying to impress my mom. We came here every year and watched for them. He told me all kinds of facts about eagles. When he got sick he started to tell me the same facts over and over. At first I was scared that I was losing him, but then I realized he was only telling me the ones that meant most to him."

Miles wraps his arm around me and pulls me closer to him. My head rests comfortably on his shoulder, and I watch the eagles take another plunge toward the water. I don't know how long we sit there. Miles occasionally kisses the top of my head or traces his finger along the lines of my palm.

And while sitting here with Miles, I remember the thing Dad would repeatedly tell me when we'd watch for bald eagles. He'd say, "Home isn't where your house is. Home is where your family is." I think I understand that now. A week ago, I would've been happy to live at Rockwell and make that my home, because Mom was there and so was Miles.

Home doesn't necessarily have to be a house. In my case, my home lives within the people I love.

The sun vanishes behind gray clouds, and rain begins drizzling.

"We better get home," I say when the drizzle turns into pouring. "It'll be dark soon, and my mom will get worried."

We get home just in time for dinner, and I can't remember anymore what I ate when she wasn't here. Mom is just finishing up with the sauce while Shane and Beth set the table. It looks so natural, like we've been having dinner together for years. Miles helps carry food to the table, and I stand in the corner shoving biscuits in my mouth before Mom catches me.

Dinner is strange, but also a lot of fun. We each tell our different stories of the mirror. Beth seems fascinated by everything that's happened. She asks questions and laughs when the explanations are nothing like she expected.

When dinner ends, no one leaves the table. Laughing at Shane's stories of Dad and him as children is much more appealing than clean-up.

Miles sits back in his chair and fidgets uncomfortably. I glance over and see his face scrunch and his arms wrap around his stomach.

"Are you okay?" I ask.

"Yes, I think I must have eaten too much."

"Rookie mistake with Carolyn's cooking." Shane smiles at Miles. "It's easy to overdose on anything she makes. You need to work up to it. Takes time." Shane laughs when he sees Miles tighten his arms over his stomach.

"I am sure you are right. Carolyn, you are a phenomenal cook. My full

36

stomach is testament to that. Thank you for dinner, but if you will excuse me, I think I will retire early." I stand with him, but he stops me. "Please, stay and finish your conversation." He winces, tries to hide it, then winces again. Rolling my eyes, I take his hand and walk with him to his room.

He sluggishly walks beside me, his other arm still wrapped around his stomach. "How silly of me to go to bed after making myself sick, eating too much."

"I do it all the time."

I sit on the side of his bed as he pulls the blankets up and tries getting comfortable. "Do you want some medicine?" I feel his forehead just to be sure.

"No, I am fine. Actually, I am extremely tired. I believe sleep will be the medicine I need."

"Good night." I kiss his forehead before leaving. Once I get to his door, I hear his breathing deepen. He's already asleep.

"He okay?" Shane glances up from his plate of cheesecake.

"Yeah, he's tired. Poor guy has had to adjust to a lot lately."

"Something tells me he'd adjust to a lot more to stay by you," Beth says, smiling. I smile back, knowing he would.

After dinner, Mom walks Beth to her car, and surprisingly, I'm exhausted.

"Good night, Shane." I wave at him and get a grunt in return, because he's stuck with kitchen clean-up.

The night isn't the escape I was hoping for. The deep rejuvenating sleep doesn't come, but the dream does. Again, I'm throwing myself through the mirror only to land back where I started.

My reflection taunts me, turning and walking away, knowing I can't follow it. And when I try, I only got more mad when I make no progress. As with the night before, I sit on the floor and wait until the sun rises and I can finally walk out of this dream.

"I'm guessing you didn't sleep well."

I glare at Mom as I enter the kitchen. "No, I didn't."

"Was it Miles? Is he still feeling sick?"

"He's not up yet?" That's unlike him. He's usually up, showered, dressed, and making breakfast by the time I get out of bed.

"I haven't seen him." Mom usually worries about things much more than I do, so her nonchalant attitude toward Miles is also unlike her. Now that I'm looking for something, I see it. She's nervous; her hands shake as she puts together her breakfast.

"Are you okay, Mom?" She slices the apple, putting it on her plate, ignoring my question. "Mom?"

"What? Oh yes, I'm fine. Just fine." She quickly puts the rest of the fruit on her plate and flees from the kitchen. After I see if Miles is okay, I need to make sure Mom is.

I knock on his door, and when I don't hear anything, I look inside. Miles is still asleep in bed, sprawled out, looking like he had as much sleep as I did. Sitting on the side of the bed, I carefully feel Miles' head again. No fever. His coloring looks better this morning, though. He feels me touch him and he slowly opens his eyes. When they focus, and he sees me, a sleepy smile forms.

"How are you feeling?" I ask.

"Much better. I told you sleep was the best medicine." He tries sitting up, but his eyes glaze over and his body sways.

I gently push him back on his pillow. "Stay here awhile. I can bring breakfast up."

"That is ridiculous. I am very capable of walking down to the kitchen."

I grin because our roles are reversed. Last time it was him who insisted on doing everything for me. From carrying me from the river, to keeping me locked up in my room at Rockwell. I remember how much I hated it, so I back off.

"If you feel well enough to go downstairs, then be my guest." I wave a hand to the door. Watching him stand is painful. He wobbles and keeps rubbing his eyes with the heels of his hands. "I'm guessing you don't want spaghetti for breakfast." I know the thought of him eating what he did last night will make his stomach churn, and I want that. He obviously needs to stay in bed.

"Please, Gracie, I do not wish to be sick in front of you. Let me change. I will meet you downstairs." He shuffles to the closet, so I let him have some

38

privacy, but I don't go far. After too long, he finally comes out. He looks better after a shower and a change of clothes. The color is coming back to his face, and he no longer hunches over. When he sees me, he rolls his eyes.

"You worry too much. It is as if you have feelings for me," he says dryly. He puts his arm around my shoulder; it's heavier today as he puts more of his weight on me.

"I do have feelings for you, some are not very kind at the moment." I shuffle under his weight. He's too big. Even after I try to be careful, he falls into the chair at the table. He puts his elbow on the table and rests his face on his hand like he can't keep his head up a second longer. He looks tired again. Maybe food will help. Looking through the fridge for the mildest breakfast I can find, Shane comes in behind me.

"How are you feeling, Miles?" Shane asks.

"Much better, thank you. I only need to remember that when my stomach tells me to stop eating, it is probably wise to listen."

"With Carolyn's cooking, you never listen. It's worth getting sick for a few hours." Shane would know, as he's now popping some antacids in his mouth.

I hand Miles some toast and yogurt, not really sure it's the best food to be giving him. He eats only half then pushes it aside. Mom will know what to feed him.

"Shane, do you know where Mom is?"

"You haven't heard?" he asks, surprised.

I whirl around to face him. "Heard what?"

"I should've known she wouldn't tell you," he mumbles as he walks over to the counter and switches on the TV. My heart sinks when I read the breaking news headline.

LATE MILLIONAIRE'S WIFE FOUND ALIVE

"Oh no." I sit and watch the footage of the front of my house as reporters describe the return of Carolyn Gentry. "Where is she?"

"In the other room speaking with Mr. Mitchell, your father's attorney. Police should be here soon."

"What will she tell them? I guess this is probably for the best. Now we can get everything squared away with the business, and you can start fixing everything."

"Grace, this isn't for the best. Your mother has been missing for over a year. People are asking questions. Did she fake her death? Has she been paying taxes? Where has she been? She can't answer any of these truthfully."

"How did they find out?"

"News said some people spotted her while we were shopping. I told her she can't hide a face like hers, but she didn't listen." Shane slams the cupboard shut, then presses his hands against the counter.

"What can I do?"

"Nothing right now. Carolyn and I have come up with a story. We'll let you know the details when it's important."

"It's important now." I look up at him, not giving him a chance to argue with me. He sits across from Miles and slides the bottle of medicine to him, then turns to me.

"Our story as of now is she went down in the plane crash but managed to escape with a parachute. I made sure that plane was in pieces so no one would be able to count parachutes . . . or body parts. The plane went down in Idaho where there is an exceptional amount of vacant land, mountains, forest, etc. Your mother woke, not remembering what happened or who she was. She found a cabin, belonging to an elderly couple who had just moved there after retiring. They took her in and nursed her back to health. She stayed with them for a few months, helping around the house and surrounding land until parts of her memory started to come back. She finally remembered everything. Who she was, where she was from, her family. So she made a miraculous return to us."

Geez, it sounds like something out of a book. "Don't you think everyone is going to start looking for this couple?"

He smiles, a little wickedly. "That was taken care of before your mom went missing. Who do you think paid for that couple's retirement?"

"Are you serious?"

"The less you know, the better. I'm not sure what's going to happen in

40

the next few days, but it's best if Miles stays out of the way in case they start questioning him. Grace, you'll be asked questions too. Tell them what happened from your point of view. Your mother was in a plane crash and couldn't be found. You held a funeral and buried tokens of her. While in England over Christmas, your uncle received a call from your mother. We both rushed home to see her. That's all you need to say. Anymore questions they ask that are outside of the basics, you say you don't know, because in all honesty, you don't."

This is all so ridiculous I don't know if I should laugh or cry.

Mom comes into the kitchen looking awful. It looks like she's been up all night. Her eyes are swollen from crying, and her face droops, which is something since her face is so skinny.

Beth comes rushing in from the back door. "I just saw on the news. What can I do?" She gives Mom a hug, and it seems to snap Mom out of her daze.

"Nothing right now," Shane says from the table. "Beth, it's best if you're not here for the next little while. They'll want to talk to you if they think you know anything. It's better if you stay clear." Shane sits back and twists the medicine cap between his fingers. I know him well enough now that I can see his calm face, but his eyes are brimming with anxiety. He always tried to put on a strong face for me after my parents were gone. I recognize it now.

"I want to stay. Tell me what to do," Beth insists.

"You need to go home. We'll call as soon as we think it's alright for you to come back. Beth, only talk to the police. If anyone else calls or comes by, turn them away. If the police do want to talk, tell them what happened as you saw it, nothing else." He looks up in a way that gives Beth no room to argue.

"Okay. Please call me if you need anything." She hugs Mom, rubs her hand over my head, and goes out the back door.

"What do we do now?" I look to Mom for the answer, knowing Shane will answer it.

"We wait and hope our story sticks."

Miles takes my hand, feeling the seriousness of our situation. The doorbell rings, and Mom and I jump.

41

I guess it begins sooner than we thought.

chapter four

I pace the length of the kitchen over and over as Mom talks to the police in the other room. Every so often I can hear her laugh, and that helps calm some of my nerves.

"It'll work out, Grace." Shane offers me a chair, but I shake my head and continue pacing. "Why don't you go downstairs and find Miles? This is going to take a long time, and your pacing isn't going to help the outcome."

"I can't help it."

"Go downstairs," he says again. "Miles was asleep when I last saw him. He might need something. He doesn't look good."

I shoot him a glare when he uses dirty tactics to make me leave. Using Miles as artillery isn't fair, but it works, so Shane doesn't care.

I go downstairs and find Miles sound asleep on the couch. He still looks so sick, especially against the black leather of the couch. I pull his blanket up over him, and then pull another from the back of the couch and make a bed on the floor. I try watching the rest of Miles' movie but don't make it very far before falling asleep.

There's a reason I don't take afternoon naps. I can never quite wake up from them. Someone is moving my limp body, but all I can do is grunt at them. When I hear Miles laugh, I open my eyes.

"How long have you been on the floor? You should have woken me." He puts me on the couch and offers me the blankets he gathered from the floor.

"I didn't want to wake you. You're the one who said sleep was the best medicine." All the muscles on my left side are numb from lying on the ground too long. "Do you feel okay? Do you need anything?"

"Stop fussing. I am fine."

He doesn't look fine. Somehow in the last day he looks skinnier, weaker. His usual ruddy cheeks are now pale, his eyes a little swollen. Even his black hair is wiry and faded.

"Stop watching me, Grace." Peering out of the corner of his eye, he catches me looking over him.

"I'm worried about you."

He puts his arm around me and pulls me into his shoulder. "I only need rest, which is what we are doing."

I nod only because I know the more we fight the more tired he'll get. He smiles at me, but it isn't his smile. It's weak, and his lips look thin. The sun is setting, and the soft glow of sunlight that comes in through the windows makes Miles look worse. Were his cheekbones always so bony? I reach out and touch them, knowing they haven't ever been like this before.

"Maybe we should take you to the doctor," I say.

"I really am fine. I think it is the combination of the different food here and the amount. It amazes me how much food you can put into that little body, Gracie. Were you this way at Rockwell, and I just did not notice?"

"No, you guys didn't eat enough. I cleaned my plate many times and then wondered how inappropriate it would be to ask for seconds or start eating food off others plates." He laughs, slightly flinches, but quickly tries to hide it. "I'm calling a doctor."

"That is unnecessary."

"You called one for me without my consent when I got to Rockwell."

"Yes, but you were unconscious and could not talk back to me. I am now realizing how fortunate I was that you could not." I scowl as he laughs. "Also, your hand was hurt. It was gray."

"So are you." I touch his cheek and feel how cold he is, even with blankets on him. "My friend Bridgette, her dad is a doctor. He'll come here and check you. We won't go to a hospital or even need to leave the house. Please?" He gives me a warning look, and my stubbornness explodes. "I won't drop it. You know I won't. I'll only pester until you say yes, and if it

44

takes too long, I'll get Shane and Mom doing the same." I raise my eyebrows asking him to challenge me.

"Once he says I am fine, you are taking me out of the house."

"The wedding is in a few weeks. Shane reserved the room a few nights before the wedding. I can take you skiing, and by the end of the weekend, you'll wish you never asked me to take you out of the house."

"I am looking forward to it," he mutters, while his eyelids slowly lose the battle to stay open.

"Grace," Shane calls from the doorway. "You have some visitors." He smiles and inclines his head upstairs.

"Stay here." I turn back to Miles, but he's already asleep. I tuck the blankets around him, knowing they aren't helping keep him warm. "He looks worse," I say quietly when I get to Shane. He doesn't say anything back, and that tells me more than anything he could've said.

I walk upstairs and to the entryway, knowing by the sound of hysterics who my guests are.

"Grace!" Bri, Stella, and Kallie are at my side, all trying to hug and talk to me.

"We saw on the news. I thought it was joke, a horrible joke. We had to come see if it's true. Is it? Is your mom back?" I have no idea who asked the question, as they're all huddled around me.

"Well, it's nice to see somethings never change."

The moment they hear Mom's voice, they straighten and turn in slow motion to her. Bri gasps, Stella takes a step back, and Kall has her hand over her mouth. They look to me, and I motion with my head to go ahead. All at once, they throw themselves at Mom. Over their shoulders, Mom nods and smiles at me, telling me the situation from earlier is okay.

"I can't believe this." Kall holds around her waist, Stella around her neck, and Bri around her shoulders.

"How are you? We aren't hurting you, are we?" Bri steps back, pulling the others with her.

"I'm fine. It's so good to see you girls. Grace told me how horrible she was to you." Mom looks past them and scolds me with her eyes for it. "I'm glad you three are not the kind to take offense and walk away. Even though

45

she didn't speak to you, she knew you were there, and just that helped significantly."

"Wait, wait. You're here!" Bri scrambles for words. "You have to come to the wedding. Please tell me you'll come."

"I'm not sure that is a good idea. I can't even leave my house at the moment."

"We're having a dinner the night before the wedding. Grace's hotel reservations start two nights before the wedding. You should come and get away from all the vultures out there. Please come," Bri pleads.

"I don't know, Bridgette. This is not meant to be arrogant, but I'm afraid if I'm there some of the attention that is supposed to be yours will unfortunately be mine, and I could never do that to you."

"Do you think I care about that? As long as Peter is looking at me, the others can do whatever they want." Bri waves her hand in the air to dismiss Mom's worry.

"And no one would blame Peter if he did look at you. Carolyn, you're just as gorgeous as when we were fourteen." Kall smiles at her.

"Things are complicated," Mom says, but she's starting to give in.

"I'll put you on a guilt trip if I have to. Please don't make me," Bri warns her.

"Bridgette, you know I want to come, but—"

"My mom isn't coming."

That silences Mom. Stella and Kall look to the floor. That's obviously a sore subject.

I walk over to Bri and grab her hand. "Debra isn't coming?" I knew her mom was always a flake and horrible to Bri, but I never thought she'd skip her own daughter's wedding.

"She's in Prague, or France, or somewhere else foreign. I stopped keeping track of her traveling after she married her third husband, who loves to travel as much as she does. At least this time she tried to come up with an excuse for not coming home instead of just coming out and telling me she doesn't want to. They have tickets to the theater the night of my wedding, and the tickets unfortunately are not refundable." Bri attempts a laugh, but it falls flat.

46

She looks up at Mom and tries again. "Carolyn, you've been more of a mom to me than she ever was. I'm ashamed to admit it, but I wasn't crushed when she told me she wasn't coming. Maybe everyone will have a better time without her. But I'll be crushed if you don't come. You mean so much to me. I can't imagine you not being there now that I know you're back. Please."

There's no way Mom can argue with that. Through her tears, she smiles at Bri. "I wouldn't miss it."

All the girls erupt into cheers and hug her again. I smile apologetically at Mom behind their backs.

Stella steps away from Mom and turns to me. "Wait, is your souvenir here?"

"Souvenir?" Mom asks.

"Yeah, Grace told us about the man she snatched in England. Is he here?"

"Ah, you told them about Miles." Mom smiles at me.

"You've met him, what's he like? Grace won't give any details." Stella dramatically frowns.

"Whatever Grace told you about him, he's better," Mom says, and I smile smugly. "And no, Miles isn't here at the moment, but you will meet him at the wedding."

"We'll get out of your hair, but we had to come over and see if it was true. If it wasn't, we knew Grace was in need of some friends."

"Thanks, Kall."

"If you need anything, just ask," Bri offers.

"Actually," I say, "there is something you can help me with."

* * *

"Dr. Scott, thank you for coming. You're probably busy with wedding preparations, so I appreciate you taking your time to come."

"Hey, anything to get out of looking at one more swatch of fabric or another shade of roses. I love my Bridge, but a man can only take so much." He laughs while wrapping me in a bear hug.

Dr. Scott was always so nice, but I didn't realize how good he was until Dad died. After that, he stepped in and took over the role. Not in a possessive or pushy way, but because he cared for me. He asked me about boys and told me to warn them he was looking out for me. Dr. Scott is tall and really skinny. His silver hair ages him, and it also makes him look a little scary. Because his face is so skinny, his eyes pop out of his head, giving the illusion that he's always watching you. We used to joke about it as kids, but now those eyes are special to me. He's watched out for me for years.

"Ryan?" Mom stops in the doorway, smiling at him.

"Carolyn." Opening his arms for her, she rushes into them. "I don't think I could ever find the words to tell you how grateful we all are that you're home safe." Holding her like she's fragile, he sways a little while she cries into his shoulder. "Bridge tells me you're coming to the wedding. You don't know what it means to her to have you there. Both of you." He looks up at me and smiles, and I know there's not a more caring man in the world.

"I'm sorry, Ryan, your sleeve is all wet." Mom pulls away and dabs at her face.

"I'm sure that's what sleeves were intended for. Now, it seems I have a patient that needs checking." He looks to me to show him the way.

Miles is hesitant when we first come in, but once he feels the sincerity from Dr. Scott, he relaxes.

"Tell me what's been hurting." Dr. Scott listens to Miles breathe when Miles glances wearily at me.

"Do you want me to leave?" I ask. Maybe he needs to be more thorough with Miles, and me being here makes it difficult.

"No." Miles pats the couch beside him, so I sit down and take his hand. "Just do not be angry with me," he says quietly. He gives me a small smile then begins listing his symptoms. "My head has been foggy. Mostly tired I believe. When I first started feeling ill my eyesight was a little off, but it seems to be getting better on its own. My stomach has had some sharp pain, but not constantly. It only comes occasionally. The pressure is more stabbing than dull. The muscles in my legs and arms ache, like I have been lifting heavy objects. Food is starting to lose its flavor as well, but I have

48

not really had much of an appetite."

I hold back my glare. He's been sicker than he let on.

"Well, Miles, your lungs and heart sound perfect. Strong." Dr. Scott puts his stethoscope back into his bag and turns to Miles. "I wonder, have you been eating differently since you have arrived here? Grace tells me you are from a small town in England. I'm assuming the food here is different than what you're used to."

"Yes, very different. Nothing can match Carolyn's cooking." Miles looks past me and smiles at Mom.

"Yes, I believe that. I wonder if that's what's bothering you. If you go from eating plain and simple meals to some American foods, it will make an impact. My advice would be to keep your meals simple. No spicy dishes, no foods with a long list of ingredients. Try to eat as bland and fresh as possible. If you don't feel better in the next few days, call me, and we can take some blood down at my office."

"I appreciate your help, Dr. Scott. May I ask one more favor?" Miles asks. Dr. Scott nods. "Will you please tell Gracie that I am fine to go out and that she does not need to worry about me as she does?" Miles glances at me only to be met with a glare. Of course I worry about him.

"I'm sorry, my boy, it's in the Gentry genes. They worry only because they care." Dr. Scott shakes Miles' hand and tells him another time to watch his symptoms and if they continue to call him.

"I told you. I am as healthy as can be," Miles says, pulling me down next to him after Dr. Scott had said goodbye. "Now, what are our plans for the rest of the day?" He almost has me convinced to take him out, but the yawn that cuts him off midsentence ruins it for him.

"I'll make you a deal. We take it easy for the rest of the day. If you wake up tomorrow not feeling worse than you do now, we'll go out."

He considers it and kisses the top of my head. "Deal." He pulls me closer to him as he sits back against the couch. "May I ask you a question? And you must be honest." Something in his face has me worried. I nod, a little afraid of the question. He rubs his neck, which only makes me more anxious. "Are you happy I am here? Or are you having regrets that you asked me to come?" He's hesitant to ask so I fight my initial reaction to laugh.

"Do you think I'm regretting it?"

"I am not sure." He looks down at my hand in his and starts playing with my fingers.

"Why do you think that?"

"Ever since we arrived here you have been distant. When we sit by each other you sit at a distance. When I stand by you, you take a step away. I am usually the one who reaches for you to take your hand or brush your cheek. Now, I am not complaining. I have no problem showing my feelings for you. But if your feelings for me have changed, tell me now so I can find a way to change them back."

I wait to answer only because I want to be sure I say the right words. "You're right. I have been distant." He stops playing with my hand and looks up at me.

"Miles, asking you to come here was one of the best decisions I've ever made. The reason I've been distant since coming is because I didn't want you to feel uncomfortable." Annoyance flashes in his eyes, but I hold up my hand before he can say anything. "I know you want me to be myself, and I've tried. But you come from a time where men and women aren't allowed to do much together. Women have chaperones and men care about a woman's reputation. None of that applies here. I could kiss you in the middle of town with thousands walking by, and not one person would think twice about it. You could live in this house with me, and no one would question your intentions or my reputation. When we got here, I told myself to stay close but not too close. I wanted you to feel comfortable with your surroundings, and I wasn't sure you could do that if you were constantly fighting me off."

His mouth curves up as he wraps his arms around my waist. "Constantly fight you off? Have you no control, Gracie?"

I laugh and then shudder when he kisses my cheek. "When it comes to you, my control is unfortunately lacking. Why do you think I've sat away from you? I knew if I sat too close I would . . . " I look away before he can see my face, and I hear him laugh into my hair.

"Do not try hiding it, I already saw you blushing."

50

Dang it! I turn back to him, and the amusement he gets only from teasing me is in his eyes.

"Now I am curious." I can feel him smile as he kisses my hand. "What would you want to do? Had you not been unnecessarily nervous about my feelings?"

I don't know if it's his light mood that has me so serious or the fact that he brought up me wanting to kiss him, because of course I do. But every time I tell myself to wait. Wait until he's settled, wait until he's comfortable, wait until he feels better. Now all those excuses are gone, so I take my hands from his and put them on his cheeks. The moment I touch him, he looks up, and his light mood is now as serious as mine. We look at each other for a moment. I don't kiss him yet, but it's not because I'm trying to linger to make the kiss better.

His eyes are different. They're not the blue that had me hooked the moment I saw him. Gray is seeping into them, turning them almost lifeless. My hands against his cheeks are making his skin discolor further. And then he smiles, but it's not *his* smile.

I close my eyes to stop whatever thought is trying to plant seeds inside my mind. I lean forward and kiss him, knowing the Miles I'm kissing now isn't the Miles I selfishly asked to follow me here.

chapter five

Miles has been here for about three weeks, and he feels a little better every day. He has more color and energy and is able to make it through the day without a nap. He's recently started asking for seconds after he's finished off his small, incredibly boring, healthy meal.

"What are we doing today?" he asks, visibly anticipating getting out of the house again.

"What do you want to do?"

"Anything."

"Okay. I was thinking that I probably should go shopping for a wedding gift. If you're up for it, you can come with me." Maybe taking him shopping will make him want to stay at the house more often.

"I already got you a dress for the dinner and reception. I also got a suit for Miles," Mom calls from the other room, and Miles and I both laugh. My mind starts working on forming an image of Miles in a suit. The night of the ball comes to mind, and I smile but quickly hide it before he can ask why I'm smiling.

After Miles agrees to go shopping with me, I quickly shower and throw on another conservative sweater and jeans. I'm not sure I'll ever be comfortable enough to dress in anything less. He's thrilled to be out of the house, which is the only reason I let him have the window down all the way into town. It isn't Rockwell winters, but it's still cold. By the time we get to the shops, I need something to warm me up. We stop at the coffee shop before exploring the stores and run into Beth while ordering.

"You've got it bad, Grace," she says as we sit at a small table while Miles waits for our food.

"Is it that obvious?"

"I've known you almost your whole life; it's obvious to me. And I'm pretty sure to everyone else in this place." She laughs and puts her hand on mine. "You look happy. I know that look, and it only comes when you're affected by someone else."

"Is that how you felt when you were in love?" The question is out before I even think about asking it. "I'm sorry, Beth. That was rude. You don't have to answer."

Over the years, Beth has mentioned the man she fell in love with when she was younger, but I've never asked about it, because the look on her face made it seem like she still lives with the heartache.

Even though she tries smiling through it, her face falls slightly. "Not rude. And yes, that is how I felt. When you meet someone who you feel completes you, it's hard to see yourself without them. They become a part of you. That's how it was for me. I fell fast and was constantly amazed at the person I was becoming because of him. Even when he died, I felt him with me. The life we had planned with each other was still my goal, and even without him, I tried to accomplish it. But I soon realized that he completed me for a reason. There were certain parts of me that were stronger with him, and when he was gone, they were weaker. Although I tried to stay that person, half of me died with him." She turns her head, tucking a piece of hair behind her ear.

"Beth, I didn't know you before or with him, but if it was because of him that you are who you are now, I'm grateful for him. He sounds like an incredible man, and I'm sorry that I never got to meet him." My smile is careful in case I'm overstepping my boundaries.

"He was incredible, and thank you for saying that," Beth says. Miles arrives with our food, and Beth excuses herself. "I won't ruin your date, but I had to say hello."

"You are welcome to stay." Miles offers her the chair next to me, but she declines.

"No, I have some things I need to do, but thank you."

"She seems very nice," Miles says as he pushes my hot chocolate, donut, and croissant to me.

"She is."

"How do you know her?"

"She was always around. I'm not sure there's a title for her. She became part of the family. When I thought my mom died, she was there for me. Shane was so distraught that he closed up on himself. He stopped talking as much, he avoided me any chance he got, and he never spoke about Mom. Ever. Beth was all I had."

"She sounds like Annie in that way. After my mother was gone and my father began traveling, it was Anne who kept me together. It was unfair of me to rely on her as much as I did, but she helped me get through it."

"Do you miss her?" I've avoided talking about his family, but the way he talks about Annie, it's inevitable.

"Yes. I miss her making me laugh, always unintentionally. I miss the feeling I get when around her. She seemed to calm anyone or make anyone happy." He laughs to himself, and although it's so good to see him laugh, there are twinges of guilt in my gut as I listen to him talk about Annie.

"Maybe you could—"

"But, as much as I miss her and my father, I am happy where I am." He leans across the table and kisses me. "Very happy." He smiles and sits back, but something behind me catches his attention. His smile grows wider as he watches, then motions for me to do the same. When I turn, I can't do anything but laugh. Stella, Bri, and Kall have their hands on both sides of their eyes, peering through the window at us. Kall is bouncing, and they all laugh as they talk to each other.

"Um, those are my friends I was telling you about. Are you ready to meet them?" I look back to him, suddenly afraid of the interaction he's about to witness. He's unaffected as he smiles at them.

"Of course, although I am not sure I have much of a choice." He laughs as the door opens and the bell chimes. The three of them are instantly at the side of our table with wide eyes.

Miles stands and turns to them, slightly bowing. "You must be Bridgette,

Stella, and Kallie. I have heard much about you. My name is Miles. It is a pleasure to meet you." When he sticks his hand out, Bri goes to shake it, but he takes her hand and kisses it. Then does the same to Stella and then to Kall. Biting my cheek to keep from laughing, I watch their reactions. They're confused at what to do, so they smile awkwardly at him.

"Will you join us?" He motions to the table, and all three nod slightly. Miles rounds up some extra chairs and helps each of them into theirs. He excuses himself to get them some food, and I know he's giving me time to talk to them, because he winks at me before he leaves. Once he's gone, they turn to me with so many questions on their faces I only laugh.

"That's Miles," I say a little smugly as I see them watch him walk away.

"Okay, most important questions first. Does he have a brother?" We all laugh at Stella's question.

"No wonder you blushed when we said his name. Does he kiss everyone's hands like that? I didn't know what to do." Kallie runs her hand over her other where he kissed it.

"Where he comes from it's how they say hello," I explain.

"Maybe I should leave and come back in to say hello." Stella grins, and we all laugh again until Miles comes back.

"I hope this laughter is not on my behalf." He smiles at them as he sets down a donut and croissant for each. "I was not sure what you liked, so I got you the same as Gracie."

"Gracie?" Bri arches her eyebrow and turns to me. "I thought that name was off limits?"

"It is." Miles sits down beside me, wrapping his arm around my shoulder. It surprises me how comfortable he is with showing affection in a public place. He had a hard time being close to me at Rockwell when it was just him and me. "When I first met her, she told me not to call her that, and it only made me want to call her it more. I started calling her Gracie only to bother her, but the more I said it, the more I loved it. And then I realized it was not only the name I was falling for." He twists a lock of my hair around his finger, and I fight the urge to shudder. It'll only give them more ammo to tease me about later when they call and break down every second of this meeting.

55

"How did you two meet?" Bri starts pulling pieces of her croissant apart as she nestles into her seat.

"Well, I got to England and . . . "

"No," Bri holds up her hand, "I want to hear it from him. You have the tendency to hold things back."

Miles laughs. "I met Gracie at Rockwell. My sister and I were out riding and found her in the forest behind the house. She was hurt, so we kindly offered our assistance."

"Which she refused," Kall puts in.

"Of course." Miles chuckles, and I can see him getting more comfortable with them. "After some misunderstandings and prodding, I got her back to my home, although she had fainted on the way. A doctor came and told us she was healthy other than a bruised hand, so we invited her for dinner, and she instantly bewitched everyone in my house. A lot of my family's help that, I am embarrassed to admit, I never thought twice of, were drawn to her. After a few short days, I found that my entire household liked her better than me. This was something I should have been sour about, but how could I blame them?" He's talking too close to my face, something that's oddly making me dizzy. "She then naively thought it would be better for both of us to go home alone, but she did not get too far before she realized she could not live without me."

I always know when Miles is smiling without looking at him. His voice is different.

"So, she asked you to come with her, and you left your life behind and came?" Stella asks.

He laughs lowly, and then kisses my cheek. He turns back and looks at Stella with a smile that has everyone joining him. "How could I not?"

"Okay, I think that's enough of this topic." I put my napkin on the table and scoot my chair back. "Miles and I have errands to run if you want a gift from us at your wedding this weekend." I look at Bri, knowing she'll let us go without a fight. Kall and Stella aren't so cooperative. Miles laughs as we stand, and they keep asking question after question.

On our way out the door, Kall yells from the table, "We'll call you tonight, Grace." And with the looks they're giving me, I know I'm not getting out of it.

"What do we need to get for the wedding?" Miles seems so relaxed as we walk down the street. He takes my hand, and I have to keep my eyes on the sidewalk to make sure I don't fall as I try keeping up with his stride.

"We need to find a present to take to the reception. I'm guessing Mom got everything else we need." The mountain of shopping bags she came home with has to contain everything we need, and some things we don't.

"What gifts do you usually take to a wedding?"

"Usually something to help the couple get started in their married life. Toasters, towels, picture frames . . . stuff like that."

We decide on a waffle maker, because Miles says it seems easier than making pancakes, which he tried making a few weeks ago and failed at miserably. We spend the rest of the day in town, while he tries soda for the first time, along with cookies, clam chowder, and ice cream.

With the amount of food we ate, it should be impossible for me to be hungry, but as soon as we walk in the house, my stomach growls when I smell dinner cooking.

"Dinner in ten," Mom says when we come into the kitchen. Shane comes in, rubbing his hands together, excited for another meal.

During dinner we make our plans for the weekend.

"You and Miles drive your car up in the morning and check in. Shane and I need to get some things finished, and we will be up in time for the dinner."

"What do you need to finish tomorrow?" I didn't miss the way Mom's eyes slid over to Shane.

"Well, your mother and I got things finished with Mr. Mitchell," Shane tells me. "We acquired the codes and clearance to get your father's files. I'm pretty sure the mirror has been fixed or at least won't be sending out signals of being used. We wanted to test it tomorrow just in case. I was going to go through, and Carolyn would watch from my computer here."

Shane describes these recent events like they're ordinary things to discuss over dinner, but they're far from it. What he just said is the very reason I came back from Rockwell. The weight it has put on me since learning of the mirror is tremendous, and in just seconds, Shane has it

57

resolved.

"We can go through the mirror now?" I ask. Selfishly, my first thought is the reoccurring dream I've had of the mirror. I'm not sure how to figure out what it's been telling me, but knowing we can use the mirror gives me more options. Realizing how self-absorbed I am, I then think of Miles. He can go back and see his family. When I turn to him with a smile, I see he isn't as happy as I am. He's looking to his lap, his eyes frustrated. Before I can ask him what's wrong, Mom starts planning the trip again.

Tonight is one of those nights I dreamed about after Mom was gone, although it's still missing Dad. The four of us sit around the table and laugh, telling stories to each other for pure entertainment. My favorites are of Mom and Dad's early married years and Shane's childhood. I realize then that although I miss Dad immensely, he's never really gone. Through stories and memories he'll stay with us, and we can bring him to a family dinner whenever we want to.

chapter six

While everyone else falls asleep, I stand in front of the mirror, anxious to see where it'll take me. My reflection looks different, younger somehow. There's an energy coming off the mirror, compelling me to take that last step. Closing my eyes and holding my breath, I step through. The ground is solid beneath me, and it takes a few minutes for me to open my eyes, afraid I'll find myself in my room.

When I finally open them, I'm more disappointed than I thought I'd be. The green rug on the floor, matching curtains, and furniture dash my hopes the second I see them. I told myself not to expect anything, but the feeling I had right before stepping through was so encouraging I was sure there was something on the other side. But I only look at my dark bedroom, resenting it now. Walking over to the bed, I plan to sit here and wait until morning, because I know I won't be able to fall asleep.

Once I sit down, music begins to fill the room. Soft notes dance through the air to a familiar tune. It's a music box. Following the sound, I find a small music box on my dresser with a ballerina in the middle turning in circles. I carefully pick it up, thinking it's going to evaporate once I touch it. This music box is the one Dad gave me after my first dance recital. I loved this box. I danced to the tune every day, mimicked the ballerina, twirling until I found myself too dizzy to stand. The reason I'm so careful with the box now is because this music box broke two years ago. I cried for days after I threw the shattered pieces away. Why is it here now?

I quickly look around the room and see stuffed animals stacked on my bed from biggest to smallest—animals I last saw when they were boxed up and given away. As I keep looking, I realize that I am, in fact, in my room. But it's my room from years ago.

The boy band posters clutter my walls. Along with the posters is a collage of magazine cutouts of what I wanted in my life. Gorgeous actors, fast cars, fancy food, friends, and family. My fingers trail along the collage and with each one comes a memory that makes me laugh. Bri and I made this collage when we were twelve, thinking because we were almost teenagers we needed to set our sights on bigger and better things. I turn around in my room catching glimpses of objects that are now only memories.

I flip on the bathroom light and laugh when I see the picture of me, Bri, Stella and Kall, hanging on my mirror. We took that picture the first night all of us hung out together. We promised each other that night that we would be friends forever. In lipstick a big "BFF" is written under the picture.

"I can hear you in there. If you stayed behind because of me, I'm going to be upset." A man's voice comes from Miles' room, but it isn't his voice. It's older, weak and raspy. There's such a familiarity about it, I move to the door driven by pure curiosity. The door creaks as I open it and stick my head in.

"Lynnie, I thought you left. Please say you didn't stay because of me."

Lynnie?

The only person who ever called Mom that was Dad. Searching the room for the voice, I finally see him. Perched up on pillows, he's looking at me, though he can't see much considering the darkness of the room. Through the limited light I can see him, the subtle glow from the lamp on the nightstand makes him vaguely visible. His face is skinny and gray. His eyes are big because of the deep indents surrounding his eye sockets. His once dark brown hair is now wiry and brittle. The body of this man is frail and slightly shaky as he tries sitting up. This man who looks and sounds somewhat foreign to me is not unfamiliar. I recognize him instantly, but the picture I have of him isn't like this.

"Daddy?" My voice cracks as the cry starts to rise up my throat.

Is it even possible?

He sits straight up, and the frail man from before is now strong and surprised. "Gracie Girl?"

My head falls in my hands in case they'll help catch my cries, but they don't. They only muffle them.

"Gracie, come here."

I rush across the room and, ignoring his feeble frame, throw myself at him. Wrapping my arms tightly around his neck, I shake with fear and joy. He smells like his aftershave, just like he always did. His hands pat my back as he offers words of comfort, but I can barely hear him over my crying. What am I doing? Dad is here, and I'm wasting every moment by crying. Sniffing, I pull away and watch as that sweet smile of his appears.

"I'm guessing you found the mirror," he says. The excitement of this information is apparent on his entire face. From his smiling mouth to his amused eyes—eyes that are still as green as mine. At least *that* hasn't faded.

"Yes, I did." I hold his hands, not wanting to let go of any part of him. His fingers are bony and so cold.

"Look at you. You are no longer my Gracie Girl. You are a beautiful young woman."

"I'll always be your Gracie Girl." It's getting easier to talk. That or I'm getting better at talking through sobs.

"That's right, you will. Geez, Gracie, you look just like your mother." His hand is cold against my cheek.

"That's funny. Everyone says I look just like you."

He clucks his tongue. "Don't let them insult you like that. Everything beautiful about you comes from your mother." I laugh and put my hand over his on my cheek. "Tell me everything. How did you find the mirror? Where have you gone?" I hesitate, which he notices. "Are you in trouble?"

"Not anymore, I don't think. Are you comfortable?" Pulling at the pillows behind him, I fluff them and put them back behind him.

"I'm fine, Gracie. Please, tell me everything. Don't leave anything out."

I take a deep breath and begin. He's surprised to hear about Shane's rant I overheard, excited when he finds out I landed in Rockwell, confused that

61

Mom had been there for a year, and angry when I introduced Harrison.

"Harry was there?" It comes out as only a whisper. His eyes are looking into mine, but I know his mind is somewhere else. "What happened next?"

I continue with the story. A little proud, I embellish the story of hitting Harry in the nose with the rolling pin. If it were only to hear Dad's laugh, I would have done it again. I'm not sure how much I should tell him about my relationship with Miles, so I only mention bits and pieces of him. When I get to the part with Hannah, it's too hard to disconnect myself from the story. It's like I'm reliving that experience over again. Dad lets me cry and waits until I collect myself to ask me to keep going. I finish with Shane explaining about the mirror, and then something dawns on me with such clarity I feel stupid I haven't thought of it before now.

"Dad, this is great. I never thought we could go back for you. Shane told us how you died. Now you don't have to. We can save you." My spirits lift and the image of my entire family together again begins to form.

"Shane wasn't supposed to tell you that," Dad snaps at me. He didn't get mad at me often when I was younger, but when he did I knew to steer clear. His thin face makes his emotion more noticeable. It seems every line is turned down with anger.

"Well, he really had no choice under the circumstances. But Dad, do you know what this means?"

"Yes, I do. It means that nothing has or will change."

The image of my parents on both sides of me, arms around my waist, vanishes. "What do you mean? I can go back and change it."

"Gracie, the mirror wasn't created to change the world. The only change I wanted to have happen was right here." His finger points to my heart, and right then, it shatters. "The mirror is complex, and the stone behind it has rules of its own. You can't change the past without affecting the future. If you went back and saved me, there wouldn't be an order in life, and it would need to balance itself out. Yes, I may live through this ordeal, but your mother may not or you. Do you think that's something I'm willing to risk?"

Defeated, I shake my head and drop my eyes from his wary face. "Why don't you go back and destroy the machine? Before it even worked? Then nothing will have changed."

"If I did that, I wouldn't have met your mother, which means I wouldn't have you. I can't argue with you about wanting to be around for you and your mother, but it's out of my hands now. Changing the past will only create an uncertain life for all of us, if there even is an *us*. Please, promise me you won't go change things. This is how it's supposed to happen."

"No, it's not," I snap. "You aren't supposed to die. If you were, it would be because of some natural cause, not murder. I wouldn't be changing fate. I would be changing decisions, wrong decisions."

"Promise me," he orders firmly. "And you have to mean it, because I know how pigheaded you can be. You got that from me. I know how obstinate the Gentry mind is, so you better keep your word. And don't think you can go back and fix things because you think I won't find out. I will, and I will never forgive you if you traded your mother's life or yours for mine. Do you understand?"

I stare at him, wondering if he'd really be able to tell if I went back to change things, but the intent look on his face tells me he would.

"I understand." Is it possible to survive losing your father twice?

"You better get going. It's dangerous for you to be here. Imagine if your younger self walked through those doors and saw you. The mirror isn't something I want younger you finding out about now."

"When were you going to tell me?"

"On your eighteenth birthday. I had a plan to take you around the world. When I said I wanted to change what's inside, I didn't mean I wanted to change who you are. I wanted you to see the world, see different cultures. So it wasn't really change I wanted, just growing into a stronger you."

"I miss you, Daddy."

"Oh, Gracie Girl, I'm not far away." He doesn't understand how much he means to Mom and me. Does he know how our lives will feel meaningless without him? Before I can tell him, there's a knock at the door.

"In the closet, go." He waves me off.

I pull the closet door halfway closed, because the bedroom door opens.

"These women have me hauling trays like I'm some servant," Shane grunts. "Beth made food for you, and I'm in charge of carting it around."

But he stops and smiles when he sees Dad. "You're still ugly, but you're looking better."

"Since I got the looks in the family, that's a horrible insult to yourself, little brother." Dad weakly sits back and grins at Shane.

"No, you got the brains. I got the looks." He sets the tray on the nightstand, then sits down next to Dad on the bed. "Lyn's been looking into taking you to New York. She found a doctor there that specializes in illnesses that are difficult to diagnose." Shane rubs a hand over his face, his eyes losing the humor he was trying so hard to bring into the room. "She's adamant about it. I'm running out of excuses as to why her ideas are bad ones."

Dad's eyes dart to the closet I'm hiding in, he smiles apologetically, then he turns back to Shane. "Keep trying, and I'll keep refusing."

"If we just tell her what's happening she'll—"

"No," Dad refuses sternly. "You promised me you wouldn't say a word to her or Grace. It'll be more important after I'm gone that they have no idea what happened. Let them believe this was natural."

"There's nothing natural about it!" Shane jumps to his feet, his hands ball into fists as he paces the foot of the bed. "Dan, your family is watching you slowly be killed. They have a right to know!"

"And what will that accomplish?" Dad screams back. "Telling them isn't going to change my outcome. I'm still going to die." He sags back into his pillows, blowing out a frustrated breath. "Shane, I can imagine how they'll be when I'm gone; they don't need another thing to add to it. And I never want them to be scared of the mirror."

"They should be." Shane grips the footboard of the bed, towering over Dad. "It isn't fair that you're leaving it behind for them when they don't know the consequences of using it."

"That's why I have you."

Shane straightens, glaring down at Dad. "And what am I supposed to do with it? I don't know how it works. You won't even tell me where the stone is!"

"No one needs to know where it is," Dad says quietly, in stark contrast to Shane's heated words. "Shane, promise me they won't find out about this."

64

He sighs, sits back down by Dad and takes his hand. "I promise. But I think you're stupid."

"You said I got the brains in the family, so that was another horrible insult to yourself." Dad smiles through trembling lips, sits up and hugs Shane, who clings to him. "I love you, Shane. Take care of my girls."

"I will."

"Now go, so I can have my meal without looking at your ugly face."

Shane chuckles and stands. Tears roll over my cheeks as I watch Shane fluff Dad's pillows, gently arrange his blankets over him, and set his tray on Dad's lap.

"I have the looks in the family, so that was—"

"A horrible insult to myself, I know. Now get out of my house." Dad smiles as he watches Shane leave the room. The second the door shuts, Dad, in pure exhaustion, falls back onto his pillows and takes big breaths.

"You'll never meet anyone better than that man," Dad manages to say as I sit down next to him.

"He's great, but I know a man who's pretty amazing." I smile at him as I uncover his plate of cookies and hand him his cup of tea.

Over the rim of his cup, his eyes smile at me. "So . . . tell me about Miles."

Fire ignites in my cheeks at the sound of Miles' name. "Oh, well . . . um . . ."

His smile grows. "Only exceptional people can get someone to stutter. Tripped over my tongue constantly when I met your mom."

When another knock comes from the door, Dad just points to the closet, and I dart in just as Beth comes into the room.

"How are you feeling today?" she asks, taking a thermometer out of her apron and rubbing it over Dad's forehead.

"Better actually. I think it's those disgusting green smoothies Lynnie has me drinking. I've missed my tea and cookies, though." He plops a cookie in his mouth and smiles. "Thanks for making them for me."

"You're welcome." She hands Dad a napkin so he can wipe the tea that's running down his chin. "Carolyn and Grace should be home soon. Should I send them up when they get back?"

"Only Carolyn, I'll see Gracie in the morning. I hate to have her see me like this."

"Okay, let me know if there is anything else I can get you." She bends down and pulls a basket full of linens from underneath the bed. She hums to herself as she changes the pillowcases and retrieves a new blanket for Dad.

Beth's humming stops when Dad begins violently coughing. I immediately move to the door to run to him, but he sends me a look telling me to stay in place. Beth sits on the side of his bed and pats his back as if this is a normal occurrence. It's when I see her eyebrows crumple and the alarm in her eyes that I know this time is different.

"Dan, are you okay?"

He waves her off, not able to speak. She sees something in his hands and begins to back away slowly, shaking her head. Bumping into the door, she snaps out of it and starts moving.

"Dan, I'm going to call 911. Try taking deep breaths. Remember what we practiced. I'll be right back." She races from the room, and as soon as the door shuts, I'm beside him.

"Daddy?" My hands hover over him not sure how I can help. And then I see the blood in his hands, and know there's nothing I can do. "Daddy?" Oh please, let this not be it.

He hunches over as he coughs more and I look away so the image of him won't haunt my memories.

"Go," he manages to say between coughs. Knowing what my answer will be, he pushes me off the bed. "Go," he says firmly, but I can't move. Maybe I can help. Maybe he needs a drink. I hand him the cup, but he pushes it away so fast it falls from my hand and shatters.

"What do you need?" I ask desperately.

He sits back, barely pulling in air. "Grace, go now. And keep your promise, nothing changes." The coughing becomes erratic. Whenever he isn't coughing, he's sucking in breaths so fast I can hear faint wheezes. His throat is closing. He looks at me again, and I know it takes whatever strength he has left to smile.

"Love you, baby girl. Now go."

Staring, I tell myself to move, but I can't. When I hear footsteps outside the door, I start backing away. Entering the bathroom, I turn to see him one last time. But the second I see him, I know it was a mistake to look back. His eyes are closed, and although I still see his chest rise and fall, I know his eyes are never going to open again.

I slip behind the bathroom door and rush to my room. Carelessly throwing myself through the mirror, I land on my knees in my bedroom. I crawl over to my bed, clutching my heart that feels like tiny shards of glass, and with each beat it tears a little more of my soul apart.

I sit down with my back against my bed's footboard, pulling in deep breaths, attempting to forget the way Dad looked, how he breathed, how cold he was. I pull my knees up to my chest, wrapping my arms around my legs, trying to hold myself together.

It happens simultaneously. The same moment I feel nails softly tickle the back of my neck is the same moment I see something move out of the corner of my eye.

I'm not alone.

I cover my mouth with my hands, and slowly turn my head toward the mirror. In the silent darkness of my room, I see a shadowed figure dart from behind the mirror, racing for the opened window. In the silver light of the moon, I watch the person stop at the window. They're dressed in all black, even a mask covers their face. But their head turns toward me, and for just a moment, I can feel the eyes of the person I can't see, look directly at me. For only seconds, while my eyes are locked with ones I can't see, chills crawl under my fingernails, into my blood, and wrap my bones in ice.

Frozen in a moment, I do nothing but watch the stranger turn and jump out the window.

It takes minutes, maybe hours, for me to finally get to my feet, to make my way across my room. With trembling hands, I turn on my light, and then force myself to look behind me.

Everything in my room is as it should be.

Everything but the mirror.

Painted across the mirror in red, dripping paint is *THEY'RE COMING*.

I don't scream. I'm not sure I can. My body stops shaking, my heart stops racing. Altogether, my body flips a switch, just turns off. While the inside of me stops, I still feel the warm tears race down my cheeks. Disconnected, I open my door and walk down the hall to the person I need most.

Oddly numb, I knock on the door. When I see his face, everything that stalled inside me before restarts, quicker and harsher than before.

"Shane." I manage his name before I crumple into his arms, that for me, will always be open.

"What happened?" he asks, tightening his hold around me the harder I tremble. "Are you hurt?"

I shake my head, burrowing my face into his shoulder. "I went through the mirror. I *needed* to go through. It's been this aching need inside me for awhile." I push back and wipe the back of my hand across my eyes. "Shane, when I came back, I think someone jumped with me."

I stumble forward when his arms disappear from around me. By the time I turn around, he's already down the hall and in my room. I stop at the doorway, hating that I'm afraid to even go inside my room.

Shane is standing in front of the mirror, his shoulders quickly rising and falling with big breaths. In his reflection, I see the fear swimming in his eyes, but before he drowns in it, anger comes to save him.

"Tell me what happened."

I explain about my dream, how I wanted to see if it meant anything. I tell him that I saw Dad, but don't elaborate on the night. I only give bits and pieces of what Dad and I talked about, but I end the story before telling him that I overheard him and Dad talking.

"When I got back, someone was here, hiding behind the mirror. It was only for a few seconds before they jumped from the window."

Shane's breath stutters out, his eyes close, and I watch him take three deep breaths. "No one jumped with you," he finally says after he calms himself down. "I'm positive I made it so no one can jump." He walks across the room, scanning the backyard blindly while he pulls the window shut. I jump when he whirls around and punches the wall, leaving a fist-sized hole behind. "Someone is already here!" he screams, kicking my hope chest so it crashes into the wall. "And they were in your room!"

I flinch back when he grabs my vanity chair and hurls it across the room, causing it to crumble into splinters across my floor.

He stares at the broken wood, heaving breaths in and out, his clenched fists shaking at his sides. And then he looks up at me. His eyes narrow, so at first I brace for his anger, but then his chin trembles. Rare tears build in his eyes, framed in a face etched in helplessness.

"Grace."

I wrap my arms around his waist, pushing the events of the evening away so I can make room in my memories for this moment with Shane.

"I can't lose you," he says through barely restrained cries. "You're my only family. I promised."

So, for the first time in my life, I hold him a little tighter and offer comfort that I've never been able to give, because I'm usually the one needing it. Through my own cries, I smile into his shoulder. "I love you, too."

"What happened?" Mom rushes to my side, ripping me out of Shane's arm and into hers. I internally chuckle when I hear Shane grunt, turning his back to us, so no one else will see him the way I did. Over Mom's shoulder, I see Miles watching me intently.

"You're with me." Shane points to Miles. Miles hesitates, so I smile and nod at him, telling him I'm fine. "We're going to check the house and figure out why the alarm didn't go off. Grace, you sleep with Carolyn tonight. And from now on, the mirror stays in my room."

"We don't—" But I clamp my mouth shut when Shane silences me with a look.

Shane stomps out of the room, but Miles stops beside me. His hand runs down my arm in a comforting gesture. "Will you be alright?" he asks.

I wrap my arm around Mom's waist and smile at him. "I'll be fine."

He leans down, kisses my cheek, then follows Shane downstairs.

"Tell me what happened," Mom says when we climb into her bed.

The rest of the night is foggy. I tell Mom bits and pieces of what happened, trying to remember Dad's smiles and laughs and forget his coloring or the sound of his cough. Mom cries with me as we relive the moment we barely managed to live through once.

Because we both need it, I grab her hand and sugarcoat what happened in

69

my room earlier. Mom doesn't need to know how the coldness I felt when I saw the person in my room was like I was drowning in ice. She doesn't need to know how frighteningly easy it is for her daughter to shut off the heart she gave me. And she doesn't need to know that, for a moment, those unseen eyes saw me, they knew me, and I know they'll find me again.

Transitioning from awareness to sleep, I hear Mom's muffled cry, again taking me back all those years ago when I heard her crying through her door. We both cry until sleep saves us.

chapter seven

"The lodge is a few hours away, so you can take a nap if you want," I tell Miles when we pull out of the driveway.

"I feel well and would rather not miss this drive."

I know it's useless to try to get him to nap. Miles took a liking to driving from the start. The car fascinates him. The way it moves, how it operates. If he'd just stop pushing buttons he'd probably get tired.

Because I need a distraction from thinking about last night—from wondering why the alarm was still activated when Shane checked it, why all the doors were still locked, and why there was no evidence of a forced entry—I ask Miles, "Do you want to play a game? I can ask you any question I want, and you have to answer honestly. But the catch is I have to answer my question as well. So don't ask a question you yourself don't want to answer."

It's the game my parents and I used to play when we'd drive to the lodge when I was younger. Dad made it up, so he could get to know things about my life I didn't willingly tell him.

"Alright, you first." He angles his body toward me, and that cheeky grin makes me nervous. I know he's planning to ask me questions I don't want to answer. Maybe this is a bad idea.

I'll start off simple. "Have you ever broken a bone?"

"No, I have not. Have you?"

"Yes, my arm. I was trying to jump to the fourth bar on the playground when I was eight. Didn't take into account the rain or how slippery the bar would be. Landed on my back with my arm pinned underneath me." I pull up my sleeve and show him the scars I have from the screws.

His thumb brushes over the scars as he chuckles softly. "It sounds like you. Going into a situation without thinking of the danger or the consequences." He holds my arm tighter, knowing I'll pull it away.

"Your turn." I let it go, mostly because I know if I argue he has a lot of evidence why that, in fact, is very true.

"How do you know Landon?" he asks.

"You're playing the game wrong. You need to ask a question you can answer as well, but I'll answer it anyway. Landon and his family live by Rockwell. When my parents bought Rockwell, we spent a lot of time there and got to know the locals. We became friends, but after my mom was gone, we didn't talk much. The night of the ball was the first time I had seen him in a long time."

"Did you—"

"Nope, my turn. What was your favorite thing about your childhood?"

He waits a moment to answer, and I get impatient when he smiles. "That would have to be my mother. As much as I loved and respected my father, my mother was extraordinary. When we were young, she would take us on picnics, somewhere different each time. I told you she believed in magic, so every place we went had a story. By the lake, there were magical creatures who watched over the water, kept it clean and thriving. In the fields, they planted flowers. I remember one time clearly. She made a picnic on the floor of our drawing room. I thought she was mad since we did not eat any place beside the dining room. Anne bounced as she jumped on the quilt, ready for the story.

"My mother told us Rockwell was protected by the gods. As long as we loved each other, and stood by one another, home was a sacred place. The more we loved each other, the stronger the protection would be. Looking back now, I am sure she told us that to make me stop torturing Annie." The warmth of his smile has me wishing even more that I could've met his mom. She sounds fascinating.

He gestures for me to answer the question. "My favorite thing about my childhood was going to Rockwell." I look away from the road and smile at him. "We had these Rockwell balls where everyone would dress up as if they lived in 1810. My parents would match colors and spend the evening entertaining everyone. My mom let me put on makeup and made me a new dress every year. I loved those nights, dancing until I ended up falling asleep in the corner. They were always magical growing up, and now having witnessed a real Rockwell ball, I love them even more."

I can feel his gaze on me. I don't know how he does it, but I always know when he's looking at me. Fearing I'll swerve off the road if I look at him, I keep my eyes fixed ahead.

"When did you know?" he asks.

"Know what?"

"Know your feelings for me. Was it a particular moment when you realized? Or did it grow over time?"

I think about it for a minute. I can't remember *not* loving him, even though I've only known him for such a short amount of time. "The time you almost kissed me by the fire, I knew I was in trouble. I realized then that I was falling for you, and it scared me. When you saved me from the Bailiff, I fell for you more. But I didn't fully realize what was happening until I met you six years ahead of our time at Rockwell. Thinking you had a wife made me crazy." I glance at him and smile. "I thought it was Marie, actually."

"Miss Wilson?" The shock in his voice makes me laugh.

"Yes. I was so mad at you. Rose was five, and I had been gone six years. I accused you of moving on a week after I left, not caring enough to wait for me. It was stupid, but I didn't know what to do or how to act, because I thought you were married to someone else. You weren't my Miles anymore. You then accused me of not caring for you enough to stay, which I rudely yelled back at you that I left because I loved you, not because I didn't care. All along, I knew I was slipping, but at that moment I realized I had already fallen."

He grins arrogantly. "I believe there is nothing better in life than catching a stubborn woman when she falls." He laughs when I roll my eyes. "I felt something for you rather quickly. I am not sure if it was admiration or annoyance."

I don't have to look at him to know he's grinning.

"You bothered me at first," he continues. "It bothered me how I felt when I saw you with Mr. Wilson. It bothered me that you made friends with our help, and I could not have told you their names. You did everything wrong and informally, and yet you fascinated me. Because of that, my propriety was nonexistent when I was around you. Many times I wanted to be next to you and take your hand, and those times I wanted to kiss you. I was a gentleman, evidentially a weak one. I did not like that you made me want to do those things. But you bothered me most because I could never get you out of my head."

He takes one of my hands from the steering wheel and traces the outline of my fingers, endangering both of our lives. "I have told you before it was the night after the carriage ended up in the river that I knew I loved you. After I learned you tried to save me, I was angry but also touched, knowing your fear of water. Then you were gone, and I felt your absence in every part of me. It seemed I was hollow without you. And then you came back, and I discovered the holes in me were filled, and I was a better man because of it." He kisses my hand, sending shocks up my arm, effectively jump-starting my heart. "I enjoy this game. Your turn."

Taking a deep breath, I try holding in my courage along with my breath. This is a question I've wanted to ask but have been too scared to. "The mirror is fixed."

I hear him hold his breath, too. "That is not a question." The teasing he aims for falls flat. He's as nervous as I am about this topic.

"What now? Do you want to go back? Do you want to stay here? What happens now?"

"Yes, I want to go back, but only if you come with me. Yes, I want to stay here, if here is where you want to be. I am not sure what happens now. Anything can happen, and I will be happy as long as we are together. Do not give me that look," he chuckles. "You are not taking anything away from me. The mirror is fixed, which means I can visit my family if I wish, but moving here would not be a chore, only a privilege."

"You would move here? Away from your family, your title, everything?"

"I just told you I would. And my family is only a few rooms away. Staying for you has its benefits, but I am really staying for the phone and your mother's cooking." He laughs when I punch his shoulder. "Now, I will not require you to answer your own question, because I have one I want to ask," he says, and I gratefully accept. "I want to know what you were thinking of the night you came back for me. After you saw me and Rose."

Ah! I wasn't expecting that.

"You're playing the game wrong. You have to ask a question you can answer yourself." I think I have him, but he leans over his seat, his elbow resting on the console. He whispers in my ear, and I have to tell myself repeatedly to stay focused on the road. After everything we've been through, how dumb would it be if I killed us in a car accident?

"I intend to answer," he whispers. "That night I was thinking how incredibly lucky I was that you had come back. I thought you had come to warn us of Thomas and was confounded that you came back for me. I was thinking you had grown more beautiful in just two days. And I am embarrassed to admit that after you kissed me my thoughts were primarily on doing it again." He kisses my cheek, then rubs his thumb against the scar by my ear. "Your turn."

You'd think I'd be used to him by now, but my body acts like we're back at Rockwell and he's doing this for the first time. Cursing myself for shuddering, and cursing him for finding it funny, I swallow my pride and answer the question.

"I was remembering you that night. Six years in the future Miles. When I told you why I left, you asked if I had loved you. I told you I had just gone through the mirror and I loved you when I stepped through, which means my feelings hadn't changed. After I told you my feelings hadn't changed you grabbed my face and told me yours hadn't ether. Then you kissed me. I blushed when you kissed me, so I blushed when you asked me about it."

My breath comes out in a big whoosh when I finish. I chance a quick glance at Miles prepared to see him smirking or smiling arrogantly, but his eyebrows are drawn down as he looks straight ahead. His lips are pursed, which he only does when he's thinking through something. A dozen different questions come to mind, but I let him think whatever it is he's thinking through.

"Hm."

That's it? He's been begging me to tell him, and now that I finally do he acts annoyingly indifferent?

"Hm?" I ask, clearly annoyed.

"Well . . . " He rubs his hand over his jaw, then turns to me with a hint of amusement. "That was not what I was expecting."

"What were you expecting?"

"I was expecting you to say you and me had argued, or perhaps I said something that you either liked or found insulting. Those are the only circumstances under which I have seen you blush. It is quite strange, feeling as though I have to compete with another form of myself." He chuckles lowly while shaking his head. "It is also strange that you had already kissed me before you kissed me that night you came back."

"Just for the record, you did kiss me first," I point out.

"And I was wise to."

"Yes, you were. Now try to get some sleep. We still have another hour."

He must be exhausted, because he doesn't argue with me. He reclines his seat, and by the time we pass the next mile marker, he's asleep.

* * *

"You live in a remarkable world," Miles says as we start up the ski lift. It smells like fresh pine, and the smell takes me back to when I was a child. Miles has been studying everything. The reception desk, the elevator— which we rode four times—the key card to get into the room, the mini fridge, the view from our hotel room. Now he's staring at the skiers below us, the mountain above us, and the ground behind us. He's in awe of everything.

"Yeah, I do," I reply. It's fun seeing the world through Miles' eyes. The things I see every day he's seeing for the first time.

"It is much different than Rockwell," he says with a hint of sadness.

"Do you miss it?"

76

"Yes, but that is not was I was referring to." He looks over at me, and only half of his mouth smiles. "To live here and use all of these things every day is unbelievable. It would be difficult to live at Rockwell knowing everything you would be missing." His eyes dart to me out of the corner of his eye and then back to the mountain under us.

"Yes, there are some things that would be hard to live without. But one thing I loved about spending time at Rockwell with you was the simplicity that was there."

"How do you mean?"

To show him, I unzip the pocket of my pants and pull out my phone. There are two texts from Mom wondering where I am and how Miles is doing, one from Bri panicking about this weekend, two from Stella telling Bri she's dumb and to get over her cold feet, and one from Kall asking if there are ironing boards at the lodge because her dress got wrinkled on the way.

"You see? It was nice at Rockwell to unplug from everything. If someone wanted to find me, they had to go looking. Only the important things got passed along. Before I went to Rockwell, I spent so much time seeing how other people lived their lives. What pictures they posted, who they were with, and what plans they had for the weekend. I wasted so much of my life watching other people live theirs. At Rockwell, the only life I had to watch was mine, and I found it very relaxing. Well, aside from all the near-death situations," I laugh, but the sorrow of those experiences quickly follows. The image of Hannah smiling and anticipating meeting her nephew always guts me.

"You would not be sad? To leave here, and . . . um . . . spend time at Rockwell?" His gloved fingers tap his leg, and he shifts his weight uncomfortably.

"Would you be there?" I ask in a teasing voice, hoping to disguise the sudden onslaught of jitters.

"Yes. Hopefully that would be the reason you were there."

"You would only be a perk. The real reason would be those little cakes." I smile, and the fresh air becomes less stifling. He smiles too and sits back, but he sits back too comfortably, which makes the lift shift a little. His back goes rod straight, and then his entire body freezes in place. His eyes dart to the ground and then to the chair in front of us.

"Are you afraid of heights?" I watch him grip the handle bar in front of us, his gloves moaning because he's holding onto it so tight.

"It is not the height I am nervous about. It is the fall to an icy death that has my thoughts consumed." He peers over the side of our seat and gulps. Because I've ridden this lift a hundred times, I know we're safe, and knowing what he doesn't makes me laugh. When he sees me, his eyes narrow, but a little flicker of light shines through them, and that has my laugh dying.

"You find this funny? Watching me squirm?" He's too playful for the situation, and I know when he gets this way usually something follows that I don't like.

I straighten my back. "Yes."

"Grace, have I ever lied to you?"

Wait, what? Where did that come from? "No."

"And I never intend to lie to you. When I make a promise, I intend to keep it." He turns his head to me, making sure the rest of his body stays stiff.

"Okay," I drawl slowly, now cautious.

"There is a place for swimming at the lodge, correct?"

"Yes."

"I will remember the look you have on your face at this moment when I teach you how to swim. I am sure my face will look just as smug." He sits back carefully and grips his knees.

"Teach me to swim? We never talked about that."

"You do not remember? After the carriage accident, you asked me if I would teach you to swim, and I promised I would. You would not want to make a liar out of me, would you, Gracie?"

"I won't hold you to that promise," I answer.

"I will hold myself to it. When do you wish to start?"

Part of me thinks he's bluffing and won't really make me get in the water, but the other half thinks he'll throw me over his shoulder and toss me in the pool kicking and screaming. I look down at the skiers flying down the mountain and witness one skier completely wipe out. The group he's with helps him back up, and they continue down the slope.

"I'll make you a deal," I say as I look back at him, now excited. "If you can make it down the hill without falling, I'll let you teach me how to swim."

He looks down at the skiers as they effortlessly slide down the hill. "All I have to do is make it down without falling?"

"Yes."

"And all you do is balance on these two sticks?" He looks at the skis attached to his feet, and suddenly I'm nervous. Miles is probably one of those infuriating guys that are naturally athletic and immediately good at all the sports they try. I swallow the fear that's rising up my throat. I don't want to get in the pool.

We inch closer to the top of the lift, and I start fidgeting. He won't actually throw me in, will he? I chance a glance at him out of the corner of my eye and see him watching me, clearly enjoying that I'm squirming.

"Don't get too cocky. You have a long way to go."

"I do not like failing in situations. Teaching you to swim is only more incentive."

Wanting to erase that smug smile off his face, I lift the bar sooner than necessary and gladly watch him press firmly against the back of the seat. The employee is telling us to get off and quickly get out of the way of the lift.

"You ready?" I pull my goggles over my eyes. He nods and pulls his goggles down. We push off from the lift, and I quickly give him instructions.

"Keep your knees bent, and try moving your feet in the direction you want to go. If you want to stop, just turn your skies perpendicular to the slope. At first, you should probably point your skies in—"

I don't get any further in my explanation before Miles starts going much faster than me. Feeling stupid that I made the deal, I go to catch up with him. It isn't until I really have to push myself faster that I realize he's going fast because he doesn't know any other way. He's coming up to the orange safety fence that's just off the ski lift.

79

"Miles, turn!" I shout, now feeling sorry that I wanted to watch him fail. He turns his skis fast, too fast. His feet stop instantly, but the force of his stop has his body hurdling over his legs and to the ground. I hurry over to him and sigh when I see he's okay. Well, physically anyway. When I see the sheer disappointment on his face, I can't hold back my laugh, and the more I try to keep it inside, the more I laugh outwardly.

"I am glad you find my incompetence funny," he mutters, trying to get to his feet. I help him up and almost fall myself.

"I'm only relieved that I don't have to hold up my end of the deal. I'm sorry, Miles," I manage between laughs, not able to fully muffle them.

"Are you going to teach me how to use these futile devices or sit there and laugh?" His sense of humor is back, so I don't feel too bad about laughing.

"I'm sorry, I'll stop." I wipe my mouth hoping it'll wipe away my smile. It doesn't. "When you're heading down the mountain position your skis into a triangle. That way you won't go too fast."

I show him how to point the toes of the skis together. He mimics me and I slowly begin inching down beside him. I want to pull my phone out and record this, but I'm afraid if I look away he might crash into something else. His legs are bent and his arms are out in front to steady him, looking like a zombie on skis.

After falling only two more times, we make it down the mountain.

He turns and looks up to where we just came from and smiles. "May we go again?"

After a few more times down the mountain, I take him to the lodge for lunch. "You're going to be sore tomorrow." I hand him a cup of hot chocolate. I sit close to him and pull my feet under me, leaning on his shoulder. We're on the lodge's balcony with a backdrop of the slopes. A metal fire pit is casting off warmth in the middle of the surrounding couches. The afternoon sun is giving off enough heat that we don't need our big coats.

"Falling that many times will leave you bruised," I tease again.

"I did not fall that many times," he clarifies.

"No, that last run you only fell once. You're getting better. Now you just need…" I'm interrupted by a large yawn that hurts my jaw.

"You have been yawning all day. Perhaps we should go back, and you can sleep." His thumb runs across the bags under my eyes, making a nap sound much more tempting.

"I didn't sleep well last night," I tell him as we walk to our room.

"I know. How are you feeling about what happened?" This is the first time Miles has asked about last night—about the stranger in my room, the writing on the mirror, and what happened with Dad.

When I woke up this morning, I went into my room and saw my window was permanently drilled shut. There were white scraps against the wood floor where the mirror had been my entire life. My room felt weird without the mirror. I'm not sure if that's because I'm used to seeing it or I'm used to feeling it. I went down to breakfast and fell into the charade that I'm sure Shane concocted so I wouldn't have to talk about last night. He was happier than he is in the mornings, had our car packed up and all but shoved us out the door.

"Um . . . I'm not sure yet," I answer. "It was weird, but I think it was how it was supposed to be. I always thought he was alone when he died. But Shane and Beth were there, and I guess I was, too." I shake my head quickly to get rid of the image of seeing Dad take those final breaths.

"Miles, did you ski?" Mom asks as we enter the room.

"Not very well," I mutter under my breath, resulting in a very tight hug from Miles.

He locks my arms at my sides with one of his arms and rubs his fist over my head with his other hand. "I only need a proper teacher. One who will not laugh at me the entire time."

Mom points a look at me, and then turns to Miles, smiling. "Grace only laughs because she was on the other end of those lessons for too long. Did you know she refused to ski for years, and when she finally tried it, she got to the top and sat on the slope refusing to move? It took Daniel, myself, and a few ski instructors to coax her down the hill."

"Oh really?" Miles asks, grinning down at me.

"Yes, and when I say coax, I mean drag. She literally kicked and screamed the entire way down. We gained quite the audience." Mom is now laughing, along with Miles. I detangle myself from Miles before he can rub my scalp red. The fatigue from earlier only gets worse as I feel a bout of orneriness coming.

"I'm going to lie down for a few minutes," I mumble over my shoulder but am only met with more laughs.

"Tell me, Carolyn, how many times did it take Gracie to go down the slope without falling?" Miles asks.

"Oh, I'm not sure I could count how many times it took."

Again with the laughing. I close the door behind me and flop onto the bed. I don't even bother to change out of my snow pants. Curling up in a ball, I drape a throw over me and am asleep before I can even kick off my boots.

* * *

"Grace?"

My eyes flutter open, and it takes a few minutes to remember where I am. I see Mom rummaging through my suitcase, muttering what sounds like disappointments under her breath. I slowly roll over, so I can see the clock.

"It's already six thirty? How long have I been asleep?" Forever it feels like. My body sluggishly sits up.

"About four hours, sweetie. Are you feeling okay?" Mom feels my forehead, then my cheeks. "You're warm."

"It's probably because I fell asleep in my snow clothes." I stretch as I stand, annoyed by the fact that I'm going to be so sore tomorrow. The first couple skis of the season always make my body sore. I haven't been skiing in over three years, so I'm going to hurt in muscles I don't remember having.

"We're going to the lodge restaurant for dinner. Shane and I will head down and get a table. You and Miles come when you're dressed and ready." Mom feels my head again just to be sure.

82

"I'm fine, Mom. Last night was rough. I think I only slept a few hours. And I forgot how tired I get after skiing. I just needed a nap." To prove I'm fine, I walk to my suitcase and eagerly dig through my clothes for an outfit.

"You should hang those or they'll all wrinkle." After wincing because I carelessly toss shirts on the bed, she sighs and begins hanging them up for me.

Guessing it's too late to take a shower, I attempt to do something with my hair. I'm too tired to straighten it, but it's unmanageable now that it's been contained in a beanie all day. Mom already left, so I can't ask her to help me, so I throw it in a messy bun. I put on my comfiest clothes, which end up being jeans and a t-shirt. Hopefully no one else is dressed up.

Miles is on the couch waiting for me. He had time to shower. His hair is still damp and combed off his face. He's wearing jeans too, but somehow he looks fancier in them than I do. The black t-shirt matches mine, but he dresses it up with a sports jacket.

"You are alive," he says when he sees me.

"Sorry I disappeared all afternoon."

"It is alright. You needed the rest."

"What did you do?" I offer him my hand to help him from the couch.

"Shane took me around the lodge."

I glance warily at him. "Why are you smiling like that?"

He tries to stop smiling, but can't manage it. "No reason. I just enjoyed my afternoon."

Mom probably told him more stories of my skiing incompetence.

Dinner passes in laughter and stories. My cheeseburger and fries don't stand a chance. They're gone before the others get halfway through their meals, other than Mom. She finishes off her spaghetti in record time.

"Is anyone saving room for dessert?" the waiter asks.

"Yes," Mom and I say at the same moment Shane and Miles say, "No."

The men laugh while Mom and I concentrate on the difficult task of what to order for dessert.

"I'm not sure I've ever been so full," I say, wrapping my arms around my stomach.

"You say that after every meal," Miles laughs.

83

I elbow him in the side and turn to Mom. "I'm going to show Miles something. We'll be back in a bit."

"Okay." Mom's face scrunches in pain when she wraps her arms around her stomach. Maybe it's true that Mom and me have an eating problem. Shane laughs and guides Mom back to our room.

"What do you want to show me?" Miles asks.

"Come on." I grab his hand and lead him to the same couch we sat on this afternoon. The fire is still going, so it's warm enough to sit for a few minutes.

"When I was really little I would tell my dad the only way I could fall asleep was if I said good night to the stars first. He would bring me out here every night, and we would sit and watch the sky until I got too cold or ended up falling asleep." I sigh and nestle comfortably into his side. His arm is around me, lightly tracing his fingers up and down my arm.

"The last night we were here, I was fifteen and mad that my parents brought me skiing over a long weekend. I had plans with my friends and, being fifteen, thought my parents were ruining my life taking me away from them. On our last night, my dad brought me out here against many unbelievably rude protests on my part. I didn't know it then, but he was already sick. I think he knew it would be our last time out here. I remember thinking he was acting weird and then coming to the conclusion that I probably hurt his feelings by not wanting to be with him. So, I sat beside him, and we watched the stars. Dad would try counting how many stars were in the sky, and I would count how many shooting stars we saw." A shooting star flies across the sky, and I mentally start counting and then remember the conversation from that night.

"Gracie, I'm proud of you," Dad says, face to the sky.

"Be more specific. I'm good at a lot of things," I tease.

"I'm proud of the person you are growing up to be. I should probably just be proud of myself, because obviously it was with great effort on my part that you are who you are today," he teases back.

"You always say everything good in me comes from Mom," I counter.

"Don't you forget it. You're lucky to have her. Stay close to her, okay? When you get older and think you don't need her, stay close."

That won't be hard seeing as how Mom is my best friend. "Okay."

"You know I love you, right?"

"Of course I know." I sit up so I can see his face. "Why are you crying?" His face is still looking to the sky, but tear streaks run down his temples into his hair.

"Sometimes you cry because you are unbearably happy." I've seen Dad cry before, but this feels different. I nuzzle into his side, trying to ignore the warning in my stomach. "I'm excited for you, Gracie, to grow up. I want to show you so many things. There are some things that are meant for you that others can only dream of."

"Like what?" Maybe he's talking about buying me a car when I turn sixteen.

"You'll find out. I hope you find out." He flinches a little and then covers it quickly by standing. "It's getting cold. Let's get you inside." With one hand pressed against his side and the other guiding me through the hallways, we walk back to Mom.

"Where did you just go?" Miles asks when I open my eyes. "You have felt far away today."

"There's just a lot of memories here." It feels nice sitting in this spot with Miles. It's like I get a second chance at seeing these stars again without the guilt I carried for not wanting to watch them with Dad. "Another thing I love about Rockwell is you can see the stars clearly. There isn't pollution or city lights to make them fade." We sit in silence as my count rises to three shooting stars.

"Do you know who would love it here?"

I smile. "Annie."

"That is exactly who I was thinking of." He laughs at, I'm sure, the same picture I have in my head of Annie here.

"I've watched you get excited at seeing everything. I think Annie would combust." It'd be like watching a kid in a candy store.

85

Just ahead of us the few night skiers that remain are loading onto the lift for another run.

"Can we ski again tomorrow?" Miles asks.

"Are you sure your body can handle another beating? I don't want to show up to the wedding with a bruised date," I laugh, nestling deeper into his shoulder.

"No need to worry. I bet I catch on tomorrow."

chapter eight

"Gracie?"

Someone nudges me, but it's too early to even think about waking up. I curl tighter into a ball when someone rips the blankets away from me.

"Go away." My words slur as I pat around me to find the blankets. Miles laughs, and then dumps things on top of me. I peer through one eye and see my snow clothes piled on me, just as I get a glove straight to my face. I groan and sit up.

"If your hair is any indication of how you slept last night, I believe you slept very little." He tugs on a piece of my hair, and I instantly run my hands through it, noticing how big it is.

"What time is it? Seven? A.M.? What are you doing?" I rub my eyes, convinced I'm seeing the wrong time.

"I mentioned last night I wanted to ski again," he says impatiently.

"Yes, and I plan to go, but I was thinking after the sun comes up and after breakfast." I fall back on my pillow, cursing the red numbers on the clock.

"The sun is up." He proves it by throwing open my curtains. My arms fly over my eyes to protect them from further burning. Once my eyes adjust to the light, I see Miles is in his snow gear, ready to go. I push through the fatigue and slowly get up, pushing him out of my room so I can grumble in privacy.

"Can we at least eat breakfast first?" I ask as we walk out of the hotel room.

"I was hoping we could ski before breakfast. You always eat too much and then have to sit awhile until you feel better."

That should offend me, but I'm very aware I always eat too much. Still, it doesn't sit well.

Miles practically dances onto the lift and grins the entire ride up. I'm too tired to smile. My head is foggy, and the thought of skiing makes my already sore legs tired.

"Are you sore from yesterday?"

"No. Are you?" he asks, smiling. I only huff. Of course he wouldn't be sore.

We reach the top, and I start giving instructions again. "Remember to keep your toes pointed together. Also, just as you did yesterday, be careful not to—"

"I remember." He pulls his goggles down and easily pushes away from the lift.

At first I get mad that he isn't putting his toes together. I keep watching him to be sure he doesn't end up hitting a tree. It isn't until he stops that I realize we're already down the mountain. He takes off his goggles and turns to me, beaming.

"Good job, Miles."

"When do we start?"

"Start what?" My legs are heavy when the lift starts taking us up again.

"Your swimming lesson."

"Excuse me?" My voice comes out in a squeak.

"You told me yesterday that if I made it down the hill without falling, I could teach you how to swim. I just made it down the hill without falling." He points behind him to the bottom of the slope.

"Yes, that deal was made yesterday and ended when you fell right off the lift."

He shakes his head. "Not once did you specify when the deal ended. You said I only had to make it down the hill. You did not say I had to make it down the hill only on that run."

88

I want to smack that smile right off him. "It was implied."

"I did not hear any suggestion of the kind."

"Well…" I have nothing. Folding my arms, I sit back and think about our conversation yesterday, word for word. He's right, and I hate the situation even more because of it.

"If it makes you feel any better, I worked very hard to see that scowl on your face," he teases. "While you were sleeping yesterday afternoon, I asked Shane if he would come with me. It took a few times, but he did not laugh at me, and because of that, it freed up more time for me to learn."

That's why he had that smile yesterday. I'm mad at Shane now, too. Because I have no other options, I go the route I think has the most success.

"You won't make me get in the water if I don't want to." And the second I see his face, I know that was the worst route to take.

"Will I not?" He angles his body to me, no longer nervous about the height.

"No, you won't," I challenge, staring him right in the eyes.

"Gracie, I will teach you to swim even if I have to toss you over my shoulder."

I surprise him by laughing. Didn't I say the same thing?

We get to the top of the slope and I quickly push off from the lift. I begin coming up with excuses as to why I can't get in the pool. Some are along the lines of faking sick, but it's the wedding dinner tonight, so I can't miss that. Maybe I'll eat too much at dinner and not feel good after. But that happens all the time, so he won't let that excuse stand. I know this lodge better than him. I can just hide until the pool closes. If I do that, I'll have to hide all day tomorrow until the wedding and then until we check out on Sunday. Then I feel stupid when I begin imagining what hiding places are better than other hiding places.

I glare at the snow I'm zipping over while I remember what it felt like in that carriage, how scared I was. At the time, I really wished for nothing more than to know how to swim.

Maybe it won't be so bad.

No, it's definitely going to be that bad.

I don't have to wait long for Miles at the bottom. I can see him smiling from a mile away.

"I really do enjoy this," he says when he stops beside me.

"I'm glad."

He reaches out and tucks a piece of hair underneath my beanie. "Are you still angry with me? And for absolutely no fault of mine?"

"No, I'm not mad at you. I'm actually really happy that you're happy. Even if you're happy because you're making me do something horrible and I think a little less of you because of it."

"I am glad you think less of me. It gets tiring being perfect." Now I just roll my eyes and head back to the lodge. "Do you want to go again? We can make another deal?"

"No, I'm hungry." I ignore the 'of course' he mumbles under his breath and head in the direction the pastry smell is coming from. Mom is on her way out of the little café when we go in.

"Hi, Mom."

"Hello," she says with a mouthful of muffin. "I'm sorry I didn't get you two anything. I didn't think you would be up yet, Grace."

"I wouldn't be if someone didn't act like a small boy and wake me up to go skiing."

Miles laughs behind me. "Good morning, Carolyn."

"Good morning. I take it by the smile on your face you get to have a swimming lesson today," Mom says.

"You knew?" I glare at her.

"Of course I knew. It's about time you learn to swim. I'd throw you in myself, but he's bigger than me and could handle your tantrum." She waves goodbye and goes on her way. Because I ate so much the night before, it feels like my stomach is stretched out, which means there's more room to fill. I'm starving.

"The dinner starts at six tonight. I have some things to do with the girls a few hours before. If you're really going to be mean and make me get in the pool, we can do it before I go with them. But after lunch." Maybe I can conjure up a cramp.

"Shane told me he would take me on another hill this afternoon. One that is more challenging than the one you thought I could not make it down," he points out. "Seeing as today is most likely the last time I will ski, I will let you off the hook for this afternoon." I blow out a breath in relief, but he doesn't let me get too comfortable. "We can swim after the dinner."

"Okay," I quickly agree. The dinner will go for a few hours at least, and I can easily waste time talking to people. By the time we leave the dinner, the pool will be closed. Before my smile gives me away, I fill my mouth with a chocolate chip muffin and internally smile when this muffin reminds me of the little cakes from Rockwell. And I find I miss being there more than I ever thought I would.

* * *

Miles leaves with Shane a little after lunch to tackle some mountain. Mom and I go help set up for the dinner. Bri changes her mind a few dozen times on where she wants the flowers, the ribbons, and the pictures of her and Peter. She goes over the seating chart, changing it twenty times, and ends with it looking the same as it did in the beginning. The more we tell her to calm down, the more she panics. By the time we make it back to our room, my head hurts from looking at so many roses, tying ribbons on back of the chairs, and going without food for five hours.

"Better grab a shower before the boys get back," Mom calls over her shoulder before vanishing into one of the bathrooms. I jump in the shower, letting the hot water soothe my sore muscles.

Luckily Mom is around to help me with my hair. She does some twisty thing on top that has it out of my face but still lets it be down. When she leaves, I put on my dress and keep tugging on it. It feels too tight. Not like the ones at Rockwell that flow and don't hug your every curve. My dress is a pale rose color that stops at my knees. It's flashier than Mom's. She probably planned that. I wobble a little in my heels. It's been a long time since I wore any. As silly as I thought those slippers were at Rockwell, they were quite practical. At least you could walk in them.

"Hi, Shane." I smile at him looking uncomfortable in his suit. "Is Miles getting ready?"

"Yeah." He fidgets with his tie, trying to loosen it. "They make these too tight."

"No, you tie them too tight." Mom walks over to help him retie his tie. How is it possible for Mom to look so elegant in just a black dress? There's no embroidery or design on it. It's plain, and I know that's what she's going for. She's worried she'll get a lot of attention, so she's trying to blend in. She doesn't know it's impossible for her to blend in.

"We'll meet you down there, sweetie. I told Ryan I would get there early in case something goes wrong." Mom drags Shane from the room with him mumbling the entire time. I sit on the couch and wait for Miles. After several minutes, I begin pacing and then decide to save my feet the ache and knock on his door.

"Miles?" When he doesn't answer I knock again. There's still no answer, so I open the door and peek my head in. I look around and finally see him sprawled out on his bed, asleep. He's dressed, save his suit jacket, which is laid across the back of a chair in the corner. His arm is draped over his eyes as he takes big, heavy breaths. I contemplate just leaving him here and bringing food back for him, but I know the look I'll get if I do, so I wake him up.

"Miles." I nudge him a little, and he doesn't even stir. For a second I think about throwing his snow clothes at him as payback. "Miles, wake up." I nudge again. He moves slightly, his arm sliding from his eyes. When he opens them, they look sleepy.

"Gracie." He smiles lazily and closes his eyes again.

"Hey, it's time for dinner. Do you want to stay and sleep? I can bring you back some food."

He slowly sits up and rubs his eyes. "I do not trust you with my food. My dinner will be half eaten and my dessert will not make it to me." He stands and stretches, wincing a little when he does.

"Are you sore? Did you get hurt today?" Knowing Shane, he probably took Miles to the most difficult hill. And knowing Miles, he went willingly.

"No, I was not hurt. Perhaps I am sore." He puts his jacket on and tucks in his shirt again. The way he moves is different. It's slow and a little off balance. "Are you ready?" He turns with a smile just as I'm going to ask if he's okay. I nod, and we walk to the dinner, me watching every move he makes.

The dinner is fun. Bri and Peter wanted it to be low key and casual, just a fun night for each of their families to meet the other. The food is great. I feel like I'm eating double the amount I usually do, but that's probably because Miles doesn't eat anything so it seems I'm eating mounds.

"Stop watching me, Gracie." He looks out of the corner of his eye at me.

"Are you sure you're feeling okay?"

He sighs heavily and tries hard to keep the smile on his face. "I'm fine, perhaps a little tired."

"Anyone would be tired with the way you skied today. The boy didn't let up, even after I quit," Shane congratulates Miles. Miles looks satisfied by his input and turns to me with an I-told-you-so look.

The dinner is a little bit of a blur. I watch Miles for most of it, and when I'm not worrying about him, I'm worrying if he still wants to swim after. Hopefully he's too tired.

"Well, I'm exhausted," I say dramatically. "Better get a good night sleep so we have energy for the wedding tomorrow." I say it louder than I usually would as we walk into the suite.

"Nice try." Miles grabs my hand before I can escape into my room. "We had a deal."

"And you're exhausted. Maybe you can teach me tomorrow."

"And give you the opportunity to come up with excuses?"

"The pool is probably closed. It's late."

"The pool closes at midnight. You have a few hours," Mom chimes in.

"Thanks for that," I sarcastically snap at Mom before turning back to Miles. "I didn't even pack a swimsuit."

"I packed one for you. And Miles," Mom says.

I point my glare right at her. "Don't you want to get out of that dress, Mom? And into some pajamas? To go to bed?"

"That was so subtle, Grace," Mom laughs and walks back to her room.

Miles starts walking to his room, but I stop him. "Miles, I really, really don't want to do this, but I will because I said I would. But I'm worried about you. Are you sure you wouldn't rather go to sleep?" He knows it's genuine, so he stops smiling so big and wraps his arms around me.

"I am very tired, but I would really like to go swimming first. Perhaps our lesson will just be a short one."

* * *

"Are you ready?" Miles calls through my closed door.

"Almost," I reply, standing there fully clothed staring at my swimsuit. Since Miles has been here I've been scared of wearing something that would make him uncomfortable, and now I'm going to walk out there in a swimming suit.

A swimming suit!

My cheeks are getting hotter and hotter as I reach for it and wonder if Miles is as mortified as I am. It's one of those tankini suits. At least Mom packed a conservative swimsuit, but it doesn't make me any less mad at her. Why did she even pack a suit for me anyway? I've never gotten in the pool here.

I reach for the doorknob, but my hands are so sweaty it won't turn. I rub my palms down my towel to dry them off and finally manage to open the door.

Miles' back is to me when I come out so it gives me a chance to get my nerves under control. He's wearing black board shorts with a navy blue rash guard on top. The big red towel is thrown over his shoulder as he watches Sports Center aimlessly. I take a deep breath and walk out from the hall.

"Are you sure you don't want to just sleep?" I ask, standing pencil straight when he turns to me.

As embarrassed as I was just looking at the swimsuit is nothing compared to how I feel at this moment. When he turns, his eyes widen before they quickly look away. Then realizing that he shouldn't be looking away he looks back. But when he looks back his cheeks flush crimson, and he looks away again.

And I stand there feeling like everyone in the entire world is staring at me.

He glances back at me with a shy smile while rubbing his neck. I know I should say a smart remark to break the thick tension in the room, but I can't think of anything clever to say. So we both stand there, uncomfortable, staring at each other.

"Lets get this over with," I grunt as I throw the towel over my shoulder and stalk out, but not before grabbing the leftover brownie on the counter from dinner. Focusing on eating the brownie and not Miles in a swimsuit next to me, I lead the way to the pool, hoping every step of the way a sudden lightning storm has come and closed the pool. But to my disappointment, the pool is open, but luck is on my side, because there isn't anyone else here to witness my humiliating performance.

The pool is heated, so contrasted with the cold night, it's throwing off steam. I wrap myself in my towel when we get closer, the cold breeze making me shake harder. When I turn back to Miles, I expect him to still be bashful or to not look at me. But he's smiling. That big, smug, mischievous smile.

"I told you that you would see this face on me when I watched you get uncomfortable. It is my turn to gloat. Get in the water." He motions with his head to the pool, and I gulp loudly.

I slowly make my way over to the shallow end, feeling like I'm going against nature. I'm made for land, not water. My breathing quickens when I step on the first stair, and then it stops completely when I get to the second.

"Maybe this is a bad idea," I say to Miles, staring at the water lapping against my knees. "Maybe we should try this during the day, so I can actually see what I'm—"

I don't get much further before Miles grabs my waist and tosses me in the air.

"You jerk!" I scream, plugging my nose and holding my breath just before going under.

Once under, I'm wholly convinced I'm going to die and never inhale air again. The bitter chlorine coats my tongue, and I fight the urge to just stay still and wait for Miles to get me.

Stupid Miles.

I kick out my legs, jam my toe on the bottom of the pool, then straighten so I'm standing with the water at my waist. Okay, I'm still in shallow water. I'm not dead yet.

When I hear Miles laughing, I turn, wishing I had something to throw at him.

"You are a—"

"Genius?" He laughs again as he walks toward me. I back up, a little afraid of him now. "Oh, do not be so dramatic, Gracie. I came swimming this afternoon so I would be familiar with the area. There were young children splashing in the water right where you stand." He smirks as he inches closer to me. "I would have never tossed you in if I thought you could not touch. There is a line that divides the shallow area from the deep."

"Where?" I panic, twisting my body so I can see how close I am to the death line. It's still a ways from me, but I quickly turn to face it so I can keep my eye on it.

"Did you know I taught Anne how to swim?"

I take a step away for every step he takes toward me. "No," I answer his question and tell him to stay away in one word.

"It was the summer after my mother passed away. I felt she needed something to get her mind off of grieving. I threw her in the lake." He grins.

"How surprising." My heel hits the stairs after making a circle around the pool. I sit on the first stair but it's too cold now that I'm wet, so I sink down to the third one. Miles sits beside me and chuckles when I scoot a few spots away from him.

"She did not come to the surface right away," he continues. "I was terrified. Without another thought, I dove in after her. I could not find her at first, I twisted and turned, yelling her name."

I wrap my arms around myself. "I hate this story."

96

"After I had worn myself out searching for her and started crying like a small child, I turned to the dock to make that long journey to the house to tell my father I had just killed Annie." Why is he laughing?

"When I turned to the dock, Anne was standing on top, drenched and furious. Her smile was wicked, happy that I was beyond worried for her. I tried apologizing, but she only yelled at me. Then I said I had a cramp, because I had been swimming so fast to find her. I was hoping she would jump in after me and I could teach her then. Do you know what she said to me?"

He turns with a smile, and I shake my head. "She said, 'I hope you drown.' And she stomped off that dock, upset. I was wounded until she got to the trees and looked over her shoulder to make sure I was still above water. The next day I taught her properly how to swim."

"Why did you think it would be a good idea to throw me in when you learned that wasn't a good move when you did it to Annie?"

"Because I wanted you to forget you were in water, and you have." He motions to where I'm sitting, and I bite the inside of my cheek, so I won't give him the smile he's looking for.

Miles' head tips back so he can see the sky. The water I'm sitting in is forgotten when I notice how different his profile is. A little skinnier face maybe. His eyes are sunken in. It's more than tired. When he sees me looking at him, he rolls his eyes and pushes off the stairs.

"Come on." He holds his hand out to me, and I push myself back into the stairs.

"How about we call it a night? You got me in the water. Let's call that a success."

"You can either take my hand, or I will toss you in again." He will, too. I see it in his eyes. My eyes dart from him to the entrance of the hotel. He's partially submerged in water, so I can get out of the pool faster than him. I just need to make it in the hotel before him and to my room. And then lock the door.

"I do not think so." He grabs my arm and pulls me off the stairs. Instantly, I curl my knees to my chest and go rigid. It's like he's dragging around a ball in the water. Inching closer to the death line, I try prying his fingers from my arm.

"Okay, I get your point. You can teach me in the shallow end." His fingers are like iron clasps on my arm. They won't budge. He stops at the line and grabs my waist, and with fully extended arms he moves me across the line into the deep end.

"What are you doing?" I shriek and grab onto his arms.

"Do you trust me?"

"Before or after you threw me in the pool?" I look back at the depths behind me and begin imagining the pool water suddenly rising in gigantic waves.

"Grace."

I turn back to him and see he's no longer teasing. "Yes, I trust you. But you should know it's a little less than I did when I woke up this morning." I try smiling, but my teeth are chattering too much, so I think it just looks creepy.

"Move your arms back and forth and kick your legs." I do as he says but instantly stop and grab his hands when they leave my waist. "I am not going anywhere. If you go under, I will pull you up before you realize you are under. Now kick."

"This is stupid," I mumble but do as he says.

"It will not be so stupid the next time you find yourself in dire circumstances concerning water. Now, I have a question for you." I only nod. My entire concentration is on not dying. "You told me you would like to spend some time at Rockwell." My eyes snap to his. Whenever Rockwell is mentioned my stomach flips. His face looks like his stomach is doing the same. I nod again. "My father told me he was going to try to acquire a special license for Annie to be married at Rockwell. Anne wants a spring wedding: May to be exact. I was hoping when the time comes, you will go with me to her wedding."

Why is he so nervous? Does he think I'll say no?

"I would love to." My breathing is labored. Whether that's because I'm basically drowning or because of our conversation, I don't know. Good thing there's steam coming off the water so he can't see my breath as I pant.

His eyes narrow, looking flustered. "Gracie, I was hoping that if you came back with me that perhaps you . . . " He looks past me for only a second and then back. "You would stay awhile. Perhaps see if you could be happy there."

Happy there.

Happy at Rockwell.

Stay at Rockwell.

My mind can only form bits and pieces of what he's saying.

"How long would I stay?" It comes out much more distressed than I planned. There's panic laced with curiosity in that question. He doesn't miss it. Irritation covers his face fast.

"I am not asking for anything permanent, Grace," he snaps but quickly calms himself as he reaches for my hand. "Not yet anyway. I would like you to come back with me and spend some time with me now that I know who you are and where you come from. Last time you were frightened, and I want you to experience Rockwell differently. I would like to know my options."

"Miles, will you let go of my hand," I ask through a mouthful of water. Without my right arm I'm slowly sinking.

"Sorry." He laughs unsteadily, and lets my hand go. "So?"

"So . . . " And then I think of life there with Miles. No Bailiff lurking in the shadows, no confusion concerning Mom, and not wondering about the mirror and how to get home. Rockwell would be my home. The thought is actually not scary at all. "Okay."

I'd agree a thousand more times just to see that smile on him. "Have you noticed you have been swimming on your own these last few minutes?" He gestures to me, and I just then notice he's further than an arm's distance away from me. And we're in the middle of the deep end, further from the death line than I want to be.

Because I'm concentrating on everything that's going wrong, I stop moving, and am now under water. My eyes sting as I open my eyelids to see where Miles is, and then they narrow when I see he isn't moving. He's going to let me drown? I feel like stomping my foot, but that's meant to do on land! And when I think of stomping my foot, I quickly start kicking my legs and push my arms down to push me up. Sputtering out water when I surface, I hear him laughing before I can see him.

"Were you just going to watch me drown?" I pant as I try keeping my head above water.

"If I thought you were in any danger of drowning, do you think I would be laughing?"

"Probably," I shoot back. "Can we stop now?" Everything in me is tired.

"Yes, but this is only the first lesson. I taught you how to not drown. Next time I teach you how to actually move in the water." He takes my hands and drags me to the shallow end. I race up the stairs and glare at the water, tightening my towel around me.

"Are you still afraid of the water?"

"It's not something you get over in one night." I wipe my face and scowl at him for laughing at me. Again.

On the way back to the room, I stop at the café and pick up some fruit. Probably should eat something healthy after all the junk I've eaten.

"I told you to get a cookie." He holds his cookie above his head so I can't steal another piece.

"I didn't want a cookie when we ordered." I pop a slice of pineapple in my mouth.

"I told you to get one because I knew you would eat all of mine." He takes a bite of his cookie, and I didn't know it was humanly possible to be this jealous of Miles.

Once back in our room, Miles overexaggerates the telling of our lesson. I leave Miles to finish his animated story and listen to the trails of laughter that follow. After showering, I peek in on the main room and find Miles asleep on the couch. The poor guy is exhausted. I sit by him and gently touch his forehead.

"He doesn't look well," Mom whispers behind me.

"No, he doesn't. You think he's getting sick again?" I feel his cheek that's just as hot as his forehead.

"I think he's probably trying to experience everything and is running himself ragged."

"He's stubborn. The more I tell him to rest the more he'll want to get up and move."

"Sounds like someone I know," Miles says with his eyes still closed.

"Then you should know how frustrating it is to watch."

He opens his eyes while arching an eyebrow. "Yes, I know how incredibly frustrating it can be."

"It's late," Mom says. "You two both get some rest. Miles, there's nothing planned tomorrow until the wedding, so please don't feel the need to get up so early."

"What she's saying is don't wake me up at seven to go skiing," I add. Mom leaves to go to bed just as Miles shuts his eyes again. I get up and grab a throw from the back of the couch and drape it over him.

"Good night, Miles." I lean down to kiss his cheek. He moves his head, so I end up kissing his mouth. I've kissed him countless times and not once have I felt like I was the only one doing the kissing. His mouth is on mine, but his lips don't move. I pull back, but he only smiles with closed lips, eyes still shut.

"Night, Gracie," he mumbles, and it seems he falls asleep immediately after.

chapter nine

I shuffle out of my room the next morning, annoyed that my body is as sore as it is. It hurts to even breathe. I sit down next to Shane at the table. He doesn't notice me, just continues to pick at his croissant. His hair is sticking straight up, and he has an indent across his cheek like he fell asleep on something hard.

"Is Miles still sleeping?" I ask, noticing there are two croissants left, which means Mom and Miles haven't eaten, which is weird.

"Um, yeah."

"What's wrong?" I put my croissant aside when the warning in my stomach sends out alarms. Shane still won't look at me, using his drink in front of him as an excuse. The cup twists in his hand, he blows on whatever is inside, then he continues passing it back and forth between his hands.

"Nothing. Maybe I didn't sleep well." He takes a drink, keeping his eyes on the contents of his cup rather than me.

I turn my head when I hear Miles' door open and see him shuffling out still in his swimsuit from last night and a wrinkly black t-shirt. The second I see him, I turn back to Shane, furious.

"You thought you could hide it from me?" I ask accusingly.

"He told me not to say anything," Shane whispers.

"And you." I turn, pointing at Miles. "You thought it would be a good idea to keep this from me?"

"I am fine," he defends himself.

I walk to him, and the closer I get, the worse his color becomes. "You're sick again." I lay my hand on his cheek, feeling that the fever has gotten higher than it was last night. Yesterday I thought he was only tired because he had done so much. But he's starting to take on that slate gray color again. He looks skinnier now that I'm looking. And his blue eyes are starting to go gray, too. He actually looks like a walking corpse.

"I am fine, Grace." He brushes past me to the table.

"Fine, then eat." I drop a croissant in front of him and watch his mouth pucker. With shaky fingers, he breaks off a small piece of bread and puts it in his mouth. The second he swallows, he glares up at me, but it doesn't last long before he puts his fist to his mouth and runs for the bathroom. When the bathroom door slams, I sink down onto a chair.

"Shane, why didn't you tell me?"

"He asked me not to. My room is next to his. I heard him fumbling around early this morning, so I looked in to see if everything was okay. He said his head hurt, that he was looking for the medicine Carolyn packed. I gave him a few aspirin, but he couldn't keep them down. Just after five, we finally got them to stay down with some water. He was so exhausted I had to practically carry him from the bathroom to his bed. Made me promise I wouldn't tell you."

"Did he think I wouldn't notice? Shane, did you see him?" I glance at the closed bathroom door, hating that he's in there.

"Yeah," is all he says.

Mom comes out looking just as tired as Shane. Her hair is a scattered mess, and she's still in her pajamas. At least she knows to avoid eye contact with me altogether.

"You both knew and didn't say anything? Why didn't anyone wake me up?"

"There was nothing you could have done. No need to tire you, too." Mom's voice is stern and cutting, which I know means I can't argue.

Because I want to scream and yell, I push back from the table and go to my room. I pace to the bed, to the window, to the dresser, and back again. The numbers on the clock bug me. I want to pick the clock up and throw it against the wall.

That's exactly what I want to do. I want to hit something. I want something to feel what I'm feeling. The closest thing to me is my suitcase, so I rip it open and start throwing whatever is in there. Pants, shirts, my dress for tonight, brushes, and shoes. The sound of my blow dryer shattering against the wall makes me snap out of it. I groan as I drop to my knees, picking up the broken pieces of my blow dryer. I keep blinking so the pinpricks in my eyes won't turn into tears.

"That was impressive."

I turn and see Miles leaning against the door. The humiliation of being caught in a tantrum is small compared to the hurt I feel, and the anger. Ignoring him, I pick up the ruined appliance and drop it in the trash can.

"It was wise of me to wait to come in, or I fear I would have had something thrown in my direction."

"This isn't funny, Miles."

"Watching you toss items around your room was quite funny."

"This isn't funny," I say louder, him finally catching on that I'm not in a teasing mood. He walks to me, taking my hands in an attempt to comfort me, but his hands are so cold it does the opposite.

"Grace, I am fine. Yes, I am sick again, but I think it is only because of new experiences. I was sick when I first arrived here with you, but I grew accustomed to the changes. This is no different. Just give me time, and I will be fine."

I slip my hands out of his and take a step back. "How did you feel the night you found me with Harry? When you sat by my bed while I slept?" If it's possible, whatever color he has left in his face fades. His eyes flash with the anger he'll always carry for Harry.

"I am not sure I could put into words what was going on in me that night."

"So you can understand how I feel now." Somehow, whenever we start fighting, my voice goes up a scale, bordering yelling. I can't help it.

"This is not remotely close to that situation," he argues.

"You're right. This isn't the same. This is worse." I hold up my hand to keep him from talking. "When you sat by me, you knew what was wrong. You knew how to take care of me. You knew that Harry couldn't hurt me anymore. You knew I would be okay. But I have no idea what's wrong with you. I don't know how to take care of you, and I don't know that you'll be okay. I hate that you're sick here, and I hate that you keep ignoring it like it's nothing. It isn't nothing, Miles."

I have to take a breath, have to calm down a bit. When I feel somewhat less irritated, I continue but much more cautiously as I'm walking on very delicate territory. "Maybe you should go back to Rockwell for awhile. Until you feel better."

The shock comes before hurt paints every line of his face. He opens his mouth and then shuts it without a word. He tries disguising his wince, and at first I think it's because I told him he should go home, but when he winces again, I know it isn't because of me.

"Are you okay?" I get my answer when he grabs his side and runs from the room. My eyes close when I hear the bathroom door shut.

I throw on my boots, grab my jacket and run from the hotel room. I need air. My brain needs air. Sometimes with Miles, it feels like my head is going to explode. He's so frustrating. I wasn't telling him to go back to Rockwell forever. Just until he gets better and we have some time to figure out what's hurting him.

The cold air is a smack to the face, one I really need. Winding down the stairs from the balcony, I keep walking. Where to, I don't know. I just need some space. The laughter of skiers and the small breeze rustling through the pine trees should be calming, but I'm wound too tight. I shake my hands out as I make my way across the flat ground to the trees. Knowing better than to venture into them because I know I won't find my way back out, I stop and pace. But once I hear the crunch of snow behind me, I know I should've hid in the trees.

"You have a terrible habit of leaving before I am through speaking with you."

"You shouldn't be out here," I tell Miles. He looks worse in the sun.

"Was I supposed to stay in the room, rest, and wait for you to return? To give you enough time to come up with some plan to get me to go home? I do not think so." He's dead on his feet. His shoulders slump, and every time he blinks it seems to take all of his energy just to open his eyes again.

105

I square my shoulders and look him right in the eye. "If going home would help then you—"

"I am not going," he says with finality.

"You may not get a choice. If going home is—"

"I am not going."

"Stop interrupting me." It drives me crazy when he does that.

"Then stop speaking nonsense, and I will not have to."

"It isn't nonsense. It's true, and you know it. If the roles were reversed, you would do the exact same." When he balls his hands into fists, I almost smile. I have him.

"The situations are not reversed, and I am not going. You can whine and argue, but I will not go back."

Whine and argue? My temper is steadily climbing to murderous. "Why? Why won't you go and just see if you get better?"

"Because I know I will!" he screams, his loud voice echoing through the trees. "I have never been so sick in my entire life. I know it is because I am here, and I know it will go away if I go home. But I do not want to go home, because when I ask you to spend the rest of your life with me, I want you to be able to choose where you wish to spend that life. I do not want you to choose Rockwell because you think I cannot take care of myself here."

I match his tone and scream, "You can't take care of yourself here!" And I regret saying it immediately. "I mean, you can take care of yourself, but something is happening to you, and if you think I'm going to sit aside and watch you whither away, you have another—"

"I only need more time."

"Stop interrupting me!" I actually stomp my foot, and I have to give him credit, he tries really hard to hide his smile. By the time he controls his smile, his icy mood comes roaring back.

"I am staying, so this discussion is over." Miles stands his ground, staring at me in a way I know he thinks he's winning. With one last glare, he turns and begins stomping away.

There isn't a person alive that can make me this mad. No one. Because I'm going to combust any minute if I don't release some of the rage inside

106

me, I bend down and scrunch snow together in my hands, and throw it at his retreating back. When the snowball hits just below his shoulder, he stops, looks over his shoulder at the remaining snow on his jacket, and then faces me.

"That haughty tone of yours may work with people who call you Mr. Denley and see you as the next Lord Denley, but I see Miles. And right now, I don't like you. You can't dismiss me like I'm inferior to you." I throw another snowball at him, but he blocks his face with his arm. And then he does possibly the worst thing he could do. He smiles, thinking I'm funny. At the moment I'm the opposite of funny. I throw another one at him.

"That dismissal did not come from Mr. Denley. It came from me. And I dismissed this conversation, because it is ridiculous and getting old. I am not leaving, and you cannot make me," he says, sounding like a stubborn ten-year-old boy. "How many of those will you throw at me?" he asks while blocking my shots.

"As many as it takes to wipe that arrogant smile off your face or pop your big head. Whichever comes first."

My arm is beginning to ache from hurling snowballs at him, but the more I throw, the funnier he thinks it is. And then he catches one in his hand right before it hits his face, and he laughs. Loud. If the snow hasn't melted under me yet, it's going to.

"Why do you always laugh when I'm getting mad at you? There's nothing funny about this."

"When you are angry for legitimate reasons, I do not laugh. I laugh now because you are angry over something very silly."

Silly? I really think I might actually kill him. "Go get some sleep. If you stay I'll only throw more snowballs at you, and I'll feel guilty later for throwing them at someone incapable of defending himself. You look awful."

I turn around and stomp into the trees, but just before disappearing completely, a snowball smacks into the back of my head. I stop. Another hits me in the back.

"Incapable of defending myself?" There's defense mixed with teasing in his voice. I swallow the smile and try fixing a glare on my face as I turn and get hit right in the stomach.

"Did all your years of propriety lessons ever tell you not to throw snowballs at girls?" I pick one up and throw, but he dodges, making me extremely furious.

"Yes, but you just said you do not see Mr. Denley when you look at me, so I do not have to act like Mr. Denley." To my delight I dodge a snowball, but I get hit by the next. "I can do this all day, Grace. Tell me you will stop worrying about me, and I will let you go without further humiliation." He picks up a really big ball of snow, and while smiling at me, starts smoothing it in his hands.

"Humiliation? I think the only one humiliated here is you, or you will be. You can't hit me if you can't catch me."

He understands my challenge much quicker than I thought he would. He's charging at me before I have time to think of what to do next. A scream that's half laughing, half startled slips from me, and I start running. Laughing doesn't help keep my breathing steady. Well, it wasn't steady to begin with. I should probably exercise more. My legs don't go far before they start aching. I chance a glance over my shoulder for him, but he isn't there. There's only one set of footprints in the snow behind me. Retracing my steps, I go back to find him. Coming around a large pine, he comes into view. He's sitting in the snow, propped up against a tree, holding his stomach.

"Miles, are you okay?" I crouch down beside him and feel his head. I grab his chin that's drooped down to his chest and pull it up so I can see his face. When I manage to get him to look at me, I freeze. There's no pain, fever, or distress. He's smiling so big his eyes are disappearing.

"You didn't," I hiss.

His hands grab the back of my knees and pull, putting me flat on my back in the snow. He holds both of my wrists in one of his hands, infuriating me because he can do that, and with the other hand, he grabs a handful of snow, holding it above my face.

"Your greatest strength is also your weakness, Gracie. You care for people too much. It was bound to get you into trouble." He laughs as he smashes the snow in my face. Good thing he has my hands, because I gladly would have smacked him. I scramble away from him, about to pick up snow to toss it in his face, but he leans against the tree, exhausted, so I drop the ball at my feet. I sit next to him and lay my head on his shoulder, feeling the rise and fall coming too fast.

I pick up his hand and compare it to mine. Mine is a dark pink from being healthy and also from the cold. His is white with dark blue veins bulging from underneath too-fragile skin. I look up at him and see a hint of blue creeping into his lips. Whether that's because of the temperature or him not getting enough oxygen, I don't know.

"I told you I'd feel guilty about throwing snowballs at you." I trace his boney cheek with my finger, and panic swarms around in my stomach when my frozen fingers feel warm compared to his cheek.

"Please do not be. Then I would have to feel guilty for throwing them at you." He lays his head against the tree and closes his eyes.

"Come on. Lets go back and you can rest." I stand and hold a hand out to help him. He takes it and uses it more than I'm capable of giving. We both struggle to get him to his feet. I turn to leave, but he holds my hand tighter, stopping me.

"Before we go back there are three things I want you to know and understand. First, I am going to the wedding and reception this—"

"I don't think that's a good—"

"Stop interrupting me," he mimics my tone from earlier. "I will rest for the remainder of the day, but I want to go this evening. Second," he says before I can protest the first, "I love that you love me enough to fuss over me, but you need to stop. If I get too sick, I will tell you."

"No, you won't."

He smiles. "You are probably right, but you will be able to tell and come up with some outrageous plan to get me better. Third." He steps closer to me and tucks a piece of hair behind my ear. "Third, I will go back to Rockwell if the situation warrants it, but I will only go if you come with me.

109

I do not intend to be left at Rockwell again without a way to you. If you really wish for me to go home, you will really have to want to go with me."

If that's what it takes to get him better, I'll do it.

"Deal. Now let's get you some sleep."

* * *

"Bri, you look gorgeous," I tell her when I enter the bridal suite. She's sparkling. Literally. The silver beads on her dress throw off a sparkle anytime the light hits them. Her dress is a rich cream color, fabric wrapping around her waist and gathering on her right side. The skirt of the dress is big. Really big. The layered fabric is all bunched together with small beads dotted all over. A tiara instead of a veil completes her look.

"I told myself I wouldn't cry. Not until I say 'I do.'" Bri wipes her eyes with the tissue Mom offers.

"We better get seats. I want to get good ones so I can see you the moment you enter the room and everything after." Mom hugs her, which makes Bri tear up more. I hug Stella and Kallie on my way out, complimenting them on how beautiful they look in their bridesmaid dresses.

Mom and I leave Bri to go find our seats. We take the corner from the bridal suite, and I stop. Just outside the wedding room doors is Miles. He's wearing a black suit with a dark gray vest underneath. Mom must have gotten him one of those fat ties that if double knotted looks like a small cravat.

"You matched his tie to my dress?" I ask her when I see the gold tie.

"I couldn't help myself. Hopefully no one notices and thinks we're trying to steal the attention from Bridgette," she says, but I don't look at her. I can't. Shane comes up to Miles, pulling at his tie, and they both start laughing about something. Shane catches sight of us and waves, and when Miles turns, I feel like I'm reliving that moment from the ball all over again. I'm not sure if Mom is still next to me anymore, and I don't know if Shane is still by Miles.

When Miles sees me, a slow, sweet smile appears. He looks almost shy. Mom says something next to me, but I don't hear her. I do hear her laugh as she walks to Shane, and they both go inside. Miles and I walk to each other, and I tighten the grasp on my clutch. To my relief, he looks a little better. Some red is coming back to his cheeks, and his eyes don't seem so sunken in. The way he moves is easier, smoother.

When we reach each other, his arms wrap around my waist. His breathing sounds better, too. It isn't as labored and heavy as before.

"Are you finished assessing my health?" he whispers in my ear.

"You look better." I pull back, studying his face again.

"I told you, I only need time." The pride he stuffs into that statement oozes from him. I start into the room, but he stops me. He pulls me around the corner to a hallway with no exit.

"Last time I did this incredibly wrong." He takes my other hand in his, intertwining his fingers with mine.

"Did what wrong?"

"The last time I saw you in a gold dress I stuttered over my compliments, which I saw you took great satisfaction in," he points out. "But this time I mean to tell you how lovely you look without stammering. Gracie, you look lovely. Wait, I just said . . ." His mouth clamps shut as determination dissolves to frustration. I laugh at him again. He doesn't know that I find him more charming now than if he had the most romantic words to say.

"Thank you, Miles. You look very handsome yourself." I place my hand on his tie and smile. "It looks like your cravat. I've missed that." I've missed a lot of things from Rockwell. Things I didn't think I noticed while I was there.

He takes my hand from his tie and kisses it. Smiling, he kisses it again and slides it in his own to lead me to the wedding.

* * *

"What is a girlfriend?" Miles sits down next to me, handing me my piece of cake.

My eyes narrow. "Why?"

He fidgets in his seat. "Yesterday, I went to the pool to become familiar with it for our lesson. I met a woman there who seemed intrigued that I was

111

not from here. She asked a lot of questions about England. Most of those questions I had no answer to. She then asked if I had a girlfriend. I assume it means how it sounds—a friend that is a girl. So I said yes, but I think I offended her. She stopped speaking with me and left."

His face scrunches as he thinks about it. He takes a sip of his drink, and then says, "Just now, when I went to get you a slice of cake, I got speaking with a woman behind me in line. She asked me about England. I did not know England was so popular. She asked if I had a girlfriend. Remembering how the other woman reacted, I thought that perhaps I had not given enough credit to the women in my life. So I told the woman I had many girlfriends. She was so disgusted with me I thought she might slap me."

I look over at Mom and Shane who have already started laughing.

"What?" Miles asks when I join in.

"Miles, a girlfriend is a woman you're dating, or courting. A woman you have romantic feelings for. Usually men only have one girlfriend."

Pink creeps into his cheeks when realization sets in. "What that woman must think of me! A rake of the worst kind, I am sure." He looks behind him searching for the woman. His concern only makes us laugh more.

"She'll be fine," I tell him.

"If we can have everyone's attention please," the DJ's upbeat voice sings through the speakers. "It's time for the couple's first dance as husband and wife. Please welcome on the dance floor, Mr. and Mrs. Warren."

Peter pulls a crying Bri onto the dance floor. The song starts, and they begin to sway. I remember Bri mentioning when we were younger that Peter had absolutely no rhythm in him, so I understand the slow steps they're taking. Halfway through the dance, Dr. Scott asks Mom to dance. They join the newlyweds on the dance floor, and others begin to follow.

"May I have this dance, Gracie?" Miles bows before me and offers his hand. If he was wearing his cravat, I would've thought we were back at Rockwell. We walk out on the dance floor, and he pulls me in close.

"Miles, the dancing here is different. It's not choreographed like at Rockwell." Making a fool of himself in front of me is alright; in fact, I enjoy it too much. But being embarrassed in front of a group of people he doesn't know is another thing.

"It is not so hard. We are only stepping back and forth. And I asked your mother to teach me. Although you enjoy seeing me embarrassed, I was not prepared to humble myself in front of others."

"It's not that I love seeing you get embarrassed as much as I love seeing that you aren't perfect."

"Hold your tongue, Gracie. My ego would be mortified to hear you say such things."

His arm around my back pulls me closer, and I feel him laugh when I lay my head on his shoulder. While dancing, I watch Bri and Peter light up the room. They smile at each other, happily ignoring everyone else.

"Smile!" Mom appears and holds up her phone to take a picture. Miles still holds me in the dancing position, so we turn our heads and smile.

"May I cut in?" Shane asks when the song ends. Miles bows to him and gives him my hand, and then remembering that people don't bow to each other, he laughs and walks over to Mom, asking for her next dance.

"They look happy, don't they?" Shane flicks his head toward Bri.

"They are happy."

"Don't get mad at me, but I've noticed the look they give each other is the same one passing between you and Miles."

Instantly put on defense, I only smirk. "You know I care about Miles."

"No, *I* care about Miles. Your mother cares about Miles. What you feel for him is entirely different. This is just as uncomfortable for me to discuss as it is you, but Dan would kill me if he thought I was giving you up without asking questions." Shane scowls at whatever is behind me and mumbles something under his breath.

"What do you want to know?" This is weird, but it's also really sweet for him to care.

He looks down at me. The glare he aims for disappears behind sheer awkwardness. "Do you want to marry him?"

I trip over my foot and clear uncomfortable lumps from my throat. "You just skipped a lot of steps, Shane. I was prepared to say that I loved him, but that was as far as I was going."

He forces out a laugh, and then hearing how shaky and fake it is, he stops and resorts back to glaring. "Are you telling me you haven't thought about it? You haven't thought about what happens after the next few days or weeks? You haven't asked yourself if you want him to stay, or if you want to go home with him?"

"Of course I've thought about it. I just haven't come up with the answers yet."

In fact, that's all I've been thinking about lately. One way or another, I want Miles in my life. Whether we live here or at Rockwell. Although, if we do return to Rockwell, the mirror situation will have to be fixed so I can come back here to shower.

Shane and I clear our throat at the same time, then do it again because it's so awkward that we're both trying to fill the silence by doing the same thing. I look up at him when he stops dancing, and when I see his chin stubbornly try to stop trembling, the tension in me begins to wash away.

"Well, I'm not sure it means much to you, but the Denleys are as good as they come. Not that you need my blessing, but it's yours if you want it." He looks at his feet, trying to disguise his sniffing.

Not knowing how to respond, I just hug him, giving us both a few extra seconds to suppress whatever is trying to come out. A fast song comes blaring through the air, so I give him a quick squeeze and whisper, "It means everything to me."

He nods, then, saving us both from having to talk more about our feelings, grabs my hand and tosses me into a spin. Soon I get lost in the amusement of it all. I laugh as he dips me and laugh harder when he keeps tripping over his feet. Glancing over at Miles, I see that he didn't only take lessons on slow dancing. How is it possible for him to blend in so well when I stuck out like a sore thumb at Rockwell?

The relaxed ambience of the room transforms into a cheerful party. Laughs echo throughout the room as people dance and let go of their responsibilities for a night. They smile at each other as they spin to the music, and hollers sound as the newlyweds begin swing dancing.

The song ends, and I'm attempting to catch my breath when Miles comes back and asks for my next dance. Mom and Shane go sit at the table, and my feet beg me to join them. That's what I get for letting Mom talk me into wearing heels.

"You can dance," I pant, wiping my forehead in case sweat is dripping down my forehead.

"To avoid puffing myself up I will say thank you and not make you dwell on how fabulous I looked." Miles straightens his tie and smiles.

"You adapt to situations really well. Maybe in the summer I should take you hiking, but you'll probably be good at that too." As my imagination runs away with all the things I want to do with Miles, I don't realize he isn't talking back, or that we've stopped dancing, not until his finger hooks under my chin, bringing my eyes up to his.

He looks down at me, and I watch his eyes bounce back and forth between mine. "I need to tell you something. I have wanted to for some time but have never found the right moment or my courage to do so. I am afraid if I do not tell you now, it will only become harder."

My heart takes off in a sprint at the same time I cut off my breathing so fear can't rush in with each inhale. My gaze falls to his tie so I can get my thoughts in order. And then, remembering what Shane just told me, my breathing comes in gigantic waves.

Is Miles going to propose? Is that why Shane asked me about marriage? Did Miles ask his permission?

Of course I want to spend the rest of my life with him, but now that it's in front of me, I'm not sure what to do. I'm not ready to choose yet.

His hands grab my shoulders, gently pushing me back. Summoning any courage I have left in me, I brace myself and look up.

The fear I had for his question vanishes and is replaced by a deeper, more haunting fear.

I've seen Miles in pain. I've seen his face twist until he's almost unrecognizable.

But I've never seen him like this.

I reach out for him just as he crumples into my arms.

And that's when I hear it.

chapter ten

I hear the cough that has permanently slithered into my memories. The cough that has my heart suddenly sinking. He draws in a deep breath, and I hear how swollen his throat is getting. Wheezing, he bends over and covers his mouth. His body helplessly seizes, as there isn't time in between coughs to catch his breath. Unsteadily, he grabs my arm and stumbles toward me. His hand feels too warm and wet. I push his hand down my arm to take his hand, and I see a smear of red left behind.

We're gaining an audience as Miles coughs louder and more violently. Mom and Shane are by my side before I can yell for them.

"What's going on?" Shane takes Miles from me, wrapping Miles' arm around his neck to support his weight.

"I don't know. He just started coughing. Mom, he's coughing up blood." My arm trembles as I lift it to show her. "I'll take him back to the room. Will you ask Dr. Scott if he'll look at him? I know it's an inconvenient time, but he needs help."

"Of course. Shane will help you." I feel her pat my arm, but my body feels disconnected somehow. The people around me sway, but there's no music. I'm spinning, but my feet are planted to the floor.

"Grace," Shane takes my arm and gives me a shake, "I can't carry both of you. Either sit down at the table or buck up and follow me." He turns and leaves, and my body follows even with my thoughts far away.

Once Shane lays Miles on the bed, I can see Miles better. His face has no

116

color. Those blue eyes that are always so vivid are sunken in, glossed over and unfocused. Red streaks shoot out from his irises, coloring the white of his eyes a dark pink. He stares at the ceiling, and I know he isn't seeing anything. Miles is still here physically, but I feel it right when I see him that he's *only* here physically. The strong presence he has, the charm that exudes from him, the smile that makes me lose my thoughts—they're all gone.

"Tell me what happened." Dr. Scott opens his doctor's bag and sits on the side of the bed.

"We were dancing; he was fine. Then he started coughing and couldn't catch his breath. He buckled over, and that's when I noticed blood in his hands."

Although he tries to hide it, I see the concern in Dr. Scott's eyes before he blinks it away. Mom wraps her arm around my waist as we watch Dr. Scott examine Miles. When he finishes, he lowers his head and his skinny fingers dig into his eyes, rubbing away what he doesn't want us to see.

"If this were any other patient I would tell you to take him home, make him rest. I would tell you there's nothing wrong with him other than an accelerated heart rate. But . . ." He stands, buckles his bag together, and turns to Shane. "Maybe we should talk in private."

I step to the side to block his path. "Whatever you tell him, he'll just tell me when you leave. What's wrong?"

Warily, he picks up his bag and looks at Mom and then to Shane. "His symptoms are minimal, but because I've seen them before, I noticed them immediately. The red eyes, shallow breathing, gray skin. His heart is strong, but there's a slight stutter to its beating. Most would miss it, but I've heard it once before. With Daniel."

I want to gasp, or at least react to what he said, but I already knew. Deep down I knew it was the same, but wouldn't let myself see it. The cough is so different, so rare, that right when I heard Miles, I knew it had to be the same as Dad's. And that means . . .

"Someone's trying to kill him," I whisper.

I turn to Shane for an answer. He always has the answer. But he's grasping the baseboard of the bed, staring at Miles with the same helpless expression I saw when he was looking at Dad.

"I don't know the details that surrounded Daniel's death, but I remember the symptoms, and Miles' are identical. My advice would be to get him to a hospital, flush out whatever is in his system. I'll call and tell them you're on your way and to be ready."

I nod, but I know the hospital can't help him. It didn't help Dad.

There's only one way to save him.

"Dr. Scott? Do you have anything in that bag that will make him comfortable for the drive? Maybe something that will knock him out for awhile?"

"I've already sedated him. He should be sleeping for a few hours." He clamps his hand on Shane's shoulder, squeezing it. Once he leaves, I start giving instructions, and the more I give, the more I believe I'm doing the right thing.

"Mom, will you pack our bags? Shane will you get the car? We should go home. I don't want to go to the hospital." I don't need to look at them to know they agree with me. Shane leaves as Mom shoves clothes into our suitcases. Trying to be as careful as possible, I sit beside Miles on the bed. He seems more relaxed now, his breathing coming at a regular rhythm, but his face is wrong. It isn't Miles. A hand touches my shoulder, but I don't want comfort right now. I stand up and shrug it away, wiping my eyes with the back of my hand.

"I'm so sorry," Mom whispers.

"I just want to go home."

I sit in the back with Miles on the ride home. Shane says things to me occasionally, but I only nod, not really listening to him. I hold onto Miles for the two-hour ride home, but it feels like only seconds. The car starts up our driveway, and I frown at my house. It looks different, too. Even with the lights shining, it looks empty.

"Can you carry him by yourself?" I ask Shane.

"I can manage." Shane opens the door and starts grabbing at Miles.

I leave them behind and head to my room. I dress in a haze, going through the motions robotically. I press my hand to my stomach, begging myself to stay calm for the next few minutes. Just a few more minutes.

"Not in there," I say to Shane when he opens Miles' bedroom door.

When Mom sees me, she blinks, sending tears down her cheeks. "Miles is going home." I smooth my dress—the one I wore when we came here—and walk into Shane's room, to the mirror. "Shane, give me a ten minute head start and then bring Miles. I need to talk to his dad and make sure Annie isn't around to see him."

Their reflections in the mirror are mixed. Mom is crying, aching because she knows I am. Shane is nodding, knowing as well as I do that this is what's best for Miles.

I close my eyes and step through before I can talk myself out of it. There's no point in trying to think of where I want to go, because of course I don't want to go there. But that's where I need to go, so as soon as I step through, I land on solid ground in the attic. Being discrete, I step lightly through the hallways, hoping no one will notice me, especially Annie.

I peer in the library and see Matthew and Annie sitting in front of the fire. Their backs are to me, so I don't immediately leave. Her head is resting on his shoulder while he reads out loud. It hasn't been too long since I left Rockwell, but seeing Annie puts a knot in my stomach. I missed her more than I thought. The desire to give her a big hug and tell her how sorry I am is overwhelming, so I quietly shut the door and go downstairs.

Thankfully, Lord Denley is reading in the drawing room. He smiles when I enter, and I battle back tears because he looks so much like Miles— the healthy, safe Miles. His smile fades when he sees my face, and I bite my cheek to keep from crying as he walks toward me.

"Miss Gentry, is everything alright?"

"No, but it will be." I sit down and take a few calming breaths. They don't help. He sits beside me, looking at me, quietly asking what's wrong. "Miles is sick, and I think from the same thing that took my dad." Swallowing hard, I quickly continue, wanting to put him at ease. "My dad was poisoned, and we think that's what's happening to Miles. If he comes back here, he'll be fine. A few days of rest, and he'll be back to his normal self."

And I won't be here to see it.

Lord Denley doesn't speak, but I need him to. I need to hear that he isn't mad at me for almost taking his son away permanently. I want him to tell me that he'll take care of Miles in a way that I can't. He gently takes my hand, but it only makes me feel worse.

Lord Denley forces a smile. "I appreciate you caring for him, but we both know there is nothing I can do. Miles would never agree to come back without you."

This makes me smile. "He doesn't really have a choice at the moment. The doctor gave him something that will have him sleeping for a few more hours. Shane should be arriving in a minute with him. When he wakes up, he'll be here, and I'll be gone."

"You will not stay?" he asks, surprised I'm not planning to.

"No. Whoever is trying to hurt him is doing so because he's associated with my family and me. If he's here and I'm home, he won't be hurt anymore."

"I know this was not an easy decision for you."

"It was, actually. Once I realized what was happening and what needed to happen to keep him safe, it was very easy."

"Thank you." Those two words, said so genuinely, give me the added strength I'll need to get through the next few minutes.

"Will you come to the attic with me? Shane may need help getting Miles to his room. I also came before him to make sure Annie isn't around to see Miles. He doesn't look like himself." My head falls, wanting to hide the guilt I feel. Lord Denley stands and takes my arm in his, guiding me up the stairs. He opens the library door, and I step aside so Annie can't see me. I'm not saying goodbye to her, too.

"Mr. Wilson, may I have a word with you? No, stay there, Anne. This is something you cannot hear."

"A surprise?" I forgot how high she can squeal. She giggles as Lord Denley steps out, followed by Matthew. Before he can acknowledge me out loud, I put a finger to my mouth telling him to stay quiet. He looks at me and then to Lord Denley.

"Mr. Wilson, Miles has come home, but he is rather sick. He is not looking well, and I was hoping you could keep Annie distracted for the next few hours while we bring him to his chambers. I do not want Annie seeing him in his current state. We will tell her tomorrow morning that he has arrived home. Can you do this for me?"

Matthew's eyes slide over to me and must see something that worries him. "Will he be alright?"

"Yes, after a few days he will be Miles. I believe the only thing we have to fear is his mood when he wakes. Miss Gentry cannot stay with us." It surprises me that they both laugh.

"Will we draw straws again as to who has to tell him dinner is ready?" Matthew laughs until he sees I'm not. "Annie and I are reading, and I am afraid I put people to sleep when I read. I will make sure she does not come out of the library. June is in there with us as well. I can always count on her for making people do things they do not wish to."

I walk away, not bothering with a thank you, and hear Lord Denley follow me. The dust of the attic burns my nose and stings my eyes. At least that's what I tell myself when the water begins pooling in them. Sitting on an old trunk, I watch the mirror and wait.

It isn't long until Shane comes through. Shock covers Lord Denley's face when he first sees Miles. He hesitates helping, staring at his son like he would a ghost. He snaps out of it when Shane asks for help. I don't miss how uneasy Lord Denley is when he reaches for Miles or when he wraps Miles' arm around his neck.

After getting Miles onto his bed, the two men talk in the corner as I sit down beside Miles. He's home, and now he's safe. It helps a little, knowing I'm doing the right thing. I move the hair away from his face, smiling when I see the small cut from my botched attempt at saving him last time. Remembering how mad he was at me for staying in the carriage with him makes me laugh. No doubt he's going to react the same when he wakes up. 'What were you thinking?' I can hear him say.

"Lord Denley, can I have something to write him a letter? He'll want an explanation when he wakes up." I watch Miles sleep peacefully and am grateful that this is the image I'm leaving with. Hopefully this memory will erase the one of him at the wedding, struggling to breathe.

I go to his desk and stare at the paper. What do I say?

Miles,

Don't be mad at me. This really was the best way to make sure you are safe. The doctor said your symptoms were just like my dad's. Someone is purposely hurting you, and I won't keep you around after knowing that. I never want to see you like that again, and I won't. Hopefully we can find out why it happened and why it happened to you. For now, you need to stay with your family, and I will be with mine. Once we figure this out, and you're no longer in danger, I will come for you. But until then, get better.

Enjoy being with your family. Especially your father, now that he's home for good. Help Annie plan her wedding. I know it would mean a lot.

And remember, just because I'm keeping you from one danger, doesn't mean there aren't any here. I hate leaving you knowing Thomas can hurt you and your family, but right now this is the safer option. I'm so sorry you have been tangled in our mess.

This isn't really a goodbye. We'll see each other again but, hopefully, under less dangerous circumstances.

You asked me to give you more time, and the only way I can do that is if I give it to you in <u>your</u> time.

Get better.

I love you.
Gracie

There's so much more I want to say, but it won't do any good. He doesn't need to hear how much I hate myself for putting him in the position to get hurt. He doesn't need to hear how much I'm going to miss him. He doesn't need to hear that leaving him now is the hardest thing I've ever purposefully done. But I know that if I say those things, it'll hurt him that much more.

Setting the letter down on the pillow next to him, I start burying the pain. I've done it before. I know how to do it again. While watching Miles, I carefully push aside the raw ache, replacing it with determination and satisfaction that I'm doing the right thing. I know how to not cry, so I bury the pain and focus only on what I have control over.

"Let's go." With no goodbye to Lord Denley and no final glance at Miles, I turn and walk out of the room. The further I get from Miles, the tighter the seal inside me becomes. By the time we reach the attic, I feel better. Ignoring the stranger staring back at me in the mirror, I step through.

Mom finds me the instant I'm back in my room. "Grace, I'm so sorry. We'll fix this. I'm so sorry." I let her cry a moment longer, and then gently push her away when I begin to feel that familiar itch in my throat.

"I'm going to take a shower. It's been a long day."

Mom searches my face, trying to find the daughter that went through and not recognizing the one that came back. Before she notices too much, I leave and hear Shane come through just as I shut the bathroom door.

"What happened?" Mom whispers, thinking I can't hear. She never did realize that I've been able to hear through these doors since I was little. My back slides down the door, and then I sit with my head resting against the wall and listen.

"She's doing the same thing she did after she thought you died. She turns herself off—doesn't feel anything. You see Grace, but she's empty. I thought she was over that when I found you two at Rockwell, but I guess not."

"She misses him already."

I scramble to the shower, flipping it on so I won't hear anymore. Rummaging through a drawer, I pull out my brush and roughly tug it through my hair for a distraction.

I slip into the shower and focus on not crying. It won't help. Tears aren't going to make Miles come back.

Mom and Shane are gone when I come out, but I know Mom won't leave me alone for long. I get dressed, crawl into bed, and reach for my phone to silence it. Tears I've evaded begin building when I see the background picture on my phone: the one Miles and I took at the lodge.

I tell myself I did the right thing. I have to *convince* myself I did the right thing, because at this moment, the right thing feels wrong. My chest shouldn't ache, and my eyes shouldn't burn from producing too many tears.

I curl into a ball and clutch at my shirt, wishing with every pound of my heart that the next beat won't hurt so much—that maybe, with time, my heart can beat normally without him.

chapter eleven

It's been five weeks since we took Miles back. Thirty-seven days to be exact. I thought it would get easier over time, but every morning I wake up, and it's just as bad as the day before. Maybe worse.

Mom and I are in foreign territory. After we took him back, I woke the next morning to grocery bags full of chocolate, chick flicks, ice cream, and tissues. Mom doesn't know how to help a daughter who's hurting this way. I don't know what to do with myself, either. One thing I do know is that no matter how much chocolate or ice cream you eat, it never makes you feel better. In fact, it makes you feel horrible. Downright sloshy and gross.

Mom sits down next to me, eyeing me with worry like she has been for the last thirty-seven days. "Our attorney is coming over this morning for a meeting with Shane and me about the company. He requested you be there. He has some business he wants to discuss with you."

"With me? Why?"

"I don't know. He wouldn't tell me." Mom shrugs in a bad attempt to seem unaffected. You can actually see the burning curiosity all over her.

"Do you know?" I ask Shane over my second bowl of cereal.

"I have no idea." He shrugs like Mom did.

* * *

"Mr. Mitchell, it's nice to meet you." I shake the chubby hand he extends to me. He's my height, very round, and has an insane amount of white hair. His brown eyes look huge behind his thick glasses. When he smiles at me, he transforms into a cute old man that probably has grandkids who adore him.

"Grace, I apologize that this is our first meeting. You can understand this last year has been complicated. I have meant to schedule a meeting with you; I apologize." He sits in the chair beside mine at the dining room table. Digging through his briefcase, he brings out a folder with my name written on top and sets it on the table with his hands clasped on top of it. He studies me and then Mom and Shane.

"My first request is going to sound strange, but it came straight from Daniel." Mr. Mitchell takes off his glasses and cleans them with a white cloth from his pocket. He puts them back on, very unsteady, and continues. "I was asked by Daniel to relay some business to Grace when she turned eighteen years old. On her eighteenth birthday, I thought of contacting her, but seeing as Carolyn was still missing, I thought I would wait. And then I was thrown into the matter of the company and whose responsibilities were what. I apologize again that this is the first you are hearing from me."

"It's okay," I say, not sure if I'm supposed to or not.

Mr. Mitchell nods. "Carolyn and Shane, seeing as Grace is now eighteen and, therefore, an adult, the business I have with her is to be conducted in private."

Now I know why his hands are shaking slightly. Mine would be too if I was on the other end of Mom's glare.

"Excuse me?" Mom asks slowly.

"Now that she is an adult the business—"

"No, I heard you. I just don't understand." Mom looks to Shane for backup.

"If Grace is okay with us sitting in on the discussion, I don't see why we can't," Shane argues, glancing at me with a look that's telling me I don't have a choice.

"I'm sorry. Daniel gave me very specific instructions to speak with Grace in private. In fact," he reaches into the folder and pulls out a piece of paper, "here is a letter from Daniel explaining." All three of us perk up at the thought of hearing something from Dad. Mr. Mitchell hands it to me to read.

The paper shakes in my hands as I read it out loud. "I wish I could be there to see the look on Lynnie's face when she found out she's not included in this meeting." I look up at Mom, and the glare Dad wanted to see is fading as her eyes fill with tears. "And Shane is probably gripping whatever he's sitting on." I glance up again and Shane smiles, bringing his hands up to rest on the table. "I've had a lot of time to think about this. When you're forced to stay in bed every second, you have a lot of time to plan. After I'm gone, most of the business will concern Carolyn and Shane, unless, heaven forbid, anything happen to them and Gracie is thrown into the company. But if that happens, I know she will rise to the occasion, just as she always has."

Mr. Mitchell hands me a Kleenex and then another.

"Now that Grace is eighteen, there are some things I wish for her to know. I'm hoping she's aware of the special circumstances that surround our family and the company. If she doesn't, Shane, take her aside this second and tell her. Take her to meet the Denleys. She will love them."

Mom's chair scrapes against the floor; she hurries around the table and sits down with her arm around me.

She takes the letter from me and reads, "I want to give Grace my old journals, so she can keep them with her. I want her to hear how I lived, how much I loved her mother, and my hopes for her life. But, there are stipulations that need to be discussed between Mr. Mitchell and Grace. Lynnie and Shane, I know you'll want to argue, but let Grace do this on her own. Every second I lie in this bed, I think about you three, and I hope you're doing well. Shane, I hope you're taking care of my girls, but I also hope you're living life and are not burdened by responsibilities I selfishly put upon you. Lynnie, I hope you're dating." Mom laughs, wiping her eyes clear. "If you find someone who loves you a fraction of how much I love you, you will live blissfully happy. And Grace," Mom grips my shoulder, "I have more to say to you, but for now, I love you. It is my hope that you are all happy. I love you."

Mom puts the paper down, gently stroking it. Shane is looking out the window, his head turned so I can't see whatever he's trying to hide.

Mr. Mitchell gives us all a few minutes and then softly says, "If today isn't a good time, I can set up a meeting with Grace at her earliest convenience."

"No," I almost shout. "No, I'd really like to talk to you today." I want to know what Dad was thinking—why he's having Mr. Mitchell only talk to me.

Mr. Mitchell waits patiently as Mom and Shane take their time leaving the room. "Will you follow me outside, Grace?" He picks up his briefcase and tucks the folder under his arm.

"Outside?"

"Yes, come along." He looks over his shoulder frequently to make sure I'm following him. This is weird.

We get to his black Mercedes and, after putting his briefcase in his car, he turns back to me. "Daniel was very specific. He told me that if I conducted the meeting at your home, I was to speak with you outside so no one else would hear. He suspected your mother and uncle would try to overhear, which I'm assuming is why they are both looking out the window at us now."

I glance over my shoulder and smile when I see Mom and Shane acting casual in front of the big bay windows of the living room.

"In the letter you just read, Daniel stated he wanted you to have his journals," he says while opening his trunk and pulling out what looks like a toolbox. Flipping up the metal clasps, I open the box and suck in a breath. Eight leather bound journals are stacked neatly inside. It's the closest I've felt to Dad in years. The bridge of my nose stings when my fingers brush along the spines of the journals.

"Grace, Shane and Carolyn now know that these are in your possession. These journals are not secret and can be read by everyone. But…" He reaches into his briefcase and, with his back to the house, hands me an envelope. "There is one journal that is for you, and you only. Daniel went to great lengths to make sure it stayed hidden and also for you to retrieve it alone. I cannot stress enough how private this journal is. Inside that envelope is a letter from him stating the same. I was also told to tell you that

128

no one, not even your mother, can know of this journal. If you aren't comfortable with these conditions, you are to destroy the letter and its contents. If you choose to never have the journal, that's your decision."

"What's in here?" I ask, looking at the envelope that's pressed against my chest. There's no way I'm destroying it.

"I only know there is a letter. I have never opened it, as you can see by the seal." He points to the letter. I could never be a lawyer. My curiosity would get me fired within minutes.

"Mr. Mitchell, thank you. I can't tell you how much this all means to me." Kneeling down by the journals, I pick one out and hold it to me.

"Your father was a good man. He helped me get my business off the ground. He told me he saw great things in my future. Without him, I wouldn't be who I am today. I'm sure a lot of people can say that about your father." We shake hands before he climbs into his car. He rolls down his window and says, "Read that letter alone, and when finished, destroy it." He smiles sweetly at me, waves, and then drives away. With my back to the house, I fold the envelope so it'll fit in my pocket. After making sure it's hidden, I turn, lock up the box and haul it inside.

"What was that all about?" Mom asks, looking at the box in my hands.

"Dad's journals. He wanted me to have them. Mr. Mitchell said the journals are for everyone to read." I set the box on the table and open it.

"They smell like him." Mom slowly takes one out. A mixture of leather and cologne fills the room. "If these are for everyone to see, why did your meeting have to be private?"

"Carolyn," Shane warns.

"I know. I'm sorry," Mom snaps. "I just hate there has to be secrets." She sits, opening a journal and soon is enthralled with what she's reading. Once I feel I'm okay to sneak off, I go to my room and lock the door behind me. Not patient enough to sit in a chair, I sink down to the floor just inside my room and rip open the envelope. A small silver key falls out, clinking against the ground. I hold it in my hand as I unfold the letter. A few preparatory breaths later, I open my eyes and start reading.

My Gracie Girl,

This may seem odd to you that I've excluded your mother in this, but there are reasons. Reasons you will soon discover. I assume Mr. Mitchell has given you the eight journals. Read them. I want you to learn about me and pass down the stories to your children (which I'm hoping won't happen until you're fifty).

Grace, the journals I gave are an open book. Anyone can read them. But there is one journal I've kept separate. The eight I have given to you are stories of my life growing up, learning about the stone, meeting your mother, building the mirror, and discovering how amazing fatherhood is.

The journal I have kept private also tells of the stone, meeting your mother, building the mirror, and fatherhood. But there are stories in that particular journal that no one knows, and no one aside from you will ever know. Most of the entries in this journal are not happy. Some are frightening but essential. Some, Gracie, are awful, and I pray you won't think differently of me after reading them.

I'm ashamed to admit that I became obsessed with building the mirror. Something drove me to it, and I couldn't sleep until it was finished. I love it now. But there may come a time when the mirror may need to be altered or even destroyed. This journal contains the answer to that problem if it should arise.

I know what you're thinking. Why not give this to Shane? You will see if you read the other journals that Shane was very emotionally tied to some of the experiences and sorrow we went through. You will be able to trust no one more than Shane in your lifetime, so please don't think I don't trust him now. But there are things Shane shouldn't know, and I'm tormented with the fact that I've kept them from him.

I'm sure I'm confusing you more, but this letter will make sense once you've read through the journal.

Because of the contents of it, I've kept it hidden. Take the key that was contained in the envelope to the bank your mother and I go to. Bring your license. Ask for Mrs. Dohnute (pronounced doo-noot, not donut. I know your mind). She will then take you to a safety deposit box. This is a different

130

box than the one Shane and your mother are aware of. Inside will be the journal.

I'm sure Mr. Mitchell warned you how important it is to keep this secret. Be careful where you take it and when you read it. Your mother, bless her heart, is innately curious. Especially when it comes to you. It breaks my heart, but she can't read what's in there. I know you'll take care of it.

I'm assuming you know about the mirror, whether Shane has just recently told you or you found out by others means. I was hoping to give it to you for your eighteenth birthday. I had plans to take you all around the world. The Great Wall, Iguaza Falls, Taj Mahal, Cristo Redentor, Machu Picchu, Gettysburg. But more than these amazing places, I wanted to take you to amazing times.

The Rockwell balls your mother and I hosted were not just for fun but for education. You needed to know how to act when I took you to the real Rockwell. It's magnificent. I know you would be so happy to go back and see it.

The world holds wonderful things for you. You're smart. You get that from me. (Don't tell your mom I said that.) You have an amazing talent to meet people and genuinely care for them. That's not a talent many people possess.

I hope you already know, and therefore I'm just being repetitive, but I love you. I'm sad that I won't be there for your important milestones. When you graduate high school, move to college, fall in love (although I'm hoping that also doesn't occur until you're fifty). I wish I could be there to walk you down the aisle, but Shane promised to take my place.

Trust yourself. As smart as you are, you're timid. You can reach much greater distances if you would only allow yourself. Keep counting stars, eat like you won't be able to eat for days, laugh at things no one else sees, and love like I know you're capable of.

Now, because I feel like I'm in a cheesy made-for-TV movie, I'll end this letter. I gave you the journals so you'll know I'm not far away. And I'm not. As long as you're living, there will always be a piece of me living, too.

I love you, my Gracie Girl.

Dad

Finally, after reading it three more times, I can make it to the end without crying, and when I finish, I need to move. I need to get to that journal and figure out what he's saying. I pull out my phone and text Bri to call me.

"Hey, Bri," I say when I answer the phone.

"What's up?" She sounds like a blissfully happy newlywed.

"I haven't seen you since you got home from your honeymoon. Can I swing by and see you and your new apartment?"

"Sure! We're still unpacking, but if you hurry, there might be some cookies left over."

"Okay, thanks. See you in a bit." I shove my phone in my pocket, along with the key Dad gave me, and run downstairs. "Mom, Bri called. I'm going to see their new apartment." I orchestrated it so I could truthfully say *she* called. A little deceptive, yes. Mom would see right through me if I had called Bri to plan something. Dad's journals are on the table, and if I planned to do anything besides reading them, she'd question it. She's questioning even now.

"Will you be home for dinner?" she asks with her eyebrows rising in a you-aren't-fooling-anyone look.

"Yes." I take a step toward the garage.

"Tell Bridgette I said hello," she says and continues reading.

I race to my car, rolling down the windows so I won't feel smothered by the guilt, and, hoping there aren't any cops out, I speed to the bank.

* * *

"Grace Gentry," Mrs. Dohnute says as she comes into the small meeting room. Because Dad told me her name sounds like donut, that's all I imagined when I thought of her. So I pictured a plump little old woman who brings fresh cookies to work everyday and has candies in her pockets for her grandkids. This woman is the opposite of that. She can't be much older than thirty with a very thin, but kind of scary strong, skinny face with a pointy nose. Her business suit doesn't have a wrinkle on it, and no hair is out of place in her sleek bun. She looks all business.

"Mrs. Dohnute." Curse Dad for making me say her name with a laugh! "Thank you for seeing me on such short notice."

"I wouldn't have if it dealt with anyone other than your father. He was a good man." It never gets old hearing people say that about him.

"Thank you. Um . . . I'm not really sure how this is supposed to go. I have the key to the safety deposit box my dad left for me. Do I give it to you? Or—"

"No. I will go get it and bring it to you." All business. She strides out in her expensive high heels, leaving me fidgeting in the huge chair. In no time at all she comes back in with the small box, places it on the desk, and turns to me. "When you're finished, lock the box and signal for me. I'll take it back."

The door shuts with a bang, making me jump. That woman is a little scary. Wasting no time, I pull the key from my pocket and, after a few shaky tries, get it into the lock and twist. Why am I so nervous? It's only a book. Dad's warning about the contents and its secretiveness have me wary though. I open the lid and see the journal. This one doesn't look like the others. The others are black leather, the size of a notebook. This one is dark green leather with a brown ribbon that comes from the back to tie in the front. How am I supposed to keep this hidden? It's huge. It's the length of a textbook, but gratefully not as thick. I should've brought a backpack with me, but that would've been weird.

I lock the empty box back up, say goodbye to Mrs. Dohnute (it's still funny) and race home. I feel like I'm in some spy movie, creeping through the house. At one point I even hide behind the counter when Shane comes in to get something out of the fridge. Once inside my room, I lock the door and instantly start reading.

June 14, 1991

From the moment I touched the stone, there are feelings in me I'm too ashamed to admit to anyone.

I know I've become obsessed. I know I'm being a recluse and withdrawn from everyone. Shane tells me daily he's worried about me and tries to find small ways to get me away from the lab. I can't describe it to him, but whenever I leave the stone, it feels like a part of me deadens. When I'm away, all my thoughts are consumed with when I can go back.

The stone is like nothing I've ever seen. It's small and looks so insignificant, but the power it exudes is phenomenal. It's not just the power that's so captivating. There's something about it that calls to me. It's as if something in me was made from part of the stone, and if the stone stopped existing, my whole being would too.

What scares me most is I know this is how I'm feeing. If I were blind to my reaction toward it, that would be different. But I can see the changes. Every time I look in the mirror, I have to look twice at the thin man staring back at me. I see it in myself when I skip meal after meal, or when I snap at Shane when he expresses concern for me. The stone is slowly consuming me, and the more time I'm with it, the more I want to be consumed. With the stone, I don't feel like I need anyone else. It's bringing something into my life that is literally magic, and I know I won't find anything or anyone that will ever make me feel like this.

Chris keeps asking when the machine will be done. Truth is, I could've finished weeks ago. I'm too scared to finish. What happens when I do? I don't know Chris well, but something tells me I may not leave this lab alive when I turn the machine over.

And what happens to the stone? What happens when I turn it over and become nothing without it? I'm not going to find out. If Chris gets in my way, I'll take care of him.

I can't live without it.

July 2, 1991

It doesn't get easier working with Chris. He lingers, hovers, and sometimes belittles. I keep wanting to tell him that he asked me to help because he couldn't do it, so why is he so condescending when I, in fact, am smarter in this area than him. But I don't think that would go over very well.

A few weeks ago, I decided to get the machine working and hoped I could use it to my advantage and ensure the stone stays with me, but it won't work. I've gotten close to getting it to work, but something keeps stopping me. My math is right. I've gone over it dozens of times. I think someone doesn't want me to finish.

Shane started out hating this job and warned me about the others. Everyone but Gwen. He was smitten the first time he saw her. Won't admit it though. My tough little brother actually has stars in his eyes when he's around her. He'd punch me right in the mouth if I said it out loud, but he's a goner. He's so busy trying to not notice her, he doesn't see that she looks at him when he's working. She gets all red in the cheeks and looks away before he can catch her staring.

I continue to read, fascinated with every word of Dad's. I dog ear corners of pages I want to read again. My stomach hurts when he tells stories of Shane trying to talk to Gwen and failing miserably. Then I get to the entry that tells about that day.

July 25, 1991

I'm not sure where to begin. These last two days have been a blur but eye-opening at the same time. Everything that happened with Chris I've included in my other journal, so I won't linger on those events. What I will say is wherever Chris is, I feel sorry for those people. I know where I sent him and can only hope he finds happiness there and not take his anger toward me out on anyone.

Before going through for the first time I connected the machine to a small receiver that I attached to some ribbon to hang around my neck. It connected to the machine, so all I needed to do was twist it and it would bring me back to where I started. I was really hoping the machine would

135

take me to New York or maybe China, somewhere further away than just the building next door. But I needed a way home in case I ended up someplace bizarre. And I did.

What happened when I first stepped through I haven't told anyone and will never mention it again after this journal entry. What happened changed me. I stepped away from Shane and entered into nothing. That's the only way to explain it. It wasn't light enough to be day and not dark enough to be night. There was no sun, moon, or stars. Gray is a good word to describe it. No grass, food, buildings, or other people. It was me, alone.

Looking back I think I was caught between time. Obviously I was curious, so I kept walking around. With every step, I started to lose myself. First I started questioning myself. Why was I here? What am I doing here? But then the questions changed. Why would I want to leave here? The more I asked, the more I panicked. Then the voices came, and because I was the only one there, the voices seemed like they were screaming. The voices weren't telling me anything I understood, but the chills that came made me want to get away from them. I ran faster, deeper into this unknown.

The voices stopped, and the only noise was my own screaming. My brain felt like mush. I couldn't form a coherent thought, but then suddenly, my brain switched on and started feasting on itself. With every thought came the opposite. I wanted to leave, but wanted to stay. I wanted to run, but I wanted to sit down and not move.

I wanted to live, but I wanted to die.

I really wanted to die.

My body, crumpled on the ground, felt a heaviness looming over it. A blackness waiting for me to grow weak enough so it could have me. The despair and desperation I felt was too much. I wanted it to have me. Maybe then I wouldn't feel the pain, the fear, or the ache in my bones to want it over. As I lay on the floor, I gripped my chest. That's when I felt the key to go home around my neck. I closed my eyes in gratitude. In my mind I repeated, "I want to go home."

I twisted the receiver and the blackness started to ooze from my body. As

I'm writing this, I feel like some of it never left. That experience is something you don't forget.

But the important thing is I got away from it. When the dark left, it was replaced by an overwhelming amount of light. It was warm, and my soul sucked it in like somehow it would heal it. When I got enough strength to stand, I wandered through the big trees I found myself in. I could hear talking, so I made my way to it.

Just out of the trees stood a tall, beautiful building. A little worn and aged but beautiful. There was a tour going on, so I'm assuming it was a museum or some old house. The tour group moved on, but one woman stayed behind, lingering in the gardens. I had $52.28 in my bank account, and I would have given every cent to go on that tour if it meant I could be by her.

The next thing I knew, I was at the edge of the garden just looking at her. Other people who saw me probably thought I was some creep leering at the woman. I wasn't staring because I thought she was beautiful, which she was. Actually, she was uncomfortably beautiful. The kind where you think you shouldn't even breathe the same air as her.

I was staring, because she looked so familiar to me, like we had met before. The second our eyes met, it seemed I had found the other half to my magnet, drawn together by some unseen force. I forced myself to walk to her, because everything in me wanted to sprint. I wasn't looking where I was going, my thoughts were consumed with this woman and the pull she had over me. The gravel under me was loose, and because I was in the company of the one woman in the world that literally took my breath away, I fell. Embarrassingly fell. Like body flailing, arms swinging, knees scratching, face in the dirt kind of falling. The very worst kind.

She tried to muffle her laugh, but I'd fall a hundred more times if I could hear that laugh again.

"Are you alright?" she asked through tiny fits of laughter. My body wanted to scream that no, I wasn't alright. My wrist, I was positive, was broken. Trying to be macho and nonchalant, I pulled my wrist behind my back and bit my tongue, so I wouldn't whimper like a small boy.

I told her I was fine. She didn't believe me. I assured her it was nothing, that my ego was more hurt than my hand. She gave me this look. A look that I swear could look deep into me and know my innermost thoughts.

"Fine, if you are well, catch this." She tossed her purse at me with no warning. I reached out with both hands and instantly recoiled my hurt one, causing her purse to land in the dirt. I didn't know the woman, but I knew she was trying so hard not to laugh. I grumbled, she laughed, and then she offered to take me to the hospital.

Her name was Carolyn Weston. Would it be premature to say I loved her, and the second she told me her name, I repeated Carolyn Gentry in my head? There was just something about her, the way I felt about her that told me I belonged to her.

She was right. My wrist was broken. Not exactly broken, but a non-displaced fracture. Hurt like the devil though.

I asked if I could buy her dinner, seeing as she just took me to the hospital. I braced myself for her rejection, so it didn't register that she said yes.

"Oh, okay. Thanks for your help. Bye." That's what I said when she said yes. I never thought a woman like her would say yes.

"Daniel." She stopped me from walking away and said, "I would love to go to dinner with you."

I grinned like an idiot and just looked at her.

We went to dinner, and I don't remember a time I've laughed so much but also felt so much. Carolyn was something.

I tried grabbing a cab, but she asked if we could walk. I didn't know her house was a few miles away. If I had known I would've been the one to ask. I got to know her better. She was an only child and always wished for siblings, and for that reason she wanted a big family—lots of kids. Her dad was a surgeon. Her mother taught culinary arts at the local college. Carolyn didn't want to be a cook or doctor. She wanted to design clothes. I hung on every word she said, filing it to memory.

We got to her apartment at 3:38 in the morning. I knew it would be inappropriate if I got down on one knee and asked her to come home with me. And that's when I remembered how I got there and how I was getting home. There were things that needed to be taken care of before I came back for Carolyn.

I asked if she believed in fate, because at the moment I could feel I was fated to be hers.

"I'm starting to," was her reply, and I resisted the urge to fall on my knees and beg. Trying to be the gentleman my mother wanted me to be, I got her number, kissed her goodnight, and watched her walk inside. My spirits were in a different sphere when I reached for the key and twisted.

After I twisted it, I looked around and knew I was still in England, but it was different. Half the apartment buildings were demolished to only stones. The sky was filled with so much smoke it blocked out the sun. Streets were deserted. Garbage littered the sidewalks. A newspaper rustled in the wind and landed at my feet. It read March 15, 2040. I had to look at it a few times after rubbing my eyes to make sure I was seeing it right.

A familiar voice filled the desolate streets. Through a glass window I saw what looked like a press conference, with Chris in charge. He said he wasn't happy with how everyone was behaving. He heard rumors of revolts, and then showed a video of what he did to take care of those people who thought of going against him. I saw the machine, the machine I had been working on for months. The video showed him going through and finding those people. What he did to them is something I'll never be able to forget, nor able to put into words. It was barbaric. He wanted to make a statement, so it was fouler than it had to be.

"Be mindful of your intentions, because your consequences are in my hands," Chris warned. The screen went to static, and I took a step into the nearest alleyway. My first thought was of Carolyn. It had been about fifty years since I met her, but that didn't stop me from sprinting to her apartment. I remember she said she lived on the second floor, 208. I pounded on her door, pleading she would answer, and I could see she was safe.

139

A teenage boy answered. He was dressed in rags, filthy, and the smell coming from the apartment made me take a step back. I asked if Carolyn Weston lived there. He told me I shouldn't be asking for people, that if they found out they would kill me. I asked again. He left the door open and went to a back room. I didn't go in, afraid his apartment would look worse than he did. He came back with a small black device. He handed it to me, told me to type in the name of who I was looking for. I typed in Carolyn's name, thrilled to see her picture and pushed it with my finger.

The picture that followed was devastating, and I felt a piece of my heart die. It was Carolyn, up against a wall with a dozen others with guns pointed at them. She was the only one not turned around, with that stubborn look on her face, daring them to shoot her. I shoved the device back at the boy and asked what it was. He said they called it the Death Journal. Chris and his followers gave them to every person so they would know what happened to those who stood against him.

After that my body didn't work right. I sagged down the wall, smelling the stench of death around me and thought of Carolyn. Her bright, sunny, loving personality was destroyed because of something I made. I killed Carolyn. And then I thought of Shane and instantly knew he wasn't there either.

I clutched at the key, begging through sobs for it to take me home. I promised to whoever was listening that I could fix this if I just went home. Twisting the key, I closed my eyes, and when I opened them, I was stumbling out of the machine and Shane was there to catch me.

I latched onto him like a lifeline. Shane was here, safe. The lab I left was the same smelly one I returned to. The concern in Shane's face made me grow up in mere seconds. I planted a smile on my face and told him I was in love.

Shane saw through me and asked me again what happened. I didn't tell him about the space I went to before Carolyn, hoping if I didn't talk about it, it would leave me somehow. It hasn't. I told him about the future, sugarcoating what I really saw and left out what happened to Carolyn.

The events with Chris are already recorded, so I won't repeat them. But I *will say the guilt I feel for sending Gwen through is like I've swallowed a pile of broken glass. I didn't know what else to do. Chris gripped her hand when he went through. I know if I told Chris to leave Gwen here, he would know he shouldn't go. I've never seen Shane's face like that. And what made it worse was it was entirely my fault. Shane asked where I sent them, and I told him to the last place I went, to the future. I told him they would be okay, that they'd find a home there. He looked at me, and I started shaking my head before he could ask. I wouldn't send him there too. He wanted to be with Gwen, but Chris, Tom, and Harry would love to see him dead. I'm too selfish to let my brother go.*

So I lied. I told him I disconnected the stone from the machine, and now the machine was useless. I lied to his face when I told him there was no way he could get to Gwen.

A piece of my soul died that day as I watched my brother walk away from me.

As I write these memories, my thoughts are consumed with the stone. My good sense tells me to forget, to leave it in the past. But I can't. That stone haunts and thrills me. But for now, I'll push it aside.

Because at the moment, I'm on a plane, heading to London to find Carolyn. My life feels empty without her. Or maybe it feels like I started living when I met her. Either way, I know I can't live the rest of it without her.

After I finish reading, I just sit, staring at the book that now looks dirty against my sheets.

While I was reading, I was trying to picture what he was describing, but now I have a picture of guns aimed at Mom, and Dad wanting to die in a blank existence. Why did he want me to read this?

I slam the journal shut and hide it beneath my pajamas in my bottom drawer. I feel like I need to take a shower to get rid of how that book made me feel. Once I've calmed myself down enough, I go find Mom. I just need to see her.

"Hey, how was Bridgette?" Mom asks while stirring potato soup. Just the sight of her has my eyes watering. When I see her, I see the picture Dad formed in my mind. She drops the spoon in the pot when I wrap my arms around her arms. "Is everything okay? Is Bridgette hurt?"

"What happened?" Shane demands.

"Nothing. Nothing happened." I push away from Mom and smile through tears. I look at Shane, who has that face where he wants to be scared but masks it with anger, and then to Mom, who looks like she wants to cry with me. "I'm sorry. I'm really fine. It's just everything that happened this morning. With Dad. I'm good most days, but days like this when I remember him so clearly, they make me miss him."

Mom hugs me before I can see the tears that are brimming in her eyes. She did that a lot right after Dad died. I always knew when she wanted to cry, because she would either hug me really tight for a few minutes or go to her room. It was rare when she cried in front of me.

Dinner starts, and I want to ask Shane about Gwen, but I don't know how. Tomorrow I'll read the other journals and see what Dad said about her in those ones. Then I'll ask him.

It's unusually quiet during dinner. I assume everyone feels the same pang of misery I do. We all miss Dad.

chapter twelve

I'm an idiot to think I'd actually be able to fall asleep. Even after taking a sleeping pill, I'm still wide-eyed, staring at my ceiling. I keep glancing over at my bottom drawer, hearing the book call to me. It's my curiosity, but it's also a need. I need to know what Dad wants me to know. Flipping on my lamp beside my bed, I retrieve the journal from my dresser. It feels heavier than it did earlier today. I climb back into bed, and for the remainder of the night I read.

August 10, 1995

It's been the happiest four months of my life. I never thought marriage could bring so much into my life. I never knew so much had been lacking until I finally made Carolyn mine.

As happy as I am with Carolyn, the stone has remained in my thoughts. It's become an obsession that's becoming very hard to resist. Because of this, I think I've come up with a way to keep it, but also keep it from controlling me.

Chris had the idea to make a machine to magnify the abilities of the stone, so I did. I built the machine again, but as I stared at the huge machine in the lab, I thought I should make a machine in the form of an everyday household piece of furniture. If, heaven forbid, someone came looking for the stone or the machine, they would never find it. No one will ever find the stone; I'm positive about that. Even if they did, it would be useless to them. That was an accident.

One day, before I married Carolyn, I was examining the stone. I was trying to discover what it was made of. I also wanted to know if it could be damaged. I was careless, only looking at the stone, when I slipped with the instrument and made a huge gash against my palm. Instinctively I grabbed my hand but pushed more blood from the cut. The instant my blood touched the rock, I felt it. I felt it all the way to my bones. The stone looked the same. Black, insignificant, and ordinary. Oh, but it called to me. Maybe more now that it's mine.

The stone is hidden, and I know without a doubt no one will ever find it. But the mirror is in plain sight and more beautiful than I thought imaginable.

I'm showing Carolyn tonight. She's either going to kill me or start crying.

She's going to kill me.

December 11, 2000

I write with a very heavy heart today. I've debated, for weeks, whether I should write this down or take it to my grave. Selfishly, I want to die with this secret. But if I write it down, maybe one day I can give it to Gracie, and she'll see what happens when you use the mirror for other purposes than what it was created for. I'm a coward, because I'll never give this to Gracie unless I know I'll be gone before she reads it. I could never look at her if she knew the truth. Most days it's hard to even look at myself.

Ten months ago, Lynnie told me we were going to have another baby. I was thrilled, but as the news settled in, I was nervous. How could I love another baby as much as I love Gracie? It didn't seem possible. I kept that fear to myself and did anything Lynnie told me to. I even went to the grocery store at two in the morning for chocolate milk, because she needed to have it at that moment. When I got home, she was asleep at the table with a glass out

144

ready for her milk. That woman is amazing.

Lynnie didn't want to find out if we were having a boy or girl, which drove me crazy. I like to plan things. What if we had a boy? We had nothing blue! We would bring a newborn home, and I would be out scrambling to buy things for a boy. Lyn knows better than to send me to the store for baby things. I'm useless. I went to doctor's appointments with her, heard the heartbeat, turned my head when they weighed her (her rule), and started to love this baby.

At 35 weeks, Lyn was put on bed rest. That meant me and Gracie got to spend a lot of time together. I had no idea how exhausting that little girl was. How was it possible for one little four year old to run around in circles for three hours and not tire out at all? I was tired after the first hour.

One night in early November, Lynnie woke me up. She told me something was wrong and we needed to get to the hospital. I grabbed her hospital bag, my bag, called Shane to come stay with Gracie, and started the car so it would be warm. I went back up to our room to help Lynnie downstairs, but she'd fallen back asleep. I walked over to her, amazed that she could fall asleep so fast. When I reached the bed, I saw the sheets turning crimson. Immediately I started shaking her, yelling at her to wake up. I called 911 while screaming at Lynnie.

Just before the ambulance arrived, I felt the room get colder, the air turned bitter, and the world became darker. I knew at that moment Lynnie was gone. I held her in my arms, but she wasn't there anymore. The EMTs came and started CPR while strapping her to a gurney. Shane arrived when they put her in the back of the ambulance. He didn't ask me questions. Grief must have been apparent on my face. He hugged me and told me he would take care of Gracie. The ambulance ride was grueling. At one point, I was actually restrained, because I kept yelling at them to do something, to go faster.

At the hospital, I was left in the waiting room. I paced, broke a chair, and then was left in a small room with no furniture to break. I paced more. Then a frizzy-haired old lady came in and told me she was a social worker for the hospital. She explained what they were doing with Lynnie and asked if I needed anything. I told her I needed my wife.

145

When the doctor came in, I fell to my knees. He tried explaining what happened. Hemorrhaged, she needed hospital care but it was too late to save her.

The doctor told me Carolyn died. I'll never forget how I put my hand to my chest, confused that my heart was still beating. I gave my heart to Carolyn the second I met her, and she took it with her when she died.

He then told me the baby survived. A little girl. She had a hard time breathing at first but was doing well. He asked if I wanted to see her.

I walked into the nursery and immediately knew which one she was. She had the same dark curls Gracie did. For the remainder of the night, I sat in the corner, rocking Maggie, named after my mother, telling her stories of Carolyn. I wished there was a way I could go back and save her.

That's when it hit me. I felt stupid for not thinking of it earlier. I knew that was the reason I felt so impressed to build the mirror. It was for this exact moment when I could go back and save my wife. I kissed Maggie, swaddled her tight, promised her her mother would live, and went home to the mirror. Luckily Shane and Gracie were still sleeping. I didn't feel like talking about what happened or what was going to happen. I stepped through, telling the mirror I wanted to go back one month.

It was odd, having an in-depth conversation with another form of myself. I told him (me) everything that happened and what he needed to do. I went back to my time with new memories. New memories of hugging Lynnie for the longest time when she came home from the grocery store. She laughed as she swatted at me, telling me her lasagna was going to burn, but I held her tighter.

After that she got really irritated with me. Everyday I asked how she was feeling, how many times the baby had kicked that day, and if she wanted to lie down. We made it to 37 weeks, and she didn't even have to go on bed rest. To say I was relieved would be an understatement.

There was a problem in the European branch that the manager there couldn't solve. Something about two co-workers selling trade secrets. It's hard to remember now. Lynnie assured me she was fine for the day. I could go to London and be back by that night. It wasn't too far, considering I only had to walk into Gracie's room to get there. I told her to call me if she felt the slightest discomfort. She promised.

At 10:06 a.m. London time, I got a call from Shane. The second I heard his voice, I was already heading to my car to get back to the mirror at Rockwell. Shane told me Lynnie went into labor. He was at the hospital with Gracie and would leave with her when I got there.

I was to the hospital in less than three hours from Shane's phone call. I'm not sure what my face looked like, but every nurse I saw just laughed and pointed me in the right direction. I asked the desk which room she was in, and when the nurse didn't meet my eyes, I knew something was wrong. But Lynnie couldn't die again. I went back and changed it. It couldn't be her. The nurse told me to wait in the waiting room, and the doctor would be out shortly. Again, I was confined to a room where I couldn't break anything. After what seemed like hours, the doctor found me. I asked about Lynnie. She said Lynnie was recovering well from the surgery. I asked, 'What surgery?'

Lynnie hemorrhaged again, so they had to do an emergency c-section. The bleeding wouldn't stop, and Lynnie was dying. The doctor told me her and her team did everything they could but eventually had to do a full hysterectomy.

Then she told me about the baby. Apparently Lynnie found out at 35 weeks there was something wrong with the baby. A heart defect that made it so the baby wouldn't live outside the womb. There wasn't any indication at her big ultrasound. A mistake this big never happens, the doctor told me. It seemed the defect appeared out of nowhere. It was no coincidence they found it the same time I went back and changed fate. Lynnie's blood pressure was high, and she was already starting to bleed. Lynnie refused to deliver then, hoping that if she gave the baby more time, her lungs would develop enough to survive.

The doctor told me the baby didn't survive the delivery.

She left, and I was left alone in that small room, thinking over what was

147

happening.

Lynnie had known for three weeks and didn't tell me. Everyday she feared for the baby, put her life at risk trying to save her. She did it all alone. How did I not notice?

Lynnie's room was dark when I went in. The curtains drawn, lights off except for one in the corner. When I stepped behind the curtain, I saw her. She looked like they had taken her heart out during surgery. The lights in her eyes were gone, the smile that made me do anything was nowhere, and I knew it would take a lot of time to see it again. She was staring into the corner, but when I looked, there was nothing there. And then I remembered having Gracie and the little bed they wheeled her around in. That corner was where they would park that bed. A bed that held a baby. A baby we didn't have.

When she saw me, whatever strength she had to even hold up her head up was gone. She fell into me and sobbed. I kept telling her I was sorry for being gone and sorry for the baby. I told her I loved her and that Gracie loved her. The cries that came out of her that day will haunt me forever.

They will haunt me because I wasn't sitting there grieving a baby lost. I was sitting there grieving that I'm the one who was making my wife cry so hard she couldn't catch her breath. I changed the past. In the previous life, I lost Lynnie but got Maggie. This life I lost Maggie but got Lynnie.

I killed my baby.

A week later, while I lay next to her in bed, I asked why she didn't tell me about the baby. I didn't mean to make her cry again, but tears exploded from her. She told me a few days before she found out I became obsessive about her and the baby. Constantly asking if she was okay, how I could make her more comfortable, how the baby was doing. When she found out about the baby, she didn't have the heart to tell me, because I had been so excited.

I wanted to tell her it wasn't excitement that had me obsessing over her. It was terror that I was going to lose her again. I was so worried about her physically that I never saw how much emotional pain she carried around.

148

She then asked me if I could use the mirror to go back to save the baby. She didn't understand, and I only did because I had witnessed it. I told her no, that it was too dangerous. She told me she would give up her life for the baby. And I told her that's exactly why I wouldn't do it.

I slept on the couch for the next week, or on Gracie's floor so Lynnie wouldn't have to get up with her. When Lynnie let me back in our room, she asked me again, and I tried explaining what could happen if we went back. You don't get to choose whose life you take. I told her if she went back and saved the baby, she was giving up someone else's life. It could be hers, mine, or even Gracie's.

Later that night, I found her in Gracie's room, rocking Gracie while she slept. Lynnie cried over the loss of the baby and the fact she couldn't have any more. I sat on the floor next to the rocking chair and silently cried with her. The guilt was crushing me, causing physical pain. I knew I needed to tell Lynnie what happened, but I didn't. She would never understand what I did. She'd give up her life for the baby the same way I'd give up mine to save her and Gracie.

I didn't know the mirror had to find a balance. I didn't know it would take Maggie. I didn't know so much would change. And I didn't know, I couldn't know, I would break my wife the way I did.

That experience taught me a lesson I wish no one else will have to learn. You can't relive moments or fix moments you didn't want to live in the first place.

So I guess the purpose of telling this story is a warning for whoever is reading it. The mirror is not meant for changing the past. If you try, you will live with unbearable guilt for the rest of your life.

I have a little sister?

The memory of her is Dad's in another life, but I impossibly miss her. My heart breaks when I think of Dad carrying this secret around. It breaks again when I think of Mom and what she's had to go through. I think of

149

Shane staying with me, keeping me happy when he probably wanted to go into the other room and mourn. Thinking of all the pain my family went through, the series of cracks my heart already has widens, and soon I feel it beating in pieces.

* * *

I need to talk to someone. Mom listens and is always supportive, but I know she won't understand. I need Shane.

I peek my head in Dad's office and find Shane at the desk. He's kneading his palms into his eyes, a stack of files on the desk in front of him. The room smells like cedar from Dad's wooden chest in the corner. Dad spent so much time in his office he started to smell like cedar, too.

"Do you have a minute?" I ask when Shane looks up at me.

"Yeah, kid. What do you need?" He subtly pushes the files to the corner of the desk and stacks papers on top of them. When he looks back, I see his eyes go nervous. "Should I get your mom?"

"No." I quickly wipe a tear from my cheek and sit in one of the brown leather chairs across from the desk. "I want to talk to you." The feelings I have are weird to me, so I know they'll be hard for Mom to hear. Shane has become the one person in my life who I feel I can tell anything to. Even Miles I'm worried to tell some things to.

Shane gets up and sits in the chair next to me, glancing at the door. He looks like he's silently praying for Mom to walk in. He never did well with emotional women. "What is it?"

"Do you ever . . ." I watch my hands tighten around each other as I search for the right words. There aren't right words. "Do you ever get mad at Dad for building the mirror?" I whisper, too ashamed to say it any louder.

"Yes," he answers, and I let go of a big breath. I look up at my big, strong uncle who, at the moment, looks so lonely.

"I miss him everyday, and I know why he did it, but I'm selfish enough to think about a life we would've had without it. I wonder if it would hurt this much." Hearing myself say it out loud, I feel like a jerk.

150

"Well, I think no matter what life you have, you'll hurt. It's part of living. If your dad didn't build the mirror, you probably wouldn't have this house or the friends you have, or Miles." He swallows loudly, shifting in his seat uncomfortably.

"Yeah, I guess. But sometimes I think that if he didn't build it, maybe right now Dad, Mom, you, and me would be sitting around a kitchen table laughing at stories you and Dad tell about when you were kids. You wouldn't be so scared for your family. Maybe you'd even be married with a little brood of your own." I smile, thinking about little cousins running around the house.

"Whether your dad built the mirror or not, I wouldn't be married." Shane's demeanor darkens as he sits back in the chair, gripping the armrests.

"Because of Gwen?" I regret asking the second I see his face fall.

"How do you know about Gwen?" The question, so softly asked, was filled with such agony, I swallow the tears that I want to cry for him.

"You mentioned her when you told us the story about Chris and the others," I say quietly because the room seems to be getting smaller. He nods, and the desire to know him more is almost unbearable. "You say her name different than the rest of them."

Shane sighs, rubbing a hand over his face. "I never told your dad this, but I loved Gwen. Dan knew I liked her. He even tried coming up with these situations that conveniently put Gwen and I alone together. He didn't know Gwen and I were together every minute we weren't at the lab."

Growing up, I always wondered what Shane would look like if he were in love with someone. Now I know I've seen it my entire life. He's still in love with Gwen. Twenty years have gone by, and he still loves her.

"When Dan sent Chris, Harry, and Tom through, Chris took Gwen with him. I thought my life was over at that moment. I went home after and fell on my bed, wondering what I was going to do the next morning. Who was I going to wake up to see? I refused to talk to Dan for awhile after. He left for England to find Carolyn, and I sulked for more weeks than I'd like to admit. Time passed, and eventually I forgave Dan. It really wasn't his fault; he was trying to save me at the time, and he had no idea how deep my feelings

151

went for Gwen." Shane's grief looks fresh, like he's reliving the moment of losing her all over again.

I pull my legs up to my chest, resting my chin on my knees. "You never thought of getting married? It's been twenty years."

He shakes his head and smiles. "No. After Gwen, I didn't think there was someone else out there for me. And then . . ." He glances away, the leather under his fingers moaning. "And then life happened and circumstances got in the way."

I want to ask what circumstances, but he doesn't look like he wants to talk about it. "Shane, do you ever feel like the mirror is a double-edged sword?" I laugh at my question. "I mean, sometimes I think I can't live without it. A lot of times I find myself thinking about it even when I don't need it at the moment. I feel whole when I'm next to it. The sound of it is starting to become as important as breathing. But other times, I feel like it's stripping away parts of me. Because of what it's brought into my life, I'm changing. Sometimes I can feel it," I point to my heart, "right here. It almost feels like my heart is pumping *because* of the mirror and not for me anymore. And sometimes I get scared, because there's this inkling inside me that says I'm no longer me. It's like without the mirror, I don't know who I am, but with it, I'm losing whatever I have left."

I feel stupid talking about it. It's impossible to take all the differing feelings inside me and put them into the right words.

"I understand more than you think." He props his elbows on his knees and leans toward me. "I explained to you about your dad, about when he got the stone. There was one night where we got in a really big fight. He'd been in the lab for three days straight. Hadn't seen the sun, no sleep, nothing to eat. I finally forced him out to get something to eat for both of us. When he left, I picked up the stone intending to run with it. I was planning to take it to the ocean, drop it in, and try picking up the pieces it left behind. That night was the first time I held it."

He studies his hands as they turn back and forth. "The second I picked it up, I immediately knew that if I threw the stone into the ocean, I might as well jump in after it with a boulder strapped to my feet. It became a part of me the instant I touched it. Thoughts of destroying it became repulsive, and

152

I vowed to keep it safe without even knowing I planned to. I gripped it tighter, closed my eyes and felt the air change. When I closed my eyes, I was thinking that nothing else in my life could ever make me feel like the stone did. When I opened my eyes, I was at Gwen's house."

The corner of his mouth moves into a small smile. "The second I saw her, I forgot about the stone. The feelings I had for the stone were nothing compared to what I felt for Gwen. I can understand when you say you don't know who you are without it, because you haven't figured out who you are. Dan hadn't either when he first got it. It almost ruined him. But then he met your mom and had you. He had the mirror for fifteen years, and it never affected him like it did in the beginning. Dan found a balance. The obsession that comes with the stone was balanced with his obsession for his family. He loved you two so much that whatever he felt for the stone didn't control him. It still held onto him. Dan could never get rid of it, but it wasn't as strong as his feelings for you two."

Shane scoots his chair so it touches mine and takes my hand in his. "I know it scares you. It can magnify feelings in you that you aren't used to feeling. You just need to find a balance. You have your mother who is a very rare woman. She's good and kind and loving. If you have her around, she'll bring something to your life no one else can. At the moment you don't have Miles, but you do overall. One day we'll figure this all out and go get him. And . . ." his hand tightens over mine, "you have me. I'm ornery, hotheaded, and impatient. Sometimes I'm hard to get along with, but for the past eighteen years, you've been my balance, Grace. The stone can't touch me, because I have you. When it comes down to it, you can be surrounded by thousands of people who love you, but it's going to be you who has to decide which way to choose. I'll tell you now, it's always easiest to choose the stone and fall back on the feelings it makes you feel. But you'll discover really fast that what isn't easy is usually what's worth fighting for."

I nod, afraid I'll start sobbing if I open my mouth.

I stand to go to bed, but he stops me before I leave. "Grace, I know these past few months haven't been easy and you've seen things no one should have to see. I want you to know I'm proud of you for how you're handling it all. And I want you to know that I . . . um . . . " He shoves his hands in his pockets and looks like he's glaring at me. "I want you to know that I love you. I don't say it a lot, but I hope you know."

I wrap my arms around his waist, losing the ability to keep my crying quiet, which is unpleasant for both of us. "I love you, too."

As I tighten my arms around him, there's a part of my heart that turns away from the stone, turning toward Shane.

"Go to bed," he says unsteadily. Turning before I can see him, he leaves the room, muttering to himself.

chapter thirteen

"Thanks for taking me to lunch, Beth. It's nice to get out or the house for a bit." It's nice to get away from that journal. I hate how it's making me feel.

"It's just as nice for me. I haven't seen a lot of you lately, and I miss you." Beth eyes me, finding something to worry about. "You look terrible."

I laugh. "Well, thanks."

"I didn't mean that to be rude. I meant it like you look terrible because I can see how much you miss him." She pushes the basket of garlic bread closer to me and props her chin on her hand, waiting for me to talk.

"I do miss him. A lot. But I'm really trying to be the kind of girl that knows life keeps going even if you aren't with him. I thought it would get easier over time, but . . . well . . . it's not." I grab a slice of garlic bread, ripping it into pieces over my plate.

"Grace?"

"Hm?"

"Have you ever thought of going back for him?"

I look up with a smile. "More than I'm willing to admit. I keep thinking maybe I should go back and stay at Rockwell for awhile. I can make sure he's feeling better, and when he is, we can come back, or . . . " I frown and look away. The bread now looks like mush because of my incessant tearing, but I keep playing with it to keep me occupied.

"Or you would say goodbye to him and come back alone?" Beth guesses.

"No." I shake my head, feeling my hands go sweaty. "Or I would stay there with him."

"Forever?" she gasps.

"No. Well . . . maybe. The mirror works so I could visit anytime I wanted. Mom and Shane could come too. Maybe even you could come visit. I think you'd like it there." I smile at Beth who's now shining with delight. "Whenever I think about my future with Miles, I always imagine him in his cravat and boots and me in those dresses. We would go to parties and laugh at the customs they all find so important but will fade in only a few years. Our kids would grow up without the distractions kids have today. But we could come here anytime. If anyone got sick or needed something not available there. We could come for birthdays and Christmas. It would be just like I married and moved a few cities away. I'd only have to walk to the attic to get back."

I sit back in my chair, seeing I've torn apart another piece of bread. The picture I just painted was drawn in my mind awhile ago. It wasn't until Miles left that I realized how much I really want it.

"Why don't you?" She reaches across the table and pats my hand.

"Why don't I what?"

"Go back for him. You're obviously miserable without him, and the life you've imagined with him sounds really great. I've been in your shoes before, Grace." Beth gets uncharacteristically quiet. She's told me a little about the man she used to love. She watched him get sick and eventually die. That was one of the reasons Beth helped me so much after I thought Mom was gone. She could empathize with me.

"When he died, I was broken," she says in a low voice. "I couldn't be the woman I was before him, and I couldn't be the one I was with him, because he was gone. So I had to be the woman I was because I had known him. Grace, if I had the opportunity to bring him back, I would have. Don't let this chance pass you by. What's keeping you here?"

"Well, I have Mom and Shane. And you."

She clucks her tongue and waves my answers away. "Excuses. You just told me you would come visit anytime. Why aren't you skipping out on me and running home to the mirror?"

I shift in my seat, squashing the hope of seeing Miles again that tries growing. "Beth, someone killed Dad. And now someone is trying to do the same to Miles. He would have never been sick if he hadn't followed me here. He's safer there. He's better off without me."

She cocks an eyebrow. "If you asked him that, would he agree?"

"Of course not. He would call me stupid and drag me back through the mirror with him. He doesn't see it though. How my life is affecting him. He sees it now that it isn't *my* life, but our life together. He's stubborn."

"Sounds like someone I know." She laughs and nudges me, then gets serious again. "I wish you could hear yourself talking. Even the way you speak is sad. No one can go through the mirror, Grace. Shane told me that no one can go through but you and him. If you go back, no one can hurt him. But if you don't go back, it's you that's hurting him."

I nod, too annoyed to speak. Beth has good intentions, but that doesn't make it easier to hear. I can imagine what Miles has been feeling since he woke up at Rockwell and I wasn't there. He would've first been mad, then irate, then irritable until nobody wanted to be around him. And then, when the anger wore off, the pain would come. I hate that he's going through that, because I know what it feels like to be left behind.

The more I think about it, the more I want to run from the restaurant and back to the house, but if I leave now, I'll be going home to Rockwell, not the home I grew up in.

And that scares me enough to grip the table and tuck my feet behind the legs of my chair to plant me in place.

* * *

I'm not sure how long I've been staring. I didn't plan to come here, but I suddenly found myself sitting on the floor of Shane's room, knees curled up to my chest, inches from the mirror. Just staring.

While sitting here, I'm getting better at rationalizing in order to make myself feel okay with going back. Beth is technically right. No one can get to Miles. He'll still be safe, and we'd be together.

But then my rational thoughts break through my rationalizing, and I remember that I don't know everything about the mirror. I don't know how

Miles was being hurt before he left, and I'm not sure no one will follow me. I'd never forgive myself if I went back and something else happened to that family.

"You can see yourself better if you turned the lights on," Mom says from the doorway.

"I wasn't really looking at me."

I hear Mom argue with Shane, then he seems to be pushed as he stumbles into my room.

"Hey, kid." He rubs his jaw while he pulls an old chair over to sit next to me. "Um . . . your mother wants—" Mom clears her throat as she sits down on the floor next to me. "Your mother and I," he clarifies, "wanted you to know that Miles is doing fine."

My head whips around to Shane. "What?"

"I've gone back a few times. Miles hasn't seen me. I only talked to Lord Denley, but he said Miles is well."

I look back at the mirror. "Is he happy?"

"No," Mom answers, wrapping her arm around my shoulder. "Lord Denley said his health is back to normal, but he has been in a very sour mood since he got back." Mom laughs, and I want to laugh too, but I just continue staring.

"Grace." Mom puts her hands on my shoulders and turns me to face her. "I want you to know that it would be okay if you wanted to go to Rockwell. To live there. I know you think you can't now, until we find out who has been trying to hurt Miles, but after. When everything calms down, I hope you wouldn't use Shane or me as an excuse to stay."

"Did Beth call you?" I smile because this has Beth written all over it.

"Yes. She was worried about you. I also want you to know that if the situation comes that the mirror needs to be broken or turned off or however the thing works, please don't feel obligated to stay here for us."

"Mom, I—"

"No, let me finish. I won't lie. I would miss you every second. But you need to experience life with Miles. You need to love and have a chance at a family. Shane and I met our soulmates already, and even though they're gone, we wouldn't trade the time we had with them. You need to have that time. I want you to promise me that if, heaven forbid, you have to choose between living with us or living with Miles, you'll choose Miles."

Does she think that's an easy promise to make? It's like I get a choice between food and water. Both are vital, and without one of them, I'll die. How do you choose between the family who raised you and the family you want to make?

"You don't have to promise now. Just think about it. I don't want you to be this sad forever."

I chuckle and lay my head on her shoulder. "Am I that bad? I thought I was doing pretty well."

"Well, you haven't stopped living, and you've tried to be happy. I'm proud that you've been trying. But I don't want you to pretend to live happily. I want you to *be* happy."

* * *

"Is it someone's birthday today?" Shane asks.

I grin over my dinner plate. "It can be mine if you're buying presents."

"March 5th. It's an important date. Why?"

"I don't know." I shrug while spooning another mountain of mashed potatoes in my mouth.

"Does March 5th mean anything to you?" he asks Mom and gets the same answer. He sits in the chair across from me with two deep lines between his eyebrows.

"Why?" Mom slaps my shoulder when I talk with a full mouth.

"All day this date has been bugging me. Something happened today but I can't remember what. You sure nothing happened today?" He looks at me as if he knows I have the journal and I know information he doesn't.

"Yeah. I promise. Nothing rings a bell."

He grunts and starts buttering a roll.

Mom studies him a minute and then turns to me. "Grace, Mr. Mitchell and I were talking this morning about settling the confusion my return has caused. He brought up . . . well, he brought up Rockwell and if we wanted to continue doing—"

"Rockwell," Shane whispers, examining his roll. His eyes go big as he drops the roll and shoves away from the table. "Rockwell!" he screams and races from the kitchen with Mom and I right behind him. "I'm so stupid. I should've realized before. I can't believe I missed it." He frantically flips through the pages of Dad's journals. When he doesn't find what he's looking for, he throws it to the ground and picks up another.

I stand next to him and try figuring out what he's searching for. "What's going on?"

Shane finds the right page and starts reading. "Rockwell has become a second home to me. I love it there and have come to love the Denleys. Because of this, I started to dig into records to find out why the wing was destroyed. It took awhile and a little bribery to find the right newspaper from back then. It said the wing caught fire on March 5, 1811. Every year on March 5th, I go back and make sure it doesn't happen. But every year nothing comes close to causing a fire that size. I've come to realize that maybe something happens in the future that effects the past. Maybe in my future I go back and cause something to happen and start a ripple affect. Maybe it will be Lynnie or Gracie who change it. I'm not sure, but whatever happens hasn't happened yet. And whoever changes it hasn't done so."

"We have to go." Shane throws the book down and runs for the stairs.

"Go where?" Mom and I ask together.

"Don't you understand?" He whirls around on the staircase. "Dan could never find out what happened because it hadn't happened yet. Tom wasn't there yet. He's there now." Not another word needs to be said as the three of us run for the mirror.

"You two stay here. If Tom is there I don't want either of you close," Shane demands, blocking the mirror with his arm.

"Are you serious?" I scoff.

Mom lays a hand on my shoulder. "Shane, you have two options. We can all go together and watch out for one another, or you can go on your own and Grace and I will follow shortly after. Your choice."

Shane's face turns red and, feeling the urgency of our situation, caves. "You do exactly as I say. No one leaves my side, and no one gets smart."

160

His glare focuses on me. Mom and I nod, Shane leads Mom through, and I follow right after.

The oxygen in the attic is so minimal I keep taking huge gulps of air. There's no fire in the attic, but I can smell it. There's screaming from outside the window, orders where to take water and what to do with the injured.

Shane mumbles a string of profanities as he opens the door and a plume of smoke shoots into the attic. He takes Mom's hand, she takes mine, and we start our way into it. My nose burns as I try blinking to wet my dry eyes. I decide just to hold my breath, and gratefully, we're already starting down the staircase. Once in the foyer the smoke isn't as thick, and the second I'm out the front door, I grip my knees and suck in the fresh air.

"Miss Gentry?"

My head snaps up to see Matthew. He's completely covered in soot, his shirt is torn in parts, and the hair on the right side of his head is singed away.

"Mr. Wilson, what happened?"

He grabs his sleeve, wipes it across his face and barrels past me without answering my question. I glance back at Shane and Mom, mouth *sorry* when Shane's eyes narrow at me, and then dart after Matthew. I try stopping him, and am surprised when he roughly shakes me off.

"Annie is still in here!" he yells over the roar of the fire, and without giving me the slightest glance, runs into the smoke.

I hesitate for a moment, because the thought that creeps into my mind has my feet sinking into the floor.

Thomas killed Annie in another life. I thought I saved her from that, but I brought her death with me.

My legs finally move when I can no longer see Matthew. I pull my sleeve up over my nose to block out the smoke and match my steps with his. I keep gagging on the smoke that's beginning to accumulate on my tongue.

"Most of the rooms are destroyed," he tells me as we run up the stairs. "I checked them all before they burned and she was not there. She is not outside, in the kitchen, or anywhere on the main level. She must be up here somewhere." He rubs his sleeve across his face again, and while we're both running into an unknown, his eyes lock with mine. "Mr. Denley is missing as well."

I only nod, but that information has my feet moving faster, my heart pounding harder. We run through the upstairs hallways, checking each room we pass.

"Where is she?!" he screams, slamming his fist into a door, causing it to loudly rap against the wall.

"Have you checked the library?" I ask, not staying put to hear an answer. I'm running down the blackened hallway, hoping my memory is accurate enough to get me there.

"Twice," he answers, but he follows me in anyway, only to be met with more disappointment when we find it empty. There's no fire in here yet, but the smoke is thickening above us, crawling along the ceiling. A sound, much like a whimper, escapes Matthew's lips as he runs frantic hands through his hair. I hear another whimper when he turns to leave, but I grab his arm to stop him.

"Do you hear that?" I whisper. I pull him closer to me and back up towards the wall. It wasn't Matthew whimpering. That's Annie. I grab a fistful of Matthew's shirt when he tries running beyond the bookshelves to the back of the library. "Don't move," I warn him.

I have no proof, no evidence to go on, but I know Thomas is the reason Annie's whimpering. And I know if Matthew goes charging back there, I'll see both of them dead. Raising my finger to my mouth, I tell Matthew to be quiet so we can silently make our way past each bookshelf.

"Get her here! I know you can!" an unfamiliar man's voice yells.

"If you believe I could conjure Grace here, do you think I would be here without her? I have no way to her!"

Miles. My heart loosens when I hear his voice but breaks when I hear the anger in it.

"Then take me to her. Take me to her now!"

"Again, if I could take you to her I would not be at Rockwell."

A low, throaty laugh sends chills up my arms. "Do you hear that, little Annie?" Thomas asks, who I can now see through the last bookshelf. The fire from the other parts of the house sends a harsh light through the windows, casting a red tint about the room. I can't really make out Thomas' hair color since it's practically all singed away and wiry. Blood is running down his arm, soaking his dirty sleeve. What I can clearly see is the gun he's digging into Annie's temple, and Annie's tears making a clean path down her blackened face.

Thomas smiles at Miles, who's standing across the room with his back to me. "Little Annie, did you hear your brother? He just said if he could get to Grace, he wouldn't be here. He loves her more than he loves you." Annie bites her lip when Thomas tugs on her hair. "Don't!" Thomas shouts, keeping an arm around Annie's neck while pointing the gun at Miles. "I explained this, Miles. You get Annie when I get Grace."

An idea forms, and before I have time to think of the consequences, I crouch down and pull Matthew down with me. "Do you have a weapon on you?" I ask as quietly as possible. Unwilling to look away from Annie, he reaches in his boot and pulls out a measly excuse for a knife. "It'll have to work. This is what I need you to do."

* * *

"Remember what I told you," I whisper to Matthew. "Don't do anything until I tell you to." I take a steadying breath, nod at Matthew, then move around the bookshelf.

"I'm here, Tom." I step into the light coming from the window, and as much as I want to keep my focus on Tom and Annie, my eyes shift to find Miles. His head whips to the side, and his eyes find mine instantly.

For one small moment, the fire stops burning, the beams stop cracking, and the smoke gets a little weaker. While his body is still braced for a fight, it's his eyes that tell me everything.

They tell me he's missed me as much as I've missed him.

They tell me he's mad at me, but the anger is slipping, because I see a light come into his eyes that I know has been missing since the day I brought him back.

And, without any words spoken, they tell me that our time apart was as agonizing for him as it was for me.

Tom breaks Miles' and my connection when he laughs. "Grace Gentry in the flesh." His hand tightens around Annie's neck at the same time he takes two big steps away from me. "Didn't I tell you?" He turns his head and talks to the empty space next to him. "I knew it would work." His laugh turns to a cackle, and combined with the way his head twitches to the left and the fact that he's talking to no one, he looks crazy.

I take a cautious step forward, lifting my palms up so he sees I'm no threat. "Let her go, Tom. You have what you want."

Tom's insane laughing immediately stops, and those dark, piercing eyes roam over me. "I'm two hundred years and a few thousand miles away from what I want." He repositions his arm around Annie, so he has a better hold of her and slowly smiles at me over her shoulder. "Although little Annie is beautiful."

Miles steps forward at the same time Matthew jumps out from behind the bookshelf. Matthew's arm wraps around my arms, pinning them to my sides. Then I feel cold metal against my neck, and see Tom's gun aimed at Matthew.

"I do not know who you are and why you want Miss Gentry," Matthew yells at Tom. "But if you want her, I get Annie."

Tom's face reddens, making a bulging vein appear down his forehead. "You, boy, know absolutely nothing. Did you know that Grace is the reason I'm here? Did you know that she's the reason the Denley's house is burning to the ground? Are you aware that Grace is the reason Harry was in this house to begin with?" Tom wipes his mouth with the back of his hand and moves his gun back to Annie's head. "And did you know that when Grace landed here at Rockwell, she involved the Denleys in a story that has no happy ending? Your precious Grace is a murderer hiding behind glass you can't see."

Matthew's shaky hand tightens the knife against my neck. "I do not care who she is, and that is why I will willingly hand her over to you in exchange for Anne."

Tom smiles, sardonically, and dips his face into Annie's hair, inhaling deeply. "She is a pretty little thing."

"Do not touch her," Matthew's demands calmly, but somehow more threatening than if he were to scream. "I will count to three, and if that gun is still at Annie's temple, your Miss Gentry will be on the floor. One."

"Matty, stop," Annie whimpers, then yelps when Tom pulls her hair so hard her head whips back.

'Two."

"Mr. Wilson." Miles steps toward us, and I subtly shake my head, letting him know everything's okay. Miles stops, but his eyes never leave the knife at my neck.

"Three."

"Wait!" Tom screams when Matthew pulls my head to the side, exposing more of my throat.

"No!" Matthew screams back with such anger, I wince when the blade slides a little against my skin. "Give me Annie now or pray Miss Gentry is still of use to you dead."

A low growl rumbles up Tom's throat as his eyes bounce from Matthew to me to Miles. Like a trapped animal, he surveys all of us, tyring to figure out the plan that's most beneficial to him. When his eyes fall on Miles, a slow grin forms. "Very well, we'll do it your way." He takes the gun from Annie's temple and aims it at Miles. "You get Annie. I get Grace." He looks right at me, that grin turning into a sneer. "I get Grace, or I kill Miles."

Annie falls to the ground when Tom throws her away. Matthew is immediately by her side, picking her up in his arms and darting from the room. I don't watch them leave or try to lessen Annie's worried protests that they can't leave Miles and I here. Without another word, I walk to Tom and willingly hand myself over.

"If you want to get to the mirror, we need to go now," I tell Tom. Nerves that I'd managed to keep at bay are now rushing to the surface when I see his eyes. Brown eyes are usually warm, but his are dead. "Shane's downstairs and has probably started looking for me." I glance at Miles, holding up my hand to stop him when he steps toward me.

Tom laughs, wrapping his arm around me like he did Annie. "Do you think I'm stupid, Grace?" he whispers in my ear. "Do you think I'm stupid enough to leave Miles alive so he can run to Shane and tell him where I am?" He presses his cheek harder against the space just behind my ear, and I feel his breath in my ear when he quietly says, "I'm not stupid, Grace."

Miles and Tom both make a move, and time slows down enough for me to see the consequences. Miles is charging Tom, but not as fast as Tom raises his gun.

"No!" I scream, kicking off the ground to throw Tom off balance, but I'm too late.

The gunshot sends vibrations throughout my entire body, and when they stop, everything inside me stops. Watching Miles fall to the ground forces my heart into a stutter, every irregular beat hurting more than the last. His head cracks against the bookshelf when he hits the ground, and then he just lies there. He isn't moving. Why isn't he moving?

"Miles." My voice cracks as I say his name over and over. "Miles, get up."

"Best be on our way." Tom tightens both of his arms around me and begins pulling me, and with each bookshelf we pass, I fight harder. I buck and kick, throw my head back to hit something, anything. A sharp pain zings through the back of my head when I hit something hard. Tom hisses out a breath and drops me on my hands and knees, and I scramble to get back to Miles.

"Harry said you had fight." Tom grabs my ankle, and like I'm nothing more than a disposable twig, he drags me across the floor. I try to grab onto anything we pass, but he tugs me harder. Wood splinters shoot up my nails as I try clawing my way free. I frantically grab onto both sides of the doorframe, jamming us so we can't move forward. Tom drops my ankle, snatches a fistful of my hair in one hand and my arm in another.

He chuckles close to my ear, pulling my body more against his. "You're a feisty little thing. Maybe when you get me where I need to be, I'll keep you."

The smoke is too thick to see anything, and the smell is too bitter to keep breathing, but all I can think about is Miles bleeding in the other room. I have to get back to him. Without another thought, I start moving any part of my body that can hit Tom. I stomp on his foot, elbow him in the stomach, reach around and pinch the sensitive skin on the back of his arm. He finally lets go of my hair, using his free hand to backhand me across the face. Black dots immediately swirl through my vision as I spin and sway, but I don't hit the ground. Arms catch me before I fall, arms that have always caught me.

"I've got you," Shane whispers. He helps balance me on my feet. I notice only one of his arms is around me, which means the other has a gun pointed at Tom.

"Put it down, Tom."

Tom laughs, the same as before, but it does something to me.

Something dark slithers around inside me, slowly and gently wrapping ribbons of hate around my heart. Even as I tell myself to cut them, Tom's laugh pulls them tighter, squeezing a heart that, terrifyingly, I'm losing.

"Press your luck, Shane," Tom says ecstatically. "You know I'm quicker than you. I can get my shot off before you even think of pulling the trigger."

"Not with me here."

I turn out of Shane's arm and see Lord Denley's pistol on the other side of Tom. Lord Denley is badly burned—red, blistering patches trail down his left cheek and across his neck. Cradling his left arm against his chest, he raises his right a little higher, getting his gun closer to Tom.

Tom looks back at me, and another piece of my heart is enveloped in hate when I see in his eyes the craving to kill. Defeated, he unwillingly lowers his gun to the floor. Shane reaches out and points it at him along with his other gun.

"That's probably the wisest choice you've ever made. We have some talking to do, Tom. You can cooperate, and we'll talk outside. If you don't, I'll bind you to a chair in the other room and walk away whistling."

"Big talk for such a coward. You don't have it in you. Never have." Thomas laughs as he turns his whole body to Shane and raises his palms up. "Do your worst."

"Look away, Grace," Shane demands, and I quickly obey.

But he wouldn't actually kill him, would he? I press my hands to my chest and hold my breath when I hear the trigger click. But nothing comes.

"You lucky dog," Shane laughs. "I loaded my gun before I came here last time, and that one empty chamber held the bullet that is currently in

Harry. Do you want to try again?" Shane aims his gun again, and I cover my ears.

"What do you want to know?" Tom surrenders, and I blow out a breath of relief.

"Good thinking. Outside, move." He nudges Tom in the back with the gun.

"Wait." I stop them. "Miles is in the library. He's hurt. I can't get him out by myself."

"I will help you," Lord Denley says, pulling his arm closer to him.

"No, I will help." Matthew emerges from the smoke, looking more ragged than before.

"Is Annie safe?" I ask Matthew as we run back to the library.

"Yes. She is outside with June helping the injured."

"Good."

"I am sorry about what happened earlier. I became carried away, and my only thought was of Annie. Did I hurt you?"

I smile at him, but I really just want to sit down and cry. "No. You did good."

He gives me a slight nod, rushing past the last bookshelf to get Miles.

"Can you get his shoulders? I'll get his legs." I try to pick up both of Miles' feet, but Matthew ignores me and lifts Miles' arm and, with some effort, throws Miles' body over his shoulder.

Matthew grabs my hand and yells, "I cannot see well. I will follow you."

I lead us both blindly through the smoky hallways and down the stairs. Once outside, Matthew drops Miles on the grass and tears at his shirt to look at his wound. Mom is at his side with a candle, examining how badly Miles is hurt.

"Grace, go with Shane," Mom orders, pressing a dirty cloth against Miles' left shoulder. Ignoring her, I step up closer to Miles to see how I can help. I have to do *something*. But when the candle gets closer to Miles, I instinctively shy away as blood runs down Mom's arm. While walking away, I hear vague orders of different tools that are needed to get the bullet out. My stomach lurches into my throat at the thought of those tools going into Miles. And that it was my fault.

chapter fourteen

Under a large tree on the side of the house, Tom is sitting down with his hands behind his back. The light from the fire turns everything a dark orange, and the further I walk away from Rockwell, the colder it gets.

Shane isn't pointing his gun at Tom anymore, but it's tucked in his belt in case he needs it. When Shane sees me, he begins to tell me to go back to Mom, but I shake my head.

"Stay behind me," he orders. I stay a step behind him, but position myself so I can still see Tom. "Start talking, Tom. How did you get here? What were your orders once you arrived?"

Tom fidgets with the rope around his wrists, then realizing he isn't going anywhere, sighs and leans against the tree. "You always were such a fool. The only reason you came into the group was because we needed your brother, and he wouldn't come without you. You were useless."

"Nice try. I already hate you. Your insults mean nothing to me. Start talking, or I'll ask Grace to leave so we can talk, just you and me," Shane threatens.

"That day, when Dan said he finished the machine, Chris ordered us through, and we all walked into that prison without even questioning Dan. He just wanted the stone for himself."

"My dad didn't send you away because he wanted—"

"No Grace," Shane stops me. "He doesn't deserve an explanation." Shane lays a hand on my shoulder and squeezes. "Don't listen to him. He's only trying to get in your head." I nod as he turns back to Thomas. "What happened when you got there?"

"I'll tell you if you explain your niece's interruption. I would love to hear what excuse Dan gave you for sending us away. You talk, and then I will."

"You're in no position to negotiate," Shane snaps. "I'm the one with the gun, while you're tied to a tree."

"I'm not stupid, Shane. You want answers much more than seeing me dead. I'll talk, but I want to hear what Dan said."

Shane growls as he turns and paces. After looking at Thomas a few times, he finally starts talking. "Dan got it working while all of you were out partying. Because of the man Dan was, he wasn't going to let anyone else go through before he knew it was safe, so he went through. It took him to the future where he found you three had taken the machine and created a world you wouldn't believe. You caused a global war.

"Dan was scared that what he helped create would ruin the world. He tried talking to you all, but you were so blinded by Chris' greed that you turned on him. What was he supposed to do? Turn over the machine and hope for the best? So he sent you through, hoping that he sent you somewhere you could create lives for yourselves but also keep you away from the stone." Shane concentrates on bringing down his temper. When the temper dissolves, the vulnerability comes. "Tom, you knew Dan. Do you really think he would have intentionally sent you through, knowing he was condemning you? And all for rights to the stone?"

Shane sits down on the grass and digs his palms into his eyes. I glance over at Tom and see his temples jumping as he glares at Shane. It isn't the evil glare he gave me earlier, more a wounded one. He tries shaking it away, but he only glares harder at Shane for making him feel whatever he's feeling.

"Your turn, Tom. Start talking."

When Tom talks, his voice is quiet, calm. "We recreated the machine from what we had in the future, but we could only use it when the original one had been used. When we did use it, it only took us to the original mirror's destination, and once there, you were stuck. Chris asked Harry to

170

go first. After Harry went, we sat by that mirror for days waiting for another jump, but nothing came. Chris became obsessed. We took shifts watching the machine, all day and all night. When you got tired, you traded with another. We did this for another few years. One day, on my watch, a power surge came. Chris ordered me through, and I found myself in a forest, looking at a beautiful woman." Tom's eyes run from my feet to my eyes. "I watched her. She was scared, and hurting, and then she looked right in my direction, and I knew she was Dan's. Lucky for her, Miles came to the rescue."

I remember that feeling from the clearing. It's the same one I have now. I want to rub my arms just to make sure nothing is crawling over my skin.

"What were you supposed to do when you got to the other side?" Shane asks.

"Chris gave us orders to find Dan or you, and then take back the machine and come for him. But I landed here. To my excitement, I heard rumors of an abhorrent bailiff who, gratefully, was still alive. So I paid a visit to Harry, and together we made a plan to break him out of jail and find you. Harry was different though. The machine didn't matter anymore, only revenge. Revenge on a girl who ousted him. Stupid Harry, he could never let the little things go. But, outsmarted once again by a young girl, Harry died." Thomas looks past Shane to glare at me.

"I'm the one who pulled the trigger. Grace was only a victim of your brother."

Tom and Harry are brothers? They look nothing alike, but the way my blood boils under cold skin is the same with both of them.

Shane shifts to the side to block Tom from seeing me as Tom keeps talking. "Yes, I learned of that when you and I met next. You got away from me that time, so I tried finding a way to get you to come to me, or me to you. And then I heard some interesting news. Gossips travels fast around this town. The younger Miles Denley had vanished along with Miss Gentry. It was like they disappeared, I heard them say." He looks at me and says, "You should know, Grace, your reputation is ruined. Miles' too."

"Do you think I care about that?" I ask, stepping beside Shane.

171

"You might if you heard what everyone is saying about you. Tearing a family apart, ruining a gentleman, vindictive—"

"Enough!" Shane barks.

But Thomas smiles at me. "Then just a few weeks ago, the rumors started swirling again. Miles Denley was back. A few people I talked to said he was on his death bed; others said he would throw fits of rage, because he was abandoned by Miss Gentry. That's when I knew the machine was used. I couldn't get to you, so I decided I would bring you to me. And what better way to do that then to send up smoke signals?" He inclines his head to the house that's slowly crumbling to ash. "I knew Grace would come running. And if she came, you came. And as happy as I am to see you both, I don't really need you here. I only needed you to go through the mirror so it could power ours."

"To get Chris and Gwen here?" Shane asks.

"Only Chris. Gwen has been here for three years." Tom said that to get a reaction out of Shane, and it works.

Shane staggers back a few steps while staring at Tom. "Here?"

"Well, not *here*. She's been in modern day for three years."

Bewildered, Shane runs his hands over his face. His eyes dart back and forth fast, and when he looks at me, I know he doesn't see me.

"You're lying," he whispers.

"I'm afraid I'm not." Tom gleams while watching Shane pace. "Chris told me to power the machine as much as possible, because there are a lot of people waiting to come."

They're coming whispers in my ears.

Harry warned me that he didn't want to live to see the day they came. I always assumed it was Christopher and Gwen, but there are more.

"I'm sick of this, Tom. Explain or you are no longer useful to me." Shane pulls his gun but keeps it at his side.

"I told you Dan sent us to a prison. Everyone had a number they used for everything. We didn't have a number, so we couldn't even buy food. Some people there didn't like having their movements monitored, so they rebelled. Those people didn't like having their movements known because they weren't exactly lawful people. Chris took care of them, led them. He

172

promised a new world where they could live their lives freely, away from prying eyes. He told them of the machine, although at the time it didn't work. Chris has a way of making just about anyone do anything. There are hoards of angry people, waiting to see a power surge so they can follow Chris. They'd follow him anywhere."

My breath catches when his words catch up to me, and the understanding that this is all much bigger than any of us thought.

"One problem, Tom. I fixed the frequency of the machine. It won't give any power to yours."

That creepy smile comes back as Tom watches Shane. "What makes you think it's *your* machine, in the present, that powers it?" Tom isn't laughing anymore. His eyes are solely focused on Shane, the murderous gleam I saw earlier coming back. "We figured out a few things before we came here. Found them out from you and Dan, right before we killed you both. And then we went searching for Carolyn, and when we found her we—"

Shane grabs Tom's collar and shoves him against the tree. I hear the crack Tom's head makes when it bounces off the bark.

"Go to your mother, Grace," Shane growls, still face to face with Tom.

Tom's eyes roll over to look at me. "You don't want to know what I did to your mother? You don't want to know how—"

I'd already started running away when Tom turned those vile eyes on me, but even from far away, I can hear when his agonized screams start.

"How is he?" I ask, kneeling down beside Mom and seeing Miles is still unconscious.

"It's bad, Grace. He needs help," Mom says frantically.

I look up at Annie. "Who was the doctor you called for me when I came?"

"No, Grace." Mom puts her hand on my shoulder. "He needs our doctors."

I'm shaking my head before she has a chance to finish. "No, he isn't coming back. Not yet. Let's see what the doctors can do here first. If, after they've done all they can do, taking him back is our only option, then we'll figure it out."

"I'm telling you now that this is our only option. I'm not a doctor, but I know that if we wait, we will be staying longer for a funeral." Mom wraps another piece of cloth around his shoulder.

"So we pull him from one dangerous situation into another?"

"We pull him from this, get him healthy, then if you still want him to come back, we bring him back."

She makes it sound so easy. It isn't like I can ask him to go back. He's already going to be mad at me for bringing him home to begin with.

She turns back to me with a glare I've never seen before. "I don't have time to argue with you. This is no longer your choice. I care about him too much. He's coming back." She brushes me off and turns to Lord Denley when he kneels beside Miles. "Where did the fire start? Can we make it through?"

Lord Denley wipes his face with a handkerchief and talks while examining his son. "It started in the north ballroom. If you hurry you should make it through. I will follow and make sure the mirror is safe."

Mom and Lord Denley start talking of other things, but I'm not listening. Off in the distance, I see Shane kneeling down with his head lowered. Even from here I can see his body shaking. As I get closer, I can hear the cries. I've heard Shane cry once, and that was the day after Dad's funeral when he sat in Dad's office. He didn't know anyone was there. I sat outside the door and listened to him cry so hard he couldn't catch his breath. It guts me now just as it did then.

He stands slowly, wipes his eyes with his arm and turns to come to us, but stops when he sees me only a few steps away. The feelings on his face are so painful I start to feel them, too.

He walks toward me and hugs me, grips the back of my dress like I'll save him from demons I can't see. "I'm so sorry, Grace," he whispers through uneven breaths. The question is on my tongue, but I can't ask why he's sorry. Not when he's like this. A new round of cries erupt from him, and I don't realize it's because of Mom until she takes him from me and holds him. He talks too quietly for me to hear what he's saying, but the growing fear in Mom's eyes scares me too much to ask.

After Mom calms Shane down, he starts talking with Lord Denley, and Mom avoids eye contact with me as she wraps a blanket around Miles. I

174

reach for her hand, and her eyes close when I touch her.

"Mom?"

"Please, Grace, not now." Her hand slides from mine, and when Shane arrives they start to move Miles.

"Where are you taking him?" Annie asks. "Father, he should stay here." She blocks our path, but Lord Denley gently pulls her to the side. Annie has been such a source of light for me, so it's hard to recognize her at the moment. Her eyes are dark, missing the glow they usually have. And her face twists in such an unfamiliar way I don't realize she's glaring at me until she starts screaming.

"This is your fault!" She points her finger at me. "None of this happened until you came here." To see Annie not bouncing is a little scary. I've never heard her talk with such disgust before. "Miles is better off without you." She turns to her father and cries, "Please, do not let them take him. I can take care of him." She shoots me another glare over her shoulder.

"Anne, you know nothing of what you speak. Miles is in far better care where he is going than if he were to stay here. And you know as well as I that Grace will do everything possible to make sure he comes back to us." He looks up at me with eyes only a father can have. They plead with me to save his son, while also holding back a flood of emotions he doesn't want Annie to see.

"Lord Denley . . . " I want to apologize. I want to apologize for everything.

"You must hurry." He motions toward Mom, who's almost to the house with Shane and Miles.

"Oh, Grace, I am sorry." New tears fill Annie's eyes as she hugs me. "I did not mean one word I said. I am just so frightened." She ducks her head into my shoulder while she tries to calm her breathing. "He told me there was a maid trapped upstairs with a hurt leg," she says quietly. "I followed him to the library, but there was no maid. He frightened me, Grace."

"I know." I pat her back as she clings to me. "He scared me, too."

"Miss Gentry, hurry now." Lord Denley takes Annie from me and points to the house. I wave at them, smiling when Matthew steps up to Annie and she falls into his arms.

175

Trying to help where I can, we all carry Miles back into the burning house. Annie's shrieks can be heard over the cracking wood when Lord Denley steps through with us. Once inside, we huddle together so no one gets separated.

When we get to the attic door, Shane goes up the stairs first to make sure it's safe.

"Let's go." His muffled voice is barely heard over the wails of the house. We quickly run up, and the men make plans for the mirror. There isn't a chance for me to be involved as I'm taken directly to the mirror. Mom stops me just in front and points to it, giving no room to argue. I look at Miles, and although I'm so scared to bring him back, I'm selfishly thrilled.

As soon as I step into Shane's bedroom, I collapse to the floor, gulping down the fresh air. My lungs stickily cling together. The air I'm pulling in isn't expanding them. Breathless and achy, I prop myself against the wall and begin counting. I'll give them one minute to come before I call Dr. Scott, knowing that's who Mom will call for Miles.

I don't count long before frozen pinpricks slowly trail up my spine. The abrupt knowledge that I'm not alone has me stiffening, staring at the mirror, mentally screaming for Shane to hurry.

If I'm not alone, I want to know before it's too late. After one deep breath, I pick myself up and run to the lamp by the bed.

The light stings my eyes, but I can see clearly enough.

Across the room, sitting at the window seat is a man. Every inch of him is filthy, from his hair to his shoes. I can't tell what color his hair is since it's covered in so much dirt. His clothes are too big and torn all over. The second I see him I know I should run, but something in his face tells me he won't hurt me.

He's maybe a little older than me. One of his eyes is bruised and black, his lip bleeding and puffy. Although his face is colored and swollen, I can see he's really good looking. As I watch him, I can tell he's more confused than I am.

I take a step closer and stop immediately when his eyes meet mine. Although they're hard to see beyond the swelling, his eyes are unmistakable. I know those eyes. The kind of green that looks fake, like

176

something you'd find growing on the side of a river. If the green weren't rare enough, the gold flakes speckled throughout his eyes would convince me. This man, this dirty, disheveled, lost man has eyes exactly like Dad and me.

"Are you alright?" I ask, feeling an unknown connection to him.

"I don't know." His voice is low, his lips trembling slightly.

"Why are you here?" I take another step closer to him.

"I don't know. I said I wanted to go home." His eyes briefly glance at the mirror.

I feel stupid asking, but I have to know. "When did you come from?"

He looks up through his lashes and cautiously answers, "2040."

We stare blankly at each other, neither one of us knowing what to say. I hear grunts and moaning as Shane and Mom pull Miles through.

"You'd think since he's been so sick he'd have lost a few pounds." Shane and Mom laugh breathlessly at his joke until they see me. Tears are making a clean trail through the black soot on my face.

Shane sets Miles on the bed then comes to me, oblivious to the other guest in my room. "Grace, what happened?"

Words are lost, so I incline my head to the window. Mom gasps when she sees him, and I know she's seeing Dad in him like I do. She comes to my side as Shane reaches behind him for his gun.

I stop his hand from grabbing it. "You don't need it. He isn't here to hurt us."

Shane doesn't believe me, but he keeps the gun tucked away. "Carolyn, go call Dr. Scott. Tell him whatever you need to. I think we may be past the point of avoiding his questions. Grace, get some towels and warm water."

Shane gives orders, never once looking away from the stranger. Mom leaves, but I'm too stubborn. The man intrigues me. There's a pull he has over me, a familiar connection I can't describe. I go to the bathroom and grab a few towels, get one wet from the faucet and hurry back. Shane rolls his eyes in frustration when he realizes I'm not going anywhere.

I sit beside Miles and clean his face, taking comfort that he still has color.

"Ryan is on his way to see Miles. Grace, do you want to clean up before he gets here?"

I decline Mom's not so subtle offer to leave the room.

"Grace?" The man looks at me and then to Miles. "Miles?"

Shane itches to get his gun, but sticks his hands into his pockets instead. The man stands and takes a step to me, but Shane moves, blocking his path. The man doesn't seem to notice Shane's apprehension. His eyes are focused on me. Through his beat-up eyes, tears start to appear. And then he smiles, and I catch my breath at the sight of it. I'd know that smile anywhere.

"Are you Grace Denley?" he asks with such enthusiasm and hope it overshadows the shock of hearing that name.

"My name is Grace Gentry," I stutter.

"But that's Miles Denley, right?" He points to Miles, who I suddenly become protective of. Sitting closer to him, I position myself between him and the man.

"Yes."

The man's face turns into pure joy as he watches me take Miles' hand in mine. The tears fall like weights from his face, and he flinches when tries to wipe them away.

"What's your name?" I ask, holding Miles' hand tighter, anxious to hear the answer.

His smile grows as he straightens his back. "My name is Miles James Denley III. But you always called me James."

There isn't much else to do but stare.

Stare at this man, this familiar man, and wonder if this is really happening. My reply is stuck in my throat as I gape at him. The eyes that are entirely Gentry and the smile that is unmistakably Miles are now beaming at me.

"Are you saying . . . "

That smile of his turns teasing, a teasing smile I know too well. "Hi, Mom."

chapter fifteen

"Mom?" It comes out half laughing, half surprise with a little bit of hysterics. My heart is pounding but not in a scared or anxious way. In a—I recognize and know this man—kind of way. Suddenly, he looks younger to me.

"How old are you?" I ask. Maybe if I keep asking questions, I'll find out that this is all a joke.

"Twenty-two. My birthday is October 21, 2018."

2018? I'm going to have a baby in three years? Luckily I'm already sitting, because my legs are going numb. Mom walks over to him, placing her hand on his cheek. He puts his hand on top of hers and, closing his eyes, he smiles. The more I see him smile the more I'm convinced that this is real.

He opens his eyes and looks at Mom. "Hi, Grandma." I know that face. Somehow I know he only said that to get a reaction.

"Grandma?" Mom scoffs, and I'm sure that's the reaction he was looking for. He takes her hand from his cheek and holds both of hers in his and laughs. At the sound of his laugh, Mom turns to me with wide eyes, noticing too, how much it sounds like Miles'.

"You always hated when I called you that. Said it made you sound old." James laughs again and pulls Mom into a hug. He's quite a bit bigger than she is. If what he's telling me is the truth, it all makes sense. He has Miles' big shoulders and height. The same nose and mouth. His eyes are mine, and now that my eyes are adjusting to the light, he has the same caramel colored hair as me.

"What did you call me then?" Mom is warming up to him, her arms slowly wrapping around his waist.

"Nana, but Gramps didn't want to be called Papa. He insisted on aging like everyone else."

"Gramps?" Mom and I ask at the same time.

James pulls away and looks at us, confused. "Yeah, Gramps. The two of you got hitched a few years before I was born."

The disappointment in that statement is crushing. My initial thoughts were if my, um . . . son, could come here, then surely Dad made it to the future. It's ridiculous and impossible, but I'm beyond the point of staying in a safe reality. Anything is possible at this point.

"And I'm guessing by the looks on your faces that marriage hasn't happened yet." James steps back from Mom and starts pulling at his hands. If Miles were awake, he'd laugh at that.

"Hold on a second." Shane steps up to James. "I think everyone is getting ahead of themselves. How do we know you are who you say? You could have come looking for Chris. This could all be a trap!"

In only takes a second for Shane to point his gun at James, and it takes an even shorter amount of time for Mom and me to stand between them. It was instinct. I didn't plan to do it, but the sight of Shane reaching for his gun had me moving before I thought to.

"Chris is here?" The infuriating way James says his name makes me smile; he isn't so bad. "Where is he?"

"Why do you want to know?" Shane doesn't lower his gun, and the mention of Chris has him shaking.

"Me and Chris have unfinished business."

"What?"

"I promised him the next time I saw him, I would kill him."

Silently we stand there staring at each other. James' breathing is heavy behind me, and Shane's is quick in front of me. I trust Shane wholeheartedly, but there's a trust I have in James that I can't describe. We're all saved from this stare down by the doorbell.

180

"That must be Ryan," Mom says but doesn't move. She waits until Shane puts his gun down. "Shane, I know you're looking out for us, but please don't pull your gun on him again. Almost gave me a heart attack. Now, I'll go answer the door and try explaining to Ryan our situation. Grace, stay with Miles. Shane, take James to get cleaned up. And if I hear any arguing between you two men, you'll both be hearing it." She gives everyone a stern look before leaving.

"She's just the same. Nicest woman you'll ever meet, but cross her and she'll tear you to shreds." James laughs until Shane turns back and glares at him.

"I don't trust you, but I can't deny the similarities you have with my family. But don't think I won't be watching you. My family is everything to me, and nothing has stopped me from keeping them safe this far. And be careful what facts you let come out of that mouth. No one should know what happens in the future. It'll change things, and you don't want to mess with fate. Trust me."

"What if some things need to be changed?" James asks. It's subtle, but I don't miss the glance he gives to Miles and me.

"Keep it to yourself," Shane grunts, then stalks out of the room.

"Will he be okay?" James looks down at Miles endearingly.

"I'm not sure, but seeing as you're alive, I'm assuming he'll be fine." James won't exist without Miles.

"It doesn't work like that, Mom."

Mom? Will I ever get used to that?

No. I won't. It's weird.

"Enough," Shane snaps from the doorway, flicking his head to the bathroom for James to follow. Now that they're gone and my mind is getting back to the realm of normal, Miles has my full attention.

"Grace, I was hoping the next time I saw you, you would be in better spirits." Dr. Scott hugs me quickly, then expertly removes me from Miles' side before I know I'm being moved. "Carolyn, I'll try my best, but you have to listen to me if I say he needs better care. And while I'm working, you start explaining. Grace, don't go far, I may need an assistant."

I swallow the vomit that rises up my throat. Just the thought of watching him stick things in anyone, let alone Miles, is nauseating. But I don't say anything. If he needs me, I'll be here.

Dr. Scott works fast at prepping the area. He has all the tools he needs. I'm in charge of holding towels in case Miles starts bleeding out, which has me swallowing again.

Dr. Scott holds an instrument just over the bullet hole. "Carolyn, are you sure about this? I'm doing this blind. It's not deep. I can see the bullet, but I'll be digging. If I hit an artery, or anything vital, he'll bleed out before an ambulance can get here. I'd never agree to do this for anyone but you, but you have to be positive this is what you want."

Mom looks at me, and we both agree this is our best shot. We can try taking him to the hospital but with that comes questions that we don't have answers to. Dr. Scott takes a deep breath and gets to work.

"Start talking."

Mom tells him the truth, leaving out just one detail. She tells him Dad created a machine that would recreate the way people travel. There were people who wanted it for themselves, so they killed Dad, and now for some reason we don't know, they're going after Miles. But since we're trying to keep Miles hidden, we can't take him to the hospital. Dr. Scott nods, acknowledging he's listening while he works.

After what seems like weeks, I hear him sigh followed by a clink as he drops the bullet into the metal tray. I lean against the wall while my muscles seem to melt. I didn't realize how tense I was.

"I've never seen that kind of bullet before." He glances up at Mom, curiously, then begins stitching up Miles. Would he believe us if we told him what the mirror did? Where it went? If someone told me before seeing it for myself, I would've laughed at them and then probably been scared they were unhinged. I let my mind wander to distract me from hearing the tugging of the thread and Miles' low moans.

"Grace, find a seat before you pass out," Dr. Scott orders while stitching. I'm grateful for his instructions and find a seat.

After what seems like days, Dr. Scott finishes sewing him up then slathers something over the wound. After bandaging it, he gives Miles a shot in the arm. "If he doesn't wake within twenty-four hours, or the cut seems to open or get infected, call me. I gave him some morphine, but here's a prescription for pain relievers in case he wakes and finds he needs them." He hands the white piece of paper to Mom. "Will you walk me out, Carolyn?"

I'm not stupid. My parents did the same thing when they wanted to talk about things they didn't want me hearing. I let them go without arguing. I'll ask Mom about it later.

I grab a blanket from the closet, wrap it around me, and climb on the other side of the bed.

I don't know how it's possible after everything that's happened today, but I know sleep will come easily. My eyes close, and my mind starts to race through images that are stored in my head.

I think about Miles being back and what consequences are going to follow.

I think about James and the repercussions of him being here.

And I think about the mirror, because now that I've been in Shane's room for awhile, I can sense it in my blood again. And it scares me that it feels like I'm breathing right and that I haven't been for weeks.

* * *

The room is quiet when I open my eyes. I have no idea what time it is, but it's still dark out, so I roll over to fall back asleep.

But thoughts of sleeping quickly vanish when I roll over and my eyes are looking directly into Miles'. He's lying on his side facing me with a look I don't recognize. I knew he'd be mad, and while there's definitely anger in his eyes, there's something else there, trying to soften them. I gulp loudly and see his lips twitch, only a little before he corrects it.

The gauze over his wound is still mostly white, which is a good sign. I reach out and gently touch it, looking up at him when he takes my hand.

"How are you feeling?" I ask. In the quiet, early morning hours, all I can manage is a whisper. He doesn't answer at first, letting me squirm as he traces his fingers along my palm.

"I am angry with you." His voice doesn't get higher than a whisper as well, but it's enough to cause my nerves to dance. I missed his voice.

"I know."

He closes his eyes and brings my hand to his mouth, kissing my palm. "I have been so angry. I should be much more angry now, but . . ." His eyes open, and the anger is replaced by hurt. As hard as he tries to hide it, I can see the pain I caused him. "Do you realize that was the second time you left me, thinking I was better off without you?"

I nod, but then too stubbornly won't let it go without an explanation. "You were dying," I remind him.

"And do you realize this is the second time you have come back for me?"

"I know that. I wouldn't have brought you back this time if you hadn't gotten yourself shot," I snap.

He smiles, but it isn't his smile. It's dark, leaning toward menacing. "If I had not been shot, you would have left me there?"

"Once I made sure everyone was out of the house and safe, yes, I would have left you." I feel horrible saying it, but I won't lie to him. He lets go of my hand and rolls onto his back, glaring at the ceiling.

"What did the doctor say regarding my shoulder?" His voice is placid, and I swallow the desire to make it happier.

"He got the bullet out and stitched you up. If it reopens or seems to be infected we need to call him, but he said you should be fine."

"So I can go back?"

"Yes." Does he want to go back?

He nods, and the silence between us is becoming unbearable. There are so many things I want to say but know he won't hear them how I intend them to be heard. He sits up, swinging his legs to the floor. After a minute, he stands and walks to the window.

"Do you want me to go back?" he whispers, so quietly I'm not sure that's what he said. I walk over to him, afraid to see the light in his eyes darken further than they already have. When I get to the window, he turns to me so quickly it takes the words right from me. His good arm wraps around my waist, pulling me closer to him. When we can't get any closer, he whispers in my ear, "Do you *want* me to go back?"

184

My eyes close as I think of the right answer. Of course I don't want him to go, but he needs to. Shaking, my hands move up his arms, careful not to hurt him, and rest them on his cheeks. When my eyes open, I see we're only inches from each other, and unintentionally, my eyes drop to his mouth.

"Grace, do you want me to go back?"

He never says my name that way. I really do love that he calls me Gracie, but when he says my name this way, because it's rare, it makes my stomach jump. Because I haven't in so long, I pull his face closer and kiss him softly. And immediately know it was a mistake.

This isn't the plan.

The plan is for him to heal and then ask him to leave. But I didn't take into account how much I've missed him.

The moment our lips touch my will crumbles. I can't remember the answer I was going to give him. I can't even remember the question. The kiss is short, but overwhelming. I pull away just enough to see his eyes, and I see the feelings I have swirling around in me are also in Miles.

It's useless to lie; I won't do that to him, but the truth may hurt more. My mouth hasn't moved far from his, so I talk quickly before I'll be tempted to kiss him again and end up throwing my resolve out the window.

"No, I don't want you to go, but you need—"

I have more of an explanation, a reason why my wants aren't what he needs, but he hears the words he wants to hear, so anything else I have to say is useless. He grabs my chin and closes the small space between us.

Miles and I have kissed before. Some are sweet and short, others much longer and deep. But this one is different. The desperation in this kiss is so apparent it only makes both of us put more into it, trying to convince the other how much we love them. He knows I love him, and I know he loves me, but because of the situation we're in, it's vital to take measures that we don't want to. The more he kisses me, the less selfish I feel, selfish for wanting him to stay here with me.

Once I start rationalizing him staying, I know the kiss needs to stop before I end up begging him to stay. My hands push against his chest, and when I see his face, my anger comes.

"Why are you smiling?" It isn't that he's smiling that makes me mad. It's

185

the arrogance in it. Now that he sees how his smile bothers me, it gets bigger.

"Because I know that you want me here as much as I want to be here." He moves in to kiss me again, but my hands slap against his chest to stop him.

"Yes, I want you here, but that doesn't mean you should stay."

His mood is much too high to say anything that will get through to him. "The only reason I would return home was if you did not want me here. If your feelings had changed, which I know they have not, or if you wanted them to change, I would leave. Do you want your feelings for me to change?" He takes my hand from his chest and puts it at my side so he can step closer to me.

"It is getting easier to make you blush. Do you wish to change that?" he asks, his smile going cocky as his thumb rubs against my cheek. His hand slides from my cheek and rests on my neck. "Do you wish to change how fast your heart beats when I get close?" I hold my breath, because I can feel my heart pounding against his hand and I want it to stop. How embarrassing that he's noticed that. He moves his hand from my neck, down my arm and takes my hand. Bringing it to his mouth, he kisses it, then smiles. "Do you wish to stay still when I touch you? And no longer tremble?"

Oh my gosh, say something, Grace! I'm very aware how he makes me feel, and the fact that he knows it makes all my symptoms worse. I can feel my heartbeat throughout my entire body, my hands are shaking profusely, and to my embarrassment, my face is on fire.

He cups my face with one hand; his hurt arm staying close to his side. He kisses me, just barely, but enough to make me want to kiss him. But when I move in, he stops my face just before we kiss. I can feel his breath on my lips, but I can't shake my head to get rid of the fog; he's holding me too tight.

"Is it your wish to not want me?" he asks in a low voice.

I give up. Now that he knows I want him with me, I can talk until I run out of breath, and it still won't be enough to convince him. And if matters aren't bad enough, I feel warm tears streak down my face.

He pulls back but keeps his face close to mine, so my eyes are all he sees. "Gracie, I know why you did it. Believe me, I would have done the same if our roles were reversed. But you must hear me when I say I wish to stay with you. Please let me make my own decisions. I know it is hard for you not to take care of me, but believe it or not, I have managed to care for myself for almost twenty years. Yes, situations are different now, but I would like a say in what happens in my life, especially if that involves you. And remember this," he squeezes me into him and kisses me, "the next time you think I am better off without you. Remember that we always find a way back to each other."

chapter sixteen

"Your mother told me we have a guest but said you needed to explain," Miles says, fussing with the sling Dr. Scott sent over this morning for him to wear.

Curse you, Mom! The blush starts at my neck all the way through my face and to the tip of my ears.

"My curiosity is peaked." He brushes his thumb over my fire-hot face.

"Um . . . " This is so awkward. How do I start? Are you hungry? Mom can probably make pancakes. By the way, this is James. We end up getting married, and he's our son.

"Gracie, you are killing me." We stop just outside the kitchen where breakfast is cooking. It doesn't help when he looks at me with those big, pleading blue eyes. It just makes me more nervous.

I hold my breath and take the leap. "He came last night through the mirror. From 2040." Miles nods, a little wary. "We call him James. His full name is . . . " Ah . . . breathe! "His real name is Miles James Denley III."

Miles smiles at the name, but then the realization comes. And so does his blush. "Oh."

It's more awkward than I imagined it would be. I look at my hands, pulling at the other while Miles rubs his neck. In silence. Uncomfortable silence.

"So . . . " I say, hoping he'll say something. Anything.

"So . . . are you going to introduce me?" He smiles that crooked smile and the tension fades some.

"Yeah." I take his hand and start toward the kitchen. "It's really weird. He's known us for over twenty years, and we're only just meeting him."

"It is nice to know I put up with you for twenty years."

The awkwardness is gone as I swat his shoulder. "You'd be lucky if I gave you twenty years."

He whirls me around to face him and kisses me hard, knocking the breath out of me.

"It seems the habit of you two kissing whenever the urge hit started early."

I push away from Miles when I hear James and see James leaning his shoulder against the wall, watching us.

Miles lets go of me and turns to James. "You must be the reason Gracie has a hard time looking me in the eye this morning."

James grins. "And you must be the reason she's the color of a tomato."

This just keeps getting worse.

"James, I assume." Miles sticks his hand out to him.

"Yep." They shake hands, both looking intriguingly at each other. It really is a sight to see them side by side. James is taller than Miles. Not as big though. But their smile is exactly the same. Even though James has my green eyes, they have the same glint to them as Miles' have.

James' eyes slide over to me, and I recognize the teasing smile. "Mom started to keep a journal after you two came back from the fire. She said one of her favorite parts of having you back was so you could kiss her."

"James!"

"Did she?" Miles looks down at me and I know I'm outnumbered. One sensible girl against two ten-year-old boys trapped in men's bodies. I *had* thought of keeping a journal, because I love reading Dad's so much, but I don't want to anymore.

"I'm hungry." I turn around and walk into the kitchen.

"Of course," James and Miles mutter under their breath. Once hearing the other say the same thing, they laugh.

"I'm happy everyone has met," Mom says, pouring batter onto the hot skillet. She questions me with a look, asking how I'm holding up. I just glare at her, but she knows it's meant for the boys.

"I think we're in trouble," James laughs, smoothly taking the spatula away from Mom.

"I usually am." Miles sits down by me and takes my hand. "But I would take her wrath any day." He kisses my hand, and my anger goes down a notch. I smile, not able to stop myself. "James, thank you for the tip. Perhaps if I indulge her in her favorite thing, I will not be in so much trouble." Before I can narrow my eyes, he pulls me in and gives me a big, loud kiss on the mouth.

"Boys," I mutter, turning to the cinnamon pancakes James puts in front of me.

"If you give her kisses, and I give her food, you and I will be unstoppable." James sets the syrup beside my pancakes and goes back to the skillet, smiling.

"I like that idea," Miles says in my ear. I feel him smile against my hair when I shudder.

"Okay, enough teasing for one day." I concentrate on my pancakes and settle into the situation. It doesn't take long before I get comfortable sitting around the big table, laughing with Miles, James, and Mom. I want this. This weird, impossible life. I want it.

James stands and folds his napkin by his plate. "If you will all excuse me, I have a friend I need to visit." He doesn't look at me. He talks mostly to Miles, and the way Miles' eyebrow arches has my curiosity peaking.

James leaves to visit this *friend*, and Mom and I take the time to catch up on much needed laundry. Miles offers to help, although he slows us down. Mom dumps the clothes from the basket on the floor, and I plop down next to it.

"I forgot how easy it is to do laundry when you have the machines, but I also forgot how many clothes one person can go through." Mom laughs while tossing me socks to pair up and fold. I hear her catch her breath, and when I look up, I see one of Dad's shirts in her pile of clothes. "How did this get in here?"

"Oh, it was probably one that you let Miles borrow." I recognize the graphic.

"It's funny." Mom smiles at the shirt. "Even after washing his clothes, they still smell like him." She puts the shirt to her face and inhales.

"Are you alright?" I ask.

"Yes. I miss him. And sometimes I get sad that Daniel was all by himself that night. There was no one at home to see him, and sometimes I wonder if someone had been home if it would have made a difference." She looks up and puts on her fake smile. "At least he got to see you before, so that's comforting."

"Beth and Shane were there, too. So he wasn't totally alone," I say, grabbing the shirt Miles is trying to fold and fold it myself.

"Beth wasn't there," Mom says, not looking up from the laundry.

"Yes, she was. She was changing the sheets."

"Grace, maybe you were mistaken on the night you went to. Maybe it wasn't the night he died. Beth was at her house when you and I got home. I found Daniel. I . . . " She puts the pants she's folding down and takes a few deep breaths.

"She's right," Shane says, strolling into the room. He stops when he sees we're folding laundry, and it looks like he wants to walk right back out. "Beth made a tray of food for Dan, and I took it up after she left. I called Beth later that night to tell her he died. She was at home."

I turn back to Mom. "No, she—"

"Grace, let's be done with this conversation." Mom tosses the pants aside and starts folding at an alarming speed.

I know what night I went to, and I know it was the night Dad died.

I stand and pull Miles up with me. "I want to show Miles something. We'll be upstairs."

Mom waves us off, still looking down at the clothes.

"What are we doing?" Miles asks on the way up the stairs.

"Why do you think we're doing something? I could have just wanted to get out of doing laundry."

"Because you get a certain look on your face when you have a plan. You are very serious, and you get a crease, right here." His finger runs down the middle of my eyebrows.

I smile, pull him into Shane's room with me, and stop at the mirror.

191

"Miles, I know I went to the night he died. That's not an experience you mistake. I'm going back, and I want you to come with me." I turn and extend my hand to him.

Half of his mouth pulls up. "It would be a pleasure to meet your father."

"No, we aren't talking to him. I want you to come with me, because I need you. And also because you need to make sure I'm not seen. By anyone." I know I sound crazy, but I have to make sure I'm right.

"Gracie, are you alright?" He steps up behind me and wraps his arm around my waist, resting his chin on my shoulder. I look in the mirror at him, and moments like these make me fall in love with him all over again.

"I will be. Let's go." I squeeze his hand, think of Dad that night, and step through.

Once in the past, I can hear me talking to Dad in his room. The sound of his voice is gut wrenching. It isn't as strong as I convinced myself it was. I pull Miles to the door and peek out into the hallway. No one is there, so we dart down the hall and into the bathroom right at the top of the stairs. We keep the lights off and sit on the floor, slowly opening the door just a crack, so we can see the door to Dad's room.

"What are we watching for?" Miles whispers.

"That." I point to Beth, who's coming up the stairs. She walks into Dad's room, and I close my eyes to listen.

"How are you feeling today?" I hear Beth ask.

"Better actually. I think it's those disgusting green smoothies Lynnie has me drinking. I've missed my tea and cookies, though. Thanks for making them for me."

"You're welcome. Carolyn and Grace should be home soon; should I send them up when they get back?"

"Only Carolyn, I'll see Gracie in the morning. I hate to have her see me like this."

I squeeze Miles' hand a little tighter.

"Okay, let me know if there is anything else I can get you." I hear her humming begin and the sound of her airing out sheets. Then everything happens, just like last time, but harsher than before.

Dad's cough.

Beth stops humming.

Dad's wheezing.

Beth's frantic pleas for him to breathe.

Dad's last breaths.

Dad's last everything.

I snap out of it when I see Beth scramble out of the room, closing the door behind her. Her hands and head rest against the door, her shoulders rising and falling with big breaths.

"Move," I whisper. Why isn't she running for the phone?

She turns around, and the second I see her face, Miles' hand clamps over my mouth.

Beth is smiling euphorically. And when she starts laughing, I push myself further into Miles. If he lets me go, I really think I'll barrel out of this bathroom and throw her down the stairs. Tears pool above Miles' hand over my mouth as I watch Beth saunter down the hall. She reaches the stairs and begins whistling a song.

I peer out of the bathroom and watch her grab her purse from the table in the entry. Her laugh echoes through the house as she closes the front door and leaves.

"I am sorry," Miles whispers, removing his hand from my mouth. "I am so sorry."

"We have to go." I push up from the cold floor and run to my room. I try ignoring the cries coming from Dad's room—my cries. I quickly take Miles' hand and go through.

Like before when I came back from seeing Dad the first time, I fall on my knees the instant we're back.

Miles kneels beside me and gathers me close. "Shane! Carolyn!" he shouts, hugging me tighter when I jump. Frantic footsteps race up the stairs, and I watch Shane and Mom burst through the door.

"What happened?" Mom kneels beside me, but Miles won't hand me over.

"Is she hurt?" Shane asks, crouching down by me.

I shake my head. "N-n-no."

"Would you like me to tell them?" Miles asks. I want to tell them but

193

know my words will be incoherent. I nod and cry more when he begins.

"Grace felt she was right about the night Daniel died. We just went back." Miles looks over his shoulder and glares at the mirror.

"Grace, we've talked about this. You can't keep going back. It's too dangerous to—"

"No," Miles stops him. "It is good we did go. Beth *was* there that night. Grace remembered her helping Daniel, changing his bedding, and then rushing from the room to call for help when he began coughing. This time, however, we watched as Beth came out of his room. She was in no hurry."

"She laughed!" I scream. "Beth turned from Dad's door and laughed. He was dying, and she didn't do anything. She left the house whistling!" I'm on my feet, feeling my whole body tremble.

"Are you sure?" Mom asks quietly, clutching her chest. I just give her a look, and the tears she was holding back start falling.

Shane hasn't moved since we told them. He watches his fists tighten and then closes his eyes, and his whole body seems to go lax.

"What do we do?" I ask.

Shane leaves the room for a moment. He comes back with my phone, handing it to me. "Text Beth. Tell her to come over."

Me: Beth, want to come over tonight? Mom and I are watching a movie.

I look back at Shane and wonder how any of us are going to stand having Beth step foot in this house.

Beth: Be there in twenty!

"She'll be here in twenty minutes," I read from the text. "What do we do when she gets here?"

"You do nothing," Shane orders firmly. "I want all of you to leave the house. I'll talk to Beth. Alone." He leaves the room, punching the door on his way out, making it bounce off the wall and slam shut.

Mom is out the door, running after him. "When are you going to realize that we're in this together? You can't keep pushing us out of this."

194

"I promised Dan that I would do anything to protect you and Grace." Shane whirls around. "I promised him!"

"And we appreciate that, but you have to understand we love you as much as you love us. Grace and Miles can leave, but I'm staying." Mom widens her stance, like she's bracing for a fight.

Shane glowers at Mom, then looks past her to me. "No use in fighting. Grace will stay if you do. I have a plan, but you have to follow my instructions. No one breaks."

Why does Shane only look at me?

* * *

Beth's car pulls up, and I worriedly look at Shane. He nods for me to go, so I grab the bowl of popcorn and go sit on the couch. I repeat over and over to stay calm, to stay focused, but when I hear the door open the house feels darker, the air bitter.

"What are we watching?" Beth asks, plopping down next to me and taking a handful of popcorn.

"We haven't decided," I snarl, but quickly smile to cover it.

"Are you still sad about Miles being gone? I'm so sorry he got sick." She smiles the smile I used to see as sweet.

"Me too. Those few weeks were torture," Miles says, strolling into the room. He hands Beth and me a drink, then sits down next to me.

"Miles? I didn't know you were here. When did you come back?" Beth's eyes are so wide, I really think about jamming my finger in one of them.

"Just a few days ago," he replies.

"I'm glad you're feeling better." Beth sits back, taking big gulps of her drink.

"I am as well. After a week of being home, I felt much better. After three weeks, I was myself again and came back." Miles wraps his arm around me, squeezing a bit for support.

"Grace, did you go get him?" she asks.

"Yes." I look at the black TV, praying I won't break down sobbing right here and now.

195

"When? What day did you go?"

"Um . . . I'm not sure. A few days ago, maybe." I take an unsteady breath and Miles pats my shoulder.

He stands and turns to us. "I need to refill my drink. Can I fill yours?"

Beth jumps up with a smile. "Sit down. You're back and should be relaxing. I'll refill our drinks." She takes Miles' cup before he can decline and grabs mine out of my hands. Once she's out of the room, Miles sits and pulls me into him.

"How are you doing?" he asks.

"I want to hurt her," I confess, but my voice is so weak the threat sounds funny.

He chuckles and sits back. "I know how you feel. Especially seeing as she is most likely adulterating my drink." When he hears her come back, he quickly shifts so he's right next to me with one arm around me and his other in the sling.

"Here you go, Miles." Beth hands him his glass, but I take it seeing as Miles' hands are occupied.

"I'll take it," I say when Beth won't let his glass go. She looks at me in a panic and then to Miles.

"I'll just set it down on a coaster until he's ready for it. Here's yours, Grace." She sets Miles' down and hands me the other one. I look at the drink in my hand and wonder why she's trying to poison Miles and not me. She killed Dad. Why doesn't she want to kill Mom and me, too?

"You okay, Grace?" Beth asks, reaching her hand out for mine. I flinch away from her, and turn to Miles, apologizing, because I can't take it anymore. I can't be in a room with her anymore.

I stand to leave, but Shane is in the doorway. "Beth, I didn't know you were coming by," he says carelessly, sinking into a chair.

"Grace invited me over to watch a movie." Beth eyes me curiously as I'm hovering at the edge of the room, wanting to run away.

"Oh good. I have just the movie to watch." Shane pulls out his phone and adjusts the channel on the TV until pictures from his phone pop up on the screen. He scans through the ones of Bri's wedding and then stops on a video.

196

The video starts off showing the kitchen. I look at Shane and then to Beth, who's looking at the video confused. I see her eyes go wide, and I quickly look at the screen to see Beth in the kitchen. She pours the soda into two cups, glances over her shoulder, and takes a small bottle out of her purse. Dropping just a little liquid in, she swirls the cup around and then picks up the other, plants a smile on her face, and walks off.

The screen goes black and all eyes point to Beth. She looks to the floor as her chin quivers and then glances up with tears building in her eyes.

"You don't deserve to cry," Shane growls, standing up and tossing his phone across the room. It hits the wall and shatters, making Beth jump.

"You don't understand," she cries, but Shane is already hovering over her.

"Please tell me. Tell me how I don't understand how you could be a part of this family and then kill Dan. You killed him!" His fists are so tight it's making his arms shake. I can see he wants to hit her, but with the control I don't have, he doesn't.

Beth's face twists, and then crumples as she begins bawling. "I was so scared. Chris would kill me if he found out I was with your family. You have no idea what he's capable of."

"How do you know Chris?" Shane yells, making me take a step back even though I'm across the room.

"I was engaged to him," Beth admits, looking up at me. The man she always told me about is Chris? I mourned with her over him. I let my heart feel something for him.

"Is that why you killed Dan? So you could get Chris back here?"

Beth's expression turns terrified when she looks back at Shane. "No. Chris can't know I'm here. That's why I thought Dan had to be killed. I thought if Dan was gone, no one could use the mirror. Shane, no one should use it now. It'll bring Chris back." Her head falls into her hands as she sobs loudly.

"Enough." Mom comes in the room, patting my shoulder absentmindedly. Her focus is entirely on Beth. Beth goes silent and still but keeps her face in her hands. "Beth," Mom says, more murderous than I thought she was capable of, "if you didn't want the mirror to bring back

Chris, then why did you push Grace through? And why did you go to great lengths to make Miles just sick enough, but didn't kill him?"

Mom's usual calm and pleasant demeanor melts as she steps toward Beth. Her face is consumed in rage, and when she talks, it sounds like she's trying to harm Beth with only words. "And why did you try to persuade me to go back for Miles and bring him for Grace? You told me you thought he would feel better, and we should bring him back for Valentine's Day and surprise Grace. You even asked if you could go with me, spinning the plan like it was all for Grace. For someone who is terrified of Chris, you are giving him plenty of ways to get back."

Beth's face is still in her hands when her shoulders start shaking. My heart wants to go out to her; she's obviously terrified of Chris. But then I hear the same ugly laugh she had the day Dad died.

Her hands fall to her lap as she sucks in air between laughs. She looks up and sits back in her chair, smiling while tears still run down her cheeks. "Everyone told me Dan was the genius, but he never pieced it together like you just did, Carolyn."

Mom lunges, but Shane catches her before she can get to Beth. He holds her tight as Mom stares down at Beth, whose smile has grown.

"So, I'm assuming you'll now force me to tell you everything, and if I don't cooperate, you'll kill me. Isn't that your job, Shane? Kill anyone who hurts your family?" Beth baits.

"I'm thinking about it," Shane threatens while handing Mom off to Miles.

"Go ahead then. Get it over with," Beth says, crossing her legs slowly. When Shane doesn't do anything, she smiles. "You're weak, just like Dan was."

Shane's gun is out and pressed against Beth's forehead before I have time to blink. Beth doesn't even flinch. In fact, she pushes her head into the gun as she keeps her eyes on Shane.

"Go ahead," she says. "I wouldn't mind seeing what death feels like. It's only a matter of time until Chris comes and changes everything." Beth stands, and Shane's gun stays on her. "I told you, you have no idea what he's capable of."

Shane lowers his gun, but keeps his finger on the trigger.

She smiles as she looks him up and down. "I knew you didn't have it in you."

"But I do." James comes in the room behind me with his gun pointed at Beth. When did he get back? And where is everyone getting guns?

"And who are you, handsome?" Beth looks over him, and the smile fades. She glances at Miles and then me. Her high laugh turns my stomach sour. "The resemblance is uncanny."

Beth's laugh instantly dies when James shoves Shane to the side and points his gun at her. "I've killed you once before. I'll do it again," James snarls.

Beth no longer finds the situation funny. She looks at James, and the fear she pretended to have earlier is now very real. Her eyes don't blink as she stares at the gun pointed right between her eyes.

"Shane, get everyone out of here," James orders, but then changes his mind when he grabs onto Beth's arm and drags her out of the room.

"What are you doing? Let me go!" Beth fights against him, but she looks like a twig in James' hands. Beth turns to me and pleads. "Grace, help me. Grace!"

I watch James drag her out of the room kicking and punching him. I close my eyes and listen to her scream my name. The front door slams shut, and when I open my eyes, I see Shane followed James, and Mom is on the couch sobbing. I sit next to her, knowing there's nothing I can say to make her feel better.

"I trusted her," she whispers. "I left her alone with you for days while your father and I traveled. I threw her birthday parties and gave her money when she needed it. I bought her a new car, because the one she was in was so old I was afraid she would die on her way to our house. She took advantage of me. I'm the one who hired her to come be by you when your father and I left. It's my fault she was here. It's all my fault." Mom repeats it over and over until she shoves off from the couch and darts from the room.

I want to run after her. I want to tell her it isn't her fault. Beth would have found a way to our family regardless of Mom's friendship. I can tell

Mom those reasons over and over, but she won't believe me. She needs to cry it out, and she needs to realize it on her own.

"Will you go after them?" I ask Miles. "Go make sure James doesn't do anything he'll regret." I don't have to ask him twice. Miles is sprinting toward the front of the house as I finish.

I sit back on the couch, watching the static on the TV. When did my life get like this? When did it get to the point where every minute I'm terrified something is going to happen, or someone I love is going to get hurt?

At what point did darkness encompass my life so fully that I'm constantly looking for those little beams of light? How did I not realize how dark it's become?

The answer to that is one I've known for awhile but have been too terrified to accept.

It's not my life that's losing light.

It's me that's getting used to the darkness. Once you get used to it, you don't need light anymore.

That scares me more than anything.

I lie down on the couch and wonder if Dad knew what he was doing when he built the mirror. He took the stone so it wouldn't cause death, but that's all it's brought into my life.

chapter seventeen

"Hey, wake up." Shane nudges my arm. When I see how dark it is, I shoot up quickly, looking around. "Nothing's happened," he assures me. "You just looked uncomfortable on the couch. I only woke you so you could go up to bed."

I rub my eyes to clear them. "Where's Beth?"

"Beth's gone," Shane says with no hints of remorse.

I gulp. "Like gone, gone?"

"No, your boyfriend has higher morals than James and me. You should know though, he is much more cunning." Shane weakly laughs.

"How do you mean?"

"You don't need to worry about it. Lets just say Beth won't be hurting anyone anymore."

I let the subject go, because I don't want to start feeling alright with so many people dying around me, even if they are horrible people.

I shuffle up the stairs to my room, but as I pass Miles' room, I hear James and him inside laughing. I sit down and prop my back against the door and listen.

"You know she'll be mad at you if she finds out," James says.

"I know. Whenever I do these things, I am always torn between keeping it a secret, because Grace should not know or wanting her to know so I can see her get angry with me." I can actually hear Miles smiling.

201

"Well, I guess we all got what we wanted. We didn't kill Beth, thanks to you, but she can't get out."

"I am not supposed to ask about the future, but what happened to you to make killing someone your first instinct?" Miles asks, and I hold my breath. I've wanted to know that answer for awhile, from James and Shane.

"You told me you tried to kill Harry the night of the ball when he attacked Mom. You said you didn't because your dad stopped you, but you would have if he hadn't been there. Why did you want to kill Harry?"

"I had already fallen in love with Grace by then, and the thought that he could hurt her clouded my judgment. My father said I would regret it if I killed him, and my soul has darkened enough, because the only regret I feel is that I'm not the one who got to."

Miles tried to kill Harry? I remember him that night, but I only remember his concern for me and for Hannah. I didn't see when he went into the trees or what happened between him and Harry.

"You wanted to kill Harry because he hurt someone you love. The people I love weren't only hurt. They were killed. And the people who killed them paid for it." The hate James has so much of is the same that's building inside me.

"I know how you feel, James. I know how it feels to lose someone at the hands of another," Miles says, and I stop listening to them to think about who he's talking about.

"Do you want to pretend she isn't listening?" James asks. "Or should we go out into the hall and be surprised when we find her there?"

Wait, what? Shoot!

Before I can hurry and push away from the door, it opens. Since that's what I was resting on, I fall back, my head hitting the floor. I look up, and see Miles smiling down at me.

"Were you ever taught it is not proper to eavesdrop on others' conversations?" He crouches down and helps me from the floor. With Miles and James both having that amused smile, I know whatever I say will only make it worse.

"It's not eavesdropping if you knew I was here." I roll my eyes when they laugh. "But this makes it easier to ease in. What was James talking about? Why will I be mad at you?"

"What we did with Beth. You will not like it. I know you do not like her, but you are too good to be comfortable with it." Miles reaches for my hand, and maybe for the first time, it's his hand that's shaking.

"What did you do?" I'm still not sure I want the answer, but I feel like I need it. I need to know she's somewhere she can't hurt anyone else. And I'm okay hearing about it, knowing she wasn't killed.

"We took her to Rockwell," Miles tells me, smiling at James. I'm starting to feel like a third wheel when I'm with these two.

"In the same jail cell Harry was put in," James adds.

My eyes widen as I look back at Miles. "You put her in the cell? But Harry is still there. Or . . . what's left of him." The thought of being trapped with a decomposing body has my stomach tightening.

"I know." Miles smiles. "We put her in there and told her my father knew she was there and that she was the one who had made me so sick. We left a pitcher of water for her to drink but made sure she knew we may or may not have emptied her little vile in the water. It was her choice to drink it or not."

"She'll either get thirsty enough to risk it or wish for death enough to drink it," James says proudly.

I didn't realize I had backed away from Miles until I bump into the bed.

Beth deserves that. I know she does. That doesn't make it easier to hear Miles say it. My stomach is churning with guilt, but I'm not sure if it's guilt for what happened to Beth or for what I've done to Miles. He's different. This life is changing him just as it's changing me.

I'm ruining him.

"I told you she'd be mad," James laughs from the corner.

Miles looks at me, shame and worry on his face. "No, this is much worse."

He takes a small step toward me, but I hold my hand up to stop him from coming any closer. I glance over at James, whose smile has left and is looking at Miles for what to do. Whatever expression is on my face tells them teasing won't get them out of this situation.

"Don't," I say, telling Miles to stay where he is. "Don't come after me." I quickly turn and run from the room. It isn't Miles or James I'm mad at. I'm mad at myself.

I run to the kitchen and throw food that won't expire into containers. Tossing all the containers into a backpack, I dart to Shane's room. I fold a thick quilt from his closet, tuck it under my arm, and turn and run through the mirror.

My feet hit the frozen ground of the clearing, and I'm running. I want to cry. My whole body wants to cry, but I concentrate on what I'm doing, so I won't succumb to tears in the middle of trying to make everything right. It's futile and stupid, but right when I heard Miles explaining how he proudly condemned Beth to her death, I knew I had to do something.

The small barn is just as scary as I remember. Actually, more so now that I know there's one dead person inside and another who killed Dad. The cellar doors whine when they open, and the rotting wooden stairs bounce under my weight.

There's no light, save a small lantern just at the bottom of the stairs. The sconces on the wall are cold, which means no one plans on visiting. The lantern in my hand shakes as I walk down the small hall to the end. It smells like death.

"Grace?" Beth laughs from the darkness. "You weren't who I was expecting."

I want to leave and never come back, but I need answers. "How did you do it?" I lift my eyes to hers, refusing to look away. "How did you make him so sick without us knowing?"

She pushes off the small bench in the back and walks toward me. Gripping the bars in her hands, she rests the side of her head on a bar. "You were all so worried about what was outside looking in, you never imagined what could already be inside with you." She walks from one end of the cellar to the other, trailing her finger carelessly against the bars. "Getting Dan sick was easy. In fact, your mom and Shane spent so much time trying to save him that it left me in charge of taking care of his everyday needs.

204

"Miles was a little more tricky. Since Carolyn was making big meals, it was hard to get it in his food exclusively. So it had to be little things that no one would notice. Did you know that you and Miles weren't using the same toothpaste? I put one by his sink and another by yours, and you used it without question. I used syringes so you wouldn't see puncture marks in the yogurts you gave him when he was so sick. The water purifier you used for only him would get a few drops daily. I eased back when you called Dr. Scott, because I was worried you'd catch on that it was the same situation as Dan. After a few weeks, I realized that was the best plan, though. If you thought Miles was dying of the same thing that killed your dad, you'd take him back in a second. So I snuck in one night while everyone slept. Everyone but you. I didn't expect you to come barging out of the mirror the way you did."

Hearing her confess that she was the one in my room that night is a relief. At least I know who it was, and now I know it won't happen again.

Beth stops in front of me and smiles, just like she used to, but now it's only ugliness I see. "It was a beautiful wedding, wasn't it? Bridgette was stunning."

I take a step back and shake my head. "You weren't there."

She laughs, flicking a piece of hair out of her eyes. "Again, you weren't watching for me. And you can get a lot of things done with a pretty smile and a few extra dollars. Your hot chocolate after skiing? That only cost me twenty dollars. The waiter that brought your drinks at the reception? I paid him a hundred to make sure a certain cup got to Miles."

Her smile disappears, and eyes that look too much like Tom's dead ones lock on mine. "I saw what the stone did to Chris. I saw it over and over until it consumed him into obsession. Everyone that came in contact with him is dead, and he won't stop until he gets the stone. And from what I found out from Shane, the stone is useless to Chris now, and I'd rather die in this cellar right now than be around when he finds that out."

Her faces presses between the slats, closer to mine. "You, Grace, are a plague. You carry death in your fingertips. Everything you touch will die. If you're smart, and if you really love him, let Miles go. If you believe just one thing I say, believe me when I tell you that Chris will strip you to the bone: throw away your emotions, your humanity. He has an unparalleled power to use your weakness as his greatest strength. Your weakness is Miles, and you are his. Chris will turn you into a puppet, and Miles will be the strings that control you. And when you've lost everything, Chris will kill Miles while you watch. If you want to save Miles, get him away from you as fast as you can."

She reaches through the bars and tucks a piece of hair behind my ear. Fear has paralyzed me too much to move. "I never hated you, Grace," she says softly. "You were a disposable means to an end. And when Chris comes, it's the end."

She turns from me and sits back down on the bench, pulling her knees up to her chest.

Before I can feel something for her, I quickly unzip my backpack and shove the food and quilt through the slats. "Those are from my house. It should be enough for a week or so." I put the empty backpack on my shoulder, turn and walk down the hall, leaving her behind.

"Why did you bring me food?" she asks. I was expecting gratitude, or maybe even surprise that I was being kind in light of everything she did. But the only thing I hear in her voice is humor. She's laughing at me.

I turn around, not able to see her but wanting her to hear me clearly. "Because I hate you."

I run from the dark dungeon in search of fresh air. The smell in here is making my head hurt as my mind repeatedly tries convincing my stomach not to throw up. Just outside the building, I fall on my knees and continue to suck in air. The snow seeps into my pants, but I can't get any colder than the way Beth's words made me feel.

"I knew I should not have told you," Miles says from behind me. I jump and twist, falling over a little. I look over my shoulder and see Miles leaning against the barn.

"Geez Miles! You scared me half to death." I grab at my heart, feeling it jump-start.

"James brought me. He is waiting at the house for us. Let's get you warm." He offers me his hand, which I take only to get up. Once standing, I drop it and walk away.

"Gracie." He takes my hand, strong enough to stop me, but gentle enough to let me go if that's what I want. "Talk to me. Why did you come here?"

I still face away from him but try explaining. "I came to give her food and a blanket."

"Why?" he asks, surprised. "Why would you give that woman anything?"

"Because I hate her," I repeat the words I said to Beth.

"Yes, that makes sense. I usually do kind things for the ones I hate," he quips, and it makes me smile. "Gracie," he turns me around to face him, "why did you come here?"

When he asks again, my body sags like I no longer need to fake having backbone. "Miles, four months ago if someone were to ask me if there was anyone I hated, I could honestly tell them no. I hated what direction my life had taken, and I hated that my parents weren't there. But as for hating an actual person? No. If you were to ask me now, I could say without a doubt that I hate Harry, and Thomas, and Chris, and now Beth. I hate her. I really hate her. And I hate that I hate so much." He doesn't say anything, and I can't see his face very well in the dark, so I keep talking.

"It feels like there's this box inside me. I always knew it was there but have never needed it, so it's stayed sealed. When I met Harry, that box got punctured, and ever since there's been something black escaping. With Thomas and Chris there were more holes made. And now with Beth I feel that box rattling, wanting to open so all the dark and bitterness I've tried ignoring these past few months can be unleashed. It would be so easy to lift the lid and let it take over. Maybe then I wouldn't feel the guilt, or the pain, or the fear. Maybe it would be easier to embrace living in the dark, so I wouldn't have to keep hoping it stays light. I have so much hostility inside me, and I'm scared that it's only going to grow until I start doing things that will have me hating myself."

Because it feels good to finally talk about it, I keep ranting. "And it isn't only the hate I feel. I'm mad, Miles. I'm mad at my dad for making the mirror. Sometimes I think he was careless and selfish, only thinking of himself. I wonder if he only made the mirror to profit from it, and every time I question him, I think less of him. And then I get mad for feeling it. I'm mad at you a lot. You decided to come home with me, and sometimes I think you were so stupid for following me, because I'm going to ruin you."

My screams echo through the quiet night, but I'm not finished. "I'm also so paranoid about what will happen in five minutes or tomorrow or next week. Will you still be here with me? Will someone try hurting you again? What about my mom or Shane? Will something happen in the next few years that will change our lives so James won't exist? All of these angry feelings are feeding on each other and it's changing me. I feel myself changing every day. And I'm worried that one day my mom won't see her daughter when she looks at me. Or you're going to look at me and not recognize me anymore. Or worse . . . I will have changed you so much that you *will* recognize me, because I destroyed your soul. One day, Miles, something is going to happen that will change me just enough to alter me completely."

I should be embarrassed for that, but I only feel relieved.

"Is that why you came?" His voice sounds so calm after my yelling. "Did you think giving Beth food would make up for you hating her? Because she earned your hate." I shake my head to argue, but he suddenly lets go of my hand and wraps his arm around me. I hug him back, feeling bad that I'm trying to steal some of his good. My life, that I included him in, has already stolen enough.

"Hatred could never control you. As long as there is love in your life, you will never feel the kind of hatred that could change you. Lucky for you, you have me." He squeezes me tighter, smiling into my hair. "And I will love you, always."

"I know."

"But Gracie," he pushes me back, so he can see my face, "you need to know that this box you speak of? Everyone has one. Some are better at keeping it closed, and some do not care about leaving it open. You are not a bad person for having one. You are exceptional, because you do not want it. The circumstances that have made you feel this way you had no control over. There may come a day where you do have control over what happens,

208

and please, Gracie, promise me right now you will not consciously do anything that will change your heart."

I just hold him tighter, because I know my heart is already losing its color. It's only a matter of time until it turns black.

* * *

The next morning, Miles generously doesn't bring up my tirade from the night before. He even starts off the day teasing me. After breakfast, James takes Miles outside to play football. James is excited to teach Miles how to play, since Miles had taught James to play when James was younger. The whole situation is just weird.

Mom and I finish the dishes, and then I help her study for her driver's license test. Since she was declared dead, she has to start over, which means I have the joy of seeing her take sample quizzes (and failing them) in the back of the workbook.

"I'll get it," I say to Mom when the doorbell rings.

The woman at the door is tiny. Rail thin and about my height. Her blonde hair is pulled back into a loose, curly ponytail, which matches her yellow sundress perfectly. She has blue eyes that almost look gray, but I can't really tell, because her eyes are looking everywhere but me. She grips onto the straps of her purse, twisting her hands around the leather, making it moan.

"Hello," she says, looking very anxious to talk to me.

"Can I help you?" There's something about her that makes me want to pull her in the house and make the worry lines by her eyes go away.

"Um . . . is Shane Gentry here?" Her hands twist the straps harder, causing her whole purse to shake.

"Yeah, come in." I open the door and gesture for her to follow me.

"Thank you," she says quietly. She steps in, and her eyes instantly fix on the floor. Everything around seems to bother her. The glances she's sneaking out of the corner of her eyes only have her bowing her head further. I watch her for a minute, wondering what it is about my house that has her so uncomfortable.

There's a sharp intake of breath behind me. I turn around and see Shane, frozen in place, staring at the woman. Water builds in his eyes as he gazes at her. He takes a step to the side, so he can see beyond me and look at her more clearly.

Through choked sobs, he manages a strangled, "Gwen?"

Gwen? Chris' Gwen?

He only has to take one step toward her before she runs to him. She jumps into his arms, sobbing and grabbing at his shoulders. He pulls her into him, smelling her hair, saying things too quietly for me to hear.

And then they're kissing.

My face instantly scorches. I take a step back and run from the room. Once in the kitchen, I lean against the wall and laugh. Shane is kissing a woman. I've never seen him kiss anybody.

"What's so funny?" Mom looks at me like I'm insane.

"Mom," I say through fits of laughter, "I'm sorry." I can't even talk. I'm still so embarrassed by witnessing what I did I don't even know what to say

"What's funny?" James asks as he and Miles come in.

"I'm not sure. She hasn't stopped laughing long enough to explain," Mom says, getting a little bothered by my incessant laughing.

"I'm sorry." I take a few deep breaths to calm down. "Shane is kissing a woman in our entry," I finally say.

Mom and James stiffen instantly, and suddenly it's no longer funny.

"James, don't," Mom warns right before James turns and stomps to the entry.

"What's going on?" I call after Mom, who's running after James.

I get there just after them, but the second I step in, I don't know where to look.

James pulls his gun and points it at Gwen. Shane is just as fast with his gun, but it's pointed at James.

"Everyone put your guns down. Now! I won't have this in my house!" Mom glares at both of them, but neither of them move.

"Not while she's here," James sneers.

"Put it down," Shane threatens, taking a step closer to James.

"What is she doing here?" James spits, moving closer.

Shane twists Gwen in his arms as he moves so she's standing behind him. "You have no idea what you're talking about."

"No? So she isn't Chris' sister?" James takes another step.

"Again, you know nothing!" Shane yells, his gun pointed at James becomes a little unsteady.

"You can't say I don't know anything after everything I've been through! After everything *her* brother put me through!" James' eyes dart to me and away so fast I don't get a chance to see what's behind them.

James glares at Gwen and lifts his foot to take another step, but before another breath, Shane steps forward and punches James across the face.

I flinch at the sound, but at the same time am throwing myself in the middle. James spins around after being hit so his back is to Shane. When I reach James, his lip is already bleeding. I peer around James to glare at Shane, but see Mom in the middle of Miles and Shane, arms extended, keeping them away from each other.

"That's it! Shane, take Gwen to another room. Don't come back until you calm down. Miles, take James to the kitchen and get him cleaned up. James, you don't come back until you're behaving better." Mom glares at everyone, and when no one moves she yells, "Move!"

Gwen looks mortified as James stares her down, and then he stalks off to the kitchen. Shane takes her hand and leads her to Dad's office.

"What was that?" I ask breathlessly. In just a few minutes, we had guns waving around, punches, and threats.

"I'm not sure." Mom watches and makes sure everyone listens to her. We look at each other for awhile, wondering what we should do now.

"I'll go make sure James is okay," I say.

"I'll come with you." Shane closes the office door behind him and walks up to me.

"Oh, no you won't." Mom stands in front of him, blocking his path.

Shane looks past Mom and me to the kitchen, rubbing his hand over his sore knuckles. "I'm sorry about what happened. I reacted before thinking. James has every right to feel what he does, but his anger is directed at Chris. Not Gwen."

Mom walks over to him and lays her hand on his arm. "I will ask you only once, and I will believe what you tell me. Can you trust her?"

"Yes," he answers immediately.

"And your feelings for her aren't clouding your judgment?" Mom presses.

"No."

"Alright. I believe you. I want an explanation, from both of you. And I'd like to apologize to Gwen for our family's behavior." Mom turns around and mutters, "She's going to think a bunch of animals live here."

"Not animals. Just boys," James says with a smile on his face. I turn around and see Miles and James come back into the room. James has a bag of frozen carrots on his mouth but doesn't have that murderous look he had earlier.

"I'm sorry." James extends his hand to Shane, and just like that, they're friends again. I'm never going to understand men. "You can bring her back out. I promise I'll behave." James gives a sideways glance to Mom and winks.

"I want to explain, but . . . " Shane trails off as he glances over his shoulder at the office door.

"You want some time alone with her?" I guess.

"No. I'm afraid to explain," he admits, looking at me and then to Mom. We wait quietly until Shane exhales loudly and pinches the bridge of his nose. "She'll want to be here, too." He turns and walks into the office, shutting the door.

"Explain what?" Miles asks.

"I don't know."

After thirty minutes, Shane finally emerges from the office holding Gwen's hand. She takes a step closer to him when she sees James. Gwen sits down, and Shane stands behind her, grasping the back of the chair. I sit between Miles and Mom on the couch while James paces back and forth behind us.

"I'm sorry," Shane starts. "There are things that happened that I've held onto for years. Things Dan didn't even know." His face crumples as he grips the chair harder. Gwen stands and goes to him, taking one of his hands

212

in hers. He looks at her, and I feel like I'm intruding on such a personal moment, I quickly look away and see Miles and Mom doing the same.

"When Dan and I started working for Chris, Gwen and I had already been dating for over a year," Shane explains. "That's how Chris found out about Dan. I had told Gwen how smart my brother was, and she told me about her brother who needed help with a machine. We brought our families together, but never told anyone we were seeing each other. Dan knew I had eyes for her, but I never told him there was anything more." The lines on his face deepen while he watches the fire burn. Gwen pulls one of the dining room chairs over and sits in it, gesturing for Shane to sit next to her. I don't know Gwen, but watching her with Shane, I like her. Regardless of her brother, she loves my uncle.

"The day Dan sent them through," Shane continues, "I didn't know where he was sending them. I thought maybe he was sending them to another building, another state. Maybe he sent them far enough away it would give us time to pack up and start hiding before they came back. But he told me he sent them to the future. That they had no way back, and I had no way to her. Dan set fire to the room, destroying all of the plans and the machine. I watched the machine burn, taking my dreams with it." He exhales loudly, looking so much weaker than I've ever seen him.

"Dan wouldn't have done—" Mom tries, but is cut off by Shane.

"I know. Dan would never have sent Gwen through if he knew how I felt about her." Shane and Mom nod to each other, and then he tells the rest of the story.

"For awhile, I resented Dan. I was sad Gwen was gone, and I took it out on him. But then Dan told me he was getting married, and I couldn't stay mad. Dan and Carolyn were married, and seemed to be happy. One day, Dan called me over while Carolyn was gone and showed me the mirror. I freaked out, told him he was insane, but secretly it felt like this gigantic weight had been peeled from my chest. I could see Gwen again. A few weeks later, Dan and Carolyn went to England to look into purchasing Rockwell. While they were gone, I broke into their apartment, told the mirror I wanted to see Gwen and stepped through." He looks over at Gwen and smiles.

Gwen smiles back and tells her side of the story. "I was sitting at a coffee shop, hiding behind a book, when I heard a familiar voice say my name. I cried and then yelled at him for coming." Gwen and Shane laugh together as she inches a little off her chair and a little onto his. She turns to us, and her smile fades. "You see, when Chris and I arrived in the future, my first thought was of Shane. While the men looked for housing and food, I went looking for Shane. I found him, living happily with a wife and children." She said that with bitterness, but laughs when Shane sits back and twirls a piece of her hair around his finger. It's so weird to see Shane this way.

"So," she continues, "I went to his house, scared him to death by showing up, and told him his family was in trouble. Chris would eventually find him and Dan there and kill them. Shane called Dan, and together they decided where they would go into hiding. I told them not to tell me; the less I was connected to them the better. All I heard was Dan tell Shane they could live at Rockwell, seeing as how Dan's daughter lived there and was married to the owner." Gwen looks up at Miles and me and smiles.

In another life, I still met and fell in love with Miles? Shocked and embarrassed, I look over at him and sigh when he has that triumphant smile on his face.

"It seems even you cannot argue with fate," Miles whispers in my ear. I want to glare at him, but I'm too interested in this story and where it's going.

I nod for Gwen to keep going. "They started making plans to leave, and I said goodbye to Shane, wishing him luck. I can say this now, because Shane is not married, but it was the hardest thing I've ever done. Watching someone you love leave and knowing you have absolutely no way to get to them was absolute torture."

Miles squeezes my hand, but I don't need to look at him to know what he's thinking. I've left him twice, and he's never going to let me forget it.

"Months passed, and I got a job as a waitress at one of the few places that accepted people without numbers." When all of us tilt our heads, she explains. "Everyone in the future had numbers for everything. If you didn't have a number, you were nothing to society. The four of us had nothing, so we found jobs . . . and people . . . that didn't mind.

214

"During one of my breaks, I sat down with a coffee. That's when I heard a familiar voice say my name. I looked up and saw Shane. The Shane I remembered. Not the new one with a family, but the one that I had left just months before. Blissfully happy, I ran to him and cried, and then got upset when I realized what he was risking by coming. I told him to leave, but he didn't." She sighs, looking at Shane like a schoolgirl.

"I told her I would leave if she came with me," Shane says, putting his other hand on top of hers. "She told me she couldn't, because she was the reason the machine wasn't working."

Gwen pries her eyes away from Shane and looks back at us. "When Dan tried to fix the machine, I would always sneak in after hours and change just one number in his math. I didn't want the machine to work for Dan, and I didn't want it to work for Chris. That machine was only capable of destruction, and I didn't want any part of it. I tried keeping it from working, but Dan had the same idea as me. He snuck in after I had snuck in, fixed the math and got it working. This time with Chris, I wasn't going to fail again. I couldn't have that machine work. I would switch his numbers around or even switch out good batteries for bad ones. Chris never suspected me, so for fourteen years I kept it up. But things started changing. Shane visited me every Sunday, and as the years went on, my memory started changing. The family of Shane's that I had warned started to disappear from my memory, first the children and then his wife. I could remember them, but it was almost like I had known them from a story. Because Shane had been visiting me, he wasn't looking for a wife, so he never found one." The guilt in her voice is so apparent that I ache for her. Shane whispers something to her, which has the worry lines next to her eyes smooth and her lips turn up from a frown.

"Where was I?" she asks. "Oh yes, my memory. Shane had changed his past, which changed his future. The future Shane that I had warned of Chris no longer existed. I didn't think about that, not until after."

Shane tries wiping away her tears, but they come too quickly. He scoots to the edge of his chair, bringing her with him, so they squeeze into the chair together.

215

"Chris found them," she says through sobs. "At first, he wanted to kill Grace, so Dan could watch. When Dan got to the point where he wasn't mourning his daughter, he would kill Carolyn. And then he would kill Shane," she stutters on his name and takes a minute to compose herself. "When Chris felt like Dan had suffered all that he could, he would kill him, too. But as he, Tom, and Harry watched Dan, they saw him use the mirror. They were so excited that they could use the machine to get home, they killed Dan and Shane to get to it." Gwen looks up and locks eyes with Mom. In just a look I see Gwen trying to apologize. For her brother or other reasons, I don't know, but Mom has the same mournful look on her face.

"After Dan and Shane were gone, Chris realized Dan designed the mirror so only Dan could use it. He got mad, and did things that . . . " Gwen glances away from us, gazing out the windows as tears fall from her face. When she looks back, she's broken. "Chris tethered the mirror to the machine he had built, which created a connection to the mirror used here. When someone used the mirror here, the mirror with us opened. Chris sent Harry through first. I was so scared for whoever was going to meet Harry, I volunteered to go next. I told Chris I was upset with Dan for sending me here, making me work as a waitress. I was actually offended he believed I could be so shallow. One month after Harry left, the mirror opened, and I stepped through with instructions from Chris. I was to find Beth and give her a letter."

Venom seeps into my mouth at just the mention of Beth's name. Miles releases my hand and sits forward, stretching his fingers out. Mom pulls another tissue out of the box and adds it to the collection of used ones she has in her lap.

Gwen talks again, but this time it's much quieter. "Chris loved Beth. I knew what Chris felt, not being able to be with her. Being separated by time. I had compassion for my brother and the love he had lost. I thought I was doing one right thing by him, and I slipped the letter in Beth's mailbox. After that, I left town. I didn't want to be anywhere near any of you if Chris came back. I was worried if I was connected with you, it would make Chris that much more angry. If he knew I was in love with Shane and had gone against him and kept him from coming back, he wouldn't have taken it out on me. I wish he would, but I knew he would think Shane had brainwashed his sister. I left, and I tried staying away. But then I heard about Dan . . . " She sniffles but tries holding onto her composure.

"I had been staying away, so I heard about Dan a few years after he had died. It took me another year to get here. You need to remember I was gone for fifteen years. It wasn't like I came back and picked up my old life. I took jobs that wouldn't ask questions and lived places where no one would find me. I picked peaches in Georgia, painted new homes in Tennessee, changed oil in Nebraska. My car broke down in Utah, so I stayed there and cleaned hotel rooms for a few months. I served coffee in Idaho and then finally made it to Oregon." Gwen seems ashamed of her trek across the nation. Shane, on the other hand, couldn't look more proud.

"When I got to Oregon, I first went looking for Beth. If Chris had come back, she would know. When she saw me, she thought I was with Chris, so she let me stay at her house and told me everything that happened. She told me of receiving a letter from Chris, and finding the . . . " She stops, her tear-filled eyes turning to Shane. Whatever she's about to say, I can see she doesn't want him hearing.

"What is it?" Shane asks, pulling her closer to him.

"Please don't hate me," she whispers.

chapter eighteen

Gwen turns to us and then begins sobbing her way through an explanation. "Beth told me in the letter was a dried plant. She didn't know what it was, but Chris explained that if she diluted it and put it in food or water, whoever consumed it would die."

Mom's face falls into her hands, and the cries coming from her slash against me like a whip. Across from me, Shane slowly takes his arms from around Gwen. Greif paints his face as he stands and takes a step back.

"I didn't know," Gwen says frantically. "I thought it was just a love letter. I thought it was harmless. I didn't know." Gwen pleads with Shane, but he takes another step back. "Chris told me he wrote her a poem. I think he knew that I didn't agree with what he was doing, and he knew I wouldn't deliver it if I thought he had ulterior motives. He lied to me, and I foolishly delivered the letter, thinking if I did, it made up for going against my brother."

She stands and walks to Shane, ignoring his hands when they rise to tell her to stop. Wrapping her arms around his waist, she cries into his chest. She whispers, "I'm sorry" as she kisses his cheek and then the other and then his mouth. Shane, I'm sure, couldn't be more rigid when she first touches him, but with every kiss, he thaws. When she kisses his mouth, he kisses her back with as much fervency.

Giving them their moment, I turn to Mom. "Are you okay?" I whisper, and that's when I realize I'm crying. The tremors in my voice are loud, and when I notice those, I feel the wet marks on my cheeks.

"I'm not sure," she whispers back. James sits on the couch next to Mom, putting his arm around her. He glares at Gwen, but his face softens when he turns his attention to Mom and hands her another tissue.

I look over at Miles, who has been unusually quiet. Right when I see him, I know the reason. His hands are clamped together so tight it's making the muscles in his forearms bulge. The fact that he shouldn't be able to do that with his hurt arm tells me he's beyond feeling. The red of his face and the glare he's pointing to the ground tells me he's mad, but then a small tear slides over his cheek, and now I have no idea what he's feeling.

"Miles, are you—"

Just as I say his name, he stands and swiftly leaves the room. I look at Shane, who's consoling a still-crying Gwen. Over her shoulder, he looks at me, and nods in the direction Miles went.

After searching the main floor for Miles, I start to search upstairs and find him in his room. He's sitting on his bed in the dark, staring out the window at the rain pelting against the glass.

"What's wrong?" I sit down next to him. He cares for my family, I know that, but his reaction is about something more.

Miles takes my hand, studying at it as he plays with my fingers. "When I got sick, and you took me home, I was bedridden for awhile. Annie came to visit three times a day, and even Mr. Wilson came daily. June put everything I would need in my room and much more. Walter came to give me the paper and helped me dress those first few days back. But my father stayed away. He did not come into my room once. After a week, I started to feel like myself again. I could walk around without needing Annie, although she thought I still did." He laughs lowly, interlocking his fingers with mine.

"I bet she was thrilled that you needed her," I say, trying to make him happy.

"She was, irritatingly so." He smiles. "One night, when I felt I could not stand another moment in my room, I went to find my father. To say I was harsh with him would be putting it mildly. I accused him of abandoning

Annie and me after my mother died. I told him he was weak and that we were better off without him." His eyebrows draw together as he breathes in and out slowly. "I then started to weep like a small child, asking my father if he even loved Annie and me. Looking back now, I can see I was taking out my anger towards you on my father. I was feeling abandoned by you, and he was the only one I could yell at."

"Miles, I'm sorry for—"

"No, you do not need to explain. You have already done so, and I really do understand why you did it. I am only telling you this so you know what happened. After I seemed to yell all the horrible things I could at him, he started to cry. I have seen my father cry once in my entire life, and that was when my mother passed away. You can imagine how I felt being the source of making him shed tears." He stands up and walks to the window, rubbing his face with his hand.

"Once I settled down, my father explained why he did not check on me while I was sick." Miles talks quieter now, so I walk over to him but don't touch him. He doesn't seem to want that right now. "He told me that when you brought me back, the first thing he saw when looked at me was my mother. The same coloring, the red eyes, and the weak frame. Later that night, he said I started talking in my sleep. My voice was hoarse, and when I coughed, he heard the wheeze that had haunted him since my mother. He explained he could not be around me, for it reminded him too much of my mother's final days. He agreed that he was weak, but he called me a fool if I thought he did not love me." He turns his head and looks down at me. "Do you see, Gracie?"

"No, I'm sorry."

"When I got sick, you told me I looked like your father had before he died. My father told me I looked like my mother. While listening to Gwen's story, it all made it perfectly clear. If Chris could send Beth some plant that could cause harm, why could Harry not bring it with him when he came to Rockwell? Grace, I think Harry killed my mother." He turns away from me, looking out the window like something out there will give him the answers I can't.

I don't know what to say. Although I can empathize with him, thinking your parent died of natural causes and then finding out later they were murdered, how can I say anything when it's my family's fault that his mother is gone? If Dad hadn't built the mirror, no one would have made it back to Rockwell. His mother would still be alive.

"My father told me Harry had come seeking a position at the house, but they were not in need of a bailiff, because my mother loved tending to the gardens and the grounds. She felt they were a part of her. Mother got sick soon after that, and when she died, Harry conveniently came to pay his condolences and asked if he could help in any way. My father wanted nothing to do with the gardens, so he hired Harry and left."

"Miles." I choke on his name, not having any idea of what to say. "I'm so sorry." Those words seem pitiful compared to what he deserves, but it's all I can offer.

He turns to me fast, the sadness in his eyes still lingering. "I did not tell you that to make you feel bad. Not at one point did I ever place blame on your family. I know you see it differently, but your father could not have known the events that would occur when he built the mirror. I love my mother dearly, and would never wish for her death, but . . . " He steps closer and takes my hand, lightly tracing his fingers along my palm. "But if your father had not created the mirror, you would not have come to me. And I am finding that life without you would be—"

"Safe? Healthy? Fearless? Stabl—"

"Yes, all of those," he laughs. "But I was going to say that life without you would be boring. I would live my life day to day, dutifully holding up my responsibility as a Denley. Perhaps down the road, I would find a woman I respected and ask her to marry me. We would live happily as we watched our children grow at Rockwell."

Jealousy hits me like a slap in the face. I feel the sting as I think about him living that life.

"I really do love when you grow jealous," he teases while gripping my hand tighter when I try to pull away from him. "But," he argues, "it would be a rather dull life. Now, I am sure I would love my family and take great satisfaction in them, but I would not wake in the morning feeling for anyone

221

what I feel for you when I wake. It seems in the hours I sleep, I grow pathetically miserable and miss you terribly. In the morning, you are the first thing I think of. Every day with you is never like the last. We do not do mundane and boring things. Some have been an adventure and fun. Others have been not so fun. But with you, I get to live my life, not watch it pass by."

He lifts my face to his, gently kissing me. Miles has probably kissed me more in the last few days than he has since I met him. It's probably James' smart remark about me loving when he kisses me. It's stupid to feel embarrassed about it, because it's true.

"Do you want to go back down?" I ask when I can breathe again.

"Yes," he says, looking over my face, finding something to smile at.

Gwen is still crying when we get downstairs. She's in the middle of Mom and Shane. Mom amazes me that she can find compassion for the woman who assisted in killing Dad. I know it isn't Gwen's fault, but without her, things could have been different.

James is sitting in the same place, still glaring at Gwen. I sit down next to him and nudge him with my elbow. "You promised you would behave," I whisper.

"I am behaving. I never promised to keep my thoughts decent or my hatred unknown." James doesn't whisper. In fact, he probably says it louder than his normal tone.

"Why do you dislike her so much? Have you met her before?" I ask it quietly, hoping James will match my tone. But of course he doesn't.

"No, I haven't met her. But I met her brother, and that's reason enough to hate her."

"That's enough, James," Shane warns.

"No, it's okay. He has every right to hate me. I'm not too fond of myself at the moment." Gwen pushes Shane's arm aside so she can see James. "I'm sorry for whatever Chris did to you. Words are all I can give you to make up for what he's done. But you're actually the reason I came."

James stiffens, grasping his hands together just like Miles does when he gets mad.

Gwen stands and paces from the window to the fireplace for a minute. She stops, closes her eyes while she takes deep breaths, and when she opens them, she no longer looks fragile.

"Chris is here," she says, looking at Shane. "I don't know where, but he is. Yesterday I woke up with new memories. I remember arriving here and going to Beth's to deliver the letter. But this time, before I could leave, Chris came. He told me he had plans for the future, and he knew how to make the mirror work. Whenever I close my eyes, I get new memories. I'm not sure what's happening, but Chris found his way back and arrived three years ago. It's only a matter of time until all of your memories start changing, too."

Shane and Mom are on their feet asking Gwen questions. I can't hear over James' heavy breathing and my own heartbeat.

"Let's go," Shane orders, taking Gwen's hand.

"Where are you going?" I stand to follow.

"No, you stay here with Miles and James. Your mother and I will go with Gwen to the lab. I think it's time we shut down the computer altogether. If the mirror doesn't work, Chris can't use it."

"But—"

"Stay here, Grace," Shane demands, looking past me at Miles for help.

"No, don't." I shake off Miles' hand on my arm. "Shane, you can't turn it off. What about Miles? He has a family. He'll never see them again."

"I know. We've discussed it. Miles, fill her in. We don't have time." Shane dismisses me with a wave and leaves with Mom and Gwen.

I watch them leave, feeling more helpless than I ever have before.

"Grace," Miles says from behind me, causing the tears building in my eyes to start falling. "Shane asked me the first day I arrived here what I would choose if the event should arise where the mirror must be destroyed. I did not even have to think about it. I told Shane if the time came where he needed to destroy the mirror, I would be happy to help as long as I was with you."

"You shouldn't have to choose," I cry, thinking about Annie's wedding that he won't get to see. And Rose. He'll be an uncle in a year, and he'll never know her.

"It was never a choice. Not for me." He turns me around and holds me while I cry. I feel stupid for crying, seeing as he's the one who's losing his family.

"Wait." I push away from him. "*I* have a choice. What if we leave now? We can make it to the mirror before Shane turns it off. I'll write my mom and Shane a note telling them I went with you. Maybe down the road, if they get everything fixed, they can get it working again. If we go now, we can make it." I grab his hand and start for the stairs.

He stops me, and I turn to argue. "Miles, we don't have time. We have to—"

The second I see him, I stop talking. His shoulders sag, his eyebrows pinch together, and his gaze leaves our hands and slowly lifts to mine.

"You would do that for me?" he asks in a whisper.

He's really touched at my offer, and I'm offended. "Why does it surprise you that I would? You aren't the only one who has to make a sacrifice for us to be together."

"I'm not surprised, but it is nice to hear that you would live at Rockwell. That you would *want* to live there." He blinks away the vulnerability, and his eyes lighten with amusement. "And a little presumptuous, Gracie. I have not even asked if you would marry me, and here you are, planning to move into my home." He picks me up and hugs me tightly. I laugh against his mouth when he kisses me.

"Ahem," James clears his throat when Miles pulls me closer to deepen our kiss. "You two get worse when you're older, you know." He laughs and sits down, waiting for us to unlatch from the other and sit. "How did you two meet?"

"You don't know?" I ask.

"Well, I know the story, but you told it to me after twenty years had gone by. I want to hear it again while it's fresh in your memory." James glances at Miles, and when I see Miles nod out of the corner of my eye, I sigh. They're in cahoots to distract me, and it's working.

Miles tells the story from his prospective and takes every opportunity to tease me.

"I've never seen you blush so much," James says when Miles finishes.

224

"Good. Maybe that means I stop doing it."

"Not if I have any say in it." Miles pulls me closer to him on the couch.

I look up at him and grin. "Maybe you lose your charm, and I don't find you as endearing."

He lowers his head, so he's inches from my face. "That means you find me endearing right now, and I am not trying to be. Imagine if I tried working for those blushes." He runs his finger down my cheek, and his eyes drop to my mouth. He smiles arrogantly and turns back to James. "I am not worried."

When I look back at James, he isn't smiling. He looks like Miles when Miles is upset. The creases between his eyes are deep, his mouth just a line. Then he quickly looks out the window, blinking rapidly.

"You okay?" I want to go sit by him, console him in some way. But I stay where I am and wait for him to talk.

"No, I'm not okay." He wipes his eyes with the back of his hand. "Shane told me not to say anything, but I can't help but think that's the reason I'm here. To change things. When I left my time, you two weren't there anymore. No, don't say anything." He puts his hand up so I'll stay quiet. "You two were taken away from me. You didn't tell me about Chris. No one knew he was there, actually. You two were gone, and he came, told me he could help me. He told me things about you two; about all of you that only family knew. He knew about the mirror. I trusted him. I led him through. That's what Gwen was talking about. That's how Chris got back. It was because of me. He had me take him to the year 2037 so he could stop Harry and Tom from going through the mirror, and then I took them all to three years ago."

His voice cracks while explaining his part in it. "Once I realized where we were and what he was doing, it was too late. He told me what really happened to you two and his hand in it. We fought. He threatened the only person I had left in my life. I told him the next time I saw him, I would kill him, and I meant it. I tried going home to make sure she was safe, but it brought me here. I should've known it would bring me to you two. You are my home."

He turns his head away again when a tear falls. This time, I do go to him.

225

Miles too. We sit on both sides of him, not really sure what to do. Miles lays a hand on his shoulder and it seems to melt away some of James' anguish. I want to grab his hand, to be there for him. But just as before, I sit and do nothing.

"There was a bright spot in your story. Who is she?" Miles asks, smiling at him. James' head shoots up, and the two of them share something with each other in just a smile. Miles is better than me. He's trying to distract James so James won't have to relive his pain. I want to keep questioning him and get as much information out as possible.

"Her name is September. I know, weird name, right? She's the daughter of a family friend, and I've loved her my whole life. She told me I was too young for her. Three years isn't too young." He laughs and sits back, running a hand down his face. "I asked Dad . . . " He stops and looks at Miles apprehensively. It's so weird when he calls us that. He thinks so, too, but Miles nods for him to continue. "Dad gave me advice on what to do. He said he had experience dealing with a stubborn woman."

"Of course he did," I say dryly, while Miles beams at me.

"When I turned twelve, I started giving her a card every year on her birthday. Included was a picture of a man who married an older woman. Shakespeare, George Washington, Martin Luther King Jr., Walt Disney, Albert Einstein. I asked her if she thought those women were embarrassed by their husband's age. She got mad at me." He chuckles and rubs his jaw. "I told her in the first card that if she really wasn't into me to let me know. Not that I would stop trying to get her attention. I just wanted to know how hard I needed to work. She still hasn't told me to stop. She's in love with me. She just doesn't know it yet." He sighs and looks like he can see this girl in front of him.

"It seems you will follow in my footsteps. There is nothing more rewarding than convincing a stubborn woman that she cannot live without you." Miles smiles, reaching across James to tug on a piece of my hair. They both laugh, and for a moment, I can't tell whose laugh belongs to who.

"Maybe it's not her being stubborn. Maybe she doesn't find arrogance attractive," I point out.

"I'm not arrogant," they say together.

"Arrogance is exaggerating my own importance. It's not my fault September finds me important, and I play into that," James argues.

"It is also not arrogance if you know the woman loves you and is trying to stay blind. It is not arrogance if you help her see what she cannot," Miles says. I open my mouth to argue, but nothing comes. Frustrating.

"A bunch of boys," I mutter as I get up from the couch. It only makes them laugh more. As soon as I stand, all the blood rushes from my head, and I stumble back.

"Are you alright?" Miles asks from behind me.

"Yes, just stood up too fast." I wave him off, but the next thing I know, I'm on the ground. I'm not fainting. I can see everything clearly, but that's what's so weird. Everything is so vivid, like I'm watching my thoughts and memories from the outside.

And then the pain comes.

From both sides of my head comes this stabbing pain like someone is slowly inserting a searing knife through my ears. This high pitch scream shrieks in the space around me, so I cover my ears, but it only makes it worse. The scream becomes internal. The pain shifts, so it hits all angles of my head. Someone is saying my name, trying to pry my hands away from my ears, but I just stiffen. Thoughts trying to pass to one another keep getting lost in the disconnection the fog creates in my head.

One thing is clear, and that's the sting my head feels leftover from the blinding pain. When my hands fall from my ears, I can hear my own whimpers as my body sags to the ground. Then I see Miles' and James' face right in front of me.

"Are you okay?" James asks.

"What happened?" Miles kneels beside me and pulls me to him.

"I don't know. It happened so fast, but my head. And then there was this screaming."

"That was you screaming," James says, looking at Miles, concerned.

"Your nose is bleeding." Miles hands me a tissue. I press it against my nose and pull it back to see bright red dots. We sit in silence, while Miles rubs my back and I try getting the bleeding to stop.

"I don't remember screaming. Geez, my head hurts. I wonder what—"

"Grace!"

The scream is so desperate, so scared, I push up from the ground, but Miles won't let me move. Shane comes charging into the family room, and seeing me on the ground, he drops to his knees in front of me.

"Grace." His arms wrap around me so firmly Miles' arms fall away. Shane's entire body shakes as he clings to me. Gwen comes around the corner, and when she sees me on the ground, her hand flies over her mouth.

"Shane, what is it?" I try pushing him back to see his face, but he won't let go. "Shane?"

He quickly pulls away and grabs my face. That's when I see his red eyes and tear streaks down his cheeks. His nose was bleeding, too. Years of being afraid someone else is going to be taken away comes whirling back, knocking the breath out of me. Shane sees the panic in me rising, so his face changes from heartbroken to serious.

"How did your dad die?" Slowly and quietly he asks, his eyes watching my face.

"What?"

"Tell me how your dad died."

"You're scaring me, Shane. What's going—"

"Tell me!"

I flinch at his scream, and he flicks Miles' hand away when Miles reaches for me. Shane holds my face tighter.

"He was sick. Beth killed him." I feel tears leave my eyes, making it halfway down my cheek before they pool above Shane's fingers.

He shakes my head slightly. "Think again."

"I think I would remember how he died, Shane." I feel my anger trying to plug the holes that are opening in me.

"Shane, perhaps we should all calm down and discuss—"

"Shut up, Miles," Shane hisses. He turns to me, more frantic than before. "Close your eyes."

Being angry isn't working, and the terrified look on his red face is too much. I close my eyes and listen to him.

Shane takes a minute to calm his breathing and loosens his grip a little.

228

"Grace, go back. Tell me what you remember. Concentrate on the day he died."

I want to argue with him. That day is one I try not to remember and living through it twice is enough. But knowing Shane will keep asking, I go back and picture him so sick.

"I remember leaving his room, wishing he would get up and follow me downstairs. Mom was holding my hand as I said bye to Dad and promised to come say goodnight before going to bed. She led me from the room and shut the door. I turned to ask how he was doing and she . . . wait . . ."

Wait, this isn't right. I remember the conversation Mom and me had that day. It's one I've held on to every day since. She told me to be brave. That no matter what happened, she would always be there for me. But she isn't in this memory anymore. I'm alone on the staircase. Suddenly, my memory blurs, and the harder I try to see, the faster it vanishes.

There's a new memory.

A knock at the door.

Police officers standing on my porch telling me something.

Something horrible.

I fall to my knees.

I sob as I call Shane, telling him what the officers told me.

Another new memory.

Walking down a dim hallway. It's cold. No furniture lines the hall as Shane and I make our way to the very last door.

Shane's feet drag, his head hanging in despair.

The sound of water dripping slowly is in the background, and I try matching my steps with it, not wanting to reach the door.

And then I see why I didn't want to be in that room. Lying on a metal bed is Dad. Hearing Shane confirm it's Dad sends me lunging for him. Hunching over Dad, I cry and then scream at Shane for dragging me out of the room. Just before the door shuts, I see another bed next to Dad's with someone under a white sheet.

Another memory comes and brings with it a dark emotion.

It's raining.

I'm freezing and wet but don't seem to notice.

229

Staring at the ground, my tears mix with the rain.

Shane's hand on my shoulder disappears, and I'm left alone staring at Dad's headstone.

As I shift my eyes to the right, I'm now looking at Mom's headstone.

They died together.

A car accident. Their car went off a bridge.

This isn't right. Seeing Dad sick is still so vivid, but this new memory is also clear.

I open my eyes and look through the water flooding them. "They're both gone," I whisper.

I can feel it now. The memories of losing them both that day brings with it the *feelings* of losing them. My heart aches, surprising me that I can feel it at all, since my body seems hollow. Vaguely, I sense I'm being put in a chair and Shane speaking to me.

Two different lives I remember, two different memories.

"What's happening?" I finally ask when I manage to speak. Shane is pacing, his hands in balls at his side. Miles and James sit on both sides of me, Miles taking my hand.

"I don't know. It's changing. Every minute I feel it changing. The bigger changes have a physical affect. My vision blurs and I get lightheaded. There's this pain, it's . . . " He trails off, rubbing his forehead, unable to explain what it feels like, but I understand.

"Why did it happen?"

"I told you. Everything is changing. Your parents died differently and left at a different time of your life. Your memories are different. I think your brain is trying to catch up. With both of your parents gone, I was appointed your guardian. You were just sixteen." Shane paces quicker, and when James lays a hand on his shoulder, he stops, pinching the bridge of his nose.

"It's the same as what happened to me. You're remembering two different lives," Gwen interjects, walking over to Shane. He hugs her, grips her like she'll nail him to this life. She kisses his cheek, and the fear in his eyes leaves with his tears.

Shane turns to me, still holding onto Gwen. "Grace, with your parents dying together and so suddenly, we didn't have Rockwell balls. If Chris is

230

behind this, that means Beth wasn't with us that night. The night you went through the mirror—"

"Never happened," Miles whispers. "She never went to Rockwell." He holds my hand tighter. Too much is happening or too much is disappearing. My head hurts as I try figuring out what happened and what's going to happen or what's going to fade.

"Whoa, Grace, stay with me, okay?" Shane kneels in front of me, but I can only see him through walls of water in my eyes. "We don't have much time. If Chris figured out how to use the mirror, it's only a matter of time until he changes our past. We have to go back and change it."

"Dad said we can't change the past. That worse things happen if you do." The image of Dad holding Maggie flashes behind my eyes.

"What's worse than this, Grace? If I have to give my life to balance it, I will." His tears seem to melt away with his determination.

"Why are we still here?" James asks, staring at his hands like he's looking for holes in his skin.

"I have no idea," Shane says, turning back to me. "The only explanation I have is it's like a ripple effect. Your parents dying changed your future, and because of that event, the consequences are starting to fan out. It just needs time to catch up. I need to go back. I can fix it." Shane mumbles under his breath as I sit and do absolutely nothing. My hand clings to Miles' like if I hold on tight enough, he won't vanish.

"What do we do now?" I whisper.

"We go back to right before Dan and I destroy the machine and convince Dan not to build another. He had met and fallen for Carolyn by then. He can go find her and still have you. Chris will be in the future with no way of getting back. Everything important will be the same, but the machine can no longer exist. Are you okay with this?"

"Why wouldn't I be?"

"Your entire life will be different. Your dad won't have the mirror to plan his finances. This home won't exist."

"I know that, but I'll have Mom and Dad."

Shane stops pacing, and crouching down in front of me, he looks at Miles and then to me. "If the mirror isn't invented, there is no way of getting back to Rockwell. This is final."

I look at Miles in a panic and see he's looking at me the same.

"Grace." Lightly taking my hand, Shane waits for me to look at him. "You'll remember him." His head tilts to Miles. "After we talk with Dan, we'll come back here to a new life but not new memories. You'll get new ones from the different life, but you'll always remember Miles, the mirror, and this life." He takes a deep breath. "But Miles will not remember you."

For just a minute, I'm selfish. I'm not ready to give Miles up. I'm not ready to give up our future and give up on James. I'm not ready to live the rest of my life always thinking of what could have been.

But I want both of my parents and Shane with me.

If I *don't* destroy the mirror, Miles still won't remember me. Our pasts are already different. That fact I can't change.

He can find a wife, have a family, and be safe from this world. More importantly, he can be happy.

"Grace?" Shane asks quietly. All four of them look at me, I can feel it, but I won't look at any of them.

"How much time do we—"

The screaming comes back, worse than before. The dark spots invade my vision, and the room begins spinning. I shut my eyes while clutching the sides of my head. The pain pierces through my head sending waves of confusion crashing over me. One person I can see, and that's Shane.

New memories with him. He was at my graduation, happier than I remember him being last time.

And then I see the obituary lying beside my crumpled body, pulled in fetal position on the bed. I shake with sobs while clutching the newspaper.

"Shane, don't leave me," I scream. I can't see him through the blackness but beg anyway. After a few minutes, the heaviness lightens, and I can slowly see again. I rub my eyes to clear them. I turn to ask Shane what that one was about but get my answer when I don't see him anywhere.

"Shane?"

"He's gone," Miles whispers, shocked as he stares where Shane just was. My whole body trembles as I now remember burying Shane next to my parents.

232

I can't do this. Not again.

"Grace." Miles urgently kneels down in front of me. "Look at me." When I don't move he grabs my face and forces me to look at him. The agony in his eyes is overwhelming, but there's a hint of hope still there. Hope I don't have. "Listen to me. I understand what you need to do. To get your parents back. I understand, but because I am selfish, I will ask you to look for other ways. If it comes down to a choice between your parents and me, I know you will make the right choice and save them. But if there is another way to keep the mirror so you can come back to me, please find it." His hands shake slightly as he holds my face tighter.

My throat tightens as tiny sobs come bubbling through. "But you won't remember me."

His face softens, and he brushes his thumb against my cheek. "Perhaps not. But I fell in love with you once. I believe you can make me do it again."

I shake my head. "Everything's different. You fell in love with me because I was different. I wasn't like the women you avoided. I'll be like those women, Miles. I'll come for you. I won't be able to pretend I don't love you."

"Is that what you think?" His smile is warm as he leans forward and kisses my cheek. "You believe I fell in love with you because you were different? Grace, I fell in love with you for so many more reasons. Do not lose your sharp mouth. That was the first trait of yours that had me. Call me out when you think I am arrogant. Tell me your opinion when I do not ask for it. It is difficult for me to believe that I would ever forget you. Perhaps I will not remember the memories we have made, but I know deep down I will know you."

He struggles to keep his composure. His voice trembles, and so do his hands on my face. "And Gwen told us we found each other even when we had both of our parents. We found our way back to each other. We can do it again."

He kisses me, different than any other time before. I never knew a kiss could hurt. But this one does. It rips at my insides, tears through my soul. It happens so fast I don't have time to try to memorize it. Him. He pulls away just enough to put his forehead to mine. He grips my hair at the back of my neck and through unsteady cries of his own makes me promise.

"Find me, Gracie," he whispers.

At that moment I want to promise. I want my parents, Shane, *and* Miles. Before taking that last step and ensuring the mirror will never exist, I'll try to find a way to have everyone.

"I'll find you," I promise.

He closes his eyes and smiles. "I love you, Grace."

I hear him, but combined with the screeching that's getting louder and the fog thickening in my mind, I shut down. My hands fly over my ears again as I fall on the couch, curling my knees to my chest, begging that the noise will go away and take the pain with it. This pain is different. Worse. It's the culmination of all of them put together. Losing Mom, Dad, Shane, Miles, and James hits me unbearably hard, and my body can't handle it. It gives up, sagging motionless on the couch.

When the screaming stops, it's silent. I had been begging for silence, for me to hear something other than the screaming, but now that it's happened, I'll take the screaming over hearing nothing. There's no one to hear. I open my eyes slowly, knowing I'm alone, but knowing I won't see anyone doesn't make it easier. The empty family room seems huge. I look at the spot on the rug where Miles, just seconds ago, was kneeling.

"I love you, too," I whisper just before the first wave of mourning hits. It hits hard and covers me whole. When I come up for breath, the next one hits, bigger than the one before. Each one increases in intensity, threatening to drown me entirely. And when I feel I can't take another beating, another insurmountable pounding hits me.

I'm alone. I'm completely alone.

I grip at my chest, feeling that cold burn that's quickly racing from my heart into the rest of me.

Hopefully it'll spread quickly and numb whatever it touches.

chapter nineteen

What do you do when you have no one?

Hours have passed since everyone vanished, and I'm left in an empty, quiet house. When I think my tear ducts can't produce another tear, I sit up, and the daunting thought of what to do next is excruciating. Where do I even start? Shane said something about going back, but I don't know how. Then I remember Dad's journals and how he mentioned he had answers for this exact situation.

My thoughts are interrupted when the doorbell rings. It's probably Bri, Stella, and Kall. They've texted these last few days, but with everything that's been going on, I haven't responded. I don't even know where my phone is. Thinking through excuses as to why my family is no longer here, I open the door with a fake smile.

"Hi guys, I . . . Oh, sorry. I thought you were someone else."

The stranger on my doorstep turns and grins at me.

Whoa.

That's all I can think as I look at him. He's the kind of man that if you were to pass him on the street, you would literally stop, turn, and watch him walk by. He has one of those square jaws that people talk about in books, but you never actually see on men. What's the word? Chiseled? I never thought I'd use that word to describe someone. He has very tan skin, which compliments his auburn hair. It isn't quite red, but it's also not brown. It's thrown in disarray, strands escaping the stubby ponytail in the back of his head. He has to be around Mom's age. Although his hair makes him look young, it's his eyes that age him. Those big gray eyes look at me with genuine pleasure. He recognizes me. I can see it in his smile.

Oh no, I'm staring.

Since I opened the door, his eyes haven't left mine. Something about him has me fixed on him. And while I can't tear my eyes away, the rest of my body is throwing off warning signs. My blood turns hot and races through my heart, causing it to drum.

"Can I help you?" I ask, gripping the inside doorknob in case I need to slam the door shut.

"I hope so," he croons with an incredibly smooth voice. It's deep but really sweet sounding. "I'm a college friend of Daniel Gentry. I was not able to attend his funeral a few years back and wanted to give my condolences to Carolyn." The compassion he talks with makes me actually sigh, softening my grip on the doorknob.

"I'm sorry. She isn't here at the moment." How long will I be able to keep that excuse going?

"Does Shane Gentry live nearby?" he asks.

I shake my head. "He actually was living here after the accident."

The accident.

Dad and Mom were in an accident.

Together.

This new life is the result of that. The man in front of me should know that Mom, Dad, and Shane are gone. He shouldn't have wanted to go to just Dad's funeral, but Mom's, too. My hand grips the door tighter.

"I'm sorry." He extends his hand with a disarming smile. "We didn't introduce ourselves. You must be Grace."

Curiosity and something bigger has me letting go of the doorknob and taking his hand. He grips it tight, and his smile beams. Why am I smiling back?

"It is a pleasure to meet you, Grace. My name is Chris."

Every muscle in my face falls as the rest of my body tightens. Chris. That's why he knows Dad died first. He's remembering both lives just as I am. I try to pull my hand away from him, but he holds it tighter.

"Let me introduce you to my friend." Keeping my hand in his, he turns slightly. Tom comes around the corner, standing just behind Chris. Tom looks different. He isn't as big as he was when I met him. He's leaner and stronger. His smirk is still as creepy as ever.

"Won't you invite us in?" Chris asks, and I'm mad at myself for hesitating. When my thoughts catch up, I shove the door in his face, but it bounces back when he sticks his foot in the way. I walk backwards, too scared to turn my back on him. "Well, that was rude." Chris opens the door and walks in as if he's been here before.

His eyes roam all around, taking in the house. He lingers on family pictures, especially ones with Dad in them. He picks up a small picture of Mom, Dad, and me at Rockwell when I was younger. Chris smiles at it, and then sets it gently back on the shelf.

Tom takes every step Chris does. His eyes dart everywhere, and I don't miss how his hand lingers behind him. That's where Shane kept his gun, too.

What do I do? I can try to run, but with two of them, I'm sure they'll catch me. I've been on the receiving end of being caught by Tom and Harry. I don't want to think what it's like with Chris.

"Grace, you look worried. I'm not here to hurt you. On the contrary, I have a business proposition for you. Let's sit down." He reaches for my elbow to lead me into the other room, but I pull my arm out of his reach. He nods and gestures with a hand for me to lead. The whole time to the family room, I jump from one plan to the next. None of them are going to work.

Chris sits on the couch, Tom standing behind him.

"I'm sure you're wondering what I'm doing here," Chris begins, "and I would like to explain. I've come to tell you two stories. I think you will like it. I'm an excellent storyteller." He looks so casual as he sits, his long legs crossed. He pats the seat next to him, but I sit on the couch across from him. Not only do I not want to be close to him, but Tom is standing behind him, looking ready to pounce at any movement I make.

"Do I have a choice?" I ask, glancing at Tom.

"You always have a choice, Grace. The consequences may not be in your hands, but the choice is always yours." Chris grins again, and it portrays such gentle sweetness, I have to remind myself who he is and what he's done.

"The first story is only a legend, and you can choose to believe it or not. The second story is very real, and in direct correlation with the first." He shifts so he's leaning toward me.

"Centuries ago, there lived a very poor young man named Ariston. He was a very good man. Although he was not blessed with temporal riches, he was blessed with a good heart. He was able to see people for how they really were. He saw what was inside.

"He worked countless hours every day to tend to his family's farm, but as the weeks and months went by, his parents grew older, and their contribution to household needs was diminishing. Ariston's father was in a terrible accident one day while trying to help the harvest. His father lay in bed, bleeding, crying because of the pain. His mother stood next to her husband and mixed her tears with his.

"Ariston went from the house through the farm and fell on his knees by the river. He prayed to whoever would listen to spare his father's life. He promised he would be a better son. He would work harder on the farm. He would give up his meals if it meant his parents would take them and live. During his cries, he felt the winds change. Clouds multiplied and turned black, slowly sinking lower to the earth.

"'You have no need to fear,' he heard a voice say. Ariston turned around to see a large man with pure white hair and golden robes standing on a cloud above the earth. This man introduced himself as the king of the skies. The king told Ariston that the king's job was to make sure everything has a balance, or an equal. The earth has the sky, the sun has the moon, and the ocean has the land. The king looks down on earth and tries to even out what needs balancing. But, the king said, Ariston has not been dealt a balanced life. He was born into a poor family with no hope of gaining riches. Now his father was on his deathbed, and his mother would follow soon because of the ramifications of losing her husband. Ariston would be left with a farm that did not produce enough to buy food and debts that he did not yet know about.

"The king told him there was a way to fix everything. The king would give riches to his parents, more than they could ever dream of. He would cure Ariston's father of his injuries and promised that both his mother and father would not die of unnatural causes. When it was time for them to die, they would do so because they had fulfilled their time on earth, and their moment to pass on had come.

"But the king said that Ariston must marry his daughter, and if on their wedding day, his daughter didn't come to marry him, Ariston's parents would no longer be protected, and he would be killed. The king then explained that his daughter had been engaged four different times, and each time on her wedding day, she did not attend the ceremony, which meant the four other men were killed.

"Ariston was scared, but he feared for his parents more than he feared for his own life. Ariston accepted the deal and sealed it with a handshake. Suddenly the clouds started to rise, and Ariston went with them. When he arrived in the kingdom, he was dressed in the finest clothes. The king led him to the castle, where he was introduced to his betrothed, Penthea.

"Ariston thought she was the most beautiful woman he had ever seen. Penthea was quiet and shy, but Ariston saw her heart was good. Penthea accepted Ariston, and the wedding preparations began. They would be married in one week.

"Penthea took Ariston to meet her sister, Olesia. Ariston had heard stories of Olesia. The reason the stars exist or the flowers bloom or the sun makes colorful sunsets was because the elements tried to match the beauty of Olesia. She was so perfectly made it was like he was looking at a sculpture made by angels. But as beautiful as her face was, he could see her heart was black. When other people were possessed by her smile, Ariston was turned off by it. He knew that whatever was behind the smile was corrupt. He was not drawn to her like everyone else was.

"Five nights before his wedding, Ariston snuck into Penthea's room. She was frightened, but he told her he wanted to talk and know her better. He noticed she was very quiet around her sister, and he wanted to speak with her when they were alone.

"For four nights, Ariston went to Penthea, and they talked until dawn. He learned that she loved to read and paint. She was awful at singing but loved music. He was embarrassed to tell her he didn't have many talents, but he did know how to love, and that talent was getting stronger every minute he was with Penthea.

"He asked her why she didn't attend the other weddings, but she refused to tell him. She promised him, if they got married, that on their wedding night she would tell him why the weddings never happened. It made Ariston want to marry her even more.

"The night before the wedding, Ariston couldn't sleep. He was so excited to marry the woman he loved. There was a knock on his door, and when he opened it, it was Penthea. She told him she had a wedding present for him. Opening her hand, she showed him a black stone. She explained that if he took the stone, it would take him to his parents. He could go to them for a few hours and tell them he was getting married and was happy. But he had to be back by dawn, and he only had to hold the stone, and tell it where he wanted to go.

"Ariston was happy to see his parents and grateful Penthea had given him the opportunity. He kissed her soundly, and when he pulled away, he saw her crying. He wanted to ask why, but she backed away from him and said, 'When you are ready to return, tell the stone where you wish to go, and it will take you there.'

"He visited his parents and found them healthy and happily living in a warm home with an abundance of food. He told them of Penthea and how good she was. His parents were happy to see their son in love. Ariston didn't want to wait until dawn to get back to Penthea. He hated being away from her. He said goodbye to his parents just after midnight and took the stone from his jacket. He closed his eyes and told the stone he wanted to go to Penthea.

"He opened his eyes and saw he was in her room, but she wasn't there. Remembering how she had cried earlier and the other failed weddings, he rushed to find her. He was afraid someone was holding her captive, and that's why she never made it to any of her weddings. He searched the castle for her, and just before dawn, he found her curled up on a small bench in a dark hallway staring at a door.

"When she saw him come down the hall, she began to cry again. He fell on his knees and told her he came back to her room, but she wasn't there. He asked what was making her tears and promised he would fix it. She kissed him and told him she would tell him that night, after their wedding.

"The wedding was a joyous occasion. Everyone was happy to see Penthea attend, and the whole kingdom celebrated the marriage of their princess. When the festivities ended, Ariston stole Penthea away to his room and asked why the other weddings did not happen. He told her whatever the reason he was grateful, because he could not imagine his life without her in it.

"Penthea told him the story of her first wedding. The man was visiting from another kingdom, and they instantly connected. He asked the king for her hand in marriage, and Penthea thought life could not get any sweeter. The night before their wedding, she went to him and gave him the stone. She told him to go home to his family and tell them that he was happy. He left, but what she didn't tell him was the stone knew your true wishes. It knew the desires of your heart and would take you there. So, when her first betrothed asked to go back to the woman he loved, it took him to Olesia.

"The other three men were the same. The night before their wedding, Penthea would give them the stone and then would wait outside Olesia's door, and just before dawn, she would hear them come back and find themselves inside. Some were confused as to why it took them to her; others were not. But she wouldn't marry someone who wanted her sister, so she did not show up to her wedding. Ariston asked her if she knew he loved her, and she told him she knew.

"The next year, they lived blissfully happy. Penthea wasn't as quiet, and actually had a very bright personality. The kingdom started to look at her and find her enchanting. She may not have been as beautiful as her sister, but she captivated the hearts of everyone she met.

"Olesia was not used to being ignored. She grew jealous of Penthea, because she knew Penthea had the one thing she would never have— someone who really loved her. Olesia took the stone and hid it in the farthest corner of the earth. She then poured alcohol in her eyes to make it look like she was crying and went running to Ariston. She told him Death had come to her father, asking if he could take Ariston's parents. She told Ariston his parents were ill, and that if he didn't go home right away, he would never see them again. Ariston thought that since he was now a member of the kingdom, he could return without the use of the stone. He left a letter for Penthea, telling her Olesia had found his parents in grave condition and that he had gone to see them, but he would be back before dawn.

"When Ariston arrived home, he found his parents healthy and happy. Suddenly the skies darkened, and the rain shot down like falling glass, tearing everything apart. He knew they were the cries of Penthea, and he screamed to the skies to take him back.

"Penthea ran to the king and asked for him to bring Ariston back, but the king could not, because once you have become a part of the kingdom and leave the skies stepping foot on earth, you are mortal and cannot return. Penthea could hear Ariston cry and watched him climb the highest mountains to try to reach the sky.

"One night, as she lay in her bed, she listened to Ariston cry. He begged the king to bring him back. He told him he didn't need to live in the castle. He didn't need fine clothes or food to eat. The only thing he needed was Penthea.

"Penthea sat up and went straightway to the king. She asked him to send her to earth. He called her a fool, because she was giving up everything. He told her if she were mortal she would hurt and bleed and wrinkle. She would get old and eventually die. Penthea understood this and said the only thing she needed was Ariston.

"Her father granted her wish and sent her to earth. Olesia watched their reunion, and the earth shook with her anger. She put a curse on the stone that whoever would find it would be as drawn to it as everyone was to her. At first they would find happiness, but the longer the stone was with them, the cloudier their vision of happiness became. Soon it would turn their heart as black as hers. The things that made you cringe, the things you promised yourself you would never do, would soon make you happy."

Chris sits back after finishing the story, smiling at whatever is on my face. "It's a romantic story, don't you think? Two people from different worlds falling in love with only a stone connecting them." He tilts his head, studying me with a look that has my heart dropping into my stomach.

He knows about Miles.

"Since it seems you are so interested in my stories, I will tell you the next one. Once upon a time," he smiles at his melodramatic opening, "there was a family. They were happy and loved each other. The father was an adventurer and a thrill seeker and had a love for folklore. The adventurer side of him drove him to become a pilot. He got to go to many cities and see beautiful sites. The thrill seeker in him had him climbing cliffs, diving in oceans, and jumping out of airplanes. But it was the folklore that made the other two relevant. He had heard the story of Olesia and the stone and was determined to find it. He looked in caves, under water, and through jungles to find it. A lot of the money he made as a pilot went to his search. The mother taught elementary school and had to take an extra job as a piano teacher to help make ends meet because of the father's dreams. One of their children was a twelve-year-old boy—we'll call him John—who wanted to be just like his father. His older brother was the town's football hero, destined for a greater life outside the small town. John also had a little sister, who bothered and irritated him; he tortured her every chance he got." Chris' laugh is pleasant, not nearly as sinister as I imagined. And his voice is compelling. I catch myself on the edge of the couch staring at him.

"One day this father came rushing through the door. Torn shirt, muddy pants, and all kinds of junk in a bag. He threw his things on the ground and ran downstairs to his office. The family did not see him again for three days. When he finally emerged from the basement, he told his wife he found something that would revolutionize travel. They would have everything they ever wanted. His wife laughed at him, called him a fool, told him everyone thought he was crazy, and walked out the door.

"John's dad changed that day. Instead of having a zest for life, he seemed to be merely living it. He turned to vengeance, wanting to prove to everyone how important he was. He became obsessed with his work in the basement, only coming up from the basement to eat, and even then, it was

243

sparingly. One night John heard his parents arguing downstairs. He snuck down to listen and heard his mother call his father a dreamer and a fool if he really thought a stone could be magic. He asked her just to trust him and go downstairs, but she stormed out of the house. John followed his father downstairs and told him he believed him, because his father could do no wrong in his eyes. His father was filled with so much joy that his son believed him that he confided in him. His father pulled a cinder block out of the wall and showed John a stone hidden behind it.

"His father asked, 'If you could go anywhere, where would it be?' John immediately said he wanted to go to his grandparents' house in Wisconsin. His father smiled, held his son's hand and with the other grabbed the stone. All of a sudden, John was outside shivering. He looked to his dad who motioned to look ahead. John watched through a foggy window as his grandpa sat at the table reading a paper while his grandma knitted on the couch. John couldn't believe he had just traveled five states in only a second. He was a believer, in the stone and his father.

"A few nights later while John was sleeping, he heard glass shatter and then yelling. He ran downstairs to see which one of his siblings had broken something and then happily see what consequence they got. But when he started down the stairs, he saw three masked men, pointing guns at his father. Their backs were to John, so his father could see him on the stairs. He slowly shook his head, ordering John to stay where he was. There was arguing, he only heard bits and pieces, but what he did hear was that the men were there for the stone. Acting quickly, his father tried fighting the men. He was strong and fast, managing to disarm and hurt two of them. But the third was too quick and pulled the trigger before his father could even face him." Chris takes a moment to calm down, to breathe slower, to quiet his voice. It's then that I realize this story is about him.

"The three men fled, and John watched as his father died on the floor. There was no time for him to grieve; he knew what he needed to do. He ran to the basement, grabbed the stone, and hoped it would take him back just a few hours. Elated, John found himself in his room just before bed. He watched as he and his family brushed their teeth, read books, and then got into bed. John watched himself sleep, and waited until he was needed.

"He heard the glass shatter and sprinted for his mom's room. He woke her, telling her there were men downstairs with guns who wanted to hurt his dad. Reaching for the phone, he explained she needed to call the police, but when he turned back to the bed, his mom was gone. She was so worried about her husband that the thought of calling for help never crossed her mind. She blindly ran to him. John ran frantically to the staircase and watched again when they shot his father and then his mother. The men fled, John watched his parents take their last breath, and the house went silent."

I hate the man across from me. He's taken everything away from me, leaving me only my life, so I can be tortured for the rest of it. I hate him, but I ache for him. No one should have to watch their parents die.

"John knew what to do this time. He couldn't rely on others to help; he, and he alone, had to save his family. He went to the stone again, knowing just what to do. He returned to his room the night before, waited until he saw himself fall asleep, and then put headphones on the John that was sleeping, so he wouldn't wake and ruin anything. John waited at the top of the stairs. The second he heard the glass break he called 911. He told the dispatcher three men had broken into his house with guns, and they needed to hurry. He then ran to his sister and brother's room, pulling them from their beds and hiding them in his parents' room. John's older brother was big, and John always thought he was so brave. Feeling the need to protect his family, just as John had felt, his brother darted from the room. Before John could do anything, his mother ran after his brother, pleading with him to return to safety. That's when he heard it."

Chris pauses and wipes his eyes with a handkerchief from his pocket. He deserves no sympathy from me; no matter how many times I say it, I still feel for him. Watching him wipe away tears makes me start making ones of my own. He tucks the handkerchief back into his pocket and looks up at me. I don't want to cry for him, but I know what it feels like to lose family. And as much as I tell myself that it's because of this man my family is gone, it still hurts to think of a scared little boy trying impossibly to save his family.

He continues with his story but very quietly. "Three gun shots echoed through the house, telling John he had just killed another member of his family. He held his shaking sister under the bed, telling her to stay quiet, afraid they would find her and take her away from him. He stayed strong for her, held her tight until he heard help coming. The sirens grew louder until they filled the room. He heard the yelling of orders for the men to drop their guns, and then he listened to them be arrested. The men were caught and couldn't take his sister, so he left her under the bed and, staying hidden, ran to the basement. Knowing if he used the stone again, he would lose someone else he loved, he hid the stone behind the cinderblock, just as his dad did. He sealed it there, so no one would know what hid behind it.

"If possible, it got worse after that. His sister was taken from him and placed with a family a few states away. No matter how hard he tried, he could never find her. Then, knowing how to be charming when needed, he was placed with a family as well. They tried to love him, but he was too far away to make a connection. The day he turned eighteen he left, doing whatever necessary to scrounge up enough money to find out where his sister was. After months and a few dead ends, he finally found her. He knew he was lucky with the family that had taken him in, because his sister didn't have the same fortune. Those who took her in were pathetic, using her for another hand to work so the parents didn't have to. They treated her poorly, and when he found her, she was almost transparent, barely hanging onto life. He took her away from the hole she lived in and then took care of those who claimed to have cared for her."

He waves a hand like he can dismiss killing those people with the gesture. It amazes me how anyone can speak so evilly, yet look so . . . kind.

"I'm sorry that happened to you. I know what it feels like to have your family ripped away," I say, my anger coming back. He smiles, clearly understanding what I mean. Instead of acknowledging it, he finishes his story.

"It took a lot of work, a lot of patience, and a whole lot of intelligence to get into my old house for the stone. That's when I came into great company with Tom and Harry; they helped carry out certain favors of mine. Once we tied up a few loose ends, you could say, the stone was mine. At first I only looked at it, terrified it would take me back to that night and I would watch everyone die again. After a few months, I finally tested it, but it didn't work. Well, it did, but only in the present. I could go from here to New

York in less than a second, but I couldn't get back to that day. I tried everything. Holding it a certain way or asking differently. Nothing worked. The furthest I got was I could go one day in the past, and that was when I put everything in me into it. We started looking around for someone who could help us. I wanted someone to build a machine that would take the power of the stone and strengthen it, so I could go back. But did you know there are a lot of useless people in the world, Grace?" He scoffs and then laughs when he hears Tom behind him laugh.

"We were running out of time. The disappearances of the inept people we chose to hire were starting to gain attention. And then, as if fate was on our side, we heard rumblings of some brilliant man who, if you could believe it, lived only a few cities away. We approached this man, told him of our project, and he gleefully accepted. He was slow but showed much more promise than the others we hired. After some months, I was starting to get impatient, there were things I wanted to accomplish but needed the machine. So, we confronted Dan—oh, I'm assuming you knew we were talking of your father."

I want to scream at him. I hate that he talks about Dad with such carelessness. It's his fault all of this happened.

"To my astonishment, Dan told me the machine worked. The impatience to see my family again was too great; I demanded him to show me how it worked, so I could go back and save my family in a way I couldn't before. But Dan was stubborn. He told us he was afraid the machine would be used for some great evil or to benefit ourselves. He thought I wanted to gain power from the machine, but I only wanted to save my family. His judgments clouded my vision. The only thing I saw when I looked at him were three masked men demanding the stone from me. I thought he wanted to take it for himself, take credit for its invention." He starts laughing as he slaps the arm of the couch. "Although, I wasn't too far off. This is a very nice house you live in." He chuckles as he centers the lamp on the table next to him.

"Where was I? Oh yes, your father. I immediately chastised him for his greed and told Tom and Harry to take care of him. Shane was always a thorn in my side. When he shot Harry, I knew he would have to be taken care of as well. Dan stepped in, told us he didn't want anyone hurt and that I could have the stone and machine. I didn't want to kill Dan. I only wanted what he could give me. He told me the machine worked as he flipped a switch, and I heard it hum. Excitedly, I motioned for Tom and Harry to go through and watched with such astonishment as they disappeared. I took Gwen by the hand and walked through, putting blind faith in Dan, something I quickly found out was a mistake.

"It seems I'm always one step behind Dan, constantly making mistakes. But the biggest mistake I've made can be fixed, and that's where you come in, Grace." Tom moves to flank Chris as he stands.

Chris is here because he needs me? A little bit of peace settles in my stomach. He can't take away anyone else, so I don't have to help him. More comfortable with my foreseeable death than I ever thought possible, I sit back, fold my arms, and smile at him.

His answering smile is almost blinding. "I see Dan in you. Which at the moment is very fortunate . . . for you of course."

"What is it exactly you need me for?" There's no way I'm going to help him but knowing more about the situation can always help. Chris waves Tom off and sits down beside me. The atmosphere around me changes instantly. I want to feel poison come off him. I want to cringe as the evil from his heart crawls toward me. Really, I don't want to feel the way I do.

I'm comfortable. Chris possesses an aura that has my boiling blood slowly start to simmer and then just flow. My hands that shook earlier are still, my body no longer wanting to run away. It isn't attraction for him that wants me to stay, although he's outrageously good looking. There's something about him that's charming. Charming enough for me to see only what's good and ignore all the ugly he really is.

"I have many horrible things to say about your father, but stupid is not one of them. He was brilliant. So brilliant, in fact, that he managed to recreate the machine in the form of a mirror and make it travel space *and* time. But his brilliance really peaked when he made the machine answer to him and only him."

He scoots closer, his hand resting on the couch right beside me. "It took me some time to figure it out. Longer than it should have. Why was it that

Dan, Shane, and you could use the mirror and no one else? What was it about you three that made you special? And then I realized it was because you were family. You share the same DNA as Dan, which means you can go through. Same with Shane. I didn't need Dan to use the mirror, only a part of him. So I thought I would use his grandson." My heart jumps at the thought of Chris getting close to James.

Chris smiles when he sees my face. "Ah yes, your son. Great boy, that one. Took some time to get him to trust me, but once we took away what was important, the trust came easier. I took his arm, and he led me through. We first went back for Tom and Harry, before they went through the machine, and then we all came here. You can't understand how unbelievably good it felt to be home.

"Once here, I did what I came to do: take back the stone. I had three problems in my way: Dan, Carolyn, and Shane. If I got rid of them, I'd have ownership of the mirror, and James as my key to use it. The car accident was easy to plan to deal with your parents. A few months later, Shane died from a horrible illness that no doctor could figure out. That was my first mistake. Eliminating those three changed your future. You never found out about the mirror, which meant you never met Miles." My stomach drops further at the sound of his name. If he knows about the Denleys, he now has leverage over me he didn't before. That changes things.

"Since you never met Miles, James unfortunately never existed. So, I am now here without the two entitled to use it or the one I planned to use as my key. So Grace, that leaves you. The key doesn't have to be Dan, only a part of him. And you are definitely your father."

My body wants to be scared. Parts of it jump at what he's saying, but most of me wants him to keep talking. For reasons I don't understand, I feel better when he's talking. His voice is comforting, even if the words he's saying are malicious. Of course I'm scared, that much my body does feel, but I'm not scared of Chris. I'm scared for the Denleys.

Although I don't fear Chris, I do feel my anger toward him, and the only way to deal with it comes out in the form of laughter. I laugh, hard and loud. The men exchange glances, and I can sense the confidence in Chris I felt before start to fade and turn into uncertainty.

"What makes you think I would ever help you?" I'm serious now. The charm and good I felt from him are cast aside. Although they're clawing at me with every look he gives me. Chris lays his hand on top of mine, and I have to tell myself twice to take my hand away. A third time and I actually manage to pull it free.

His smile, so sweet and caring, makes the hand he just touched start to tingle. "Miles doesn't know who you are, but I'm willing to bet you wouldn't want to see him or his family hurt."

How does he do that? How does he look so innocent while spitting out threats? Concentrating on those threats and not his effect on me, I try threatening him back.

"You need me to go through the mirror. How do you think this is going to work? You ask me to do something, I refuse, and as punishment you ask me to take you to the Denleys, so you can hurt them? If you want me to take you through, you'll have to kill me first, but that ruins the whole purpose, doesn't it? You can't hurt the people I love if you can't get to them."

Arrogantly, I sit back and fold my arms. He can't make me take him there so he can hurt them. My arrogance fades when Chris smiles, sits back on the sofa, crosses his legs, and studies me. His head tilts to one side and then the other, watching me with those stormy gray eyes.

"I've underestimated you, Grace. You're more clever than I first gave you credit for. No offense, of course."

"Of course." I smile, even when I tell myself not to.

"But the mistake is yours. I'm no fool. I may not be able to get to the Denleys now, but what makes you think I haven't already been there?" He leans toward me until our faces are only inches apart. "Where do you think Harry is?"

Memories of Harry as the bailiff are all I can see.

"You're lying." My blood starts swimming again.

"It wasn't until after your parents were gone that I realized my error. I knew there wasn't much time to fix it, so I had James take Harry to past Rockwell, knowing your ties there. I told Harry to become acquainted with the Denleys, gain their trust, and ask for their help when he needed it and then have James bring him back. But James came back without Harry and was rather upset with me. It seems James started to piece it all together."

"How long has he been there? How do I know he hasn't already hurt them?" I can't get the picture of Harry out of my mind—or Hannah.

"We came back with James just before your sixteenth birthday. I wanted to return sooner, but when you've been missing for more than a decade, it's hard to return and reclaim your old life. I couldn't be here long without people asking questions. Again, I wasn't quite prepared for the timing. I had changed your future, which meant you knew nothing of the mirror. What it was, how it worked. I couldn't come to you then and ask you to take me places, because you didn't know how. So I have been patiently waiting for this exact day when both of your pasts collided. Your past has changed, but you remember everything from both lives. You are the perfect combination of knowledge and despair: my favorite." He clamps his hands together and shifts closer to me.

"What about Harry?" My voice squeaks as my throat tightens.

"James took him just after we got here. He's been there for a few years. I'm sure he's ready to come back."

Tears fall when I shut my eyes, trying to erase what he just said. Harry has been there a few years? I can only imagine what he's done in that time.

"Don't worry, Grace. Knowing Harry, he probably found a job and is biding time until I go get him."

I nod, only slightly listening.

Chris nods to Tom, and through a smile Tom grabs his keys from his pocket and his gun from his pants.

"Wait! Where is he going?" I stand and try catching him, but Chris stands in my way.

"I want you to take me to Rockwell to get Harry, but after having this conversation with you, I trust you less now than I did before. Tom is just going for a drive around the neighborhood. If he hasn't heard from me letting him know of my safety, I'm afraid he will have to pay your friends and the doctor a visit."

He knows about Bri, Stella, and Kallie. I'm trapped, and the door closing behind Tom solidifies my future. I'm bound to this man for as long as he needs me.

"Now," Chris steps closer and tucks a piece of hair behind my ear, "will you sit again so we can talk?"

Robotically, I sit down and watch Chris crouch down in front of me, so our eyes are level. There's something big about him, something I can't figure out. While I know if I were to look inside him I'd find nothing but poison, I feel a piece inside me that is comfortable with him. That scares me way more than Chris does.

The indescribable feeling of belonging gets stronger when he looks at me like that, like he needs me. "Grace, if you tell me right now where the stone is, I will make you a promise. I'll leave you alone and not interfere in your life anymore. You hand over the stone, and I'll take you to Rockwell right now and leave you there to live happily with Miles. If you help me, I'll give you whatever you want."

I want to laugh and cry at that. Who would I be if I turn the stone over to him? And who would I be if I didn't wish I could? I shake my head and genuinely regret what I'm about to say. "I have no idea where the stone is, but it wouldn't do you any good to find it. My dad didn't make the mirror answer to him. It's the stone that's his."

Something dark flashes across Chris' face. I close my eyes and hold onto the cushions under me when furniture starts flying. Chris screams at Dad, hating and cursing him. Wood splinters against the wall. I flinch when something whistles past my ear, and then I hear glass shatter behind me.

When it goes quiet, I open my eyes and see Chris panting in the middle of debris. A few dining room chairs are in pieces, some picture frames are scraps, and other decorations are now piles of garbage by the wall. Chris' breaths are ragged and shallow, but when he sees me, they begin to slow. As he looks at me, his eyebrows smooth out, and his lips turn up. He closes his eyes for a minute, and when they open, his black eyes are gray again.

He moves toward me, scanning my face the closer he gets. "Forgive me." His smile turns angelic. "Will you follow me?"

His heels are light as they bounce up the stairs. With no other choice, I follow, but not without thinking over every scenario possible to change my circumstances. There has to be a way out of this. My head hurts when I walk in my room and see the mirror returned to the corner it's been my entire life.

"Don't look so glum. I have wonderful adventures planned for us." Chris intimately takes my hand, and I fight back the first instinct I have, which is to grab his tighter. "Now, I want you to take me to Rockwell." He's different now, excited.

"Can I change first?"

His eyes roam over my face, and he sighs dramatically. "I think you look beautiful as you are."

"If we're going to past Rockwell, I'm sure they won't be very inviting with me in jeans and a t-shirt."

"Oh, that's right." He laughs, his entire countenance lightening.

Looking through the clothes in my closet, I see I don't have any dresses to wear. Without Mom, Dad, and Shane, I haven't been to a Rockwell ball in years, which means the dresses I do have are too small. I grab a maxi dress and my wool coat to go over it. The dress is floor length, and that's all that matters. I turn to close the door and see Chris leaning against the frame, watching me.

"Do you mind?" I motion for him to leave, so I can change.

"Yes, I do mind. I like you, Grace, but I don't trust you." Reaching for the dress, he takes it from me and holds it up. He pulls it over my head, my arms shaking as I slide them through the sleeves. It fits weird over my clothes. He turns me around and buttons up the back, and the fear and danger I feel get stuck in my stomach. They try coming out in sobs, but they dissolve when they reach my throat.

"There." He pats my shoulder, and I quickly move away from him. "Are you ready?" He holds his hand out for me but senses my hesitation. "Please Grace, you're being quite rude. I have promises to keep to the Denleys. We shouldn't keep them waiting."

"What promises?" I demand.

He holds up his right hand like he's swearing an oath. "I promise I will not lay a hand on your Miles. Hopefully the others in his family have kept their side of the bargain with Harry, or I'm sad to say they will not fair so well. Harry's always had a temper, so hopefully no one got in his way. Now," he pats his chest pockets, "I left my phone downstairs. I'll be just a moment." He walks out of the room, gliding into his new life with a smile.

The second he's out of the room I run to the mirror. This is my chance to get away. I can go to Rockwell, warn them about Harry and try coming up with a plan. Then come back to this exact day, so Chris won't hurt my friends.

Through the reflection of the mirror I see Chris come back into the room. At the first sight of me he smiles, but it fades when he sees what I'm doing. The change in expression looks forced, like he's making himself look upset. The anger isn't organic. That twinkle in his eye that has me wanting to be closer to him is still there, but he's masking it for some reason.

I turn around, and with as much gumption I can manage I say, "You can't hurt the people I love if you can't get to them. And you can't get to them without me."

He looks at me, not worried, not scared that he's going to lose his only connection to the mirror. "I'll find a way. I always do." Casually, carelessly, he takes a step toward me, and that charming smile gets bigger with every step. When he's only a few feet away, I step back quickly, inside the mirror.

chapter twenty

I don't fall this time. This time I take a step from my room and stand directly in the clearing at Rockwell. The second my feet touch the ground, I'm running. I pull my dress up to run faster and maneuver over the low-lying branches. It's easier to run through the trees while wearing high tops than it was the night of the ball. As vain as the thought is, I really hope no one notices my shoes.

At the edge of the trees, I stop and examine Rockwell as I take out my hair and tie it up again, taking more care with it this time. Miles doesn't know me, but I'm hoping his dad knew my dad. If my parents died in a car crash two years ago, that gave Dad ample time to meet Lord Denley.

In case I'm being watched, I walk calmly out of the trees. With my head up and shoulders back, I try to make it to the front door as elegantly as possible. Which is stupid, because it means I'm going much slower than I want to.

"Miss." A male worker tips his hat to me as I go by.

"Good day." I incline my head to him, and by the look on his face, I'm guessing that women don't usually talk to him. Ugh, I've already been through this. I'd think knowing what to do or say would come easier this time than it was my first time in the past, but if possible, it's harder. Finally reaching the door, I knock quietly and can't hold back my smile when Walter answers the door. The ornery old man has that same permanent frown on his face, but he's endearing to me. The only acknowledgment I get from Walter is a disdainful look as he looks to my shoes then back to my face.

"Good day. May I please speak with Mr . . . I mean Lord Denley, please?" I said please twice, and he noticed.

"This way." He gestures for me to come inside, and the second I step through, my breath catches. This isn't the Rockwell I remember. Everything I'm seeing was here when I came the first time, but something is different. The house feels different.

"This way." Walter pulls me from my gawking and opens the doors to the drawing room. "May I tell him who wishes to see him?" he asks as I walk past him and sit on a chair.

"Um, yes. My name is Miss Gentry. Grace Gentry. My father is Dan . . . well it's really Daniel Gentry. I'm Grace. Gentry." I agree with his annoyed sigh. I'm acting like an idiot.

He leaves me there, and the butterflies in my stomach multiply. To distract myself, I look around the room, finding treasures I've never seen. One in particular catches my eye. Above the fireplace where the portrait of Rockwell always was is a family portrait. Lord and Mrs. Denley sit on chairs with Annie and Miles standing behind them. Everyone in the picture smiles, except for Miles. His jaw is a hard line, and his angry eyes focus on something outside of the painting.

The door opens behind me, and I take a deep breath before I turn. The relief to see Lord Denley in front of me is so overwhelming I have to stop myself from running to him and throwing my arms around him. What stops me is the way he looks at me now, like I'm just another stranger.

"Miss Gentry, it is a pleasure to meet you." He bows, and I awkwardly curtsy.

"Did you know my father?" If he does, there's someone I can talk to. If he doesn't, I have nowhere to go.

"Yes. Daniel and I have become very good friends."

I let out a big breath. "Lord Denley, I'm sorry to be so forward, but did he tell you where he came from?" A small smile comes to his mouth as he nods. "Did he tell you about the mirror?"

"Yes, he did."

256

Thank heavens. "I'm sorry to barge in on you, but I'm in trouble, and you're the only person I have left."

He motions for me to sit and asks Walter to get some food and drink for me. "Please, tell me what has happened."

"What has happened to who, dear?"

The voice is familiar but definitely new. A woman comes through the door, and I clamp my mouth shut in fear it'll drop and hang open. She's beautiful, and the smile that lights up her face is one I know very well.

Mrs. Denley gracefully crosses the room and sits next to her husband. The lines in her face look permanently creased from too much worrying. She's the perfect combination of Annie and Miles. Annie's hair, voice, and countenance. Miles' smile, nose, and eyes.

Then it dawns on me. I didn't think about it earlier, but Chris changed Harry's past, too. Which means Harry never came back and killed her. Miles has his mom.

"I hope all is well." She takes Lord Denley's hand.

"I am not sure everything is. That is what I am trying to find out. Dear, please meet Miss Grace Gentry." He looks at me, but I only see her. When she looks at me, her eyes get big and her smile makes me miss Miles.

"You are Carolyn's daughter? Oh, of course you are. You are just as beautiful as she is." She crosses the room to me, so I awkwardly stand and go to curtsy, but she crashes into me, hugging the air out of me. "How lovely to meet you. Carolyn and I have been conspiring together for some time now."

"Conspiring against who?" I ask breathlessly. Her hug is a little too tight.

"You and my Miles." She chuckles as she takes my arm to sit me down next to her. "Please tell me your mother is coming. We haven't seen them in too long."

"Evelyn dear, we can get to your plans later, but I think Miss Gentry has come with urgency. Are your parents coming as well?" Lord Denley asks.

I remember the last time I told him Dad died. I had at least found Mom by then, so this time is excruciating.

"That's why I've come. My parents have passed away." The catch in my breath is loud. Mrs. Denley's is louder. She's already crying by the time I calm myself and look over at her. Multiple tears fall at once as she puts her arm around me.

"I am so sorry." She pulls me against her, and I feel like I'm comforting her more than she is me, since her head is buried in my shoulder, crying.

"I am sorry to hear that. Your parents were fine people." Lord Denley smiles in condolence. "What can we help you with?"

"You said my dad told you about the mirror. How much did he tell you?"

"How do you think I knew you would be good for my Miles? We saw you as a little child." My head turns to Mrs. Denley and through her tears, she smiles.

"You went through?" I ask in astonishment.

"Many times. They were dear friends."

I'm shocked, but this is good. "I'm glad to hear that. Since you know what the mirror does, this will be easier to explain. There were some people that my dad was trying to keep the mirror from. They got a hold of it and went back and killed my parents. They're searching for me now. I'm not sure about all the details, but what I gathered is they need me to power it. I have no idea what to do anymore, and I have no one to ask."

Mrs. Denley pulls me closer until I'm practically sitting on her lap.

"Miss Gentry, you are safe here," Lord Denley tells me.

"I'm not sure I am. Have you been in contact with a Mr. Harrison, or Harry?" I don't even know if Harry kept his name here.

"I do not believe I have. Has he harmed you?" Lord Denley's voice darkens.

Absentmindedly, I rub the scar by my ear. "He wants the mirror, and I was told he has been here for a few years. He was told to get in contact with you."

"I will study my contacts and see if I have been acquainted with anyone recently under a different name." If Harry didn't come here, where is he? Lord Denley stands and sits on the other side of me, taking one of my hands out of Mrs. Denley's. "But if he comes for you, he will have to go through me to get you." He smiles.

"And me," Mrs. Denley says from my other side.

It's been so long since I was between a mother and a father. I love it. I miss it.

"Thank you." I squeeze their hands, appreciating their support but know I can't stay here. I'm pretty sure Chris can't get to me seeing as he needs me to use the mirror, but when have I been right about anything considering that dreaded machine? Somehow he'll find me, and I'm sure he'll hurt the Denleys in the process.

"I appreciate that, but it's probably best that Harry doesn't find me at Rockwell. You may be willing to put up a fight, but I'm not willing to let you." I stand up, but Mrs. Denley doesn't let go of my hand.

"Will you please stay for dinner? I would hate to think I have sent you off with an empty stomach." She has Miles' smile and Annie's big, pleading eyes, so it's impossible to refuse. "Oh good. I believe you and Evianna would make such good friends. She is a joy to be around, although she is not here at the moment. The next time you come you can meet her. And I want you to meet my Miles. I am sorry for the secret talks your mother and I had, but I believe you would be good for him. Especially now."

"Now?"

She looks at the fire for a second, holding my hand a little tighter. "I am not sure what to say about it. Miles is one of the best men I have the privilege of knowing. Yes, my judgment is clouded, but a mother has that right. He is charming and good. He can make anyone laugh, regardless of their mood. He loves to tease and see others smile."

Mrs. Denley's eyebrows knit together as she glances at her husband. "A few years back, he started grumbling about going to social gatherings. I thought he was becoming shy as he was old enough to really start gaining a woman's attention. At the events I could persuade him to attend with us, he would stand in the corner, glaring at anyone who dared look at him. His only words to a woman were 'good day.' It seemed to strain him to say even those two words. He has not even danced with a woman. Ever!"

Would it be rude to start laughing? I know it would, so I walk to the fireplace to keep my smile hidden. Miles, my Miles, never talk to a woman? Never dance? My fondest memories of him are of him asking me to dance, him explaining his childhood, and memories of his mother. I can't imagine

259

Miles any other way than the memories I have of him.

"And then there is that blasted scar that he hates so badly. It really—"

"Scar?" I whirl around to make sure I heard correctly.

"Yes. Just over a year ago, he was riding his horse like a rascal. You would think he would learn that horseplay is for children, but obviously I was mistaken. He went riding one afternoon in a dreadful mood. When he came back, his face was bloody. He told us an animal had spooked his horse, tossing him. I do not know what he landed on. He said he did not remember. Cut him from here to here." She motions with her finger from her right temple down to her jaw.

"After that, he got much worse. Any woman that garnered enough courage to talk to him was dismissed by only a look. He thought if they could look past his scar, they only saw his title. Women do not speak with him anymore. They are afraid of him. Can you imagine? Afraid of my Miles?" She laughs, throwing her arms in the air.

"And even the men avoid him, frightened he will pull his sword on them. Even our dear friends the Wilsons refuse to visit. We have not seen them in over a year."

Does that mean Matthew and Annie aren't together? What is this place?

"My husband said it has gotten worse as he started teaching Miles about his responsibilities he will inherit. Miles does not like to learn about finances or where the money is dispersed. Anytime my husband tries to show him our accounts, he refuses to learn and vanishes for a day or two. And then . . . " Mrs. Denley stops, taking the handkerchief from her husband and dabbing at her eyes. Lord Denley looks away, grief painting his face.

"Just after this last Christmas, something happened. I am not sure what, but he changed. He did not like being indoors, refused to go to the gardens, even tore down the mistletoe I had put around. He would not ride in carriages, refused to have tea with us. That is when he started having trouble sleeping. I assumed it was bad dreams as I found him every night pacing back and forth by the attic."

I watch her cry more with every detail. All the things he's shunning are things we did together. Maybe he remembers me. Maybe in some way, he still knows me. He told me he would.

"We threw him a ball for his birthday. We hoped it would lift his spirits, but he spent the entire evening in one of the guest rooms upstairs. I found him there, sulking by the window. I asked what was troubling him, and then I held him as he cried. The next morning he had hardened further. I have not seen him smile since Christmas."

Lord Denley wraps an arm around his wife's waist, pulling her closer to him for comfort. Although he looks like he could use some support, too.

"Why are you telling me this?" I ask, wondering why she's divulging such personal things to a stranger.

"Because I want you to be prepared for him. The man you will meet is not really my Miles. I hope you do not offend easily, Miss Gentry."

And with that warning, the drawing room doors open, and I immediately know it's Miles.

Some things may have changed, but his presence hasn't. A small part of me still holds onto the hope that he'll remember me. Shane didn't change when everything else had. Maybe because Miles was with me, this alternate life didn't affect him like it did others.

Taking a deep breath and holding it, I turn to face him, and just seeing him loosens the knot in my stomach. I would never know this Miles is different, because he looks the same. Still tall and big, hovering over his mother as she wraps her arms around his waist. His hair is still jet black but is styled differently. It's swept off his face and very neatly done. I'm sure his smile is the same but can't tell because he's frowning. And his eyes are definitely his, the blue that doesn't quite have a shade.

The scar is just as his mom described. It goes from his right temple, down his cheek, along his jaw, stopping at his chin. The scar has faded with time. It's noticeable, yes, but it isn't the first thing you see when you look at him. His eyes are still what I see first. I think the most unsettling thing about his scar is it makes him more attractive. It runs along his jaw, which makes his jaw look stronger. And I'm probably a bad person for this, but I admit I'm selfishly grateful for it if it's deterring the women around here.

"Miles, I would like you to meet Miss Gentry. She is a dear family friend." His mother steps away from him and tilts her head in my direction.

261

I'm so nervous I can feel my heartbeat in the tips of my fingers. The first time I met him, I didn't like him. He was rude, annoying, and juvenile. But I would give anything for that Miles to be here.

When his mom says my name, his head snaps up, and his eyes focus on mine. They get bigger as he stares and his look, combined with the silence, starts my hands pulling at the other to distract me.

He takes a step toward me. "Miss Grace Gentry?"

He knows my name?

He knows my name!

He has to remember me.

"Yes. How did you know her name?" His mom appears from behind him with a gigantic smile on her face.

"Perhaps I overheard in conversation." His eyes don't look away from me, something his mother is excited about. I want to close my eyes and smile when I hear his voice. Still the same, although it does lack the teasing that was consistently there.

"I am sorry. I am terribly rude. Miss Gentry, this is my son, Mr. Miles Denley."

I curtsy as adeptly as possible while trying hard to hide the huge smile on my face. The prospect of Miles remembering me is overtaking any other thoughts.

"Good day." He nods to me.

"Good day." Our eyes still haven't left each other, and my skin begins to tingle. I'm not sure if I can start up a conversation with him, so I stand, silently, looking at him.

After a few moments, he clears his throat and turns to his mom. "I have some business to finish before dinner. Please excuse me." He bows to me without looking at me and leaves.

His mom looks longingly after him just as a little ball of energy bursts through the door. It takes a minute to make sure I'm seeing her right. She's little, maybe seven or eight. Beautiful blonde curls and big blue eyes are the first things I notice. She looks exactly like a doll. Her little button nose scrunches when she turns and sees me.

"Who are you?" The voice to this sweet little girl is harsh and whiney.

"This is Miss Gentry. We are friends with her parents, Lucy," Mrs. Denley says, crouching down beside her.

"Lucy?" I ask. Who is this girl?

Mrs. Denley turns Lucy to face me. "Miss Gentry, this is Lucy Staton, my neice." I wait to see what Lucy does to greet me, but her face goes stubborn and she crosses her arms. Taking the high road, I dip slightly to her.

"Lucy, it's a pleasure to meet you."

"When can I go to my room?" Lucy asks, still glaring at me. The inner child in me wants to stick my tongue out at her or at least call her some silly name.

"After dinner," Mrs. Denley says, stroking her hair.

"I want to go now." Lucy stomps her foot.

"After dinner, Lucy," Mrs. Denley says more firmly.

"You cannot tell me what to do. You are not my mother!" Lucy screams, then huffs over and plants herself on the couch. "You never will be," she mutters under her breath. Mrs. Denley covers the offense she takes well. With a fake smile, she turns and gestures for me to come over.

"I apologize," Mrs. Denley whispers when we're far enough away from Lucy. "My sister and her husband passed away. They were both so sick, but no one could have imagined how fast the illness took them."

Did they die because we changed fates? Mrs. Denley is here, so did someone else have to die? Will everyone's death have to be replaced?

"Lucy's father has no relatives around," Miss Denley continues. "We gladly welcomed her into our family, but she is struggling. We are hoping she only needs more time."

"I do not want to eat dinner," Lucy whines, folding her arms in defiance.

"You must eat, Lucy. If you wish, you may eat in the nursery as you have been." Mrs. Denley caves, clearly exhausted and not wanting to argue. Mrs. Denley turns to me and tells me dinner will be ready soon. She walks out of the room, which leaves the rotten little girl and me. Lucy looks at me, scoffs at my shoes, and then continues to stare at the fire.

"Usually when others come for dinner they dress appropriately," she quips. My mouth would've dropped open if my teeth weren't clenched so tight. She sounds like a nagging woman rather than a child.

"Usually when I go to dinner, I don't come across bratty little girls."

Her eyes widen as she turns to me. Shock definitely is on her face. I'm assuming the others tiptoe around her, trying to make her feel welcome. I, on the other hand, have no desire to fill that pretty little head with compliments.

"Pardon me?" Her high voice is condescending. How in the world does she do that? She's eight!

"You heard me." I sound much more like the eight year old in this conversation.

Lucy stands up and plants her hands on her hips. "I am going to tell my aunt what you said."

"Be my guest." I gesture to the door. She looks at the door, then to me. With her nose in the air, she sits back down and concentrates on the fire again.

"I will not tell her. Only because she will most likely not believe me." Under her breath she whispers, "and she will probably agree with you." The selfish and mean girl turns her head from me with a pout, but it isn't a stubborn one. I hurt her feelings. Taking the higher road, only because I'm older, I sit down next to her.

"When I was your age, my parents gave me a doll for my birthday," I tell her. "I opened up the box and thought she was the most beautiful doll I had ever seen. I named her Nicole." Trying to be nonchalant about it, she glances at me with curiosity, then looks away when she sees I'm watching at her. "Do you want to know what she looked like?" I ask, knowing it's too tempting for an eight year old, even if she acts sixteen.

"Yes," she answers softly.

"The first thing I noticed when I opened the box was her big blue eyes. They looked like water in the sunlight. I envied her blue eyes compared to my green ones. What color are your eyes, Lucy?" I look down as a small smile toys at her mouth.

"Blue." She lets that smile grow only slightly. "Mine are blue."

264

"Well, you're right. You have very pretty blue eyes. The next thing I noticed was her hair. The doll had gorgeous golden hair made up of perfect ringlets. The ringlets went just below her shoulders." I watch as Lucy tugs on one of her own blonde ringlets. "I would put a ribbon in her hair that would match her dress. My favorite dress of hers was a blue ball gown, because I thought it matched her eyes." Lucy looks down at her blue dress and then touches the white ribbon in her hair.

"Did the doll look like me?" Her excitement almost makes me forget how horrible she was earlier.

"Now that you ask, I'm surprised I didn't see it before. You look very much like my doll, but one thing is different. Very different."

"What? What is it?" She sits closer to me with wide curious eyes.

"My doll had a smile on her face. It was a very small smile, but it made her face look happy." I lay my hand on top of hers. "You don't look happy, Lucy."

She looks up and tries smiling, but it leaves as quickly as it came. "I try to be happy here, but I cannot be. They are not my family." Her hand slides out from under mine, and she folds her arms again in an attempt to shut me out.

"Lucy, my parents are gone also." The second I say it that bulge in my throat gets bigger. When she turns to me with those big blue eyes filling with water, my throat seems to squeeze shut.

"There's a difference between you and me, though," I say gently. "You lost your parents but got to come live with your aunt, uncle, and cousins who love you. When my parents died, I had no one to live with. I'm all alone." Those words echo through every part of me.

"You have no other family?" she asks, pity filling her eyes. Great, a five-year-old pities me.

"None that are still living. Do you see, Lucy? You are incredibly lucky to have the Denleys. They love you very much, and I think if you stop trying to be so rude to them, you will see you love them also."

"But can I still be sad?" she asks the moment a tear falls from her eye.

"Of course you can be sad. You can cry and miss your parents. I miss mine every second. But if you start living your life here, you will soon start to find that although you will always miss them, you won't hurt as you are now. Soon the tears won't come every day, and your heart won't hurt as much. I'm not saying it goes away completely, but it does dull to where you can move on and live very happy." Am I giving that speech to her or myself? Hopefully it helps her, because it does nothing to me. She nods, then wipes her eyes with the back of her hand.

"Miss Gentry, will you bring your doll the next time you visit?"

"Absolutely." Then I bite my tongue when I realize there may never be a next time. "It's a shame you have to eat in your room every night. I was hoping we could talk more over dinner. But if you like to have dinner all alone in the nursery with no one to talk to, then that's your choice." My melodramatic sigh makes her smile. I wave it off like I'm not affected by it. When I stand, she grabs my hand but looks at her feet when she talks.

"Will you tell me more about your doll?" she asks.

"I will tell you about all of them. I started collecting them after I got Nicole. Although Nicole is still my favorite." Her head snaps up, and she smiles. "Lucy, I was right earlier when I said you were different than my doll. Your smile is not the same as hers." Her smile forms into a pout. I bend down and straighten the ribbon in her hair. "Your smile is much more beautiful." The smile comes back, lighting her entire face.

She takes my hand, and we both turn to the door, and I yelp when I see Miles standing in the doorway.

"Mr. Denley, you scared me. How long have you been there?" Geez, good thing I didn't say anything that could've gotten me in trouble. He looks at me and then to Lucy, the crease between his eyebrows softening just barely.

"Not long." He stays in the doorway, looking uptight and uncomfortable. "Lucy, go change for dinner," he demands. I give her hand a squeeze before she leaves. He watches her walk away, turning back to me with that same placid look. "Miss Gentry, dinner will be a few minutes still. I was ordered to ask if you would like to get some fresh air before dinner."

I'm sure his back is aching from standing so straight. And I'm also sure his neck hurts from keeping his nose so high in the air. Did he say he was *ordered* to ask me? I want to refuse, but of course I don't. He offers me his arm, very stiffly, and I bite back my sigh when I thread mine through his.

We walk in silence to the terrace. What do I say to him? Great weather we're having. Why are you so ornery? Is Annie engaged to Matthew? Oh, and by the way, I'm in love with you, and you have absolutely no idea who I am.

"Miss Gentry?" he asks, exasperated.

"Huh? What?" What did he say?

"How long are you staying?" he says again, acting bored out of his mind.

"Um, not long. I'm leaving after dinner."

I tighten my coat around me as we walk outside. The last time I was on this terrace was when I saw Hannah and Harry disappear through the trees. My eyes glance across the lawn to the spot, then I quickly rub at my eyes, so I won't start crying. When we stop at the railing, he drops my arm and takes a few big steps away from me, turning to look over the grounds. I want to smell my coat to see if I'm emanating some foul odor, because he's acting like it.

"My mother seems fond of you," he says formally, talking to the space in front of him.

"Thank you. I like her, too. She's great."

"She is. I love my family dearly. They are everything to me." He turns his head only slightly but turns back before he actually looks at me.

"I know."

"I am not sure you do. My family is important. I would do anything to protect them." This time, his whole body turns. He glares at me, and I swear the temperature just plummeted twenty degrees. He looks just passed me, and his face shifts. It isn't a face I recognize. He looks pained, but not the way I've seen him before.

"I apologize, Miss Gentry," he says lowly.

"Apologize for what?"

His eyes darken, turning his entire face into pure anguish. "I am so sorry," he whispers. Before I can look more intensely at him, his eyes flicker to the floor.

The only warning I have is hearing a heavy footstep behind me. I don't have time to turn, run, or even brace myself. Big, hard arms come around me, locking my arms at my sides. Then a hand clamps over my mouth. A scream bursts through my lips but is muffled by the rag over my mouth and nose. The scent is sweet and overpowering.

It starts at my fingers. The numbing. And then my toes. The numbing starts to spread like wildfire over the rest of my body. The panic in me explodes, causing me to shake and kick, trying to fight myself free. At first, I'm not sure if I'm getting tired of fighting, and that's why I can't feel my body or if it's really going numb. My eyelids go heavy, but I keep trying to get away.

And then a whisper, so quiet and calm touches my ear. "This will be easier if you don't fight."

My head may be cloudy, but my body takes an instant reaction to Harry's voice. Every cell vibrates underneath my skin. My heart beats faster, and my arms want to shake under his grip. I want to fight, but the more I fight, the faster I slow down. Every kick or jerk is in slow motion, and the sweet smell grows in pungency.

"There you go. That's better," Harry says softly as he lowers me to the ground. The ground is cold, biting at my sweating skin.

Before my eyes close, I look up at Miles, and the last picture I see is him shaking hands with Harry.

chapter twenty-one

A bead of sweat slowly slips from my temple, across my cheek, and falls from the tip of my nose. Each inhale of breath brings speckles of dust into my nose, making the itching intensify into burning. My hip hurts. I try to roll over, but my bound hands behind my back stop me.

Opening my eyes seems impossible. It's like my eyelashes are sewn to my cheeks. Noises around me are only rumblings. Deep voices are muffled; there's paper crinkling somewhere. Something heavy falls to the floor, and the jolt of hearing it makes my eyes open. It stings at first, even though there's very little light. Slowly my eyes adjust, and I notice the chairs and trunks covered in dust. We're in the attic. As discreetly as possible, I inch my head up to see where the voices are coming from.

"You gave me your word you would not harm her," Miles snarls, towering over Harry.

"And I haven't," Harry points out.

"Bringing her to unconsciousness is not harming her?" There's an edge to his voice, one I'm happy to hear.

"Mind your place, boy."

"What place is that? I did what you ordered me to and, in return, you gave your word Miss Gentry and my family would be unharmed."

"Do you need another scar? Maybe I should even it out and match the one I've already given you." Harry holds the knife up to Miles' neck. "I haven't touched your family, and I haven't hurt her. But I didn't promise anything regarding you."

"Stop," I manage to say with more than a whisper.

"Ah, Grace." Harry tucks his knife away and turns to me, smiling. "I thought you'd be out a little longer. You put up quite a fight." He crouches down next to me and angles his head in different directions to see me better. My wrists are chafing against the rope from twisting them so much.

"Trying to save Miles again, are we?" Harry pulls on my arm so I'm sitting. My neck is like a twig trying to keep my head up. It bobbles around until it rests on one of the trunks next to me. "How does it feel? To see Miles again, knowing he has no idea who you are. I'm sure it's excruciating." I quickly glance at Miles over Harry's shoulder to see he's glaring at Harry.

"You still love him!" Harry laughs, and the sound has me ignoring the skin peeling from my wrists. I pull and twist harder to get free, just so I can hit him.

"What do you mean?" Miles asks, taking a step to me.

Harry stands, turning so he can see us both. "Miles, this is Grace Gentry. You've met her before, but you no longer remember. She does, however. She remembers every moment you two shared. Every laugh. Every conversation. Every kiss."

Miles looks horrified, his eyes darting back and forth between Harry and me. If I can't get my hands free, my feet will have to do. They're still wobbly, but with all the strength I can manage, I pull my leg back and throw a kick to Harry's knee. He buckles over, falls to his knees, and gives me the perfect target. Again, I pull my leg back and smack my foot right into his temple. He screams. He swears. He grabs more rope and ties my feet together. I don't even mind being tied up this time. I deserve it and am glad I do.

"I should know better with you. Last time I met you should've been enough for me to know." Suddenly his knife is at my ear, tracing along the scar he gave me before. "Tell Miles how you got that scar," Harry says, tracing up and down my cheek.

I look Harry right in his shallow eyes. "No."

"If you haven't noticed, you are not in a position to fight." A little more pressure from the knife, and it'll break skin.

Miles takes a step to me. "Miss Gentry—"

"Shut up, Miles. Another step and her blood will be on your hands," Harry growls. Miles stops instantly. Harry's smile disappears when he turns back to me, his eyes losing more color the longer I look at him. "Tell him how you got that scar," he says again.

I raise my chin in confidence, although I don't have any. "No." Harry's head begins to shake slightly, and the knife at my face does, too. "You need me to get to Chris. You can't kill me."

He leans closer, one corner of his mouth turning up. "I wasn't planning on killing you, but I can still make you bleed."

Maybe if I bite my tongue hard enough, it'll distract me from the slicing pain by my ear. I keep my mouth shut, but my muffled screams are loud. Harry's face gets closer to mine, his sneer growing. Our noses are almost touching, and my stomach drops, taking my breath with it, when his eyes focus on my mouth. If he gets any closer I'll knock him in the teeth with my head. Before I can, I hear a crack, followed by an *oomph!*

Miles hits Harry in the back of the head. Hard. Harry's disgusting breath blows over my face just before his body sags and falls on me. Miles grabs Harry by the collar and throws him to the ground. I've seen Miles get that murderous look in his eyes before, but I also knew who he was inside. I don't know this Miles, so I don't know what he's feeling. And I'm not sure I want to know.

I look down at Harry, who's out cold, blood dripping to the floor from the back of his head.

"What was he speaking of?" Miles asks while untying my feet and hands, making sure he never touches me in the process. He still has that horribly scary look on his face. For a split second, I'm scared of him. Genuinely scared.

"Um, it's hard to explain. I—"

"Try," he demands.

"Fine." I stand up and walk to the mirror, glancing at Harry to make sure he isn't too close to take advantage of my proximity. Miles stands behind

271

me, watching my every move. I stretch out one finger and lightly tap the glass. Miles sucks in a shocked breath as he watches the glass move in liquid waves across the mirror.

"I told you it's hard to explain."

Miles bends down in front of Harry, that killer look coming back. A few minutes later, Miles finally tears his glare away from Harry and points it at me. "I apologize, Miss Gentry." I wasn't expecting an apology. Even as he says it, he still looks like he wants to kill me. "This man told me of you. Told me to let him know if I heard of you or if you came here."

"And you did." My glare matches his, now feeling betrayed.

"Yes, I did. He threatened my family if I did not listen to him. I threatened him in return, but he told me he had others with him who would harm my family if anything happened to him."

Now I can't stay mad at him. What would I have done in that situation? If someone told me they would kill my family if I didn't turn over someone I didn't even know, I would have done the exact same.

"I understand." The venom in my voice doesn't sound like I understand, but I do. To distract myself, I go over to the bag I saw Harry digging around in earlier. I find notebooks, money, a gun, a few knives, rope, and a bottle of clear liquid. Probably the same stuff he used on me. I flip through the notebooks and discover it's all about Miles and me. How we met, what happened with Rockwell, my fight with Harry, finding Mom. Everything.

Harry starts moaning, shifting his body in jerky movements. Harry told Miles he had others, and I need to know the truth before I leave. I can't leave knowing there are other people here who want to hurt the Denleys. I hold my hand up to stop Miles from hitting Harry again. I wait until Harry rolls over, wait until he can see me.

"Harry, if you promise nothing will happen to any of the Denleys, I'll take you back to Chris without fighting." I hold my hand out to him, ignoring Miles' hot glare. Harry takes it, but I don't help him up. He staggers, grunts as he stands. "Is anyone coming with us? Or are you alone?" I ask, hoping Miles is listening.

"I'm alone." Harry winces, holding the back of his head.

"Is there anyone you want to tell your plans to? Especially if they're ordered to hurt the Denleys if you don't return."

"No. It's just me," he snaps, looking at his hand covered in blood. I glance at Miles and give a half smile. Now he knows no one is here to hurt his family.

"You told me you had others with you," Miles fumes from the corner.

"I lied," Harry moans, rubbing his head. "You should be happy, boy. No one will hurt your family. Especially your beautiful sister." Harry doesn't see what's happening. He's staring at the mirror with blind anticipation.

Another crack, this time bone-to-bone. Harry is on the ground again, Miles standing over him shaking. I wait until Miles calms down. It takes awhile. A long while. Once he begins pacing, the tension in his body loosens.

"Um . . . thanks," I say, gesturing to Harry.

"Before, you said it was difficult to explain. I want you to tell me what you were speaking of."

"I really can't right now. I don't have time. I've got to get back." I can probably spare a few minutes, but the way he's looking at me . . . I just can't.

"I think I have earned an explanation."

"You haven't. You were roped into this, and I'm sorry for that. But the more distance you put between this and yourself the better off you'll be."

"What is happening in here?" Mrs. Denley comes running up the stairs with Lord Denley just behind her. She gasps when she sees Harry on the floor. Gasps again when she sees blood on Miles. She grabs his hand, fussing over him.

"I am fine, Mother," he sighs, taking his hand from her.

"Son, what happened?" Lord Denley steps toward Harry with concern.

I'm mad at Miles. Really mad. But I know it's only because it's easier to be mad than to accept the fact that he doesn't know me. But he's still Miles and still good. He was trying to protect his family. Isn't that what I'm doing? Or trying to do by going back?

273

"Lord Denley, this is Harry," I explain. "He came trying to hurt me, but Mr. Denley stopped him. He saved me." I look at Miles. He still glares, but gives a small nod to say thank you.

"Oh, you must have been terrified!" Mrs. Denley leaves Miles and rushes to me. Her hug is warm, and I take advantage of it for a minute.

"I am proud of you." Lord Denley clamps a hand on Miles' shoulder, but Miles shrugs it off. There isn't room on his shoulder with the guilt weighing it down. "I will take care of it from here." He looks down at Harry, now with disgust.

"Please, let's get some food in you. You are very pale." Mrs. Denley wraps her arms around my waist and pulls me to the stairs.

"Thank you for the invitation, but I need to go. There are things that need to be fixed. I don't want anyone else showing up here to threaten you." I smile, showing only false bravery.

"Very well," Lord Denley says, before his wife tries persuading me again.

"It feels wrong. We should not be sending her away. What danger is waiting for her? Carolyn and Daniel would want us to protect her." Mrs. Denley is crying, which reminds me of Annie. And thinking of her almost brings on a wave of emotion I can't afford to feel.

"It is not our choice, dear. If she asked for our help of course we would be there for her. But I think this circumstance is bigger than us, and we need to trust that she knows best." Lord Denley takes her hand as she cries and turns back to me. "Miss Gentry, the mirror will remain safely here if you should need to come again."

"You knew about this? About that contraption?" Miles accuses.

"Son, there is much to explain"

"Yes, there is. Everything could have been different if I had known." Miles turns to me now, angrier than before. "You knew Harry was coming here. How did you know? Are there others?"

"Yes, but they can't get here."

"Harry did," he barks.

"Yes, but the person who brought him here isn't here anymore. I'm the only one who can bring anyone here, and I would never do that!" It's embarrassing to yell at him in front of his parents, but I guess wanting to scream at him hasn't changed.

"What are you fixing? Are you going back to those associated with Harry?"

"Hopefully when I go back, they won't find me. I only need to get some things, and then I'll leave again."

If I could get back to the house and get the journal, I think I can fix this. The place Dad talked about, the place he went right before meeting mom. The nothing as he described it. If I could get the coordinates to that, I can take it back to Dad and have him send Chris there instead of sending him to the future. Chris can't hurt anyone there. But also, no one can hurt Chris. I hate him. And Tom and Harry. But I don't have it in me to actually kill them.

"I will go with you," Miles exclaims, shocking me out of my mental plans.

"No," I refuse, hearing Mrs. Denley sigh in gratitude at my rejection.

"I am a part of this disaster now, and I do not trust you enough to make sure no one harms my family." I'm pretty sure he loathes me, but at the moment the feelings are mutual.

"Miles!" Mrs. Denley throws her hand over her heart.

"No, it's alright." I hold my hand up to her and look at Miles. "I don't care if you trust me or not. You have no idea where I'm going or what to do there. I'll be better off without you." No I won't. "Stay here, I'll be fine."

"May I remind you that I just saved you from one man who had cruel intentions?" He points to Harry on the floor.

"And may I remind you how that man got close enough to me to carry out those intentions?" I scream back. His face flushes red, and his eyes flash to his parents quickly and then back to me.

"What is she speaking of, Son?" Lord Denley looks as guilty as Miles, and I feel bad for putting them in the position.

"Nothing. I'm just mad," I cut in. "I have to go. Lord and Mrs. Denley, thank you for your help. Hopefully the next time you see me it will be under better circumstances." I smile at them and nod briefly at Miles. "Mr. Denley."

I turn to the mirror and close my eyes, ignoring the bickering behind me. I want to go home. I want to go to my room, at home, in Oregon.

I repeat it before I step through, but just before I lift my foot to take what feels like an insurmountable step, I'm stupid and open my eyes and see Miles through the reflection. I promised I would try to find him again. I did find him again, but it isn't him. But if I change it, it'll change him back. Harry wouldn't have threatened him. He won't be so cold and untrusting. He'll be safe. Everyone will be safe.

He looks right back at me through the mirror, and just before stepping through, I see concern cover his face. I quickly close my eyes, so I won't have to watch me leave him again. I walk through, but something pulls at me, and then forcefully pushes me through. Everything is black like always, but I'm not alone.

My feet hit the ground hard, throwing my body down. Right when I land I know something is wrong. I said I wanted to go to my room, not outside. I stand and look around and immediately know I'm in Oregon, but down by the tree house. Why didn't it take me to my room?

Footsteps over crunchy leaves behind me have my stomach tensing, and I whirl around, bracing for whoever it is.

Miles stands in front of me, looking around in stupefied awe.

"What are you doing here?" I ask frantically.

"I am not sure. I saw you head for the mirror and it . . . opened for you. My first thought was to pull you away, afraid you would be hurt. Once I reached you there was an indescribable pull I felt. I could not deny it, so I followed you through." He looks around, his eyes getting bigger. "I followed you through a mirror," he rambles, not believing a word he's saying. "A glass mirror."

"What were you thinking?" I shout. My plan is ruined. Now I have to find a way for him to get home.

His rambling stops as he glares at me. "I just told you. I was curious."

"You idiot! Now I have to find a way to get you home." I shove past him, too upset to even look at him. Curious? What am I supposed to do now? Maybe I can take him back before I go to Dad.

He grabs my arm as I pass, stopping me completely. "If you would get your nose out of the air for a moment, you may realize I can be of some assistance," he says harshly.

"No. All you'll be is in my way." I jerk my arm out of his hand and keep walking. He *will* be in my way. Every minute. It's easier not to think about Miles when he isn't with me. Now he is, and again, he's brand new to this life. I don't have time to explain everything to him or help him feel comfortable. I don't want to worry about him. And I certainly don't want to get attached to him again. Losing Miles the first time was heart wrenching. I'm not doing it again.

"Let's go. I'm taking you home," I say over my shoulder. I'll take him home first and then figure the rest out.

By the time we make it up the hill, both of us are fuming. His stride quickens with every glare I give him, and my heart breaks just a little more every time he looks at me. Stomping out of the trees, I stop, and grab Miles' arm to do the same.

The only home I've ever known is standing in front of me, but it's almost in pieces. The cobblestone drive has stones missing. The fountain in the middle of the circle is on its side, shattered. Weeds have taken over the flowerbeds—flowerbeds that look like they haven't been touched in years. The trees surrounding the house are only stumps. Boards cover up most of the windows, and the windows that aren't covered are broken.

I cautiously walk to the house, glancing over my shoulder frequently in fear that Miles and I aren't the only ones here. We stop on the porch that's now littered with trash. I stare at the scratches and graffiti covering every inch of the front door that's slightly cracked open. My hand shakes as I raise it to push the door, but Miles puts my hand back down.

"I will go first. You stay here," he orders, walking into the house without waiting for my answer.

"You don't even know where you're going," I whisper, because once I enter, it feels like the right thing to do. Tears prick at my eyes when I see the remains of my house. Most of the furniture is gone. Whatever is left is only in pieces. Cotton is thrown everywhere. Scraps of wood and plastic make a maze to walk through. There are holes in the walls and floors. Everywhere. I take a step into the family room, and glass crunches under my foot. I look down and see the glass I'm stepping on once held pictures of my family. Those pictures now are torn in shreds.

Miles stands behind me and very quietly whispers, "Whoever was here seemed to be looking for something."

A new, hot fear shoots through me.

"The mirror," I gasp and dart for my room. Some of the boards on the staircase are missing, so I have to jump one or two at a time. Splinters shove into my hands when I fall on my way upstairs. Miles is calling after me, but I can't stop. I run into my room, and the air is abruptly ripped away from me.

The mirror is gone.

I kneel beside the spot the mirror has been my entire life. My fingers trail against the white marks scratched into the wood made by it.

"What has happened?" Miles asks as he studies the bedroom. He's seeing the ruins of what's left. I'm seeing what isn't here.

"It's gone," I whisper.

"What is?"

"The mirror. It's gone."

"Well, where is it?"

"You think I'd be sulking on the ground if I knew? It was right here when I left."

I turn to the window, needing the fresh air. Throwing it open and taking a deep breath only makes my breath disappear completely. Out my window used to be a big valley, covered in trees and dotted with houses. The valley now looks barren. What's left of the trees are only stumps. Half of the hill my house sits on is covered in singed trees and black ash. Smoke still rises from the ashes. Maybe that's why the sky is so gray. The roads are empty. That's when I notice how quiet it is.

There are no planes in the sky, no cars, no static from power lines. Birds aren't even out chirping.

The world I've grown up in is gone.

"Something's wrong," I whisper. "This isn't my home."

Dear Reader,

I was going to thank you in the Acknowledgment section, but you deserve your own page. I need to tell you that I think about all of you a lot. Wait . . . that sounds creepy. I don't mean it like that. What I mean is when I look at my sales for the day, I wonder who bought the books. I wonder if you're a mom who tiredly makes it from day to day, just like me. I wonder if you sneak your phone into the bathroom and read a few paragraphs as fast as you can before your kids find you. I wonder if you're a teenager who's falling in love for the first time. I think you might be in college, trying to figure out what to do with the rest of your life. Or you're a grandparent.

I don't know what your situation in life is, but you're all reading this now because you took a chance on an unknown author. That chance you took on me gave *me* a chance to dream bigger dreams. I wish I could give you more than some words in the back of a book, but until we become besties on Facebook, this will have to do.

So, thank you, readers, for loving Grace and Miles. I'm excited for you to find out what happens next.

Thank you,
Janessa

Social media scares me, but you can find me here:

Facebook: www.facebook.com/janessabbooks
Instagram: @janessaburt
Twitter : @nessaburt
Website: www.janessaburt.com

Acknowledgments

I'm lucky enough to be surrounded by people who encourage me to keep going. Without them, these books would still be sitting on my computer, unread. There are so many people who I have to thank, but there are a few that, without them, I wouldn't have made it this far.

My mama. Thanks for the weekly lunches during the summer. Thanks for listening to me when I needed a listening ear. Your advice is invaluable, especially when I'm having bad mom days. Thanks for giving me confidence in my writing. And thanks for forgetting to take other people dinner because you were so wrapped up in the book. You'll never know how much that meant to me. (That probably makes me a bad person.)

To my sister, Jill. Thank you for letting me talk your ear off about this book. I found plot holes while explaining the story out loud. You pointed out mistakes that needed changing. When you texted me and told me you had stayed up until 2 A.M. reading the second book, and you wanted the third book immediately, that's what got me excited to finish. Without you, I really don't know what the book would look like. And thanks for helping me design the cover. I love it.

Sophie. Thanks for teaching me about the Chicago Manual of Style (still don't know what it is), when to use commas (though I didn't understand a word of it), and something else about links and prepositions. I can't remember. But thanks for giving up your nights to edit the book. You're Super Sophie!

Neal. Thanks for reading my book about teenagers and romance. I know it's your most favorite genre. Thank you for taking screen shots of errors so I could fix them. And thanks for keeping Beeg company while I locked myself in my room to finish this book.

And to Beeg. I'll thank you in every book I write. Thanks for becoming Mr. Mom when I need to finish a chapter, write a scene, or meet a deadline. I've asked a lot of you these last few months, and you haven't complained once. It's made this process so much easier knowing that you're taking care of everything. I love you.

And thanks for buying me Symphony bars.

Made in the USA
Lexington, KY
13 October 2015